Praise for the novels of Brenda Novak

"Fascinating characters, powerful conflicts and complex emotions make any Brenda Novak book a must-read for me."
—Sherryl Woods, #1 *New York Times* bestselling author

"Once you visit Silver Springs, you'll never want to leave."
—Robyn Carr, #1 *New York Times* bestselling author

"Heartwarming, life-affirming, page-turning romance. I can always count on Novak to make me weep, laugh and fall in love!"
—Jill Shalvis, *New York Times* bestselling author

"Brenda Novak is always a joy to read."
—Debbie Macomber, #1 *New York Times* bestselling author

"Brenda Novak doesn't just write fabulous stories, she writes keepers."
—Susan Mallery, #1 *New York Times* bestselling author

"The perfect read to cozy up to on a long winter night."
—Susan Wiggs, #1 *New York Times* bestselling author, on *Before We Were Strangers*

"The author deftly integrates topics such as coming to terms with one's past and the importance of forgiveness into another beautifully crafted, exceptionally poignant love story."
—*Library Journal* on *Discovering You*

"*This Heart of Mine* had such beautiful details that it captured my full attention—and had me sniffling and smiling while waiting to board my plane."
—*First for Women*

"*This Heart of Mine* is a potently emotional, powerfully life-affirming contemporary romance."
—*Booklist* (starred review)

W9-BLI-072

brenda novak

unforgettable you

mira

mira

ISBN-13: 978-0-7783-0793-8

Recycling programs
for this product may
not exist in your area.

Unforgettable You

To the packing crew that comes to my house
two days a month to pack Brenda Novak's
Professional Reader Boxes, a subscription box
service run by my daughter through my website
featuring autographed copies of my books—
and other authors'—as well as fun reader-related
goodies. Thank you to Theresa Atashkar,
Janice Bechtel, Marilou Frary, Cindy Gabriel,
Yolanda Gliko, Leslie Henning, Dana Kelly,
Patricia King, Danita Moon, Stephanie Novembri,
Jan Plott, Jeri Ramos, Liz Schneider-Cheyne
and Brittany Walton for the hard work,
the good company, the great stories and the
many laughs. The professional reader boxes
wouldn't be possible without you!

unforgettable
you

1

Jada Brooks was pushing her brother in his wheelchair at the farmers' market on the second weekend in June, a Saturday morning that inspired the cliché "picture perfect," with nothing but blue skies and the usual mild Southern California weather, when she caught a glimpse of something that made her stop dead in her tracks.

"What's wrong?" Atticus twisted around in his seat to look up at her. It'd been thirteen years since he'd been shot, so he was accustomed to the paralysis in his lower body and could propel himself with his arms—he was adept at doing almost everything, including driving now that his truck was properly equipped—but it was more relaxing and easier to stick together in a crowd if she took over. Visiting the market while Maya, Jada's twelve-year-old daughter, helped her grandmother at the cookie store was something they'd become accustomed to doing every now and then since Jada had divorced her husband and moved back to town three months ago.

"I just…" Jada shook her head to clear it of the image that stubbornly remained. Surely, she was wrong about who she thought she'd seen. Maddox Richardson had left town right after she'd gotten pregnant, and there was nothing to draw him back. It wasn't as if he had family in the area, like she did. The only reason he'd moved to Silver Springs in the first place was because he'd been sent by the courts to attend New Horizons Boys Ranch, a boarding school for troubled teens. And when he left, it was because he'd been enrolled at a different school somewhere else, somewhere she was never even told. After that terrible night, Maddox had essentially been banished at the request and expense of her parents, which hadn't been an easy thing to accomplish given all the red tape his mother had had to go through in order to accommodate them.

Whether forcing Maddox to go somewhere else was fair to him was another subject entirely. Jada tried not to think about that. She tried not to think about Maddox at all.

Too bad she wasn't more successful at it. So many little things brought him to mind, especially now that she was living where she'd gotten to know him. Someone who slightly resembled him or laughed like him or had the same cerulean blue eyes. Even a particular song or smell could bring him back to her. His life had intersected with hers in a way she would never forget—both for good *and* bad.

"Jada?" Atticus prompted.

She blinked, realizing she'd let her words trail off, but continued to study the crowd around her. Maddox wasn't there. It must've been someone of his general size and shape with the same jet-black hair, but she couldn't see anyone who resembled him now. Whoever it was had melted back into the crowd jostling around them.

"It's nothing." She forced a smile and started pushing again. She couldn't mention Maddox's name to Atticus, regardless.

"Should we get some kale for our morning smoothies?" Atticus asked.

He still lived with their mother, had never even been in a serious relationship and talked as though he had no plans for that sort of thing. Although Jada had spent all the years since she'd had Maya in LA, she hadn't rented a place of her own since returning to Silver Springs, so she and Maya were currently living with her mother, too. She'd been trying to find the right situation to be able to move out, but there weren't a lot of homes for rent in this artsy, outdoorsy, spiritually focused community, and with her mother sick so often these days, Jada was needed at home.

It'd be different if her father was still around, but...

She steered her mind away from Jeremiah. Losing him earlier in the year to a stroke when he was only fifty-five had not been easy, especially because she felt she'd let him down so terribly and never had the chance to make it up to him, as she was trying to do with her mother and brother.

"Sure," she said about the kale. "Maybe it'll boost Mom's immune system. It's supposed to be really good for you."

Pausing in front of the closest stand, she chose a particularly healthy-looking bunch of leafy greens and was just handing the vendor her money when she heard her name.

She turned to see Tiffany Martinez, a friend she'd gone to school with from fifth grade on, hurrying toward her in a short-sleeved, button-down blouse, sandals and shorts, similar to what she was wearing herself. Because

Jada had had a baby just as everyone else was going off to college, her life had taken a completely different course, one that had put her out of sync with the group of friends she'd grown up with. For the first several years after moving to LA, she'd felt overlooked, abandoned, left behind, while everyone else went away to college and documented all the fun they had on social media. Watching them on her computer while struggling to raise a child when she was barely more than a child herself had only made that period of her life harder. But Tiffany had always been supportive and remained in touch. And everything was changing now that so many of their other friends were getting married and having children. Jada had been able to reconnect with several who still lived in the area.

Tiffany would always be her favorite, though. She was also the only one who knew Jada's most guarded secret.

"Hey, Tiff." She put the kale into her reusable tote and hung it on the back of Atticus's wheelchair. Jada had told Tiffany she was going to the farmers' market when they spoke on the phone last night, which was what had prompted Tiffany to come, too. Like Jada, she was recently divorced, only she didn't have any kids, so she was always looking for things to do when she wasn't working at the regional hospital as a nurse. They would've come together—they did a lot together—but Tiffany hadn't wanted to change the chemistry of Jada's morning with Atticus. "Glad you made it."

"I've been here for a while. I was just leaving when…" She tucked her curly red hair behind her ears as her eyes—so green and clear they were almost startling—darted to Atticus, a captive audience in his chair. "When

I saw something that... Well, that reminded me of you and made me wonder if you were still here."

So Tiffany hadn't *accidentally* spotted her and come over to say hello? She'd come looking for her? "What was it?"

Again, Tiffany glanced uncomfortably at Atticus. "A person actually. Someone we knew a...a while ago."

Jada's heart began to pound as her friend's behavior connected with the scare she'd had only a few minutes earlier. With the way Tiffany was acting, so flustered and overly aware of Atticus listening in... "Atticus, would you mind grabbing some purple onions while I talk to Tiffany?"

"Sure. No problem." Seemingly relieved to escape the girl talk, he rolled away as Jada led Tiffany a few feet in the other direction, just to be safe.

"What is it?" she whispered. "Why do you look as though the world's about to come to an end?"

Tiffany grabbed her forearms. "You don't know? You haven't seen him?"

Suspicion turned to outright fear. "*Him?* You don't mean Maddox..."

"That's exactly who I mean!"

Shit. She *had* seen him. The question was...had he seen her? And why was he in Silver Springs?

Jada swallowed hard. Had he returned because he'd learned about Maya?

That couldn't be, could it? Her family had kept her pregnancy so quiet. She had easily been able to hide her rounding stomach beneath baggy clothes as school came to an end. Her parents had kept her home throughout the summer, her final trimester, so almost no one saw her looking unmistakably pregnant. And then she moved to

LA with her newborn. Other than Tiffany, the few friends she'd kept in contact with over the years, and loosely at that, knew she'd married almost right out of high school, that she had a child and had recently divorced. But they didn't know exactly *when* she'd met her husband or had Maya. Most assumed Maya belonged to her ex.

But if anyone really pressed for details—when and where Maya was born—they could *possibly* put two and two together…and Jada was afraid Maddox might do exactly that.

"Are you okay?" Tiffany asked.

Jada felt dizzy, faint. *"Why?"* she asked instead of answering. "Why is he back?"

"I don't know. But he is. I just saw him."

"You're *sure* it was him."

"*Positive.* There could be no mistaking Maddox Richardson."

Maddox had always stood out, been unique, charismatic, appealing—and sexy as hell. She'd never met a man who could make a woman feel warm and tingly simply by looking at her.

Tiffany had also known him in school, and she clearly remembered what he was like, as well. She'd been interested in Maddox's brother, Tobias, who wasn't as enigmatic and appealing as Maddox but came awfully damn close, despite his terrible reputation and the behavior that had earned it. She'd been at the party that fateful night, too.

"Did he see you?" Jada asked.

"He did, but I don't know if he recognized me. Our eyes connected for a second. Then he looked away and kept moving."

He *had* to have recognized Tiffany. Not many people

had her shade of hair and unique, slanted green eyes. So...what did *that* mean?

Tiffany bent to adjust her sandal. "Do you think Tobias is out of prison?"

"I have no idea."

"He should be. He only got eight years, and it's been thirteen."

"But my father told me he did something on the inside—got in a fight or found some other trouble—and they extended his sentence. I'm not sure by how much." That was the last thing her father told her about it before he died, and she wasn't willing to ask her mother, wasn't willing to go anywhere near the subject with her.

Tiffany looked as conflicted as Jada felt. "I wonder what he's like now..."

"I can't imagine prison has improved him. I have no idea what the past thirteen years have done to Maddox, either."

"You two have had *no* contact?"

"None whatsoever. You know that. But I thought I saw him, too, a few minutes ago. I'd just talked myself out of it when you came up."

Tiffany looked back over her shoulder. "I'm sorry. You can't be happy about this."

Jada was facing the opposite direction. She could see that her brother was still paying for the onions. Maddox was nowhere in sight. "I'm not," she said. And yet there was a small, rebellious part of her that was feeling an unwarranted rush of excitement and expectation. What did Maddox look like these days? What was he up to? Had he gotten married? Was he happy?

She'd often tried to look him up, had been dying—*for years*—to catch a glimpse of him or find out the smallest detail of what was happening in his life. But he wasn't on social media.

"What will you say to him?" Tiffany asked.

Jada had no idea. What *could* she say to him? If she'd never gotten involved with him, her brother would be a fully functioning adult. "I'm going to avoid him, if I can." Because of Maya, that was the smartest way to handle the situation. If she drew Maddox's attention, he might figure out the truth—if something or someone hadn't tipped him off already.

"That's probably for the best," Tiffany agreed. "The mountains and hills that close off this area make Silver Springs feel like such a small town. But there are seven thousand people here. That's not so small that everyone knows everyone else. You might get lucky and never cross paths with him."

That wasn't very likely. She was running her mother's cookie store downtown much of the time. They'd at least *see* each other. Unless…

"Hopefully, he won't be staying long," Jada murmured, but she couldn't be *totally* committed to wishing him gone. She'd loved him so much, hadn't felt anything even half as powerful since, which was a sad testament to what her marriage had been like. She'd screwed up her life in so many ways—dating the boy her parents had warned her not to get involved with, getting pregnant at seventeen, marrying the wrong man while rushing to find the same kind of all-consuming love she'd lost. And now, just when she was putting the past into perspective and settling in to rebuild—slowly and with some caution this time—*Maddox* popped up in Silver Springs?

Unbelievable…

"Yeah, maybe he's just passing through."

"He could have come to see Aiyana," Jada offered. Aiyana Turner had founded the boys' ranch he'd once attended. Almost all of the students who went there adored her. She'd done a lot for troubled young men over the years and deserved the accolades. "There could be some sort of reunion going on," she added, to bolster the argument. "After all, it *is* June, when schools are celebrating graduation."

A skeptical expression gave Tiffany's true feelings away. "But does he know Aiyana that well? He didn't attend New Horizons for even one full school year. And he went on to graduate from somewhere else."

"Still… You never know."

"That may be true."

Jada put up a hand to alert Tiffany to the fact that Atticus was wheeling his way back toward them.

"Should we get anything else?" Atticus asked as he rolled up.

Jada couldn't help glancing around. "No, we've got enough. We should get going."

Atticus's thick dark eyebrows jerked together above his milk-chocolate-colored eyes. While Jada had sandy-blond hair, her eyes were the exact same color, which was part of the reason everyone told them they looked just alike. "You're done shopping? I thought we'd get a hot dog and a lemonade over at that stand." He jerked his head to indicate what he meant.

She didn't dare risk running into Maddox, especially while she was with Atticus. How was her brother going to feel when he learned Maddox was back? While it was true that Maddox wasn't directly responsible for putting Atticus in a wheelchair, he'd been very much involved in what went down that night. Nothing would've happened without him first setting those events in motion. And he'd immediately tried to protect his own brother, Tobias, who *had* been directly responsible.

"I thought so, too," she said, "but I feel a headache coming on. I should get home and take a painkiller so it can kick in before I go help Mom at the store today. Do you mind?"

He lifted his hands. "I guess not."

Jada felt bad for cutting their excursion short. She and Atticus were just beginning to find common ground. He'd been so sullen and fatalistic since he lost the use of his legs. It'd been difficult to even talk to him while she was living in LA. Her mother complained that he wouldn't come out of his room for days at a time, that he couldn't seem to get on top of the depression that coincided with the loss he'd suffered. So Jada was glad he was finally starting to function more normally and live as well as he could. She hated to put a damper on his recovery, even by saying no to something as small as getting a hot dog together. But if he saw Maddox, she was afraid it would throw him into another tailspin, and he'd lose all the ground he'd made up. "Okay. We'll be sure to get lunch next time we come," she said and, with a quick wave to say goodbye to Tiffany, wheeled him out of the market.

Maddox Richardson couldn't get away fast enough from the spot where he'd seen Jada Brooks. When he agreed to come to Silver Springs to become the principal of the brand-new girls' school Aiyana Turner was opening right next to the original New Horizons Boys Ranch just outside of town, he'd been assured Jada didn't live in the area anymore. Aiyana had told him Jada was married, with a child, and living in LA!

So…had she and her little family moved to Silver Springs? Was he going to have to deal with the possibility of running into her whenever he was in town?

Or was she just visiting?

He stood behind the corrugated metal building that sheltered the vendors so he couldn't be spotted and called his new boss.

"You're not going to believe who I just saw," he blurted out the second Aiyana answered.

"Maddox?" She sounded surprised by the lack of a hello or other lead-in. Or maybe she was reacting to the emergency in his voice.

"Yeah, it's me."

"Who did you see?" She didn't give him a chance to answer before she added, "Please don't tell me it was Atticus Brooks. He hardly ever leaves the house."

That was what she'd told him before! "It was Jada. But Atticus was with her."

There was a moment of silence.

"Did she see you?" Aiyana asked at length.

"I don't think so. I slipped into the crowd as soon as I realized, but while I was trying to put some distance between us I almost bumped into that friend she used to hang out with all the time—Tiffany something."

"Tiffany Martinez."

"That's the one. Jada might not have focused on me long enough to really see me, but Tiffany definitely recognized me."

"And she'll tell Jada."

"No question. So…what's going on?" When Aiyana had been encouraging him to accept the position, she'd told him that Jada's father had died. She'd said Jada's mother and brother were still in the area, but if he did his job and didn't bother them, didn't approach them at all, they probably wouldn't even realize he was back. Not only had it been almost thirteen years since the terrible incident that had disrupted so many lives, including his own, *he* wasn't the one who'd caused the damage! And the opportunity she was offering was simply too good to pass up, especially for someone with a checkered past, like him. It took a person like Aiyana to be able to see beyond the confusion and anger of his childhood to discover his potential as an adult.

Besides, he owed her. She'd stayed in touch with him over the years, arranged a scholarship for his college education from a wealthy benefactor (he suspected it was the professional football player Hudson King, who did so much for the school, but the person writing the checks had chosen to remain anonymous). She'd also helped him get his first job at Westlake Academy in Utah by recommending him to her friend, who was in charge at the time. He'd been excited to come work for her, to take charge of the new girls' school and do all he could to give back to her by giving back to them.

But now... He was beginning to wonder if he'd made a mistake.

"I don't know what's going on," she said. "I'll have to make a few calls."

"You haven't heard anything about Jada moving back to town..."

"No, but it's not like that sort of thing would be reported in the paper. And I've been so busy getting the students here ready for graduation I haven't been keeping in touch with what's happening around me."

"She's probably just visiting..."

"That's my guess, too."

"So it'll be okay."

"I'll call you as soon as I find out."

"I appreciate it." He disconnected, scrubbing a hand over his face as he stared out toward the Topatopa Mountains. He'd already signed the lease on the house where he was living and taken the reins at the school. It wasn't as if he could easily change his mind.

But perhaps he was getting worked up for nothing. Since Jada's mother and brother lived here, she was going to visit occasionally. And if she wasn't here very often, maybe he could manage to avoid her.

Letting his breath go in a sigh, he started toward the parking lot but had barely cleared the shade of the building and stepped into the sun when Aiyana called him back.

"What'd you find?" He stopped walking and plugged one ear so he could hear above the throng of people chatting around him.

"I think you'd better sit down," she said.

2

"What are you doing here so early? Didn't you go to the farmers' market with Atticus?"

Jada tried to set her fear and misgivings aside so they wouldn't be revealed on her face. Her mother looked worn and tired. Jada knew part of it was the lupus. Flare-ups could be bad and the past few months had been rough. But Susan was also contending with her constant worry over Atticus. He was her baby, younger than Jada by six years, and had always been her parents' favorite, which made what Jada had done in high school that much worse. She'd allowed the "golden calf" of the family to be permanently damaged; Atticus had almost lost his *life* under her watch. "We decided to cut out a bit early today."

Her mother's eyes widened. "You didn't have an argument…"

"No, of course not. I was getting a headache, that's all."

"Oh." Her mother didn't ask if she was feeling better. Jada wanted to believe she would have, if Maya hadn't interrupted by sticking her head into the front of the store from the bakery in back.

"Hi, Mom! Come see! I've been baking chocolate chip cookies!"

That she'd been baking *something* was apparent. She had a smudge of flour on her cheek and some in her hair. "On your own?"

"Grandma said I could do it by myself this time."

At least her mother seemed to love Maya, despite the fact that she'd pushed and pushed for Jada to give Maya up for adoption and, when she wouldn't, had refused to acknowledge her existence for the first two years of her life.

"She knows how," her mother said, almost defensively. "I've shown her."

"She's a smart girl." Maya was beautiful, too. She had her father's thick dark hair, which she wore long, as well as her father's big, dreamy Jake Gyllenhaal eyes. Maya was tall like him, too, but she didn't have his thick frame. In that she took after Jada's side. Maya reminded Jada of a gazelle, especially when she ran track, which was her favorite sport.

"We just have to do the red velvet cookies," Maya said.

Jada slipped behind the counter. "Great. I'll help you. You can head home and rest now, Mom."

A touch of regret entered her mother's face as she glanced around the store. As difficult as it was to keep Sugar Mama profitable, she loved what she'd created and kept trying new marketing techniques, hoping to get the store to take off. That she didn't make a lot of money hadn't been a big deal when Jada's father was alive and could help with the household bills, but now that he was gone, money was getting tight. That was another reason Jada hadn't gotten her own place. She'd been staying at home so she could pay rent, a way to help without making her mother feel awkward or guilty for accepting the money. Problem was, now that she was spending so much time trying to relieve the pressure on her mother at the store, helping with the housecleaning and encouraging her brother whenever possible, she wasn't able to make as much running her own business handling social media for a variety of companies. She'd already had to let two clients—the most time-intensive—go.

"Are you sure?" her mother asked.

"Of course. Maya and I can see to this place, can't we?" Jada said to her daughter.

"You know I'm good with the cash register, Grandma," Maya piped up.

"Yes. Yes, you are." Her mother lowered her voice as she added in an aside to Jada, "Kids these days. They can handle a computer like nobody's business."

Jada smiled.

"Should I take Atticus something for lunch? Or did you eat at the market?"

"We didn't have a chance to eat. He said he was going to fix something at home."

"There's not much in the fridge. I'd better call him." She whipped out her phone as she left, and Jada let her smile slip away. Yes, Atticus was unable to walk, but he was more capable than her mother gave him credit for. Susan needed to quit babying him. Jada felt she was making him feel *more* disabled—and deserving of sympathy—which only dragged him down. He had to get beyond the self-pity and that sense of limitation to thrive.

Jada couldn't say anything, though. Not yet. She planned to do so at some point, when they were all on stable emotional ground. But with Maddox back in town, she wasn't about to cause so much as a ripple between her and her mother and brother. She was just going to keep her head down and hope Maddox left without ever learning that *she* was in town, too.

Jada *was* back! In between the time Maddox had accepted Aiyana's job offer and actually relocated to Silver Springs, she'd moved here to help take care of her mother, who'd recently been diagnosed with lupus, and her younger brother. Apparently, Atticus had graduated from an online college with a bachelor's degree in computer science, but still lived at home and didn't have a job.

What were the chances she'd come back to Silver Springs right now? Maddox had known he was pushing his luck moving to where everything had gone so terribly wrong. But Aiyana had been nothing but confident and encouraging! He'd believed it would be okay because he'd wanted to believe it would be okay, wanted to take the helm of New Horizons for Girls. He could not have built the kind of life he'd built without Aiyana's help. She'd reached out and made him feel as though he mattered, and she wouldn't give up on him even when he tried to push her away. He longed to play that kind of a role in someone else's life, make *that* kind of a difference, and she'd given him the perfect vehicle.

Except that taking the job she'd offered now put him back in close proximity to the only girl who'd ever broken his heart. He hated that Jada blamed him for the night her brother was shot, but he knew she had reason. *He* was the one who'd talked her into disobeying her parents and taking Atticus to that party. Had he not pushed her into it, Atticus would still have the use of his legs.

He tossed his keys on his desk as he walked into his office. New Horizons Boys Ranch, at the other end of the fifty-acre compound, was bustling with students milling about campus, playing basketball on the outside courts, football on the big field or watching movies in the gymnasium. They had a two-week summer break but many students stayed year-round. New Horizons for Girls, which was separated from the boys' side by a tall fence, was completely empty. Maddox hadn't officially accepted his first student yet. That wouldn't happen for another two or three weeks.

He breathed in the smell of new carpet and paint as he gazed around at the way he'd organized his office. He'd unpacked and settled in at home, too. Had that been a mistake? Should he go get some boxes and pack up again? Because he didn't see how he was going to be able to stay here. He'd known it would be difficult if he ever ran into Atticus and hadn't been looking forward to that moment. All the apology letters he'd sent over the years had gone unanswered. Honestly? He wished that bullet had hit him instead, but it hadn't, and because he'd done all he could, he'd be willing to stand tall, look Atticus in the face and apologize again.

It was different with Jada. His emotions were so complicated where she was concerned. She was right to blame him, and yet it had almost destroyed him when she had. He'd needed her forgiveness more than he'd ever needed anything, even though he hadn't had the nerve to ask for it.

God, life was complex, especially *his* life. Although he hadn't been affected nearly as negatively as Atticus, he'd lost even more than Jada. He'd lost his best friend and only sibling for thirteen years! And everyone seemed to have the attitude that he got what he deserved, which was something he'd wrestled with ever since. *Did* he deserve what happened that night? He'd been a young, stupid kid who'd just wanted to go to a party. Maybe he'd been reckless in some of the things he'd done, far from perfect. But he'd had no desire to hurt anyone, hadn't even touched the gun. So the punishment didn't seem to fit the crime. That he was older than Tobias, even if it was only by a year, made matters worse. His mother, their teachers, everyone had expected him to keep Tobias out of trouble and therefore safe. But Tobias had a mind and will of his own. He would not, could not, be controlled. At the time, Maddox couldn't even keep himself out of trouble. He certainly hadn't been mature enough to be responsible for anyone else.

He pulled his phone out of his pocket and opened his calendar. Tobias was due to be released July 20. Maddox couldn't wait. At the same time, he was leery, afraid to find out exactly what spending so many years behind bars had done to his little brother. Tobias had been put away when he was so young… Maddox couldn't believe much "rehabilitation" had gone on. Tobias hadn't meant to shoot anyone, least of all an eleven-year-old boy. He'd been hallucinating at the time, thought Atticus was some kind of monster attacking him. But that didn't seem to matter to anyone, either.

His phone rang while he was counting the days until Tobias's release. It was his mother, Jill. She'd been calling him a lot lately. When he was young and needed her, she couldn't be relied upon. She'd been too busy going from one man to the next, trying to fulfill herself. But now that he was an adult and could offer *her* some support, she was in almost constant contact.

He was tempted to silence the ringer and send her call to voice mail. He was in no mood to talk to her. She was easier to take when she wasn't using drugs, but given her track record, he couldn't be sure she was as clean as she claimed. And she was so high-strung and emotional, if he didn't answer she'd just call him right back—or leave a long, angry message laced with every swear word she could think of.

With a muttered curse, he hit the talk button. "Hello?"

"Have you decided?"

He pressed three fingers to his forehead. She wanted him to take her when he went to pick up Tobias, but Tobias had specifically requested she *not* come. Maddox didn't want to tell her what Tobias had said, but he couldn't foist her on his brother the second the poor guy walked out of Soledad. Tobias deserved a chance to acclimate, at least to a degree, before having to deal with the one person who'd always been his biggest trigger.

"I don't think so, Mom. We need to give Tobias some space. Both of us."

"How are you giving him space if you're the one picking him up?"

"Someone's got to do it."

"So are you going to bring him to my place after?"

"No. I told you before. He's met someone. They'll be living together."

"Here in LA, though, right? Not in Silver Springs."

"Of course in LA. He could never move to Silver Springs." The only reason Maddox had been able to accept Aiyana's job offer and come to Silver Springs himself was because his brother had another place to go. Tobias had been with the same woman—the sister of a cell mate—for the past year. But letters and visits weren't quite the same as living with someone 24/7, so Maddox was skeptical as to whether the relationship would last. He hoped it would. If she kicked him out before Tobias could find work, Maddox would be left trying to figure out how to help him, which meant he might have to quit the job he'd just accepted even if he decided not to do it because of Jada.

"So if he's coming to LA, anyway, why can't you swing by?"

Because he doesn't want to see you! He's planning to start over, and you make him want to put his fist through a wall. "Because he's eager to see his girlfriend."

"After being in prison for thirteen years, he's not eager to see his *mother*?"

If she was so keen to be with him, she could've driven to Soledad a lot more often than she did.

"I'm sure he'll visit soon," Maddox assured her. "He's been through a lot—let's give him a chance to warm up to life on the outside, to heal a little, before we start making demands."

"How is wanting to see my son making any demands?"

She didn't like to be denied. She probably had reason to be offended at this, but she took offense at *everything*. That was part of the problem.

Maddox opened his mouth to say something that would pull her back from the brink of freaking out—he could hear that high pitch to her voice—but she didn't give him the chance.

"God, you kids are ungrateful!" she snapped and hung up.

Maddox scratched his head. He tried to give her the benefit of the doubt. Especially these days. Life hadn't been easy for her, either. At least she'd stuck around, more or less, and kept a roof over their heads. It was their father who'd really let them down. He'd split when they were so young they barely remembered him.

But emotions weren't always fair and they weren't

often logical. It was still difficult to forgive her for her indifference and selfishness, which left Tobias and him on the streets at loose ends until late in the night, hanging out with the wrong kind of people, when they were only twelve and thirteen. There'd been no one to care what they did, especially if their mother was drinking or using or if she had a man in the house.

He told himself he should call her back. That would be the nice thing to do. But he couldn't make himself. Not today.

He shoved his phone back in his pocket and pulled out the profiles for the students the state hoped to send them. His mother would be back in touch—just as soon as she needed money.

"Do you like living here in Silver Springs?" Jada sent her daughter a sideways glance as they slid the cookies they'd finished onto the rack in the display case side by side.

"*I* do." Maya sent her a confused look. "Why? Don't you?"

"Yeah, I do," she said, but considering what Tiffany had seen at the farmers' market—or rather *who* Tiffany had seen and Jada had briefly spotted herself—Jada was beginning to wonder if it'd been a mistake to come here, if perhaps they should return to LA.

Maya wiped her hands on her Sugar Mama apron and straightened as Jada put the last cookie in place. "So… why are you asking me like that?" she asked. "As if you regret coming here? Don't tell me you're thinking about leaving. Grandma's been nice so far. Hasn't she?"

"She has. I'm not thinking about leaving necessarily.

It's just...this place is very different from LA. I wanted to be sure you like it."

"It *is* different, but I like it better. We can't leave, anyway. Who'd help Grandma?"

Maya made a good point, but she wasn't aware of the bigger picture. Maya knew that Eric, Jada's ex-husband, wasn't her genetic father. Jada had made that clear from the onset. Maya didn't even know her father was alive. Jada had told her that he'd been killed in a motorcycle accident before she was born to protect her from ever feeling rejected, or wondering where he was, or insisting they search for him. Maybe it was wrong to lie. There were moments when Jada felt a tremendous amount of guilt. But the truth would only cause *more* problems.

For the same reason, Jada hadn't told her that it was her father's brother who'd hurt her uncle Atticus or that she was the one responsible for bringing Atticus to the place where he'd been shot—only that he'd gone to a party where there was a scuffle and someone, while on drugs, squeezed off a few shots, after which Atticus had been found bleeding on the floor.

"We'll stay and help Grandma," Jada said. "I was just checking."

"It's so hard to go to a new place. I don't want to do it again," Maya said. "I've already started to make friends here. I wouldn't want to leave Annie."

Maya's best friend was a nice girl. Still, Jada was surprised Annie seemed to matter more than Eric. She'd grown up with him as her stepfather! But when she thought more about it, she decided it was sort of understandable. They'd never been that close. Eric wasn't abusive or unkind in any way; he was just gone a lot. And when he was home, he was preoccupied, emotionally inaccessible. If he'd been more open, loving and engaged, maybe she could've made the marriage work.

She put a hand on her daughter's back to reassure her. "Okay. Don't worry."

Maya smiled in relief but didn't have a chance to say anything before the bell went off over the door and they both turned to see Aiyana Turner, a petite woman with golden-brown skin, long black hair she almost always wore in a braid, bright clothing and lots of turquoise jewelry.

Normally, Jada would've been thrilled to see Aiyana. Everyone loved her. Jada guessed they'd probably put a statue of her in town after she died; she was *that* admired. But that she would stop in today of all days, when Jada hadn't yet seen her since she'd been back, made Jada uneasy. Did Aiyana know about Maddox and why he was in town? Had she kept in touch with him over the years?

It'd be like her. She'd adopted eight of the students from her school and finished raising them, had placed who knew how many others into good homes and worked to support them all long after they left for college, arranging financial help, jobs, anything she could do to help them build productive lives.

"Hello!" Maya chirped. She didn't yet know Aiyana, so she saw only a much-needed customer and went directly into "sales" mode, as she'd seen her grandmother do. "We just finished frosting some of our popular red velvet cookies. Would you like to try one?"

They often put a plate out on the counter with various cookies cut into bite-size pieces for sampling.

"No need to bother with taste-testing for me," Aiyana said with a wink. "I know how good they are. That's why I'm here."

"You save a few dollars if you get a whole dozen…" Maya informed her.

Jada couldn't help chuckling at the twinkle that entered Aiyana's eyes as she played along. "Then that's what I'll do. I always like a bargain."

Excited to have achieved a sale—even an "up" sale, as her grandmother called it, where she talked a customer into ordering more than she otherwise would have— Maya hurried to grab a box.

"It's very nice of you two to help Susan the way you are," Aiyana said to Jada while Maya carefully packaged the cookies. "I bet she's grateful."

If she was grateful, she didn't show it. But Jada suspected her mother still hadn't forgiven her for Atticus and probably never would. "She's had a rough year."

"Yes. I am *so* sorry about your father. I caught a glimpse of you at the funeral but didn't want to intrude on your thoughts."

Jada battled the lump that suddenly swelled in her throat. "Thanks. It was very sudden." And very unexpected. She hadn't had the chance to make things better between them. That was what hurt the most.

"So sad. He was still young." Aiyana waited patiently as Maya finished with the cookies and rang her up, but then she took the bag and said, "I was wondering, providing Maya here feels comfortable manning the store for just a few minutes alone, if you and I could step outside and have a brief chat?"

Jada felt her stomach muscles tighten. Aiyana knew something, all right. She'd bought cookies to have the excuse to stop in, not the other way around. "Um, sure. Okay. You can watch the store for a second, can't you, Maya?"

"Of course. I just showed you I can do the whole thing," she said proudly.

Maya was clearly eager for the opportunity, so Jada took a deep breath and followed Aiyana outside.

Aiyana turned to face her when they were just a few steps from the door but still beneath the overhang that connected most all the stores downtown. "Jada, it's so good to have you back."

Jada felt Aiyana was sincere in that sentiment. Aiyana was sincere about everything. But she could also hear the reservation in her voice. "But I'm not the only one who's back. That's why you're really here, isn't it?"

A sheepish expression revealed the truth before Aiyana even responded. "I'd be lying if I said otherwise. But when I offered to hire Maddox to run New Horizons for Girls, I honestly had no idea you'd be moving back to town, too. This is as much a surprise to me, and to him, as it is to you."

Jada let her breath seep slowly out. "So that's why he's here? To run the new school?"

"That's why."

Oh God. Not only was he staying, he had a good job. "Then he's not just passing through…"

"No. At least, I hope he won't leave. I need him."

Jada shaded her eyes from the sun slanting beneath the overhang. "You *need* him? Are you sure? I mean…is he even qualified to run a school?" Her parents had always said he'd never amount to anything, and she'd had to admit, at least to herself, that they were probably right. Most young men in his situation never did.

"As a matter of fact, he is," Aiyana told her. "He has a master's—finished his schooling in record time once he settled down—and has spent the past three years helping to run a private school in Utah. Not only is he qualified, that school has provided him with a glowing recommendation. I don't think I could find a better candidate. And I know him and like him, which makes working with him even more appealing."

Jada rubbed her forehead. "What about my brother?"

"I'm sorry if hiring Maddox seems insensitive of me. I feel terrible about what happened. I hope you believe that. But Maddox didn't pull the trigger. As far as I'm concerned, he's as much a victim of that night as anyone else. You were all hurt to some degree—your poor brother worst of all, of course, but that doesn't mean he's the only one who deserves some consideration."

Jada stared at the cement beneath her feet. It wasn't as though she could tell Aiyana *not* to hire Maddox. There was no law against his return. She'd always felt a little torn when it came to what her parents had done after the shooting—going so far as to pay his mother to petition the court and have him moved. He had as much right to be here as anyone. "Where is he living?"

"I plan to have a house built on school grounds, but there have been more important places to put those funds in this start-up phase, so I haven't gotten around to that yet."

"Which means…"

"He's renting the back house on Uriah Lamb's property."

Jada knew Uriah. His wife used to teach her piano, not that she'd kept up with it. His property wasn't even as far out as the school. Jada could easily run into Maddox, especially because she couldn't imagine a man his age staying in all weekend. That meant if she wanted to get out, too… "When is his brother being released from prison? Or is he out already?"

"He's not out yet, but that will be happening soon, from what I understand. I can't give you the exact date off the top of my head. It's next month sometime. But I can assure you that Tobias won't be coming here."

Thank God for small favors. "Where will he go?"

"To LA. His mother still lives there, with a roommate these days to help pay the rent, a woman who works at the same bar. From what Maddox has told me, Tobias has a girlfriend who is also in LA. He'll be staying with her."

"I see." There were so many questions Jada wanted to ask, but one more than all the others. "Is Maddox married?" Although this question had nothing to do with the situation with Atticus, if Maddox was involved with another woman, if he had a child or children with someone else, he'd be much less likely to pay much attention to her—or, more important, Maya.

"No."

Jada hated the sympathy in Aiyana's eyes, but there was no fooling her, no pretending Maddox hadn't meant a great deal to her. Aiyana was far too intuitive for that.

"He's never been married," Aiyana added. "Never had any kids."

A trickle of fear ran down Jada's spine. Aiyana didn't know it, but there was a lot more at stake than upsetting Atticus—although, considering Atticus's situation, that was enough. Maddox *did* have a kid. He just didn't know it. And now Jada wasn't sure how she'd keep him from finding out about Maya.

3

On Monday, after Maddox had read the profiles of the students he'd likely be taking on in August, he'd spent the afternoon making staffing decisions and going over his fall budget, seeing if there was any way to nip a bit here or there to give more somewhere else. Aiyana cared more about girls who needed a good place to live than she did about getting paid, so he knew he'd face more financial constraints here than he would at many other jobs. But she did what she did for the right reasons, and that was what made New Horizons so special, why he wanted to be involved. He'd just have to overcome the challenges her generosity created by helping her run fund-raisers, contact alumni who might be willing to contribute and/ or cultivate relationships with those wealthy enough to help. The state paid for the students it sent but at a significantly reduced rate—something Aiyana had negotiated to make it more viable for them. She said she hesitated to ask for too much lest New Horizons never receive the students who needed them most—those who'd been bounced around the foster care system or even the court system.

He'd managed to get a few things done today, but he wasn't at his most productive. He hadn't been able to concentrate. He kept thinking about Jada. Since he'd been back in Silver Springs, it'd been difficult *not* to think of her. Every sight, smell, sound seemed to dredge up those days when they were both so innocent and in love. But now that he knew she was close by, it was even worse. He wondered how she was doing, what her marriage had been like, how old her child was, what had caused her divorce.

Most of all, he wondered if she'd ever forgiven him…

"I thought I might find you here."

He glanced up to see Aiyana poking her head into his office. It was after seven, but there wasn't anywhere else he needed to be. Now that Jada was in town, he felt like he couldn't even go out to dinner or for a drink somewhere.

"Just trying to get prepared." He pretended he was staying late because it was absolutely necessary, but he hadn't done anything here he couldn't have done at home. He just hadn't been interested in staying in his empty house for that long. At least when he'd lived in Utah, he'd had Paris to come home to. He'd broken up with her before he left, but there was still some question as to whether they might get back together. She'd been hitting him up lately, asking if she could come out and see him.

Maybe if he let her come, he'd be able to forget Jada. Except…he wasn't in love with her, and it wasn't right to say yes if he knew it wasn't going to go anywhere.

"Do you have a minute?" Aiyana asked.

He stood and indicated the chair on the other side of his desk. "Of course."

She gestured at the stack of files near his elbow. "How are things going so far?"

"Not bad. There's a lot yet to do, but we'll get there."

A small smile quirked her lips. "Does that mean you're not going to give me notice?"

"Give you notice?"

"Now that you know Jada is living here, too."

He drew a deep breath as he sank into his chair. "I'm tempted."

"I talked to her on Saturday."

To avoid eye contact, he started straightening his desk. She had the uncanny ability to see through anyone. "About…"

"I wanted to let her know you weren't aware she was living here when you accepted the job, and I wasn't aware she was here when I extended it."

He couldn't help stopping what he was doing so he could look up, after all. "Would you have thought twice had you known?"

"Probably, but only because I would've expected you to refuse."

She was right. That would've been a game-changer. "And? What did she say?"

"Not a lot. She's worried about how her brother might react when he learns you're back. But you and I have already talked about Atticus. He needs to let go of what happened that night and move on. As hard-hearted and insensitive as it might be to say, given what he's been through, there is no other choice, not if he wants to lead a happy life."

She'd told him similarly harsh truths over the years. He remembered one call in particular where she told him to quit feeling sorry for himself and get his ass in gear. He'd needed her tough love as much as her unconditional love. He could see that now. Without her, without that one person who kept checking in on him and holding him accountable, he could easily have chosen a much less productive path. "Was she terribly disappointed that I'm breathing the same air?"

Aiyana studied him. "I don't think *disappointed* is the right word."

He wished he didn't care what Jada had said, but he did. "What word would you choose?"

"Worried."

"Well, she has nothing to worry about. I plan to stay well away."

"I did make it clear that you wouldn't bother her."

"Thank you for that."

She lingered, waiting for him to look up at her again. When he did, she said, "She asked if you were married."

Every muscle in his body went taut. "Because…"

"She didn't say, but if my opinion matters at all, I think it's because she loved you, too."

She certainly hadn't done anything to show it. For months after he'd been sent to Rockport Academy outside bitterly cold Chicago, he'd looked for a letter, a phone call, anything. He'd been so devastated, so lonely, that his need manifested itself as a physical ache. His mother had been so angry that he'd let his brother get hold of a gun she wasn't speaking to him (the fact that she'd taken up with yet another man probably had even more to do with her neglect). His brother had been charged as an adult, and since the whole trial process had taken over a year, due to his age and both sides fighting over how he should be tried, he was sent to a regular adult prison. Maddox had lost the one girl he'd loved more than anything he'd ever loved before. And he'd had to live with the knowledge that her little brother, who was only eleven, had been crippled, and she blamed him. Only Aiyana had reached out to him during those terrible months when he'd come so close to running away from that overly strict school and striking out on his own. She'd forced him to see that, as oppressive as the school was, it provided him with his only avenue toward a second chance, that it was an opportunity he'd be foolish to waste, and she'd promised him that he'd receive the money he needed for college if only he'd bring up his grades and begin to apply himself.

Maddox still wasn't sure what had caused him to listen to Aiyana. It certainly wasn't the promise of college. It was her compassion and her fire, her absolute determination, not to lose him to the life he would've had otherwise, he supposed. He remembered being surprised she cared so much. "Do you have any idea what went wrong in her marriage?"

She shook her head. "None. I know Susan but not well, and Jada and I have not stayed in touch."

She'd given *him* her sympathy thirteen years ago, when everyone else had sympathized exclusively with the Brookses. "What's Susan like these days? Has she changed?"

"In my opinion, she has, but not for the better."

"What do you mean?"

"From what I've heard, she's never been very nurturing to Jada. That, of course, got worse after the…accident. You may think Susan blames you and your brother, but I'm sure Jada has taken her own share of the blame. The weird thing is…as hard as she's been on Jada, she seems to be the opposite with Atticus. I've seen him around town. He's capable of living a full life despite his disability, and yet she babies him like crazy. He never left for school, is still living with her to this day."

Maddox put several of the files he had out into his

right-hand drawer. "Well, when Jada tells him I'm back, maybe he'll decide to move."

"*I* think that would be the best thing for him."

"You're trying to make sure I feel comfortable here."

"Is it working?" she joked.

"I believe in what you're doing with the school, the kids."

"Which means you'll stay."

"Yeah. What you're trying to accomplish here is bigger than my own personal discomfort."

Her smile widened as she stood. "I knew you were the right man for the job."

He smiled, too, until she left. Then he let his head fall onto the back of his chair.

Did she tell her mother and brother that Maddox was living in Silver Springs or let Susan and Atticus bump into him one day and figure it out for themselves?

Jada stewed about that, as she had all weekend, while she closed the shop Monday night and headed home. Although it was after nine, thanks to the long days of summer the sun had barely set and the air was still warm and pregnant with the scent of flowers, so many of which were blooming in the pots that hung from the streetlights. Summer was when all the tourists came through. Her mother couldn't afford not to capitalize on the influx, so it'd been a long day for Jada. She hadn't taken time to pack anything for dinner, and she hadn't been able to leave the store to pick up something, so she was hungry as well as tired. Her daughter had left around four thirty, having been invited to dinner and a movie in nearby Santa Barbara with Annie and her family, which left Jada to finish out those last five hours on her own.

Although that meant she'd had nothing but the cookies in the shop to eat, it also meant Maya would be gone for the next two or more hours and she could have some private time to talk to Susan and Atticus—if she wanted it.

It was probably time to address the past. She and her mother had never really talked about what happened, not after the initial blaming and shaming and, when she found out she was pregnant, pressure for her to put the baby up for adoption. When she'd refused to agree, Susan had grown stony and cold and berated her at every turn. She'd acted as if Jada had caused the loss of her brother's mobility— essentially the loss of his entire future productivity—and was now foisting an illegitimate baby on the family to care for when they were already reeling. Her father had just gone silent. If Jada *did* try to talk to him, he was distant, the conversation strained—not real or honest, and definitely not what she'd needed. So she'd moved to LA and had very little interaction with her family during the next few years. As hard as it was to go out on her own at eighteen, and with a baby, it was easier than continuing to bow beneath the overwhelming burden of their disapproval and blame. It wasn't until after she married and her husband finally reached out that they began to associate again, and then very slowly. Her parents had eventually embraced Eric as if they were relieved they were no longer even remotely responsible for her well-being, as if they could finally accept her again on these new terms, and started to acknowledge Maya. And Jada had done her part to let the past go. She certainly hadn't wanted to reopen old wounds. By that point, she'd figured some kind of relationship was better than none, especially because she was beginning to struggle in her marriage, to wonder if she'd made a mistake in committing herself to a man she wasn't passionate about. She'd needed them, needed *someone*. But her father had gone to his grave before they could ever truly get over what'd happened.

She didn't want the same thing to happen with her mother.

She told herself she'd call Atticus away from his gaming console, which was where he'd be because he was always there, and confront them both.

But when she walked in, she saw her mother looking pale and drawn as she lay on the couch, watching TV, and couldn't bring herself to mention Maddox. Having him in town didn't *have* to impact them. What did it change? Nothing! His presence wouldn't alter their routine, compromise their financial picture, limit their opportunities, cost them *anything*. If they ignored him and went about their business, he could ignore them and go about his business, and they could coexist without a problem.

"How'd we do today?" Susan asked as she heard Jada step into the living room.

"We had a flurry of customers around dinnertime. I put the deposit—five hundred and forty-eight dollars—in the night drop on the way home."

"Thank God. The house payment is coming out of my account tomorrow."

"Will you have enough to cover it?"

She adjusted the pillow under her head. "Barely."

"When does your car payment come out?"

"Not for a few days."

They'd have more sales by then, but rent on the store would be due soon, too, not to mention the utilities and advertising expenses.

"Where's Maya?" Susan asked.

A hint of resentment flared up. Her mother had grown to

love Maya so much since they'd come to Silver Springs—
which was a good thing, Jada reminded herself as she
tamped those bitter feelings back down. Still, a little of
that love would've been nice when Maya was just a baby
and Jada had been so desperately in need of emotional
support. Maybe she wouldn't have made the mistake of
marrying Eric, would've been able to distinguish between
desperation and true love, false hope and a genuine connection. "Santa Barbara."

"What's she doing there?"

"Seeing a movie with Annie. Where's Atticus?"

"In his room."

No surprise. "I was wondering if he'd be willing to
help out at Sugar Mama tomorrow. I have a few things I
need to do for my own business."

"You do what you need to," her mother said. "I've
got the store."

That was the problem. Her mother *didn't* have the
store, shouldn't be working eleven hours straight through.
She was no longer up to it, and Atticus was perfectly capable. "Why can't he take my place?"

"It's hard for him to maneuver his wheelchair behind
the counters and to reach into the cases and hand customers their sacks, that sort of thing."

"We can figure out a way to make it work."

"He's tried. It's too difficult."

He could *absolutely* do it. That he wouldn't irritated
Jada. And the fact that their mother enabled his excuses
made it all worse. "Maya could go with him and do all
the reaching and handing."

"He has anxiety problems, Jada. Being in charge of
the store makes it worse. I don't want to send him spiral-
ing into another depression."

But was it really anxiety? Or a manipulation technique designed to make sure he never had to do anything he didn't want to?

Jada was tempted to ask. It was time *someone* did. Her mother was so lost without her father she was indulging Atticus in every respect, focusing so much of her attention on him that he'd probably *never* leave home. And maybe that was her intention, to make sure she'd never be alone.

Jada opened her mouth to say something but, knowing it would cause an argument, clamped it shut again and headed for the kitchen.

"What are you doing?" her mother called.

"Getting something to eat. Are you hungry?"

"No. Atticus and I ate earlier. There's a good show on. You should come watch it with me."

"I can't," Jada said. Now that she'd finished working at the store, she had her own work to do.

4

Maddox couldn't help himself. He drove past Jada's house on his way home. He'd managed not to go over on that side of town since he'd been back, but now that he knew she was back, too, it was harder.

He saw an old Buick, a car so dated he associated it with her mother, a practical, not overly expensive truck with a wheelchair lift, which had to belong to Atticus, and a newer Chevy Volt parked on the street.

That had to be Jada's vehicle right there.

At least now he knew what she drove and would be aware that she was close by if he spotted it.

He told himself to get the hell out of there. It was not so late yet that the house was dark. Someone could easily glance out the window and spot him.

But instead of leaving, he stopped completely and idled right in front of the house. Suddenly and inexplicably, he was tempted to go to the door. He wanted to tell them, while they were all there together, that he was sorry for what'd happened to Atticus, and that, although they refused to accept his apology, he was sincere. He also wanted to promise that he wouldn't bother them ever again, that they had nothing to worry about where he was concerned. He didn't like the idea of Jada cringing at the prospect of bumping into him or being hesitant to go out for fear she might encounter him. Her family would probably be looking over their shoulders, too, filled with dread as they scoured the area for any glimpse of him—as if he was a leper and might infect them if he came too close.

He hated feeling as though, just by being here, he made someone else *that* miserable.

He leaned forward so he could see out his passenger window. The drapes were open on the big picture window in front. What would they do if they saw him? Would they come out and yell at him to get away?

He wondered if they'd raise a fuss now that they knew he was in town or try to convince Aiyana that she should hire someone else.

She *should* hire someone else, he thought. Although he was eager to take charge of New Horizons for Girls, he'd feel lower than dirt if she had to fight the Brooks family and all their friends and sympathizers on his behalf. He couldn't imagine anyone else would support her if she took up for him, so she could find herself facing a formidable force alone. Very few people in Silver Springs knew him personally. What they did know was that he'd been busted for trying to steal a car when he was sixteen, had to go to a correctional school, where he and his brother had caused serious trouble, so much so that one of their own had been injured for life.

His reputation wasn't anything that would recommend him…

He waited for several seconds but no one came to the window or walked outside. Had that happened, he would've parked and gotten out of his truck, allowed them their chance to scream and rail at him. But knowing how unwelcome he'd be even though he was there to apologize made him decide to give it some time. Perhaps it'd be easier if he approached them after a few weeks had gone by and they had a chance to get used to the idea of his being in town. If nothing happened as a result of his presence, they could possibly develop some trust that he wasn't going to get in their way.

With a sigh, he gave his truck some gas and, at the end of the street, turned toward his own place, which was situated on a sixteen-acre tangerine orchard toward the end of the ten-mile-long east-west valley that held Silver Springs like a hand cupping a precious sip of water.

As attractive and affluent as downtown Silver Springs was, he liked living out away from the quaint shops and upscale restaurants. He preferred wide-open spaces and being able to smell the rich soil and citrus on the property. Known for its Mediterranean climate, with hot, dry summers and temperate winters, Silver Springs could grow almost anything—and did. Avocados, walnuts, figs, winter and summer vegetables, pears and other fruit were all produced in the area, along with a variety of fresh herbs. There wasn't a better place to grow fresh fruits and vegetables on the planet.

He loved this part of California, which was why it was so difficult to imagine leaving again, but he'd do it to protect Aiyana from any kind of backlash.

When he pulled down the dirt road that led to his house, his landlord, Uriah Lamb, a crusty old farmer with a salt-and-pepper flattop, came to stand in his doorway and peer out as though he'd been listening for Maddox's truck. Uriah lived alone in the 1920s house that fronted the road; Maddox lived in a smaller one-bedroom behind, originally built for Uriah's son, who now lived on the East Coast.

The smell of fresh-cut grass, strong and pervasive, rose to Maddox's nostrils the second he climbed out. Uriah cut the grass regularly whether it needed it or not. Maddox's landlord was always up at dawn and in bed by ten. He'd lost his wife of fifty years only eight months ago, so routine was about all he had left. He was estranged from his only son; Maddox wasn't sure why. He only knew that Uriah had mumbled something about it when he'd first seen the house.

"I've got a fresh watermelon," Uriah called as soon as Maddox drew within earshot. "Would you like to come in and have a slice?"

Eager to head to his own place, Maddox nearly refused. But then he reconsidered. What would it hurt to stop in for a minute? The old guy would be going to bed soon—would probably be in bed *now* if he hadn't been waiting for Maddox—so it wasn't as if he'd expect Maddox to stay long. "Sure. That sounds great."

Maddox had been inside Uriah's house before, when he was signing the lease, but he was once again struck by the simplicity of the old guy's existence. Although everything was dated, it was in good repair. If Uriah wasn't out working in the orchard fertilizing, pruning, fixing the irrigation system or painting tree trunks to protect against pests, he was adding electrical tape to whatever needed it, painting the fence around his house to protect it from the elements or caulking any nook or cranny that might possibly be subjected to damaging moisture. He could serve as the poster boy for the saying "Use it up, wear it out, make it do or do without."

"How's everything working back there?" Uriah asked as he led Maddox into his kitchen.

Contextual clues made it easy for Maddox to assume "back there" meant the house he was living in. "Great."

"Shower isn't leaking again…"

"No, sir. I'd alert you if it was."

"You'll have to watch the toilets. The septic tank's getting pretty full."

"I'll do that."

He put a plate with a gold pattern on the table bearing a thick, round slice of watermelon and provided a fork.

Uriah brought his own slice with him when he came over to sit down across from Maddox. He hesitated for a moment before digging in and his eyes flicked toward the stove. Maddox wondered if he was remembering all the times he must've sat in this kitchen with his wife, who was now gone. This was his first summer without her.

After clearing his throat, the old man took a deep breath as if he had to dredge up enough interest to actually eat, now that he'd gotten the watermelon sliced.

"You okay?" Maddox asked.

"Got a heat wave comin'," he said instead of answering. He might not have heard. He was losing his hearing. But Maddox had the feeling that wasn't the case this time. He didn't want to talk about the difficulty of his current situation. "S'pose to be over a hundred this next week."

"No kidding?" Maddox said. "In June? That's high, isn't it? I read somewhere the average is eighty-three."

"We've hit as high as a hundred and ten before. That's the record. Heard it on the news just this morning." He forked up another bite. "But yeah, one hundred's hot, 'specially for June."

"How long have you lived in the area?"

"Since I married Shirley."

This proved he was thinking about her; he could've used a different benchmark.

"Course, I've downsized a lot since then," he added. "Used to own three hundred acres."

"When did you sell the rest?"

He waved his fork. "Oh, over the years. Broke off chunks here and there before I put in the trees."

"What were you planting back then?"

"Tomatoes, mostly."

"You like pixie tangerines better?"

"They're easier. You'll work your fingers to the bone growing tomatoes. I'm too old for that now."

"You seem to be getting around okay." Maddox offered him an encouraging smile.

"I'm moving a lot slower than I used to."

Maddox barely knew Uriah. He wasn't sure what he was doing sitting in his landlord's house at nearly ten o'clock on a warm summer evening, but the way the old guy had used fresh watermelon to entice him to come in told Maddox he was tired of being alone. He was probably alone too much. "Where, exactly, does your son live?"

His craggy eyebrows came together but he answered readily enough. "Silver Spring, Maryland."

"Are you kidding?"

"No. That's something, ain't it?"

"I didn't realize there was another Silver Springs."

"It's clear across the country and without the *s*, but... still quite a coincidence."

"What does he do there?"

A far-off look settled over his face.

"Mr. Lamb?"

He started eating again but mechanically—raising his

fork, putting the food in his mouth, lowering it. "I'm not certain, to be honest with you."

Maddox scrambled for something to say in response. "When's the last time you talked to him?"

"It's been about five years."

What could possibly have come between them? Maddox was curious, but he wasn't about to ask. He was pretty certain he'd been invited in to make the night easier to get through, not harder. "It's amazing the way you handle this place all on your own."

"Requires constant effort," he said. "So how's that job of yours at New Horizons?"

"Great. The school won't open until mid-August, so we're just getting the curriculum ready, choosing textbooks, staffing, that sort of thing."

"You told me you were born in LA. Is that where your folks live?"

"My mother."

He looked up. "And your father?"

"My mother says he was born in Seattle. She thinks he might've gone back there when he left us."

The old guy stopped chewing. "How old were you when that happened?"

"Four. My brother was three."

"Do you have much contact with your father?"

Maddox felt nothing but contempt for the man who'd left his mother alone with two children and no support, financial or otherwise. Even if his father reached out, he'd tell him to go to hell. It was about twenty years too late for a relationship. "None. He didn't leave a forwarding address. Wasn't too keen on the idea of child support, I guess."

"That ain't right."

"I survived." His life could've been a lot easier, though. He often wondered if his mother would've been a better mother if only she'd had someone to help her.

They ate in silence for a few minutes. Then Uriah said, "Where's your brother these days?"

Maddox hadn't mentioned that he had a history in Silver Springs when he'd answered the ad that brought him to this small orchard. He hadn't wanted to damage his chances of getting the house, in case Uriah happened to know the Brooks family. He'd figured, if Uriah didn't remember his name from having read it in the paper or hearing it on the lips of all the shocked Silver Springs residents at the time, that was on him. But now that Uriah was asking a direct question, Maddox decided to be up front, partly because the Brookses already knew he was back, so it didn't matter if Uriah told them, and partly because he refused to act in any way that could be construed as being ashamed of his family. "He's in prison."

The old man's hand froze halfway to his mouth. "For what?"

"For shooting Atticus Brooks."

"Ah." He nodded slowly. "Thought I'd heard your name somewhere before. Couldn't place it."

"Then you know the Brookses…"

"Not well. I know Susan owns the cookie shop in town. My wife used to stop in and buy a dozen every now and then. Sometimes she'd take in a bag of tangerines. She felt bad for Susan's boy, for what happened."

So did Maddox. That was the thing. He wished he could have that night to live over again. He'd stop that whole chain of events. "Now that you know it was my brother who was responsible for putting Atticus in that wheelchair, do you regret renting to me?"

Finished eating, he stood up to dispose of the rind. Maddox watched him rinse his plate. "Mr. Lamb?"

"Did *you* have anything to do with it?" he asked above the sound of the water rushing through the tap.

"I was there that night, at the same party," Maddox replied. "But no."

He came over to get Maddox's plate. "Then I don't regret renting to you."

"When were you going to tell me Maddox Richardson is back in town?"

It was nearly two weeks later, on a Friday night at midnight, when her mother opened the door to Jada's bedroom and hit her with that question—spoken low so that Maya and Atticus wouldn't overhear from their own bedrooms on the other side of the house. Jada had spent every single day since she'd learned Maddox was living in Silver Springs checking to make sure the coast was clear wherever she went—watching the foot traffic outside the cookie store, peering cautiously down every aisle before entering it when she went to the grocery store, obliquely glancing at the other drivers when she was on the road or stopping to get gas and, much to the consternation of Tiffany, refusing to go to the bar or any other place she thought single people might hang out. She hadn't seen hide nor hair of him, so she'd begun to relax, to think they could live parallel lives that would never intersect beyond that brief sighting of him at the farmers' market Saturday before last.

This brought all of her cautious optimism to an abrupt halt.

"Jada?"

The accusation in her mother's voice, as if Jada had *in-*

vited Maddox back, was upsetting. But this conversation was going to be difficult enough even if she approached it carefully, so she tried to keep the pique out of her own voice. "I *wasn't* going to tell you."

She came in and closed the door behind her. "Because..."

The subtle lines in her mother's face, around her eyes and mouth, seemed more pronounced today than ever. Jada wanted to feel some sympathy for her. She wasn't well. But Jada was too defensive to feel anything other than a heavy dose of resentment over the past, and irritation that her mother would approach her this boldly, as if she were still a child. "Because I knew it would upset you, and I didn't see any reason to do that."

She fisted her hands on her hips. "You didn't think I had a right to know? He's Maya's father, for crying out loud!"

Jada knew what was at stake. "I realize that. But *he* doesn't know it and, other than Atticus, neither does anyone else." Except Tiffany, although Jada wasn't willing to admit that she'd told her friend. She'd been given strict directions not to tell a soul. Learning that she had would only make her mother angrier. Susan wouldn't stop to think about how young Jada had been when everything went down and how badly she'd needed someone to confide in who wouldn't try to tell her what to do. Jada probably wouldn't have had the guts to stand up to her parents and keep Maya, not while she was feeling so guilty and terrible about Atticus, without Tiffany insisting that it was *her* life and *her* decision, and she'd be the one who'd have to live with the regret if she made the wrong choice.

"She looks just like him," her mother said. "He could easily guess!"

Icy tentacles of fear wrapped ever tighter around

Jada's heart, but her mother always argued for the worst possible scenario. She supposed most mothers did that in an effort to keep their babies safe; she found herself warning Maya about the terrible things that could happen if she didn't watch out, too. "It's not as if I can chase him off. I don't own the area. Neither do you. We don't get to dictate who lives here and who doesn't. I'm not sure it was fair of you to do what you did last time."

"Fair of me?" she cried.

Jada clenched her jaw. "You and Dad. But never mind. Bottom line he has a great job working for New Horizons. He'll be heading up the girls' side, so he has good reason for being here."

"You know quite a bit about what he's doing."

Jada couldn't miss the insinuation. "Just the basics."

Her mouth tightened. "Then you've talked to him."

"No, I haven't. Tiffany saw him at the farmers' market and told me about it. I didn't know if he was just visiting or what until Aiyana showed up at the store and told me she'd hired him." She closed her laptop. "Who told you I already knew he was in town?"

"Evangeline, the lady who owns the olive oil and balsamic vinegar shop a few stores down. She saw you talking to Aiyana and assumed you were planning to enroll Maya."

"Why would I send Maya to a correctional school? She's a good student."

"*She* doesn't know that. She has a fourteen-year-old daughter who's giving her nothing but trouble. Purple hair. Piercings everywhere. Cuts herself. Shoplifts. Runs away every few months. Evangeline has been beside herself for the past several years, can't seem to handle her, so she's relieved to have New Horizons as an option."

"She's going to send her daughter to a boarding school that's here in town? Doesn't that sort of defeat the purpose?"

"Why would it? Aiyana's giving her a steal on tuition. She wouldn't be able to afford it, otherwise. She's spent every dime she has trying to get her shop going."

"I'm not sure it'll have the same effect if her daughter goes as a day student and comes home to the same friends and situation that had her cutting herself to begin with."

"She's going to stay there, so it'll be the same as if she's miles away. Aiyana doesn't allow the boarding students to go off campus, not without permission from their parents. And Aiyana is making Evangeline sign a contract that she will come see her every Sunday for two hours, from one to three, but won't show up any other time or give her permission to leave, except for a death in the family or holidays."

"It'll be interesting to see how that works—being so close and yet so far away." Jada wasn't being facetious; she was sincere in that comment. She'd heard Aiyana could work miracles, but this sounded like a unique situation.

"Although I wish her the best, what happens with Evangeline's daughter is really none of our concern. I only brought her up because it was Evangeline who mentioned the new principal. She asked me if I'd met him, says he seems young but capable. I nearly spilled my coffee when she told me his name!"

"I bet."

"I don't understand how Aiyana could hire a man with Maddox Richardson's background."

"Then you don't know Aiyana, because that is absolutely something she would do. She doesn't just give lip service to believing in her students. She fully supports them. Besides, she claims he's qualified."

"In what way?" she scoffed.

"He has a master's." That was a pretty lofty accomplishment given that Susan had insisted he'd never amount to much. Jada was tempted to throw that in her face, but she bit her tongue.

"That doesn't mean anything."

"It means he's qualified for the job!"

"What about his no-good brother?"

"What about him? I doubt much has changed for Tobias, since he's been in prison all these years."

"Don't tell me he's coming here after he gets out."

"Aiyana claims he's not, but I have no idea if that will change. I didn't know *Maddox* was coming back."

She wrung her hands. "I can't imagine how Atticus will react when he hears about this."

"I'm guessing he'll take his lead from you. If you act as though it's no big deal, maybe he will, too."

"No big deal?" She gaped at Jada as though she'd lost her mind. "Maddox Richardson got you pregnant before you were even out of high school, which changed the entire course of your life! You have *no* education as a result! And because of him and that evil brother of his, your own brother will be in a wheelchair until the day he dies!"

"Sex takes two." Jada couldn't defend Maddox when it came to what'd happened to Atticus, but she wasn't about to let her mother blame him for Maya. Jada had wanted to make love to Maddox every bit as badly as he'd wanted to make love to her. They could hardly keep their hands off each other. As a matter of fact, she'd never had better sex. There were plenty of times, even while she was married, that she'd lain awake, thinking about how incredibly erotic and all-consuming those encounters had been, and wondering if she'd ever experience the same depth of feeling.

"I haven't forgotten your part in it," her mother snapped and stalked out of the room.

5

Maya was lying on top of the bed on Saturday while her friend Annie Coates sat at the white desk in the corner of the room with a pencil and notebook. Downstairs, they could hear Annie's parents banging around in the kitchen and smell chicken wafting up from the grill outside, since the door to the patio stood open so Mr. Coates could come in and out without bothering to open it.

"Tell me *everything* you know about him," Annie said, poised to make a list.

Maya was so glad to have found Annie. She'd never had a friend like her. She'd only been in Silver Springs for three months, but it felt as if they'd known each other forever. "That's just it. I don't know anything! I haven't met one single person who knows less about their dad than I do."

"Because he died before you were born. You never got to meet him."

Maya frowned. "It's not only that. My mother doesn't like to talk about him for some reason. She acts weird whenever I bring him up."

Annie wrote something in the notebook she had out. "*How* weird?"

Maya pictured her mother's face, how tense it grew whenever Maya asked about her father. "That's hard to explain. Worried or something."

Annie looked up. "Maybe she misses him. Maybe it makes her sad to remember him. My mom always cries when she talks about my grandmother, who died last year."

Sad wasn't the impression Maya got, but she didn't have a better explanation. "I guess. I just wish she'd tell me *a little* more about him."

"When was the last time you asked?"

Maya brushed the crumbs from the cookies they'd eaten earlier off Annie's comforter. "When we were packing up and leaving Eric."

"She might've thought you were too young to hear about the motorcycle crash. My parents won't talk about smashed heads or dying people, either. Not in front of me. They say it's too *gruesome*."

"How old do I have to be to hear about my own father?" Maya rolled over and shoved a pillow beneath her head as she stared up at the ceiling. "In two months I'll be *thirteen*! That's old enough to hear about motorcycle crashes."

"True." Annie blew a bubble with the big wad of chewing gum in her mouth and it popped. "Did she say you could talk about it when you're older?"

Maya shook her head.

Annie pulled the remains of an even bigger bubble off her face. "What *did* she say?"

"Nothing, really. He was a wonderful man, and I look just like him."

"That's good!"

Maya lifted her head. "What's good about it?"

Annie shrugged. "She said he was nice. That's better than saying he was mean."

"But get this—when I asked her what his last name was, she couldn't remember it!"

Annie dropped her pencil. "No way!"

"Yes way! How can she be too sad to talk about him if she doesn't even remember his last name?"

Annie bent to pick up the pencil, which had rolled onto the floor. "Do you know his *first* name?"

"Madsen."

"I've never heard of anyone by *that* name."

"I *think* that's what it is. When I asked, she said 'Mad…' and then she stopped and said '…sen' really fast."

Annie bit her lip. "She might be embarrassed for having a baby when she wasn't married and all that."

"I know. *And* when she was so young. She has one of those dangly things you get at graduation in her scrapbook that says she graduated from high school the same year I was born."

"She never went to college?"

"No." Everyone who saw her mother assumed she was twenty-four or twenty-five, not thirty. Sometimes people asked if they were sisters, which made Jada squirm. Saying they were barely eighteen years apart made whoever was asking clamp their mouth shut and lift their chin, as if he or she suddenly smelled something stinky.

"I don't see how we're ever going to find out more about your father if she won't tell you anything."

"That's why we're trying to come up with ideas, remember?"

Annie blew another bubble, which made a soft *poof*

as it broke. "I hate to tell you this, but I don't even see a place to start."

"We aren't very good detectives if we give up *that* easily."

"Then…what are we going to do?"

"My mom had to show my birth certificate to get me into school."

"Which means…"

"I saw it."

"Why is that any big deal?"

"Because a birth certificate says when and where you were born. It also says who your parents are."

Annie jumped to her feet. *"Did it have your dad's name?"*

"No. And my mother used Brooks as her last name, so that didn't tell me anything, either."

"Her last name is Brooks now."

"It's always been Brooks, except when she was married to Eric."

"Then I still don't get it," Annie said, growing exasperated.

"My birth certificate said I was born *here*. That means my father had to have been alive close to that time and living here, too. It takes…you know—" she lowered her voice to a whisper so that there would be no danger of Annie's older brother hearing them in the next room "—s-e-x between a man and a woman to have a baby."

Annie giggled. "I can't even imagine letting a boy put his *thing* in me."

Maya shuddered at the prospect. "Me, either. But it can't be *all* bad if everyone does it, and my mother must've done it with my dad or I wouldn't be here."

"If your mother was still in high school when she got pregnant, maybe he was, too."

"That's what I'm thinking."

"Well, if your dad was in high school when your mom got pregnant, he was probably living with his family. Do you think *they* could still be around? His parents at least?"

"I wish, but my mom told me they moved away."

"Did she say where they went?"

"She said she wasn't sure."

Annie pulled out the tie holding her hair back and let it fall as she combed her fingers through it. "Wow. This is going to be hard."

The thought that she might never know anything more than she did right now was discouraging. Maya wasn't out to make her mother feel bad about the fact that she didn't have her father in her life. She'd once had a school-teacher pull her aside to tell her she had a very nice step-father and should be grateful for him. But Maya hadn't been complaining about Eric when she wrote that paper about her father—she just wanted to fill in the blanks. Even those kids who didn't have any contact with their father had usually *met* him—or at least seen a picture. Maya knew almost *nothing*! "It'll be easier now that I'm living here."

"In what way?" Annie asked.

"We know he was probably close to my mom's age. And we know he was living here when she got pregnant, which would be nine months before I was born. I say we go to the library."

"How will that help?"

"The motorcycle wreck that killed him should've been reported in the paper. I tried to find something about it online, but it said old newspapers were put on micro... something at the library."

"Good! We'll find out what that means, because you're right. Wrecks and deaths and murders and stuff are usually in the paper, especially here, because we don't have a lot of other news."

"If that doesn't work, maybe there's a way to learn who was living here the year I was born," Maya said. "A list or something. His name is weird, like you said, so if we look through all the school yearbooks from that time, we might find him. There can't be two Madsens."

Annie's eyes flew wide. "Of course! You're so smart! Even if we can't find any high school yearbooks at the library, we can ask at the high school. The secretary or someone else probably keeps them. Did your mother go to Albany or McGregor?"

"The colors of her graduation tassel were red and white, so..."

"The Bulldogs. That's McGregor. We've narrowed it down some already."

"Annie! Maya! Neil! Dinner's ready!" Annie's mother called from downstairs.

Maya heard Annie's brother's door open and rolled off the bed. "Do you think we'll find anything?"

"Of course I do. All we needed was a start, and now we've got that," she said and lifted her hand for a high five.

It was so anticlimactic to learn Jada was in town and then have the rest of the month go by without a single sighting or confrontation. Maddox almost laughed at himself for ever having considered moving. He would've given up a good job for nothing. A decent living arrangement, too. Because he avoided stopping in town whenever possible and mainly just went back and forth between the orchard and the school, he'd been spending a lot of evenings playing chess with Uriah. At first, he'd done it because he couldn't bring himself to say no to someone who was so obviously lonely, especially when he was bored himself and had no good reason to refuse. But it was getting to the point where he looked forward to the challenge Uriah posed. The old man wasn't easy to beat. He still had a sharp mind, but that was what made Maddox feel sorry for him the most. His body was slowing down, could no longer keep up with all that had once been so easy for him, which *had* to evoke the worst kind of frustration. It had to be sad to lose the people you loved, too. Maddox always felt bad when he saw Uriah's gaze linger on the photograph that graced his wife's piano—their wedding picture. And he was still curious about Uriah's son. The man never talked about him.

"Your move," Uriah said.

"Yeah, I know," Maddox grumbled. He'd let Uriah split his king and queen with a knight, so he had no choice except to move his king out of check, which would sacrifice his queen. Maddox had battled back from a deficit before, but he wasn't seeing a clear way out this time.

Although…he still had both rooks. Maybe he could manage to bring one of his pawns across the board and get his queen back. That would take some maneuvering, but…

After he lost his queen, Maddox captured Uriah's knight. "Your move."

"I think I'm going to win this one," he said.

Maddox scowled at him. "I haven't given up yet."

A slight smile curved the old man's lips—right before

he took one of the rooks Maddox was depending on to help save the game. How Maddox hadn't seen that coming was beyond him. It was so obvious. "Damn."

Uriah chuckled. "Your mind isn't on chess this evening. What's going on?"

"Nothing."

"It's still early, only…what, six? You need to get out, do something. It's a Friday, for God's sake. The weekend's here."

"And what do you think I should do?"

"Go to a movie. Grab dinner with a date. Get a drink. You know, burn off some of that restless energy. You're too young to be working all the time."

Maddox finished the soda Uriah had offered him. Uriah had confided that he'd once had an alcohol problem, so he didn't touch the stuff these days, didn't even have it in the house. "I'm not working all the time. I'm right here, playing chess with you, aren't I?"

"Yes, and you're doing it often enough that I know you're not doing anything else."

"That's okay." Maddox laid down his king to signify his surrender. "Let's start another match."

"No." Uriah pushed away from the board. "Get out of here."

"What?"

"You heard me. Go do something fun."

Maddox *had* been feeling cooped up, on edge, tense. "I guess I could go to Santa Barbara…"

Uriah waved that idea away with one gnarled hand. "Don't waste your time with the drive. It'll cost you a lot more if you need to take an Uber home. Just go down to the Blue Suede Shoe. They have a live band playing on the weekends."

"And if Jada is there?" They'd spoken a little about Jada, so Uriah knew Maddox wanted to avoid her.

"Let's face it. You're going to run into her at some point. You might as well get it over with so you can be comfortable in this town."

"I'm not convinced I'll be any more comfortable after. I'm sure she wants me gone."

"She might not even be there. She's probably manning the store for her mother until nine. And if I'm wrong? Maybe she'll feel more comfortable, too, if you clear the air. Let her know you have no ill intent. Tell her your brother won't be moving here when he gets out on the twentieth. A little reassurance can go a long way."

Maddox remembered the night he'd driven past her house. He'd wanted to apologize then. He'd decided to give the Brookses some time, but three weeks might be enough. "I'm not convinced she's ready to hear from me."

"Then she can say so."

Letting his breath go in a long sigh, he stood up. "All right. What's the worst that can happen? They figure out a way to get rid of me like they did before?" he joked, but Uriah didn't laugh.

"They'd better not even try."

Maddox smiled at him.

"You've grown up since then." He clapped Maddox on the back. "Let's just hope they'll give you the chance to prove it."

Jada wasn't at the Blue Suede Shoe. At first, Maddox was relieved. He sat at the bar, had a drink and watched a Dodgers game. As he listened to others talk and laugh, he realized that he was getting lonely here in Silver Springs. Coming to a "new" place, one where the only people he knew, other than Aiyana and her two sons who also worked at New Horizons, didn't want him around, wasn't conducive to him making friends.

Still, he was glad he'd come out tonight. Uriah had been right—he'd needed the change of scenery.

Oddly enough, as the night wore on and he kept watching the door, he began to feel more disappointed than relieved. He'd never had a chance to talk to Jada after Atticus was shot, to tell her how broken up he was by it all and how terrible he felt for her brother. While the prospect of confronting her remained as daunting as ever, it was also an opportunity he craved.

So instead of driving home when the game ended, he found himself cruising past Sugar Mama. He didn't want to go in if Susan was there. But if Jada was alone, and the store wasn't busy, he figured it would be a good opportunity to speak to her.

He couldn't see any customers inside the store, but the window didn't show everything. Movement told him there was someone behind the counter. Was there a second person in back?

He drove around to the alley, hoping to get a better idea of what and whom he might face, and was encouraged when he saw only one vehicle: the Chevy Volt.

That could mean Jada was working alone…

Or had her mother hitched a ride to work?

He figured he might as well find out. It'd be easier to encounter them both for the first time here, while there wasn't anyone else in the store, than in a crowded restaurant or bar.

He parked down the street, so that he wouldn't start any tongues wagging with his visit, and ambled down the covered sidewalk. He was grateful that the sun was finally setting. Normally, he loved the long days of summer, but tonight he felt obvious, awkward, out of place. Dusk blurred the lines around him, made him feel as though he didn't stand out as much as he would otherwise.

When he came close to the sign for Sugar Mama, he stopped and glanced uncertainly into the street to see if anyone was watching him.

There didn't seem to be, but he turned around, anyway. This was bullshit, he told himself. He was stupid to bother her. Everything had been going along fine. He just needed to keep his distance.

But after only three steps, he stopped again. He *wanted* to see her. Was that so terrible?

Without allowing himself to think about it again, he took a deep breath, went back and walked into the store.

6

Jada was in the back putting the last of the cookies into plastic bags and marking them as "day olds," which meant they'd be on sale tomorrow, when she heard the bell over the door and cursed under her breath. Of course, as soon as she started closing up early so she could go home and do her own work, she'd have a customer. It had been absolutely dead tonight. An *hour* had gone by since her last sale. But she should've known better, she told herself. It never failed.

Plastering a smile on her face to cover her exhaustion and irritation, she hurried out to greet her new patron and froze. An older, taller and much more muscular version of Maddox stood on the other side of the display cases. His black hair was still thick and wavy and looked as though it could use a good cut, but she liked it. It softened the harsher lines of his cheekbones and jaw.

He's more beautiful than ever. That was the first thought that went through her mind. The rest was just panic. Since she'd learned he was in town, she'd been keeping a sharp eye out for him. She'd expected to encounter him eventually. It stood to reason that if they lived in the same area long enough, it was bound to happen. But she'd never dreamed he'd just stroll into the cookie shop one night.

"Maddox…"

He shoved his hands into his worn jeans. "Jada, I hope… I hope you don't mind me stopping by. I just… I wanted to tell you a few things." He gestured toward the door. "And then I'll get out of here and leave you alone, okay?"

She could hardly breathe. She saw so much of him in their daughter. Those beautiful eyes. The proud chin. The hint of vulnerability he was trying so hard to mask with all that raw masculinity.

Thank God Maya was spending the night with Annie tonight and wasn't helping in the shop.

Jada swallowed hard. "Okay." She wanted to say a few things herself but didn't know how or where to start. It didn't seem to matter, anyway, because her throat had nearly closed off. She couldn't have said much if she'd tried.

He blew out a sigh. "I'm sorry," he said. "I want you to know that. I never intended for anyone to get hurt when I pushed you to take Atticus to that party. It's no excuse. I shouldn't have done it. The consequences of my actions have been…terrible. But I never dreamed anything like that would happen. It came out of nowhere. Tobias was always a little troubled, of course. And angry at the world. Hell, we both were. Still, I didn't know that anyone would have a gun, let alone that he'd somehow get hold of it or use it."

"Maddox…"

He held up a hand so she'd let him finish. "Anyway, it might seem as though I just went on and lived my life, as cavalier as you please, while your and your brother's

lives were destroyed. But that isn't the case. I've thought
about it almost every day since. And I'm sorry. I would
give anything to change the past, but since that's not possible, I want to assure you that I won't make what happened worse by getting in your way or bothering you or
your family now that I'm working in the area, okay?"

She blinked several times, trying to stanch the tears
that suddenly welled up, but it was no good. She could
feel them spilling over her lashes and running down her
cheeks.

When he saw her reaction, the color drained from
his face. "I shouldn't have come. I didn't mean to upset
you. I'm sorry. That's all I wanted to say. I'll leave you
alone," he said and hurried out before she could utter
another word.

Jada wanted to go after him. She started around the
counter before realizing that she couldn't leave the store
unattended. She'd have to lock up first and by then he'd
be gone, or so far away it'd create a spectacle to chase
him down. Her mother wouldn't be happy if she closed
up during business hours in the first place, but to close
up to speak to Maddox?

Evangeline might see her talking to him and say something to Susan, and Jada knew how well that would go
over. Once Susan had learned that Maddox was in town,
Jada had wanted to tell Atticus, too. Get it over with so
they all knew and could deal with the reality. But her
mother insisted that any reminder of that night would
send her brother into a deep depression. When Jada insisted he'd find out eventually, Susan had said she'd look
for the right time to tell him herself. From the way Atticus was acting, that hadn't happened yet.

Jada started toward the back. She needed a chance to

recover before she finished closing. But before she could even reach the small bathroom and blow her nose, the bell sounded over the door out front again.

Squeezing her eyes closed, she tried to summon the strength to pretend nothing had happened. She didn't want to face any customers right now.

Besides, it was closing time. She was eager to be done.

But it wasn't a customer. It was Tiffany, who'd decided that they were going out tonight even if they had to drive to Santa Barbara for Jada to feel safe.

"Jada? Was that who I *think* it was?" she called.

With a sniff, Jada dashed a hand over her cheeks before returning to the front.

"Oh God," Tiffany said after taking one look at her. "It *was* Maddox I passed on the street."

Jada nodded. She'd repressed so many of her feelings since the night Atticus was shot. She'd had to, for her brother's sake. He'd been what was important—helping him get through his many surgeries and recovery. She'd felt responsible for what'd happened throughout it all. She'd also *immediately* fallen in line with her parents' wishes, accepting their anger and punishments for her disobedience. In a way, it meant punishing herself, too, by cutting off all contact with Maddox.

Seeing him brought it all back—the pain, the anger and the fear. "Yeah."

"He came in here?"

"For a second."

"What'd he say?" She narrowed her eyes. "He doesn't know about Maya…"

"No." Her heart pounded as she thought about how he might feel if he ever found out.

"So why'd he come? Was he a dick? Did he hurt your feelings?"

The rapid-fire questions felt like bullets even though Tiffany was clearly on her side. Jada was just so sensitive, so raw. "He didn't do anything wrong, Tiff."

"Coming in here was wrong! What was he thinking? He has to know how your family feels!"

"Please—calm down. He came to say he's sorry. Is that so bad?"

A frown tugged on Tiffany's mouth. "Oh, that's how it is."

"I don't know what you're talking about."

"You feel bad for him."

"Of course I feel bad for him. There were no winners that night."

"Still, he should've just let it go. His coming in here... that had to have been awkward for you."

"It had to have been awkward for him, too. He must think I hate him, that everyone in Silver Springs hates him. You should've seen his face when...when I couldn't find anything to say. He looked like I'd slapped him."

"What'd he expect?"

"I don't know. But regardless of what anyone has to say about him, that took courage."

"He was never a coward."

"True."

"Why do you think he came back to Silver Springs?" Tiffany asked.

"You know why."

"He could've gotten a job somewhere else."

"It isn't easy to say no to Aiyana."

"True. No one can bear to let her down. I think that's why she's so effective with her 'boys,' as she calls them.

She loves them until they love her in return, and they clean up their act so she won't be disappointed in the end."

Maddox had been gone for several minutes, and Jada doubted he'd ever come back. Somehow, that made her as sad as everything else.

Tiffany watched as she wiped a fresh tear from her cheek. "Let me guess. You don't feel like going out tonight."

"No. I'm sorry."

"It's okay. What you went through wasn't easy. I haven't forgotten it, either."

"Thanks. Would you mind if we stopped by the grocery store for some ice cream and watched a movie at your place instead of going to Santa Barbara?"

"Not at all. Should we stop by your house so you can get comfortable, or do you just want to borrow a pair of sweats from me?"

"I'll borrow a pair of yours." She didn't want to see her mother or Atticus. She needed a break. She'd thought being married to a man she didn't love was difficult, but living with her mother and brother was beginning to make a loveless marriage look easy.

Tiffany helped her finish cleaning up the store so they could turn off the lights and lock the front door. Then, just as they were about to push the back door open into the alley, she caught Jada's arm. "Do you think you'll ever tell Maya about her father?"

Jada wrestled with the usual onslaught of guilt she felt for lying to her child, especially for so long. She'd always planned to tell Maya the truth eventually, when she felt Maya was old enough to truly understand and make the best decision where her father was concerned. But now she *couldn't* tell her, not while they were living in Silver Springs. Her mother would be furious, and Maddox might be even angrier. What if he demanded his parental rights even though that wasn't best for Maya?

Or *was* it best for Maya?

"That's such a hard question."

"She's going to ask about him at some point, won't she?"

"She's already been asking about him—for his name, where his family might've moved. She's hoping there are grandparents and maybe aunts and uncles she doesn't yet know. Bringing her here has rekindled her interest. That, and she doesn't have to feel as though she's being rude to Eric by pushing for this information. Lately, she's been bugging me for a picture."

Tiffany's eyes widened. "You can't give her one!"

"Not now. If we were still living in LA maybe I could have."

"Do you even have one?"

She did. One she'd kept well hidden. "Yeah." With that, she nearly pushed the door open so they could go but hesitated at the last second. "Do you think I'm doing the right thing?"

Tiffany shook her head. "I have no idea. I'd hate for her to find out that her father's not only alive but living in the same town and then be angry with you for not telling her. But...this is such an unusual situation. I wouldn't know what to do, so I don't blame you either way. I wouldn't want to give the wrong advice."

"When I was pregnant, you gave me the best advice I've ever gotten. I hope you know that."

"You just needed someone to talk to."

"No, really. I might not have kept her without you. I

was *that* scared of going out on my own and angering and disappointing my parents, who were pressing me so hard. When I think of how close I came, I feel sick inside…"

"You've paid a heavy price to keep her."

Jada felt fresh tears well up. "She means everything to me, so no price is too high."

"Hey, it's me."

Maddox changed the phone to his other ear as soon as he heard the deep and inviting intimacy that couched those softly uttered words. After several hours of agonizing over his visit to the cookie shop, and being unable to block Jada's stricken expression from his memory, he'd finally gotten to sleep. But the bottle of whiskey he'd been drinking before that, and his half-empty glass, were still sitting on his nightstand, his TV was still blaring loudly on the wall opposite his bed and he was still slightly tipsy. Otherwise, he would've been able to overcome the impulse to answer. He'd seen the name on caller ID, knew it was Paris.

He also knew how any call from her would probably go. That was why he'd been avoiding her since they'd talked the last time. He'd told her he didn't want her to come to Silver Springs, that it was truly over between them and to quit making it *more* difficult by trying to tempt him back. But it'd now been weeks when his only company in the evenings was a seventy-six-year-old grower who went to bed by ten.

"What's up?" He groped for the remote, which he'd dropped somewhere in his bed, so that he could turn off—or turn down—the TV.

"I couldn't sleep, couldn't quit thinking about you, so… I don't know. I just had to hear your voice."

He found the remote and hit the mute button. "Paris, you know this will only make it harder."

"It can't get any harder! It's being without you that's hard. It's not hearing you call my name." Her voice fell to a breathy whisper. "It's not feeling you inside me at night."

His groin tightened in response. He wasn't in love with Paris, but it was beginning to feel like a long time since he'd been with a woman. He missed having immediate access to sex, had tried to let the physical side be enough when they were together. But ultimately he'd realized he'd be a fool to settle if he was satisfied with only one part of the relationship. Paris was a nice girl overall. She was just a little too emotional, clingy, jealous and insecure. She ended up getting on his nerves to the point he'd make up an excuse to leave the house just to get a break.

He didn't think that was how it should be between two people. And if he couldn't love her the way she deserved, he needed to let her go so that she could find someone who could. He was trying to do her a favor, do them *both* a favor, even though, in ways, it'd be easier to stick with the familiar. If he moved on, maybe one day he'd find someone else, too—someone who didn't drive him quite so crazy.

That he should maintain his resolve was easy enough to acknowledge. It was easy to act on, too, in the daytime. At night, it became more difficult, especially when, like now, he'd had too much to drink and was missing the physical outlet she'd once provided. "I wouldn't be able to make you happy, so it's better if we both find someone else."

"I don't want to find anyone else. There will never be

anyone like you. So how could getting back together be a mistake? I love you, Maddox!"

He squeezed his eyes closed as he let his head fall back on the pillow.

"I'm touching myself right now," she said, "thinking about you. The way you kiss my breasts, the way you kiss me."

They'd had phone sex once before, so she knew he was vulnerable to this approach. After living with her for two years, they were comfortable together in that way. He'd also gotten used to a certain amount of sexual activity. Having that come to an abrupt end hadn't been easy. It wasn't as if he'd been dating other girls; he was living in a new place. Tonight was the first time he'd ever even gone out.

Maddox was tempted to let his hand slip beneath the covers, to do what he could to relieve the disappointment and frustration he'd been feeling.

"I'm so wet," she whispered and started to pant into the phone.

He could easily imagine what she was doing. His body responded by growing even more aroused.

But then he remembered how quickly she'd started talking about moving to Silver Springs after the last time he'd let himself succumb to a phone call like this one.

"Do *you* want to touch me?" she asked. "Or are you thinking about me touching you? I wish I was there—I want to take you in my mouth."

Maddox sucked air in between his teeth. It was so damn lonely here in Silver Springs. It would be so easy to take what she was offering. But if he did, he'd wind up back in the same relationship he'd been trying to end, one he already knew wouldn't work.

"Maddox!" She moaned. "God, I want to feel you pushing inside me."

He groaned, too, because he was trying so hard to retain control of his mind and his body. "It's late. I've got to go," he said and hung up before she could respond.

He'd done it. He'd won that round despite how long it had been since he'd had a sexual release. He felt a moment of relief, maybe even a little pride that he'd succeeded in doing what he felt was right. But even after she was gone, he remained stiff as a board, every muscle tense.

"Damn it!" He willed himself to relax, to think about anything *except* sex, but it was no good, because Jada kept coming back into his mind. He thought of how it used to be between them, how they'd been so naturally attracted to each other, so in love that just hanging out was almost as good as having sex.

Almost but not quite. He'd been with other girls, even at seventeen. He and his brother had been initiated into that world *young*. At twelve, a friend of his mother's— "Aunt Liz"—had come into his room late at night. Later that same year, he and his brother walked through the door of their apartment to find their mother giving head to some guy he'd never met.

But he'd been Jada's first. And she'd made it all new for him, completely different than anything he'd seen or experienced before. He'd never been with someone who'd felt quite the same way to him, which was why it had been so hard when everything went wrong. She was the best thing he'd ever known.

He let his hand slip under the covers, after all. But it wasn't Paris he imagined making love to. It was the adult Jada he'd seen at the cookie shop tonight, and the encounter he envisioned went much differently than the reality. After he walked in, and she looked up at him with those soulful eyes, she smiled and walked into his arms as if all was forgiven, all was in the past. Only the positive memories and feelings remained—and that included the desire.

"Of all the bad things that have happened in my life, losing you was the worst," he told her, which was true, and dreamed of her pulling him into the back of the bakery and undoing his pants.

7

Jada woke with a headache. Alcohol didn't agree with her. She typically avoided it, but she'd needed a break from everything that was going on in her life. She had so many hard decisions to make, and the hardest decisions were those regarding Maya. She had to tell her daughter the truth. Putting it off was getting awkward and forcing her to create more lies to cover the ones she'd already told. She hated that but, at this point, if she told Maya who her father was, she could chase her right into his arms. What if Maya decided she wanted him to be a big part of her life? What if she was so angry over learning that her father hadn't died in a motorcycle accident that she asked to move in *with him*?

Jada's marriage had failed. Her entire family was screwed up because of what she did thirteen years ago taking Atticus to that party. And now her father was dead and she couldn't even make amends. She'd had enough failures. She didn't want to ruin the one great thing she *did* have—and that was her wonderful daughter. She didn't like the idea of Maya being around Tobias once he got out of prison, or having anything to do with Maddox's mother. She'd heard enough about Jill to understand that

the woman had serious issues. No child should be subjected to what Maddox and his brother had known growing up. Truth be told, she wasn't even sure *Maddox* would
be good for Maya. Who could say what he was like these
days? Aiyana seemed to like and trust him, but Aiyana
tended to see the good in everyone.

"We *definitely* drank too much last night," Tiffany said
as she shuffled out of her bedroom, squinting against the
sunlight streaming in through the windows.

Jada kicked off the blankets that covered her on the
couch. Tiffany's house was an old farmhouse located in a
handy spot a block or so behind the natural foods store at
one end of town, but it was small—barely eight hundred
square feet. She had only three rooms—a kitchen/living
room combo, one bedroom and one bath—so when Jada
stayed over, she took the couch. "We should've stopped
after the first bottle. I tried telling you."

Tiffany chuckled. "Well, it was fun while it lasted,"
she said as she went to the counter to put on a pot of
coffee.

"Make it strong. I could use a caffeine drip right now."

"Me, too." She checked the clock above the sink, which
Jada could see indicated it was nearly nine. "Aren't you
and Atticus going to the farmers' market today?"

"No, I texted him last night to say we'll go next week."

"That was smart." While waiting for the coffee, Tiffany
gingerly made her way back and sank into the chair next
to the couch. "How'd you sleep?"

"Like a rock. Thank goodness. You?"

"Didn't even roll over. You know today's the Fourth
of July, right?"

"I knew it was coming up but sort of lost track of it
last night."

"You didn't hear my neighbors setting off a few early firecrackers in the middle of the night?"

"I probably thought it was a figment of my imagination."

Tiffany laughed. "So are you taking the day off, or do you have to work?"

"I have to work—at least until I take Maya to the park to watch the fireworks. I'm *so* behind." She sighed as she raked her fingers through her hair. "I'm afraid I'm going to lose the rest of my clients, Tiff. I can't keep up, not with helping at the store all the time, too."

"You're going to have to tell your mother."

"But then she'll try to manage the store all by herself. And she's not well enough to do that."

"She could have Atticus help."

"She's afraid to demand too much of him."

Tiffany pursed her lips. "It would be tough, as a mother, to know whether to push him or just…let him do his thing."

"She needs to push him. He's capable. If he can do all the stuff he *wants* to do, he can work."

"I suppose." She closed her eyes and rubbed her temples for a moment before continuing. "So are you going to have a talk with her?"

"Yes, but now isn't the time. With Maddox back in town, I'm all about trying to keep emotions on an even keel."

Tiffany got up to pour the coffee. "Which means you have to handle your own business and your mother's, too."

"Yeah." She felt a surge of guilt for putting herself even further behind by drinking and then sleeping in. "I'll relieve her around two."

A cupboard slammed as she got the cups out. "What's Maya got going today?"

"She spent the night with Annie, but she texted me before bed to say she wants to come help at the store later on."

"Not to change the subject, but…when's your mother going to tell Atticus that Maddox is back?"

"That's what I'd like to know."

"Maybe you should do it."

Jada scratched her head. Her mother wouldn't appreciate her stepping in, but she was beginning to think the same thing. She was the one who'd taken him to that party. Maybe she should be the one to explain recent events. "I'm considering it."

"Better to get it over with, in my mind." Tiffany handed her a cup of coffee. "I have to run a few errands, but I was wondering if we could talk for a minute before we both drink our coffee and rush off."

The tone of Tiffany's voice, and her manner, suggested she was about to approach a difficult subject, but what could be more difficult than the problems they'd already discussed? "Of course."

"I don't *quite* know how to say this, because I don't want you to think I'm only making things harder, or that I don't care about your brother, because I do."

Jada set her coffee on the table. "Okay…"

"Bear with me here, but when Tobias shot Atticus, he was only sixteen."

"Yes. Everyone knows that."

"He was also hallucinating."

"According to what he said in court."

"I was at that party, too."

"I'm not arguing that he was high."

"And yet they tried him as an adult and put him away for almost as long as he was alive before."

"He did something else while he was incarcerated that got him *more* time. We don't know what."

"We also don't know why, so I'm not sure we can judge him by the fact that they lengthened his sentence."

Jada reclaimed her cup, hoping it would warm her fingers. They suddenly felt like blocks of ice even though it wasn't cold in Tiffany's house. "Which means...what exactly?"

"It means he's paid a high price for his actions."

Jada understood the tragedy of that, but loyalty made her defensive. "Not as high as my brother."

"No, but to do something that terrible and to have to live with it would be the worst form of punishment—at least for me. He may get out of prison, but he'll never escape that."

Jada had to admit she agreed. She felt bad enough for bringing Atticus to the party, understood how that sort of regret could eat at a person. "So what are you getting at?"

Tiffany bit her lip. "I'd like to write him."

"Tobias? *Why?*"

"Just to...I don't know...tell him I understand he didn't mean to do what he did, that even though I love you and Atticus, I don't hate him."

Sitting taller, Jada tried to read her friend's expression. "Have you ever written him before?"

"No. I've considered it, many times, but whenever I pull out a sheet of paper and sit down to do it, I always feel like I'm betraying you and your family, so then I don't."

Jada stared into her cup.

"What are you feeling?" Tiffany asked.

"I appreciate the consideration, especially because you know about Maya, and if you ever said anything, it would destroy my life."

"If that's what you're most worried about, you can relax. I would *never* tell anyone what I know."

She looked up. "So what would you be hoping to achieve by reaching out to Tobias? You're not trying to rekindle a relationship with him now that he'll be getting out of prison…"

Tiffany's eyebrows snapped together. "Of course not! I haven't spoken to him in thirteen years. I have no idea what kind of man he is these days, but he *is* someone who had a rough childhood, who got involved with drugs before he was old enough to truly understand the consequences, and did something horrifying, for which he's been in prison for a really long time. Atticus has you and your mother, and he had your father until he was fullgrown. You rallied around him and are still doing all you can to help. Who has Tobias had? Only Maddox, who was almost the same age and couldn't do a lot to help him. That's sad. It makes me want to be kind in some way—but not if it's going to hurt you."

Jada took a cautious sip of her coffee. "It's not that I'd mind if you were kind. I just… I wouldn't want your kindness to bring him back to Silver Springs. It's hard enough having Maddox here."

"I wouldn't say anything to entice him."

The fact that Maddox had apologized made Jada feel as though his brother might be remorseful, too, which made it difficult to deny him what friendship he might receive.

"It's what Aiyana would do, isn't it?" Tiffany asked.

It was. Aiyana was a saint. But was she always right?

"It's a risk to draw his attention. He might not be contrite over what he's done. He may not even care. Or he may blame me or my family, even though he's the one who fired the gun. It could even be dangerous for *you*. What if he takes your letter as a romantic overture and shows up at your house?"

"It's not like he's necessarily become a monster. The boy he used to be certainly wasn't. He was a little rough around the edges, even wild, but he was larger than life, too, and he had a kind heart."

"So you want to take the risk."

"I'm talking *one* letter, just to make the outside seem a bit friendlier after all he's been through. It's got to be hard to get out after so long."

Jada nibbled on her bottom lip as she thought it over.

"Never mind. If you don't want me to, I won't," Tiffany said.

"No. You're right." Jada finished her coffee and stood. "We need to do what we can to help him heal, just in case he *is* a good guy down deep. What happened that night has done enough damage."

Tiffany came to her feet, too. "Really? You won't mind?"

"Will you let me know if he responds?"

"Of course. I'll even read it to you."

"Okay." At least maybe then they'd learn when he was scheduled to get out, what he did that lengthened his sentence and where he planned to go. That would be good information to have, if only to bring her peace of mind that he didn't stab someone—or do something worse to have his sentence lengthened—while he was in there.

Jada went over to rinse her cup and took a few minutes to clean up the snacks and drinks they'd had the night before.

"Stop. I'll get that." Tiffany came over to catch her hands. "I'm worried about you. You're under a lot of pressure."

Jada forced a smile. "I knew the crisis I faced before would continue to ripple through my life. I just never dreamed it would create such big waves after thirteen *years*."

Tiffany pulled her into a quick embrace. "No matter what happens, you've always got me."

Drawing strength from Tiffany's tight squeeze, Jada closed her eyes for a moment. "Thanks," she said and meant it. But it was Maya she was worried about. When the truth came out, would she still have any of her daughter's love and admiration?

After watching the fireworks at the park for the Fourth of July with her mom, Maya asked if she could spend the night with Annie again. Jada let her go over for an hour or so, since Annie's family, along with all their neighbors, put on their own show, but she wouldn't let her stay over until Sunday, and then they got to bed so late that she didn't wake up until after ten the next morning. Even after she woke up, she had to wait for Annie to open her eyes.

"Do you think your mom will be able to drive us over to the high school today?" Maya asked as soon as her friend woke up.

Annie dragged her pillow farther under her head. "Maybe," she murmured, her voice still thick with sleep.

"I hope so." They'd been trying to get to the high school since they'd made the decision to check there. They *had* made it to the library, however. Annie's father had taken them when he was off work last Wednesday, but they'd been sad to learn there was no such thing as a list of people who lived in the area. And even though the librarian was old and said she'd spent her whole life in Silver Springs, she didn't remember a teenage boy called Madsen. She kept saying, "There was a *Linda* Madsen who lived here once, though," as if it was the last name that mattered when it wasn't.

"Should I go ask her?" Annie said.

Maya listened for movement in the house. She couldn't hear any, but when she strained, she thought she could detect some music. "If that's okay. Then I can call my mom and tell her when I'll be at the store."

"Can I go with you to help at the store?"

"Of course!"

"Yay!" She flung the covers off and crawled out of bed.

As she hurried downstairs, Maya could hear her yelling, "Mo-om? Mom, where are you?"

After a big yawn, Maya reached into her backpack beside the bed for her phone. Her mother had been hesitant to buy her a smartphone. Jada had said she was too young for it, that she had to be fourteen before she could have one. But when they left Eric, her mother was feeling so bad about taking Maya away from her home and her friends that she broke down and bought her one early, and Maya was glad. She liked having a phone and living in Silver Springs much better than not having a phone and living in LA.

She checked to see if her mother had tried to reach her this morning.

Nope. She had a text waiting, but it was from Eric,

which seemed weird since the only other time they'd "talked" was right after she and her mom moved out, when she'd texted him to say she was sending an old jersey she'd been meaning to get back to her coach at school. He'd told her he'd take care of it, and that was it. It had always felt a little odd that their father/daughter relationship had dissolved so quickly and easily, as if it hadn't been real to begin with.

How are you? How's your mom?

She frowned at the message. Did he even care? He'd seemed more relieved than upset when they left. She'd heard him tell her mother that he was too much of a loner to make a good husband. Whatever that meant. Her mother didn't seem to be asking for too much—that he stop drinking all the time, that he come home once in a while and that he show a little interest in his family.

Great, she wrote and held her breath when she saw the little ellipsis sign that indicated he was typing.

Do you like it in Silver Springs?

She glanced toward the door, but she couldn't hear footsteps so doubted Annie was about to appear. I do. And Grandma really needs us. She's sick a lot.

She waited to see if he'd say anything else. She didn't want him to start being nice all of a sudden. She was afraid her mother would be tempted to go back to him. It was hard to live with Grandma and Uncle Atticus, since Grandma had to be the boss and acted like she was always mad at Jada, but it'd still been worse when they were living with Eric. At least Jada's eyes didn't look puffy every morning, as if she'd spent the night crying.

I'm glad you're happy, he wrote.

Thanks.

She finally heard Annie coming up the stairs, so she took a final look at her phone—Eric seemed to be leaving it at that—and set it aside. "What's wrong?" she asked as soon as she saw her friend's bottom lip jutting out.

"My mom says she doesn't have time to take us to the high school today. She has to help Aiyana Turner at New Horizons."

Maya remembered the small Native American woman who'd come into the shop and bought a dozen cookies a few weeks ago. "Help her do what? Another fund-raiser?" Annie's father made enough that Annie's mother didn't work, but she was always busy, helping a friend or a charity or a school.

"No, she's going to set up the music room for the new girls' section."

"Set it up how?"

"Organize the instruments and see if they need to order more. That kind of stuff. She also wants to paint musical notes on the wall."

"I know your mother was once the lead singer of a band, but I didn't know she could *paint*."

"My mom can do anything."

Maya believed it. "So why are you sad?"

"Because I can't go to the high school or the store with you. I have to go help her."

Maya frowned. "Oh. Bummer. I was excited."

"Me, too."

"What time are you leaving? Should I call my mom and have her pick me up?"

"I guess—unless you want to go to New Horizons with us." Annie gave her a pleading look. "My mom said you could come, too."

Although she'd heard about New Horizons, she'd never been out to see the school. "Why not? I could always help at the cookie store another day. We have the whole rest of summer."

"That's true! Come with me!"

"Okay," Maya said. "Let me text my mom."

Jada caught her breath when she saw Maya's message.

"What is it?" Atticus was sitting at the breakfast table, but Jada hadn't made him breakfast. She'd gotten him out of bed so he could make *her* breakfast. She couldn't baby him the way their mother did, or he'd never do anything.

She swallowed hard and set her phone down without answering. "Nothing."

"I can tell by the look on your face that something's upset you. What is it?"

He surprised her by grabbing for her phone, and since she'd just set it down, the lock mechanism hadn't kicked in. He frowned as he read Maya's text. "So she wants to help at New Horizons. Why would that make you go pale?"

She stood up so she could snatch her phone back. "I haven't gone *pale*. I just... I need her help at the store today, that's all."

"We've been *so* busy you can't handle it yourself?"

She scowled at the apparent sarcasm.

"God, I *wish* that was the case," he added. "Maybe Mom would be able to relax."

"Maybe she'd be able to relax if you got a job," Jada said and then almost covered her mouth. She'd been meaning to talk to her brother about being more productive and trying to contribute, but she hadn't planned to blurt it out like that. It was the pressure of everything going on that had her out of sorts.

He gaped at her. "Are you serious right now?"

Knowing her daughter was expecting an answer, Jada glanced between her phone and the shocked and angry expression on her brother's face. "I'm totally serious," she said. "If not now, when?"

"Who's going to want to hire me?" he cried.

"There might be a lot of people."

"Right. They'll be lining up at the door!"

"Atticus, there's still a lot you can do."

"And make what...minimum wage?"

"Why not? Isn't that where most people start when they first enter the workforce? Why should you be any different?"

"I can't believe this! That *you*, of all people, would lay into me."

Because it was *her* fault he was in a wheelchair. She got what he was saying, and it cut deeply. But how long could she go on trying to atone? She couldn't change the past, couldn't change reality. She could only try to forge a path forward, and she needed him to carry as much of his own weight as possible for that path to be manageable for both her and their mother. "I'm doing all I can," she said. "I'm just saying I could use your help."

"So I should go out and see if I can get a job at some fast-food joint where I can't navigate around the other workers or manage the tight space where they cook? Or should I apply to be the disabled greeter at the closest Walmart?"

"There's no shame in whatever work you do. At least you won't be wasting your life playing video games! It's time to grow up, Atticus. You're not a child anymore." She was shaking but so was he. Had she already gone too far, just when she'd decided that she wouldn't upset him for the time being?

She was terrified he'd end up hating her, and her mother would blame her for wrecking his life once again. But she couldn't see a better alternative than pushing him to improve his life—and help others along the way. Pitying him to the point that they demanded nothing of him wasn't going to make him happy.

"You have some nerve!" he snapped and threw his spoon at the wall, where it made a small dent and fell to the floor as he left his oatmeal uneaten and wheeled himself back to his room.

Jada heard his door slam just as her phone rang. She hadn't answered Maya's text, so Maya was *calling* to ask for permission.

Tears filled Jada's eyes as she stared down at Maya's picture. She was in *such* a mess. What was she going to do?

Because she didn't trust her voice, she let Maya's call go to voice mail so she could reply via text. But Maya called back before she could get it finished and sent.

This time, Jada answered on the first ring. "No, you can't go to New Horizons," she said without preamble. "I'm on my way to pick you up."

"But I didn't even get to ask!" Maya said, obviously offended by Jada's brusque tone.

"I got your text."

"You never responded."

"I was trying to."

"Oh. So why can't I go?"

Jada struggled to keep her voice steady. "You said you were going to help at the store."

"That was before, when Annie was planning to come with me. Now she has to help her mom set up the music room at New Horizons—that school on the edge of town where the bad kids go?"

"They aren't *all* bad," she said.

"I thought it was a 'corrective' school."

"It is, but sometimes kids who are bad act out only in certain situations or because— Oh, never mind." She felt defensive of Maddox, who'd gone to the school, but how could she honestly defend him after what'd happened? "It just won't work out today."

"Even though I don't have anything else to do?"

Atticus's music came on, so loud it shook the walls. *"Mom?"*

Jada could hear her daughter's confusion and tried to act a little less upset. "It's just not a good day, honey. I could use your help, okay?"

Maya hesitated as though she'd continue to press, but something about Jada's voice must've changed her mind because she said, "Is this about Eric? Did he call you?"

Her ex-husband? Jada found it ironic that he had once been such a source of unhappiness to her. Since they'd split up, she hardly thought of him. "No. Why?"

There was another pause.

"Maya?"

"No reason."

Leaving the rest of her breakfast uneaten, Jada got up to grab her purse and keys. "I'm on my way."

"What's that noise in the background?"

Jada drew a deep breath. "It's Imagine Dragons. I got into a little disagreement with your uncle Atticus."

"Oh. *Now* I get why you're in such a bad mood. What happened? He won't help at the store?"

Jada had only ever mentioned her opinion on how Atticus ran his life to Tiffany, and yet Maya had caught on, without hearing a word. She was so smart. That was partly why Jada was running scared. Maya wasn't a little girl anymore; she was becoming more and more perceptive all the time. "No, he won't help."

"Are you sure he *can*, Mom?"

Doubt welled up. Was she wrong for saying what she did? She hated to think she'd misjudged the situation, but she'd seen what Atticus could do, how strong his upper body was and how he could maneuver when he really wanted to. "He's not helpless," she said and, after a quick goodbye, disconnected.

Jada had no idea how long it would take her brother to speak to her again. Her mother would probably also be upset by what she'd said, especially if Atticus lapsed into depression. And now Maya was asking to go to New Horizons, where her father, who she thought was dead, worked.

Jada shook her head as she dug her keys from her purse. How was she going to keep her life from spinning even more out of control?

8

Jada could feel Maya watching her while they worked together for the first three hours at the store. When they'd relieved her mother, Jada had said nothing of her encounter with Atticus. She couldn't discuss it in front of Maya, for one. She didn't want her mother to say something in anger that might give too much away. And she didn't want to be too upset to greet customers the way she should during her shift. She figured she'd have all that waiting for her once she got home, but at least she'd be able to function somewhat normally until then.

Apparently, she wasn't acting *totally* normal, however, because it wasn't long after Maya ran out to get a couple of sandwiches for their dinner that she said, "Mom, are you going to apologize to Uncle Atticus?"

"I don't know yet. Why?"

"Because I can tell you're still upset. You've been so quiet all day."

"It's not only Uncle Atticus. I went out with Aunt Tiffany over the weekend and stayed up too late." She covered a yawn. "I haven't yet recovered."

A skeptical expression darkened Maya's face, but Jada

didn't get the chance to reassure her again because Tiffany pushed her way into the store. "Hey!"

Jada hadn't been expecting her friend. She knew Tiffany had to work graveyard at the hospital tonight, for which she probably needed to go home and get some sleep. "What are you doing here?"

"I—" Her eyes cut to Maya. "I was just in the area and thought I'd stop in and say hello."

"I'm glad you did," Jada said, but she could tell it was more than a casual visit when, after they chatted about the weather and how much Tiffany wasn't looking forward to working through another long night, she asked Maya to run to the drugstore two blocks away and get a pack of gum.

"Sure!" Maya, always willing to please, took the money Tiffany proffered and hurried out of the store.

"Grab yourself a pack, too," Tiffany called after her.

Maya waved to signify she'd heard and the door swung shut.

"What's going on?" Jada asked, turning to Tiffany. "You couldn't have heard back from Tobias already."

"Of course not. I haven't even written him."

"So…what, then?"

When Tiffany twisted around to look through the window toward the sidewalk, Jada knew she was checking to make sure they weren't about to be interrupted by a customer.

"I just spoke to Maddox."

Jada gripped the counter. "You *what*?"

"You heard me. I called New Horizons to get Tobias's address. I knew Aiyana would have it. I also wanted to be sure she thought my writing him would be a good idea, but as soon as I told her who I was and what I was after, she said, 'Maddox is right here. I'll let you talk to him.' And the next thing I knew, he came on the line. I heard a deep voice say hello and…and there was nothing I could do except ask him what I'd been planning to ask Aiyana."

Jada let her breath seep slowly between her lips. "How'd he treat you?"

"He was…nice."

The image of him standing almost exactly where Tiffany stood now conjured in Jada's brain. He'd looked *so* good her heart twisted at the memory. "Did he say when Tobias will be getting out?"

"He did. That's the thing… Tobias is being released on the twentieth."

"That's in only two weeks!"

"Yes. Can you believe it?"

"Wow." She gazed outside, also watching the door so that Maya wouldn't return and surprise them. "And he's not coming here, right? That hasn't changed…"

"No. Maddox said he's taking him to LA. Tobias has a girlfriend there he'll be staying with."

Jada swallowed against a dry throat. *That* was good news at least. "Where's his mother these days?"

"I didn't ask. I didn't want him to feel as though the town—or you, for that matter—had put me up to nosing around."

"Did he happen to mention what Tobias did to get his sentence lengthened?"

"No. I didn't ask about that, either. I was so nervous! I just said I wanted to let Tobias know that I understand he didn't mean to do what he did and that I wish him well as he starts over."

"And how did Maddox respond?"

"He said he was sure Tobias would appreciate hearing from me."

"That's it?"

"That's it. He told me he'd text the address to me, so I gave him my number, and he sent it as I was driving over here."

"If Maddox texted you…you must have his phone number."

Tiffany's eyes met hers. "I do." She lowered her voice. "Do you want it?"

Jada wished she had the willpower to say no. But she justified her weakness by telling herself she may need it one day. "Yeah."

While Tiffany read off the digits, Jada quickly entered the information into her contacts, but she didn't dare put the number under Maddox's full name. She wasn't sure why. She couldn't imagine Maya would ever look through her phone. Even if she did, she wouldn't recognize the name Maddox Richardson.

Still, Maya knew Jada's password, and her mother and Atticus certainly knew who Maddox was, so it felt safer simply putting it under *M*. "Did he ask anything about me—or Maya?"

"Nothing," Tiffany replied. "He was too polite for that. He thanked me, said if I write Tobias right away he should get it before he's released, and that was it. I had no choice except to thank him in return and hang up."

"So what do you think?"

"About Maddox?"

"Yeah."

"That brief conversation didn't tell me much."

"Now that you know Tobias will be out so soon, are you still going to write him?"

"I am. Not tonight, though. I need to get some sleep before work. I'll do it tomorrow morning."

Jada couldn't help wondering what Maddox thought of Tiffany's call, but they couldn't continue to discuss it, because Maya was back.

"Here you go, Aunt Tiffany," she said as she breezed through the front door.

"Thanks, love." Tiffany slid the gum she probably hadn't needed or wanted in the first place into her purse.

Maya blew a big bubble—to show Tiffany what *she'd* chosen with Tiffany's money. "Thank *you*," she said, grinning as it popped.

Tiffany exchanged a glance with Jada. "I'd better go."

"Thanks for stopping by."

Tiffany started to leave, but Jada stopped her. "Maybe… maybe when you write your friend, I should say a little something myself."

"You mean…include a note inside my letter?"

"I'm considering it."

"I'm sure that would mean a lot, much more than anything I could say."

Jada scratched her forehead as she tried to decide. Could she forgive Tobias for destroying so many lives? Reach out with a little kindness?

She didn't believe she could. Not when she was still dealing with the repercussions. Not when she still had so much on the line. But…what was life without forgiveness? Wasn't that what *she* craved, from her mother and brother? What she'd never been able to achieve from her father before he died?

How could she withhold from someone else the very thing she needed herself?

"Let me put some more thought into it."

"Okay," Tiffany said. "I'll call you tomorrow."

Jada nodded. "Thanks."

"Who are you going to write?" Maya asked as the door swung shut.

"No one," Jada replied and asked her to start a fresh batch of oatmeal chocolate chip cookies to distract her.

Later that evening, Jada let Maya go swimming with Annie. Annie had a pool, and since she and her mother were back from New Horizons, Jada saw no danger in letting Maya hang out at their place for a couple of hours. Besides, Jada was so preoccupied with her own thoughts—and with dreading going home, where she'd have to face the fallout of telling Atticus to get a job—that she wasn't good company. It was easier to work on her own. Then she only had to smile when she had a customer.

She didn't have to wait until she got home to find out whether she'd made her mother mad, however. Susan came marching into the store, her face utterly stony, at seven, only a few minutes after Annie's mother picked up Maya. "You *had* to do it, didn't you!" she said.

Susan had to be talking about Atticus. Jada wished someone else would walk in. She didn't want to have this conversation. "I'm sorry. I didn't mean to upset him. But he needs to take some responsibility. He can't get used to doing nothing, to feeling as though he *can't* work, especially because it's not true."

"He's *crippled*! What don't you get about that? Don't you know how hard it is just to bathe? To drive? To get inside places that aren't properly equipped?"

"I do know! But if he gives up, if he settles for nothing, then that's all he'll ever get. He needs to fight for more!"

"Easy for you to say!"

Jada curled her nails into her palms. "No, it's not! How do you think I feel, seeing my little brother unable to use his legs, knowing it's my fault? I can't tell you how many times I've remembered that night and—" she fought past the crack in her voice "—regretted taking him to that party. But if we're ever going to recover, *any* of us, we have to look ahead and not behind."

"*He* will never recover. That's the problem."

"I'm saying…in order for him to recover *as much as possible*, he has to be more productive. Besides, from a purely practical standpoint, you need his help."

"Don't tell me what I need! I'll decide that for myself," she said and whipped around to leave.

"Have you told him about Maddox?" Jada asked before she could clear the door.

She stopped as though she might continue the conversation but, after a brief hesitation, walked out without even deigning to answer.

Jada finished her shift, but when nine o'clock finally rolled around, she was reluctant to go home. She wished she could drive over to Tiffany's, especially after Maya called to see if she could stay with Annie again. Other than on rare special occasions, Jada didn't allow her daughter to stay over two nights in a row. Maya got to spend plenty of time with Annie. But tonight she didn't have the fortitude to say no, not when she was reluctant to return to her mother's house herself.

She gave Maya permission, and then she closed up the shop and walked down to the Blue Suede Shoe. She wasn't going to the club because she wanted to drink— she'd had enough of that on Friday night—but she did crave the escape music could give her, and it was one place she could while away a few hours until her mother went to bed. She doubted Susan would confront her again even if she did go home. But facing her mother's angry silence wouldn't be much easier. And Jada had no idea how Atticus might behave. They'd never had an exchange like the one at breakfast. She'd left home too early, when he was just eleven years old and recovering from the bullet he'd taken, for them to get into the type of squabbles that sprang up between siblings. It hadn't been difficult to get along while she was gone. They'd rarely seen each other. And since she'd been home? She'd been very careful to be a positive presence for both of them—until this morning.

Jada was glad to find the club crowded. There was a measure of anonymity in mixing with so many people. She'd been away long enough that she didn't know very many of them. She said hello to a few women she recognized as patrons of her mother's cookie shop and an old acquaintance from high school as she worked her way to one corner, but they were all with other friends and quickly went on with their night.

After about twenty minutes, she managed to snag a seat from which she could watch what was going on around her while sipping a soda. Someone came up to ask her to dance, but she turned him down. She wasn't interested in socializing. She kept staring at Maddox's contact in her phone: *M.* She'd never been more obsessed with one letter. But when the same man approached her again, she didn't have the heart to refuse him twice, which started her dancing almost nonstop with one guy or another.

She was slow dancing with a cowboy about her own age when she felt the hair stand up on the back of her neck and looked over to see Maddox. He'd just walked in with Elijah and Gavin Turner, two of Aiyana's adopted sons, both of whom worked at New Horizons—Eli as co-administrator and Gavin as the groundskeeper and all-around handyman.

He stopped the second he saw her. She got the impression he was about to turn around and walk right back out again, but when Elijah and Gavin looked at him in surprise, he simply pretended he didn't see her and headed back to the pool tables.

Maddox refused to let his gaze stray back to Jada, but it wasn't easy. He kept wondering if she was there with the guy she'd been dancing with or someone else. He also wanted to know if she was upset that he'd shown up. It could be that she'd left as soon as she spotted him. He wouldn't know, since he wouldn't allow himself to check. If she *had* stayed, he wasn't about to make her uncomfortable by showing her attention she didn't want.

"You okay, man?" Eli asked.

Maddox blinked before looking up. Apparently, Eli had said something he'd missed. "Yeah. Of course. What was that?"

"I asked if you wanted to get a drink before we played."

"Naw, after is good," he said.

Eli and Gavin had both left their wives and kids for a "guys' night out." Maddox suspected Aiyana was behind it, that she'd asked her sons to take him out for a little fun since he didn't know anyone else and she wanted him to feel welcome, but he knew they'd deny it if he asked, and he wasn't going to be rude enough to turn them down, just in case it *had* been their idea.

"We can go somewhere else if you prefer," Gavin said.

Obviously they'd seen Jada, too, and understood why her being there might make him feel on edge. "No, I'm fine." He figured he and Jada would have to get used to bumping into each other every now and then. Maybe if he showed her that he wasn't going to bother her again, she'd relax and tell her family they could do the same.

"Then you're ready to get your butt kicked?" Eli joked.

Maddox wasn't worried. There wasn't any way either of his companions was going to be able to beat him. He all but grew up in a pool hall. If not for his ability to hustle a game or two when he needed it most, he and his mother would've gone hungry on many a cold night, and there would've been no money to put on his brother's "books," which meant Tobias wouldn't have been able to visit the commissary, the only bright spot in an inmate's long days.

"Let's see what you can do," he said with a challenging grin and racked the balls.

Jada could've left. She wasn't there with anyone. But now she had something she was even more interested in watching, so she stayed and pretended to go about her business while keeping an eye on the back corner where Maddox was playing pool with Eli and Gavin. The Turner brothers glanced over at her occasionally, but Maddox never did. He kept his back to her the whole time. That should've made her feel *more* comfortable but somehow made her feel worse. She'd thought of him so often over the years, but he was acting as though he'd gotten over her without too much of a problem.

With a sigh, she got up to go to the bathroom.

When she returned, Maddox, Eli and Gavin were no longer playing pool. They were at the bar, laughing and talking and having a drink. Unable to bear watching Maddox any longer, Jada was just gathering her purse to go when she saw a woman with long blond hair approach him. Jada couldn't hear what the woman had to say, but she could easily guess what she wanted when he followed her out onto the dance floor.

Jada put her purse back down. She told herself she had no business being jealous but couldn't seem to pull her gaze away. He was the best-looking guy in the place; of course the women would be taking notice. But he was more than a handsome face to her. He was the first man she'd ever loved—and, in many ways, the last.

The blonde plastered herself against him, even combed her fingers through the back of his hair as they swayed to the music.

After nearly two hours of having Maddox completely ignore her, Jada quit worrying that he might notice her attention, which was why he caught her staring at him when he finally *did* look her way. Their eyes locked and, in that second or two, Jada couldn't help replaying the first time he'd ever taken off her clothes. They'd been the only two people at the park in the middle of the night in mid-October, before the weather turned cold. She could still feel the cool grass beneath her bare backside and his hot mouth at her breast. That'd been her first intimate encounter, so she wasn't likely to forget it. But even then she hadn't realized that it would be one of the most exciting and fulfilling moments of her life.

She felt herself flush and go tingly inside—and then the blonde leaned back to look up at him and say something, drawing his attention.

Suddenly, it felt as though a cold draft swept through the room.

She was losing her mind, Jada decided, desiring the

one man she couldn't have. She already had enough problems with her mother and brother.

This time when she grabbed her purse, she forced her feet to carry her to the door and refused to allow herself to look at Maddox again.

9

Maddox could feel the blonde grinding her hips against his, trying to arouse him. He *was* hard—and he had no doubt she could tell—but as satisfied as she seemed to be with herself, his reaction had very little to do with her.

That look on Jada's face! It had grabbed him by the throat, made it impossible for him to look away, because he could've sworn he read longing there. That was the last thing he'd expected to see, but he'd been with enough women to know a casual glance from one that showed interest.

Could he have been wrong?

He had to be. Maybe he'd had too much to drink. Maybe tonight he saw only what he wanted to see.

It *was* pretty dark in the room...

The song ended and he managed to disengage from the clingy blonde. She told him her name, even asked for his phone so she could punch in her number. He handed it to her but was only playing along, wasn't paying much attention. His heart was pounding as his brain fixed the memory of Jada's expression in his mind. He knew he'd go home and examine that picture for hours.

"Hey, now that you've kicked our asses in pool enough

times that we know we don't stand a chance against you, we've got to get back to the wives," Eli said.

Maddox knew Eli and his brother felt he was going to be okay on his own from here on out. They'd gotten him to the club, Jada was gone and there were plenty of women around to keep him entertained. "No problem," he said. "Thanks for taking the time."

Maddox hung out a little longer. He'd planned to stay the rest of the evening, saw no reason to cut the night short. His first public encounter with Jada was now over, so he no longer had to worry about how it would go. Seeing her would never be easy, but he felt reasonably assured she wouldn't be back tonight. He should've been able to relax and have a wonderful time. But the blonde wouldn't leave him alone, and he quickly grew bored. He walked to the back and played one final game of pool but beat his opponent so easily even *that* didn't generate more than a passing interest. He found himself wanting to leave…to find Jada.

Except he knew that was the worst thing he could possibly do.

When Jada returned home from the Blue Suede Shoe, her mother was asleep. Light gleamed beneath her brother's door, suggesting he wasn't, but she couldn't hear any noise, and she wasn't about to knock. She wouldn't risk waking their mother with a blistering argument. Whatever she and Atticus had to say to each other could wait until morning.

She needed to get some sleep, but she had a mountain of work to do on her social media business, and after her encounter with Maddox at the club, she was too wound up, anyway. She put on some music to help block out any thought of him and staged one of her clients' self-help books with a cup of coffee for a photo. Tomorrow, before she had to help at the cookie store, she'd use natural light to get some outdoor pictures, as well.

She scheduled the book post, responded to all the comments that'd been left on yesterday's posts for that author and moved on to her hair salon client in LA. T-hair-apy was a trendy, expensive salon in Beverly Hills, so she'd been posting regular tips on keeping one's hair, nails and skin young and healthy and getting some good traction using Facebook ads geared to younger women in the metropolitan area who also had an interest in fashion. She usually scheduled posts two weeks out, but she'd lost that buffer almost as soon as she moved in with her mother and started helping at the store. Now she was scrambling to get content ready for the next *day* and, as if she didn't already have enough to do, she'd created a Facebook and Instagram account for Sugar Mama. She thought it might help grow her mother's business. With the way millennials relied on smartphones, she couldn't see how any business could afford *not* to be on social media these days.

She scheduled a short video she'd taken earlier using a tripod showing her in the baking process, hoping it would pique interest and get some more foot traffic into the store. Then she opened her Adobe Illustrator program. Graphic design was almost as important as photography in what she did. She'd taken a couple of classes a few years ago but wished she'd been able to take more. Fortunately, she had a natural aptitude for it.

She finished the new Facebook and Twitter headers for her auto body client and got them loaded. Then she checked her calendar, picked a day to spend in the city and sent emails to half a dozen people to let them know she'd be stopping by. She wanted to get the owner of the salon, in particular, to do a live event. He was so eccentric and engaging; he was a big part of the reason his salon did as well as it did. She thought he could cut someone's hair live to show how he structured his cuts to fit his clients' facial features and bone structure—a before and after type event.

Once she finished her emails, she ran some metrics for a referral who was interested in hiring her, so she could show the growth that'd resulted from her efforts for others, and decided to call it a night. She was so tired she could hardly keep her eyes open and knew that, once her brother and mother started moving around the house, it'd be difficult to rest. It was even possible that Atticus would pretend as if nothing had happened between them and come down the hall, banging on the wall to wake her up to have breakfast with him.

It wasn't anyone in her family who woke her the following morning, however. And it wasn't early. It was after ten when the quiet buzzing of her phone rattling on the nightstand finally pulled her from sleep.

She tried to speak but had to clear her throat first. "Hello?" she said, her voice still gravelly. "Tiffany?"

"Yeah, it's me. You're not up?"

Jada yawned before replying. "No, but I need to be. I'm not sure how I let myself sleep this long. My mom always gets up early, and I usually hear her."

"You obviously needed the sleep."

"But I have so much to do. What about you? Didn't you work all night? Shouldn't *you* be sleeping?"

"I drank too much coffee to get me through my shift and came home wired, but I'm going to crash in a min-

ute. Since I was up anyway, I took the time to write Tobias. I was hoping to read it to you."

Reminded of her encounter with Maddox last night,
Jada stiffened. "O-kay…"

Tiffany hesitated since she'd drawn out the word. "I
don't *have* to read it if you'd rather I didn't."

She was curious, even interested. "I do. I just… I saw
Maddox last night."

"Where?"

"The Blue Suede Shoe."

"What were you doing there, especially on a Monday?"

She didn't want to say that she'd been reluctant to go
home to face her mother and brother. That sounded so
childish. "I walked down to hear the music for a bit after
I closed the shop."

"With Maddox in town? I haven't been able to get you
to step foot across the threshold!"

"Because I could possibly bump into him, like I did
last night!"

"Did he come in alone?"

"Hang on." She got up to peer out of her bedroom and
down the hall. It was late enough that her mother would be
at the store, which opened at ten. But what about Atticus?

She couldn't hear anything and, when she walked out,
she found his door open and his bedroom empty. Maybe
he'd left so that he wouldn't have to confront her.

Just to be safe, when she went back into her room, she
closed the door before continuing her conversation. "He
was with Eli and Gavin."

"Turner?"

"Yeah."

"They don't show up at the club very often now that they're both married."

"I'm guessing Aiyana asked them to take Maddox out. You know how she is, always trying to help and protect her boys—even those she never actually adopted."

"True. So…tell me about it. Did he speak to you?"

"No. Wouldn't even look at me." She decided not to mention that he *did* eventually look her way. The memory of that moment still made her think of things she had no business contemplating. She wanted to believe she reacted that way, even though it had been years and years since they were together, because it had also been months and months since she'd been with a man. She hadn't slept with anyone since Eric. But could that be all it was? Because she'd been to the club several times since she'd been back in Silver Springs and no one else she'd met made her fantasize about wet, openmouthed kisses and large hands touching her body in the most intimate of places.

"Then it was okay?" Tiffany asked.

Embarrassed, even though Tiffany had no idea where her thoughts had drifted, Jada dropped back on her bed. "I guess."

"Good! Maybe now I can get you to go out with me on the weekends again!"

Considering how seeing Maddox at the club had made her feel, Jada was hesitant to make a commitment, so she steered the conversation back to the topic Tiffany had called to discuss. "What'd you write to Tobias?"

Paper shuffled in the background before Tiffany started reading. "'Dear Tobias, after so long this is for sure a blast from the past. I don't know if you'll remember me—'"

"Of course he'll remember you," Jada broke in.

"I doubt it." Tiffany laughed. "I had *such* a crush on him, even though he was a year younger. But he didn't seem to feel the same about me."

"He was too busy struggling with life in general." It was true and yet Jada had been reluctant to admit that. Looking at the situation through his eyes only made what'd happened that much more difficult. She couldn't sympathize with the man—actually, he'd been a *boy* at the time, which made it even worse—who'd fired that gun, because that made her feel disloyal to Atticus, her mother and even her father.

"He was so good-looking, all the girls wanted him."

Jada didn't think he was anywhere close to being as handsome as Maddox, but she didn't say so. "They both had plenty of admirers." Which was why she'd felt special when Maddox had chosen her—and then foolish when her brother nearly lost his life. "He was hot, no question. Go on…"

"'I don't know if you'll remember me,'" she read, starting back a bit. "'But your brother recently accepted a job here in town, so I asked about you and he gave me your address. I hope you don't mind. He said you're about to be released. You've got to be looking forward to that. Or maybe not. It has to be scary at the same time, going in as a boy and coming out as a man who's missed everything the rest of us did in those years. Technology alone has changed a great deal. But I wanted to let you know before the big day that I forgive you for what you did. That probably sounds funny. What business is it of mine, right? I wasn't one of the major players. Still, I'm so protective of Jada and her family, I was hurt and angry, too. But you've paid a terrible price and, for me, it's enough.

More than enough. All I want is for you to be able to heal and be happy.'"

Jada was blinking against the tears that were welling up at the thought that someone so troubled *could* finally find peace. Did he deserve it?

Who could say? It wasn't up to her, anyway. "That's *really* nice."

"It's okay?" Tiffany said, sounding uncertain.

"Yeah."

"Good." She seemed relieved.

"That's it?" Jada asked. "You kept it short and sweet?"

"For the most part. Then I try to lighten it up by giving him a Release Cheat Sheet."

"What's that?"

"Basically it's a glossary of current tech. You know, stuff like, 'Hulu: a paid TV service where you can watch old TV series. Netflix: another paid TV service where you can get other TV shows, movies and original programming. Apple TV...' etc. I go over paying for things with your phone, live-streaming as opposed to disks, saving files in 'the cloud,' Pandora and a bunch of other cool apps he might like—everything that's new since he went in."

"That's thoughtful, Tiff. And sweet and sort of funny. I bet he'll love it."

"Thanks. I'm also sending him a hundred bucks to help him get a start. I can't imagine being released from prison without having had the chance to even finish high school. He's going to feel as if the rest of the world went into fast-forward while he was gone."

"Maybe he *has* finished high school by taking classes while doing his time."

"It couldn't be the same. He's going to feel so lost. There's no other way he could feel."

"True." Slumping against the headboard of the bed, Jada closed her eyes. "Send him two hundred dollars."

"*What* did you say?"

"I'll go in half with you."

There was a brief pause. "Are you sure, Jade? That isn't why I read you my letter. I just wanted to see if you were okay with what I was saying, and you mentioned you might want to send a few words."

"I've decided I don't want to send a letter." Jada stared around her dated bedroom. Her own family needed money, but she was already doing all she could to help them, and she felt the money would make a bigger difference to someone who had nothing. All Tobias had ever really had was Maddox, and Maddox had enough to deal with when it came to his unstable mother, if Jill was even still alive. "But I'd like to help a little financially."

"Can I *tell* him half is from you? Because I'm sure that would mean the world to him."

Jada understood why. She'd be offering a bit of forgiveness herself. That was a big step for her. But if Tobias could recover and make something of his life, why would she ever want to stand in his way? How would it help the situation for him to go on suffering?

Besides, *she* was the one who'd brought Atticus to that party against her parents' wishes, so she had to carry her fair share of the blame. "Yeah, go ahead and tell him."

When Jada heard the front door open and close, she knew Atticus was home. It couldn't be Maya; Maya had called to let her know that Annie's mother was going to drop them both off at the store so they could help Susan.

As she heard further evidence that she was no longer alone, she silently cursed herself for not getting out of the house when she had the chance. It'd been a day since they'd spoken; she didn't think another few hours so that she could focus on her work without being interrupted by a big, emotional scene would make it any worse. But she'd been on her computer, hadn't even showered yet. The only problem with running a social media company was that there were unlimited things she could do to try to enhance engagement, and the more creative ideas often took a great deal of time.

She tried to ignore the fact that her brother was home but ultimately felt too bad hiding out in her room. She'd meant well when she'd told him to be more productive; there was no reason for a rift between them—not if, by simply having a talk with him, she could help him understand why she'd said what she had.

Finally setting her computer aside, she went out to find him slapping a sandwich together in the kitchen.

"Hey." She noted his angry, jerky movements and immediately understood that this conversation probably wasn't going to go as smoothly as she'd hoped. "What's going on?"

"When were you going to tell me?"

A trickle of foreboding ran down her spine. "About…"

"What do you think? Why is it such a big secret? I'm not man enough to take the truth or something? You and Mom gotta protect me?"

"You're talking about Maddox."

"As I thought, you already know he's back. Does Mom?"

Jada hesitated, unsure whether or not she should reveal Susan's knowledge.

"Yep, she does," he said, assuming the truth by her silence.

"She only found out a day or two ago."

When he shot her a dirty look, Jada knew her attempt to pass it off as recent, and therefore less suspect, fell flat.

"Why didn't either one of you tell me? Why am I the last to learn?"

Jada folded her arms as she leaned against the doorframe. "Mom asked me not to say anything. She wanted to break the news herself."

"Break the news..." He shook his head before setting his plate on his legs and rolling to the table.

Jada sat, too. "I'm sorry. I felt you should know, but I didn't want to step on Mom's toes. In case you haven't noticed, I'm not exactly her favorite child."

He shot her a disgruntled look. "I wish you *were* her favorite. Being her favorite doesn't come free, you know. I hate the pity she feels for me."

Jada tried to hold back the comment that rose immediately to her lips but couldn't help herself. "Maybe she'd quit feeling sorry for you if you quit feeling sorry for yourself."

He shoved his plate so hard it slid across the table and almost fell off the other side. "Damn it, Jada! Are you *trying* to piss me off again?"

"No. I'm trying to *help* you. I love you."

"You have a very unique way of showing it!"

She stood and reached over to put his plate back in front of him. Fortunately, the sandwich was still on it. "How'd you find out he was back? Don't tell me you ran into him..." She hadn't wanted Atticus to be blindsided, knew that would be hard on Maddox, too.

"I haven't seen him. Donte told me."

"Who's Donte?"

"Friend of mine."

"You've never mentioned him to me before…"

"Was I supposed to turn in a list of all my friends?" She arched her eyebrows and stared him down.

"He's been gone, going to school and stuff," he said, ultimately wilting beneath her withering glare. "We've done a lot of online gaming together, though, stayed in touch."

She ignored the gaming part. She hated that her brother was so addicted. "How'd *he* know Maddox is back if he's been gone?"

"He has an interview with him this week."

"He…what?"

"He's been teaching math the past two years in LA and will have to go back next month if he can't find something around here. He's hoping to get on at New Horizons. They're hiring for the new girls' side."

"I see."

Atticus glowered at his sandwich. "Who would ever have thought Maddox Richardson would come back here—much less be in charge of half of New Horizons?"

Jada studied her younger brother's face. He was so handsome, with his high cheekbones, pretty eyes and sculpted chin. "Aiyana claims he's really cleaned up his act."

He said nothing.

"Maddox came to the store the other night."

He'd just taken his first bite, but at this he stopped chewing and spoke around his food. "What for?"

"To apologize."

He quickly swallowed. "To *you*?"

"Yeah."

"You don't think it's weird that he'd apologize to you instead of me?"

"He didn't pull the trigger. He's just the one who talked me into going to the party that night. That's what he feels bad about."

"Is that what he said?"

"Basically. He told me he'd give anything to be able to go back and change what happened, but of course he can't. I feel the same." She reached out to take his hand. She half expected him to yank it away from her, but he didn't. He looked over, his eyes filled with hurt, frustration and anger.

"I'm sorry," she said. "I'm *so* sorry that I put you in an unsafe situation."

He gazed down at their clasped hands for a few seconds; then the tension suddenly drained out of him, and he hunched in on himself. "I know. It's not you I'm mad at," he said. "It's *me*."

She let go of him so he could continue eating. "What are you talking about?"

"You were right, Jada, about what you said. I've known it for a long time."

Her chair scraped as she moved it closer. "So what are you going to do about it?"

"I've been looking for a job. It's just…hard to get out there and risk the rejection. I don't like the way people look at me, as if being crippled means I have no value. It's a tough thing to face."

"But you *do* have value, and you can prove it to them. You have such an agile mind. And you're so strong. You compensate for the loss of your legs much better than I ever could."

"It's not enough."

"It *is*. What is it you'd like to do?"

He took the top off his sandwich and rearranged the pickles. "I don't want to work at the cookie store. I know that."

"I understand. That's Mom's dream. What's yours?"

"Something with computers."

"You could do social media, like me. I could show you—"

"No, I see everything you do. I don't have the artistic talent for that. If I could choose anything, I'd like to work with kids. You know, teach them how to use a computer."

"Then start looking for a job like that. There are a lot of schools in this area, including some really prestigious private schools. Maybe you could work as an aide or student teacher until you get your credentials? I don't know what all is required, since I've never chased anything like that, but have you gone online to see if anyone's hiring?"

He smashed the top back on his sandwich. "Yes."

"And?"

"New Horizons is hiring."

Suddenly, Jada understood that he was upset about more than their argument from yesterday and finding out Maddox was back in town. He'd finally found a job he thought he might be capable of doing, even if it required a little more education than what he had now, but applying for it meant asking the brother of the man who'd shot him to give him a chance.

She scratched the back of her neck as she considered the situation. "I bet he'd try to make it work."

"No way! I'm not even going to apply. He won't want to see me every day, won't want to be reminded of what happened, especially if he regrets it. And I don't want him to give me the job out of guilt or pity."

"If he gave you the job, I highly doubt it would be out of guilt or pity. You'd make a great teacher. But surely there's got to be someplace else you could work." Someplace where he could work with people with whom he didn't have such a terrible history…

He wheeled his plate over to the sink. "Yeah, I'll keep looking," he grumbled, but she could tell he wasn't optimistic.

10

Although Maya had her own room, she often slept with Jada. They'd watched a movie together on Jada's computer and, since it ended, they'd been lying together, talking in the dark about Tiffany and Annie and how wonderful it was to have close friends. The conversation had drifted from Annie helping at the cookie shop to whether the cookie shop was going to stay open and how they could make it more successful. Jada told Maya that she'd started a Facebook page and an Instagram account for Sugar Mama, hoping that might help, but she felt Maya had an even better idea. Maya thought her grandma should start making ice cream sandwiches with her cookies, like a place they used to frequent—and was always crowded—in LA.

"We *definitely* need to talk to Grandma about that," Jada said.

Maya tried Jada's rings on her own fingers and held out her hands to admire what she could see of them in the moonlight filtering through the blinds. "Do you think she'll go for it?"

"She might." Susan could be resistant to change, but she was going to have to do *something* or she'd lose the shop, and updating and revamping what the store offered would be smart, especially because it would give Jada more to plug on social media. A double whammy.

"I hope she will," Maya said. "It's so sad Grandpa had to die. She's lonely without him."

"Yeah. What she's going through isn't easy."

"Will it be expensive to offer ice cream at Sugar Mama?" Maya asked.

"It won't be cheap, what with buying the freezer and all. And Grandma doesn't have a lot of extra money right now. But I believe it would be worth the investment. With any luck, she'd earn it back by selling more cookies."

Maya returned her rings. "I *really* want the shop to make it. I *love* it."

"So do I." Jada could feel her eyelids getting heavy, but she didn't want to miss out on any of this time with her daughter. These days they stayed up late talking quite often, but it was a relatively new thing, just since they'd left Eric. Jada enjoyed the fact that they were growing even closer.

"Mom?"

Jada had begun to fall asleep. "Yes?" she said, rousing.

"Will you tell me about my dad?"

The fatigue she'd been battling immediately evaporated. Jada had had to dodge a lot of questions like this lately. Maya seemed to be getting more and more curious about the man who'd provided the other half of her genetic code. But Jada had never been quite as apprehensive as she was tonight, when she knew Maya's father was living in the area. "What do you want to know, honey?"

"What did he look like?"

"I've told you."

"Tell me again."

Jada drew a deep breath as Maddox's image conjured in her mind—a far fresher image than her poor daughter would ever guess. "He was big, about six foot two."

"How much did he weigh?"

Then or now? He'd bulked up a bit, but it was a nice improvement. "Probably two hundred pounds."

"Wow! That sounds like a lot. Was he fat?"

"No, not at all." Jada couldn't help chuckling. "That's a good weight for a muscular man of his height."

"And he had black hair?"

"That's right."

"Like mine?"

"A little darker than yours but close."

"What color were his eyes?"

Maya already knew that, too. She just liked hearing it again. "Blue."

"We're the same there."

"Yes, you are."

"What was his middle name?"

"He never told me that."

"And you don't remember his last name?"

Jada could hear the disappointment in her voice and knew she had good reason to find that odd. "We weren't together for very long, honey. And it's been more than twelve years."

"But you loved him, right?"

There was no doubt of that. "Yes."

"Then how could you forget his *name*?"

That wasn't an easy lie to justify, but Jada had to make the attempt. "We were just kids." She hated to minimize what she'd felt for Maddox, even if they had been young, but she couldn't give too many details, not until she was ready to divulge the truth. And with everything that was going on, she definitely wasn't prepared for the truth quite yet.

"Was he nice?" she asked.

"I've told you many times that he was."

She fell silent for a few seconds, but Jada could tell it wasn't because she'd drifted off. "I wish he'd never gotten on that motorcycle."

Jada couldn't help wincing. She'd fabricated a *death*. What had once seemed like the easiest way to handle the situation—to quickly and easily eliminate all questions and keep her daughter from ever reaching out and bringing Maddox back into her life and the lives of her family—now felt like the worst plan ever, because it was going to be so hard to back away from. Or should she simply maintain what she'd said all along? She was so wedded to the lie she felt as though she didn't have much choice.

"That's why you should always wear a helmet," she mumbled.

Maya leaned up on one elbow to look down at her. "But you told me he *was* wearing a helmet."

"Right. He was," Jada said, hoping to cover for her mistake. "You can still be hurt, even killed. But at least it's a little bit safer if you're wearing a helmet."

Maya dropped back onto the pillow. "I'm *never* going to ride on a motorcycle."

When Maya seemed to accept her response, Jada let her breath seep out. She was relieved but also guilty, because she knew she was trading on trust. "I'm glad to hear that."

"Was the accident in the newspaper?"

Jada felt another spark of alarm. "Why do you want to know?"

"Because I'd like to read about it."

After adjusting the covers, Jada shifted to be able to see her daughter's face. "I doubt it was in the paper, babe."

"Do you know that for sure?"

"Um…no."

"So will you check for me? Please?"

A twinge of pain alerted Jada that she'd curved her fingernails into her palms and was squeezing too tight. She forced herself to ease up. "Yeah, I'll check," she heard herself say.

"Thanks, Mom." Happy to have achieved a commitment, Maya gave her a big kiss and rolled over to go to sleep.

As Maya's breathing deepened, Jada reached over to get her phone off the nightstand. She did a bit of reading—various news articles and surfing—hoping that would help her relax again. But it was no good. She was too worried about the lies she'd told Maya and what might happen in the future.

Ultimately, she went into her contacts and scrolled to the letter *M*. As frightened as she was, she was inexorably drawn to the man with whom she'd created Maya, even still.

She felt a smile tug at her lips as she realized that, if she texted him, he'd have no idea who it was from. Because of Tiffany, she had Maddox's number, but he didn't have hers. Neither did anyone in his circle. All she had to do was erase her voice mail greeting and, even if he called, he wouldn't be able to tell it was her.

God, you're gorgeous, she wrote. She didn't really plan on sending that message, but then Maya stirred and lifted her head and, in an impetuous move akin to suddenly jumping out in front of a bus, she turned so that her daughter wouldn't be able to see her screen, even if she was looking, and hit Send at the same time.

Maddox was sleeping when he heard his phone ping.

Reluctant to open his eyes, he tried to ignore it. He had to work in the morning, knew it would help if he felt rested. But he had the terrible feeling his mother was on meth again—she'd acted bizarrely when he spoke to her last—so he couldn't go on sleeping. She could be in trouble.

He nearly knocked the lamp over as he grabbed his phone but managed to right it at the last second.

He blinked several times to clear his vision as he read the text. Had he read that right? And who was it from?

He sat up all the way and stared down at the number. His phone didn't recognize it and neither did he. He didn't even recognize the area code. But that didn't mean anything these days, not with the portability of cell phones.

Was it the blonde he'd met at the Blue Suede Shoe? If so, how'd she get his number? She'd entered her contact info into his phone, but he hadn't done the same.

Who is this? he wrote.

No response.

Hello?

He wondered if it could be Paris. Maybe she was out partying and using someone else's phone. But if that were the case, why wouldn't she answer him? What was the point in hiding her identity? She'd already made it clear she still had feelings for him.

After ten minutes or so, when he received nothing more, he prodded again.

Paris? He thought that might provoke her into answering, but it didn't.

Hey, you texted me, he wrote.

Still nothing. He was about to assume it was someone with a wrong number and set his phone aside when he got a response. It isn't Paris.

Who is it, then?

Again, nothing.

This is Maddox Richardson. Are you sure you have the right guy?

Absolutely.

This was getting more interesting by the moment. Are you the woman I met at the Blue Suede Shoe?

He thought it had to be her, but this time he got an answer almost immediately. Definitely not.

Mystified, he thought back, trying to remember if there was anyone else he'd encountered recently, maybe a new teacher at the school. But no one he'd hired had his personal phone number. Are you going to tell me who you are?

Again, there was a long wait, as if the person writing him had to think each answer through. Was this person shy? Or maybe playing a game with him?

At last he heard another ping. No.

Why not? he asked. But it didn't matter what he

wrote after that. Whoever had paid him that compliment didn't respond again.

"I hear your life has gotten a little more interesting."

At first, Maddox thought Aiyana was referring to the text he'd received last night and wondered how she could possibly know about it. But then he realized Eli or Gavin must've told her Jada was at the Blue Suede Shoe on Monday. "Yes. The first 'run-in' is officially over."

He didn't tell her that he'd seen Jada once before *on purpose*.

She took the seat across from his desk. "And? How'd it go?"

"It was fine. We pretty much ignored each other." Until he'd finally allowed himself to look over and found her staring at him.

"Jada's a nice girl. So's her daughter, Maya."

"Did you ever meet Jada's husband?" Maddox couldn't help wondering what that man had been like, and why his relationship with Jada didn't last.

"I met him at her father's funeral. Didn't have a chance to say much."

"Did he seem nice?"

"Nice enough. He was older."

"How much older?"

"About thirteen years."

That was a bit more than Maddox had been expecting. "Did they seem to be in love?"

"It was tough to tell. She'd just lost her father, so she was grieving and probably not acting like she normally would."

"Was he trying to comfort her?"

"I didn't see them interact. She stood apart from her

mother and brother, which gave me the impression she wasn't feeling particularly close to them, even though they shared the loss. But she wasn't clinging to her husband, either. She mostly held on to Maya and he just stood behind them."

"What would make her marry a man entering his thirties if she was only eighteen?"

Aiyana crossed her legs and smoothed her ankle-length skirt. "From what I've heard, she headed to LA almost as soon as she graduated. After what happened to Atticus, I think things were difficult for her at home and she wanted to get out as soon as possible. Maybe this guy offered her the love she needed. Or maybe it was only the security."

"What do you think split them up?"

She shook her head. "I couldn't even venture a guess."

It made Maddox sad that what happened might've chased her into a bad marriage on top of everything else. "They had only the one child?"

"Yeah."

"I'd like to meet her."

"Maya? She's darling. Tall with big blue eyes and thick dark hair. She helps out at the cookie store sometimes."

"Then I'll hope to spot her somewhere else," he said with a laugh.

She laughed, too. "I don't blame you. Anyway, I came by because I want to run something past you."

"I'm all ears."

"You know Cindy Coates…"

"I don't *know* her, but I've met her. She's the one who painted the music room for us, isn't she?"

"That's her. And she brought her daughter, Annie."

"Yes, I met her, too."

"She made an interesting comment to me before she left, something I've been thinking about ever since."

"What's that?"

"She said it might be easier to rehabilitate the girls who are struggling in our student body if we have more of a mix—some girls who are doing well and don't need help, so they could set an example, befriend and uplift the others."

"If they *would* befriend and uplift. I'd hate for there to be a division, to have some girls who feel they aren't valued as highly as others, just like in regular schools."

"We could keep an eye out for that, be careful to avoid it where possible. Anyway, I'm tempted to try it for a year to see how it works, and I wanted to get your opinion."

Having fewer girls with deeply rooted problems and more people to carry the load of loving and helping them didn't sound like a *bad* idea. "This would be the year to do it. Since we're just opening, enrollment isn't as high as it should be going forward, once more people hear about us. We could fill the rest of our slots with local girls who have a good track record. But how do we find them and approach them?"

"Cindy said she could do that. She's done a lot of work in the schools, knows most everyone in town. She said she'd even enroll Annie. Annie is a great student and so sweet to everyone. She'd be ideal."

"Since we have the room, I don't see any reason *not* to try it."

"Great. That's what I've been thinking, too. I just wanted to be sure you didn't have a problem with it."

"Not at all."

"So would you like to call Cindy and get her started?"

"Have you got her number?"

She stood and scanned through the contacts on her phone before jotting the digits on a sticky note, which she tore off and handed to him. "Here you go."

She was just leaving when Maddox called her back. "Aiyana?"

"Yes?"

"What area goes with a 626 area code? Do you know?"

"That's LA, I think. Why?"

He shook his head. "No reason."

Jada's mother remained aloof for the next several days, behaving as she used to behave when Jada displeased her as a girl—by giving her the silent treatment. Atticus must've told their mother he knew Maddox was back in town. She probably blamed Jada for telling him, even though it wasn't her, but Jada wasn't going to bring it up even to address the misconception.

She tried to avoid her mother as much as possible. Susan would get up early and open the store. Then Jada would go in, often with Maya—or sometimes Maya and Annie— around two so her mother could go home and rest. And once she closed the shop at night and drove home, she'd work on her social media business in her bedroom, and the cycle would start over the next day. Between her mother's illness and Jada's work hours, they didn't have to see each other a whole lot, which was just fine with Jada. Since she'd been gone from Silver Springs for almost thirteen years, and left at such a young age, she wasn't used to interacting with her mother on a daily basis, anyway, was happier without the constant conflict.

So it was a surprise when her mother called her on Tuesday afternoon with something other than instructions for ordering more supplies or baking a certain batch of cookies. Jada was at Sugar Mama, but it was the hottest time of day, which meant it was also the slowest time of day, so she was on her computer searching for prices on freezers and ice cream makers. She wanted to put Maya's idea down on paper, to show her mother what it would cost and how quickly they might earn back the investment before pitching the idea. Maya had been at the store with her earlier but Annie's mother had picked her up so that she could go swimming with Annie.

"I just saw him," her mother said without preamble when she answered.

"Atticus?" Her brother had been gone a lot more than usual. Jada knew he was with his friend who was trying to get a job, and she hoped that Atticus was trying, too. But she hadn't asked him how that was going, hadn't wanted to keep pushing now that she'd made her opinion clear.

"No. Maddox Richardson! I *knew* it was only a matter of time."

Jada gripped the phone that much tighter. "Where'd you see him?"

"At the grocery store."

"And? Did he give you any trouble?"

"Just having him around is trouble!"

"I know," she said with a sigh. "But did he try to talk to you or anything?"

"I got the impression he was contemplating saying something. He looked at me as if he was about to approach, but I gave him a look that let him know he'd better not, and he immediately turned around."

Jada hadn't forgotten Maddox's apology. She wondered if he'd been about to apologize to her mother, too. If so, she was glad he'd been perceptive enough to change his mind. Susan was not the forgiving sort. She was too miserable right now, with her health and just losing Jeremiah, to think of anyone else and what might be best for them. "In other words, he stayed out of your way."

She didn't comment on that. "Maya looks just like him, Jada," she said. "Have you seen him?"

Fortunately, Susan didn't pause long enough that Jada had to answer that question.

"It's *obvious* she's his!"

The fear Jada had been feeling dug in deeper, this time with sharp talons. "Only to us," she insisted, using logic to battle her own panic as well as her mother's. "Because we know. As far as everyone else is concerned, Maya belongs to Eric."

"Except that *she* knows he isn't her father. All they have to do is talk to her. She'll tell them her father died in a motorcycle crash right here in Silver Springs!"

"That story will work." So long as it wasn't Maddox who was doing the asking. He might wonder at that, but no one else had followed her life closely back then. "No one has any reason to delve into it, Mom."

There was a long silence. "You'd better pray you're right, or you could lose that little girl."

Little girl. Maya wasn't so little anymore. But Jada didn't want to lose her, all the same.

After she hung up, she scrolled to the text exchange she'd had with Maddox a week ago. There wasn't much there, and yet she'd read it over and over, was always tempted to say just a little more. And, this time, she did.

11

Who's Paris?

Maddox had just finished unloading his groceries when that text came in. Although he'd been at New Horizons in the morning, there was a construction crew there this afternoon, finishing the baseboard and some other details in the conference room down the hall, so he'd left to take care of a few of life's other necessities. But he should've stayed at the school. Then he wouldn't have bumped into Jada's mom, who'd given him such a baleful glare he still felt scorched by it.

He left the rest of his groceries on the table as he sat down and considered his new message from the unfamiliar number. At least *it* felt friendly. "Shows you how pathetic my social life is right now that I'd be excited by this," he muttered as he considered his response.

I'll tell you if you'll tell me who you are.

He got up and finished stocking his cupboards, but there was nothing waiting for him when he finished. Apparently, his secret admirer wasn't going to state his or her name. He'd have to figure out who was texting him using other questions.

Okay. Can you tell me this: Are you a woman?

The answer came right away. Do you get hit on by a lot of men? Lol.

He smiled, which felt good after what he'd experienced at the store. He knew he shouldn't let what the Brookses felt toward him bring him down, but he couldn't help it. There've been a few. I have nothing against gay people, but I'm not gay, so it's kind of important to establish that in the beginning.

In the beginning of what? ;-)

"Surely, you contacted me for a reason," he said to himself but wrote, Is this meant to go anywhere?

If it doesn't, it isn't because I'm a man.

So you ARE a woman.

Yes.

Would I recognize your name if I heard it?

I'm not willing to talk about my name.

What are you willing to talk about?

The weather? How bad I want you?

Maddox felt his eyebrows go up. Definitely more intrigued by the second subject. Especially because he'd gone from being well liked where he lived in Utah to being anathema after coming back to Silver Springs. But do you even know me?

We've met.

You've got to be the woman from the Blue Suede Shoe.

Why? You've never met anyone else? ;-)

He scratched his head. I have, but I'm new to the area, so I don't have much of a social life at the moment. I would guess this has to be spurred by something recent.

Maybe. Maybe not. If you don't have much of a social life, what do you do when you're not working?

I play chess with my landlord, who's almost 80. Nothing against him. He's a cool dude. But it's definitely not what I was anticipating life would be like when I moved here.

I'll play chess with you.

When?

Today, if you want.

In person?

'Fraid not.

Online? Is that the best you can do? He hoped this wasn't one of his mother's friends, hitting on him. The idea of that made him cringe. But he was bored and lonely enough to see how it played out. Whoever it was had him intrigued by her approach.

Doesn't sound like you have a lot going on. Why not make a new friend?

So now you want to be my friend?

What I imagine doing with you when I close my eyes has nothing to do with friendship, but maybe I'll have to take what I can get.

He blew out a breath. Was there a reason she was concealing her true identity? Or was it just a fresh way to get to know someone?

If so, he had to admit she'd incited his curiosity. Can we establish some parameters to make me feel a bit more comfortable? he wrote.

What kind of parameters?

Are you single?

Yes.

Good answer. How old are you?

Not anywhere close to 80.

I'm more worried about you being under eighteen.

I'm not a minor.

You're not going to be a student at New Horizons…

No.

Can you send a picture of your driver's license to prove it?

Nice try. Quit trying to figure out who I am.

I have to ask one more thing—you aren't a friend of my mother's…

I've never met her. Happy now?

Vastly relieved.

Great. No more of those types of questions. Do you have a good chess app?

No. But I can download one. Which one do you recommend?

She was gone for several minutes before she wrote, Chess Online+.

He looked up the app and downloaded it before he responded. Are you good at this game?

I'm not bad.

I'll be surprised if you can beat me. I've been playing a lot over the past few weeks.

We'll see.

Can you tell me how you got my number? Did I give it to you?

Maybe.

Damn. No clues there. What do you do for a living?

I work for myself. You?

I work for a school. You don't know that?

Maybe I do. ;) So who's Paris?

My ex-girlfriend.

How long were you together?

I'm not saying anything more until you tell me something about you.

This is the first time I've ever sexted a guy.

When did you sext me?

What do you mean? I've said some pretty provocative things...

At this, Maddox laughed out loud, which felt damn good after how crappy he'd been feeling when he returned from the store. Telling me you want me isn't bold if you won't also say who you are.

Guess you've got me there.

So...? Will I ever see you?

Let's get to know each other a little first.

The possibility was tantalizing...

He was about to ask if she'd give him a clue as to
where they might've met when she wrote, I've got to go.
But it's your move.

He opened his new chess app to see that she'd named
herself MysteryWoman23 and started a game.

As Jada served the small family who'd just walked into
the cookie shop—tourists from Arizona, they said—she
couldn't quit thinking about her exchange with Maddox.
It had been reckless of her to text him in the first place.
She knew that. To keep it going was begging for disas-
ter. But after hearing about her mother's encounter with
him at the grocery store, she'd felt she had to do something to make sure he understood he wasn't universally
hated in Silver Springs. She couldn't imagine how hard
it would be to face the history he had here, even for the
sake of a good job, and she admired him for having the
courage to come back and apologize.

Since she couldn't tell him those things—or anything
else—as herself, she'd done the next best thing. But the
problem with being anonymous was that it made her feel
safe to reveal her true desires, which could turn into a
costly mistake if he ever figured out who she was.

She worried about that, but Aiyana didn't have her
cell phone number. Neither did Eli or Gavin or anybody
else who worked at New Horizons. In Silver Springs,

only Tiffany, her family and a few old friends could give her away, and what were the chances Maddox would approach one of those people? He wasn't the type to run around asking if anyone recognized the number of the woman who was texting him. She was pretty sure he'd wait for her to reveal herself. No doubt he expected her to, at some point; he didn't know she couldn't.

But being found out wasn't the only danger. Any interaction with him made her crave more.

After she boxed up a dozen cookies and wished her latest patrons a good day, she ignored her concerns and took out her phone again. She was eager—more eager than she should be—to get back to him.

Like her, he'd moved the pawn in front of his queen forward two spaces.

She loved chess, used to play the computer all the time. When Maya had been little and Eric had been working such long hours, she'd needed something to entertain herself. But once she'd started her social media business five years ago, she'd been too busy to play. She hoped her skill at the game would come back as she moved her second pawn.

Queen's Gambit, huh?

The chess game had a message feature, which he'd just used.

Why not? It's been an effective open for decades, maybe centuries.

Where did you learn to play?

Her chest constricted. My father taught me. The same father who'd feel betrayed that she was even in contact with him.

I don't suppose you'll tell me who your father is...

Was. But she wasn't going to give him even that much information. No.

How about any other clue to your identity?

No.

You're not making this easy.

You're not enjoying the game?

I didn't say that.

She wondered where he was. At his rental house on Uriah Lamb's orchard? She didn't ask, but nothing interrupted their game, so she knew he was somewhere he felt free to do as he pleased. They played straight through the next hour and a half before he won.

Glad I didn't put any money on that one, she wrote him.

At least you gave me a challenge, he responded.

I'm rusty. But it'll come back to me. Want to play again?

Instead of answering, he started a new game, but the bell went off over the door before she could make her first move.

Jada slid her phone in her back pocket as Maya came in wearing a sundress over her swimsuit, her hair tangled from having been wet. "What are you doing back? I thought I was supposed to pick you up after I close the shop."

"Annie's parents just took us to get a hamburger, so I had them drop me off. I didn't want you to have to close up alone. You're always working." She offered Jada some of her ice cream shake. "Oreo cookie."

It was nice of Maya to be concerned about her. Jada smiled as she accepted the shake and took a sip, but she was sort of sad she was no longer able to play chess. Her head was completely filled with Maddox—both with memories of the past and the desire to see him again. She felt slightly breathless at the thought of him, like a giddy teenager.

Fortunately, all that began to dissipate as they talked and laughed about Annie's older brother and his friend getting caught sneaking out the night before. By the time they'd boxed up the remaining cookies and cleaned, Jada felt more like her normal self, more like the responsible mother and dutiful daughter and sister she was trying to be. But then she went into the bathroom to let Maddox know she wouldn't be able to play for a few hours, and the second she saw he had a message waiting for her, the attraction she felt reared up again.

Did I lose you?

She stared at those four words. They'd lost each other, which was the greatest sadness of her life. What might've happened between them if Tobias hadn't shot Atticus?

Maybe there was nothing to feel bad about. Maybe she

and Maddox would've drifted apart, regardless. They'd been so young.

He didn't mean it like that, anyway.

Only for tonight. I have some things I have to do.

What things?

Work things.

I thought you worked for yourself.

I do, but that means longer hours.

At this time of night?

Afraid so.

Can't you just tell me who you are? Why all the secrecy?

She had a good reason for that. But why was she still bothering? Where did she expect this to go?

Nowhere. She was just trying to fulfill her craving for him in the only "safe" way she could—even though, in her more honest moments, she knew that "safety" could be an illusion.

Mustering her self-control, she typed her reply. Would you rather I leave you alone?

She held her breath as she awaited his response. She was praying he'd say yes. She needed something to stop her from contacting him since she didn't seem capable of stopping on her own.

And yet she was infinitely relieved when she received his answer.

No.

Good, because I'd give almost anything to be able to taste you right now, to run my lips up your warm neck and find those perfect lips. Her pulse was racing as she stared down at those words, but something inside her dared her to send it, and she pressed the button before she could chicken out.

You have me so confused, he wrote back. How do we know each other? Are you from Utah?

I'm much closer than that. ;-)

So you're here in Silver Springs? How'd you get my number?

It wasn't hard. You've been at New Horizons for a while now.

That's a yes. You are in town, even though you acted as though you didn't know where I worked.

She thought it over, couldn't see any danger in admitting that much. He'd never in a million years think it was her, especially after all the things she'd said about wanting him.

Yes.

Did Aiyana give you my number? Is she behind this?

I suppose it's possible...

Damn it! Why won't you tell me anything?

Are you sure you don't want me to leave you alone? I'll
stop bothering you if you tell me to.

    His answer was immediate. It's fine for you to stay
in touch.
    "Mom? You about done in there?" Maya yelled.
    "Be right out," she called back.

Okay, I'll talk to you later.

    You're getting better, by the way, he wrote.
    "Mom?"
    Despite Maya's impatience, she hesitated when she
saw his response. At?

Sexting.

    Lol! You have no idea what I'd like to say and do to
you, she responded and shoved her phone in her pocket
before leaving the bathroom.

    That night, Maddox kept checking his phone. He was
hoping he'd hear back from MysteryWoman23, or that
she'd at least pick up the game of chess he'd started.
With his brother getting out of prison on Monday and his
mother doing drugs again, he needed the distraction. Jill
kept calling him, drunk off her ass—or high, he couldn't
figure out which—and telling him he was a good boy,
that she loved him, that it wasn't his fault Tobias was in

prison. And then she'd get maudlin and cry about the fact that she'd let them both down as a mother, and he'd have to tell her to get off whatever she was on and call him when she could speak more coherently.

He received a text from Paris, asking what he was doing tonight, which he didn't answer, but he didn't hear from his new chess partner. He didn't hear from her on Wednesday, Thursday or Friday, either.

It was Saturday afternoon when he was doing laundry and cleaning house that he finally decided to text her. She'd come on pretty strong to back off *that* quickly. He felt he was justified in asking her what had happened.

Hey. You've sure been quiet. Have you already moved on to someone else?

I wish it were that easy.

Then where have you been?

I've been trying not to contact you.

Because...

Because I realize that wanting you is just going to drive me crazy. You're all I can think about.

That's bullshit, he wrote. You don't want me badly enough if you won't even tell me your name.

When she didn't write back, he regretted answering so sharply. Forget it, he wrote a few minutes later. I'm just in a bad mood. I'll leave you alone. It's not like you owe me anything. I don't even know who you are.

"You're pathetic," he muttered to himself as he shoved his phone halfway across the table.

But then he heard a ding, knew she'd sent a reply and couldn't resist getting up to see what it was.

What's wrong?

He almost ignored that and went on about his business. But this person provided him with someone to talk to, and because he didn't know who she was, didn't have to face her in his regular life, he didn't have to worry about what she might think. Besides the fact that my brother gets out of prison on Monday, after being shut up for thirteen years, and I have no idea if he'll be able to acclimate? Or that my mother's back on meth or crack or something, and I have no idea whether to try to get her into another rehab facility or just let her live her life since rehab never works for her, anyway?

You can't force someone to stop using.

Exactly. They have to want to get clean.

I'm sorry for what you're going through.

Were you already aware that my brother was in prison? How well did she know him?

No. What'd he do?

Maddox grimaced. Of course that would be the next logical question. He'd been a fool to take the conversation in that direction. On second thought, I don't want to talk about it. He'd already driven past the alley where Jada parked when she was at the store three times today. He didn't need to be reminded of her or what'd happened back then.

What do you want to talk about?

I don't know. Just make your move on our chess game, I guess.

Should I let you win? ;-)

I hope you didn't let me win last time.

No, but I'm better now. I've been brushing up online.

Instead of playing me…

Chess isn't what I want from you, Maddox.

That she'd used his name made the statement much more personal. What is?

I want to feel you inside me. I spend half of every night imagining it.

You say that and then go silent for days.

Nothing.
Come over. Let's meet. I'll make you dinner. No matter who she was, he figured he could tolerate one meal.

Can't.

Why not?

I have plans.

Tomorrow, then.

If you can beat me at chess tonight, maybe I will. ;-) But I can't play until after ten.

Because...

Work.

Fine. It's a date. But if I win, you'll make good, right?

We'll see...

That was hardly a commitment. You have nothing to worry about with me, no reason to hide.

No response.

He finished cleaning and watched a football game he'd recorded earlier. He wasn't sure he'd really hear back from her, not after her recent withdrawal, but he did. She didn't text him again but, at 10:20, she finally made a move on the game he'd started Tuesday.

You kept the appointment, he wrote.

You doubted me?

You don't have a very good track record.

I didn't know I'd made any sort of commitment before.

Telling a man you want him isn't exactly a casual comment.

Lol! Point taken. Your move.

They played for nearly two hours before he managed to capture her king.

Damn it, she wrote when she lost. I thought I had you this time.

You almost did—but I had a lot of incentive. ☺ What time are you coming over tomorrow? Or should I pick you up?

I'll come there. Give me your address.

He typed in his address. When should I expect you? I'll throw a couple of steaks on the grill, if you like.

She didn't respond. He waited ten minutes, fifteen, thirty.

Hello? Don't tell me you're reneging...

A quick rap at his door caused him to straighten in surprise. What the heck? It was nearly midnight. Had MysteryWoman23 decided to come over *immediately*?

He set his phone on the coffee table before striding to the door, which he swung open. But there wasn't anyone on the stoop. Instead, he found a homemade hot apple pie on his doorstep.

She'd been there, and he'd missed her!

He jumped over the pie and ran down the dirt lane past Uriah's house. She had to be close; she'd just knocked.

But he couldn't find anyone, couldn't see any taillights heading away from the orchard, either.

"Shit," he cursed as he trudged back to get the pie and his phone.

He'd finally heard back from her. I didn't renege. I made you a pie. Hope you like it. ;-)

You could at least have said hello.

I wouldn't have been able to stop at hello.

Would *he* want to stop? He was beginning to get the feeling he wouldn't… At least I got a consolation prize.

After he ate a piece, he realized it was a better consolation prize than he'd expected.

Pie's good. Amazing, even. Not what I was originally hoping for, but at least you didn't leave me empty-handed.

Glad you like it. 😊

He wasn't sure what was going on. It was so strange. But he liked this woman so far, enough that after pacing back and forth for several minutes, he decided to give her a call. She was the one who'd provided her number, after all, by texting him. If she hadn't wanted him to have it, she shouldn't have done that.

He put the rest of the pie in the fridge as Mystery-Woman23's phone began to ring.

12

"Holy shit," Jada muttered as Maddox's number came up on her screen. She'd prepared for the possibility that he might try to call by removing her voice mail greeting. But the fact that he was actually doing it freaked her out. What if she wasn't just getting home, with her phone in her pocket? What if she'd been watching TV with Maya and left her phone nearby while going to the bathroom?

Maya would've seen the *M* on the screen and might even have answered…

The possibility terrified Jada. She'd been careful not to let anything like that happen so far, but the longer she communicated with Maddox, the greater the chance he would discover who she was. In order to keep her identity a secret, and make sure no one on her end realized she was talking to him, she'd have to continue to guard her phone *every second*.

Could she even do that?

If not, she could always get a new number. She had that as a bailout at least. Was it time?

"Mom? Are you back?" Maya called as soon as Jada shut the door that led into the kitchen from the carport.

Maya had been watching TV with Uncle Atticus—

Susan wasn't well, so she was in bed—while Jada baked the pies, one for them and the other for Maddox. She'd told Maya and Atticus she was running the second pie over to Tiffany. "You're still up?"

"You said I could finish the movie with Uncle Atticus!"

"I thought it'd be over by now. It's getting late."

"There're only a few more minutes. Come watch it with us. It's really good!"

"I would but I have to clean the kitchen."

She was fine, she told herself. Everything was fine. And yet she could feel her life starting to spiral out of control. Not only had she been texting Maddox and playing chess with him, she'd baked him a homemade apple pie and delivered it *to his house.*

He could easily have caught her. Had she not parked and hidden in the trees until he went back inside, he would've been right on top of her. She'd seen him take off running to catch her…

She needed to cut off her dialogue with him as soon as possible.

She promised herself she would, but after telling Maya she was going to clean up the kitchen instead of joining them for the rest of the movie, she slipped into the bathroom so she could see if Maddox had left her a voice mail.

Sure enough, he had.

She held her breath as she listened to his deep voice. "Hey, it's me. I guess you'd rather not talk. I just… I wanted to thank you for the pie. I've had maybe three or four homemade pies in my whole life. My mother was never one to cook, and my grandmother died when I was a kid, so it was really a nice gift. Thank you. But next time, I hope you'll stick around and say hello."

She listened to his message three times before she slipped her phone in her pocket. He had no idea how bad she'd wanted to stay.

She started to unlock the bathroom door but paused to text Tiffany while she was thinking about it.

Hey, if anyone asks—like my mother, Atticus or Maya—I dropped off a homemade apple pie at your house tonight, okay?

Does it matter that I had to work and wasn't even there? came her response. I'm just leaving the hospital.

No. They won't check your schedule.

Got it. Where did the pie really go?

You don't want to know.

Jada, is something going on I should be aware of?

It's complicated.

That means it involves Maddox Richardson.

Maybe...

Oh shit. Don't tell me he got the pie...

He did. But he doesn't know it was from me.

He's got to have some idea.

Jada quit texting and called Tiffany instead. "What are you talking about?" she whispered so that no one else in the house would be able to hear. "Why would he have to have some idea?"

"He just messaged me a few seconds before you did."

"And?"

"He gave me your number and asked if I recognized it."

So he *was* beginning to search for her. She'd gone too far, piqued his curiosity a little too much. "What did you say?"

"I haven't replied yet."

"Tell him you don't know!"

"I will, of course. But…what's going on?"

"It's a long story, and I can't talk about it right now."

"Is Maya asleep?"

"Not yet. She's watching a movie with Atticus."

"Then come over after."

Jada rubbed her eyes with a finger and thumb. "Okay, I will." Maybe Tiffany would be able to set her straight…

"Oh my God!" Tiffany exclaimed the minute they both got out of their cars and converged on her small house. They'd been on the phone while driving over, and Jada had just told her she'd been texting with Maddox. "What have you been thinking?"

Jada hung her head as she followed Tiffany to the front door. She'd been asking herself the same thing, and yet she couldn't seem to quit interacting with Maddox. Even when she wasn't in contact with him, when she was doing other things, she was thinking about him. "He won't figure out it's me."

"He could!"

"How?"

Still in her scrubs, Tiffany let them in, tossed her keys on the counter and dropped her purse on the floor as she plopped onto the couch. "What about a crisscross directory? You know about those, right?"

"Yes, I know about those. I've searched online. Unless you're a police officer or something and have access to special databases, you're not going to find me through a crisscross directory."

"Maybe he's friends with a police officer who will check."

"I doubt it. If he had a cop friend who'd do that for him, he wouldn't be asking you."

"Well, he could ask someone else here in town." She grabbed her purse, got out her phone and showed Jada his text.

Jada frowned as she perched on the chair nearby. "You reached out to him in order to write his brother."

"So?"

"He feels safe asking you. And since you won't give me away, it'll be fine. Who else has my number he'd feel comfortable asking?"

Tiffany didn't look convinced. "This makes me *really* uneasy."

"Me, too," she admitted.

Tiffany gaped at her. "So why'd you start it?"

When Jada didn't answer, a knowing expression came over her face. "Because you're not over him. Even after all these years."

"The years mean nothing, Tiff. It feels like we were together only yesterday."

"That's not good."

"I know."

Tiffany typed a response to Maddox and showed it to Jada. No clue. Why?

"That'll work," Jada said and watched her friend hit Send. It was so late she didn't expect Maddox to respond, but a ding sounded a few seconds later.

It's nothing important. Thanks for your help.

"At least he's not running around telling everyone he's been hearing from a mystery woman, and he's trying to identify her," Tiffany said.

"I knew he wouldn't do that."

"Yeah, well, let's hope he gives up easily. I still can't believe you made him a pie."

"He was feeling bad about his brother."

"You're the last person who can nurse his wounds."

To their surprise, Tiffany's phone signaled another message.

"Maddox again." She turned the screen so Jada could see it.

How's Jada?

"What should I say to this?"

Jada couldn't help feeling gratified that he'd ask about her, but she couldn't afford his attention, couldn't have him wondering and thinking about her. "The less, the better."

She's good. Again, Tiffany checked with Jada before sending her reply.

"Okay," Jada said, and off it went.

Did you ever write Tobias? Maddox asked.

I did.

I appreciate you reaching out to him.

I hope he can build a happy life. So does Jada, by the way.

Jada didn't think it was wise for Tiffany to bring her up again, but this time she sent the message without asking first.

So do I, Maddox wrote. If you'd ever like to go out for a drink, let me know. You probably can't consort with the enemy, but if you wouldn't consider it too much of a betrayal to have a drink with an old friend…

Tiffany looked up at her.

Jada shook her head. "Absolutely not."

"I would never tell him anything."

"I don't care. I can't feel comfortable if he gets that close."

"You delivered a pie to his house tonight! How's that not 'close'?"

"If you go out with him, I'll die of jealousy."

Tiffany laughed. "There's the truth. But he has no interest in me. He makes that clear when he adds that bit about being old friends. It's code for 'don't think I'm interested in you romantically.' I bet he just wants to learn more about *you*."

"Even if that's the case. You can go out with anybody but him, and that includes my ex."

She laughed again. "Wow, you really have it bad."

"I never got to see the relationship through to its natural conclusion, whether that was a breakup or…or something else."

"Your parents would never have accepted him, even if Atticus hadn't been shot, Jada."

"But if Atticus hadn't been shot, I could've told them to stuff it."

Sobering, Tiffany reached out to squeeze her hand. "I know. I'm sorry. So what do I say now? I can't tell him I can't go out for a drink because it would make you jealous."

"Say that a drink sounds good, that you'll let him know when you have a free night and then never contact him again."

"Okay." Tiffany sent that before setting her phone aside and giving Jada a probing look. "You've been lucky so far, flirting with him without letting him know who you are. But you're going to quit, right? You're going to stop texting him and playing chess with him and all that?"

"Yeah, I'm going to stop." Jada felt some conviction when she said those words. She wanted to believe them, but she found a text from him when she got home wishing her a good night and couldn't help responding with, Night.

The following morning, Maddox was awakened by a collect call from the prison. After listening to the usual recording, he pressed the appropriate button so he'd be able to speak with his brother. "Hey, man, what's up?"

"I'm down to my last day in here," Tobias said. "That's what's up."

For years Maddox felt this day would never come, but he didn't say so. "How does it feel?"

"I can't wait, man."

Maddox hoped that was true, but his brother had to be a little nervous. "I'm excited to see you."

"Let's go out for a thick steak. Will you have time before you drop me off?"

"Of course. We can do whatever you want. My treat."

"That's great. Thanks. What's going on with Mom?"

"What do you mean?"

"I haven't heard from her in, like…forever."

"No letters?"

"Not for weeks. And she hasn't been out to see me, either."

That came as no surprise. She'd never visited him much to begin with. And these days she didn't have a reliable car. Maddox considered telling Tobias she was back on drugs but hesitated to hit him with that. The road ahead was daunting enough. "She's fine, I think. Probably seeing another guy. You know she always disappears when that happens."

"She's still chasing around?"

"I doubt she'll ever change," Maddox said with a laugh, but it wasn't really funny. Their mother's preoccupation with men had often left them feeling as though they didn't matter to her and yet Maddox could sort of understand why she was so willing to sleep with any guy who came her way. She'd never been able to find the love she needed and seemed to believe a cheap substitute was better than nothing. "I bet your girlfriend's anxious to see you."

"Tonya? Not as anxious as I am to see her. I've just about missed my sexual prime, rotting away in here."

Maddox wondered if his brother had ever been sexually assaulted. Tobias had been a tough kid when he was sentenced, one who'd essentially grown up on the streets. But he'd been imprisoned with adult men, some of whom would see him as fresh meat. Maddox had always worried about the abuse that must go on inside the prison, but Tobias had never said a word about that sort of thing, and Maddox wasn't going to come out and ask. If something that terrible had happened to him he wouldn't want to talk about it after, so he wasn't about to bring it up with his brother. "Hopefully she'll be willing to help you catch up a bit."

"She talks like she wants that as bad as I do."

"You've got a lot to look forward to. Of course, there will be some tough adjustments, but—"

"I'll be fine." He broke in as if he was eager to steer the conversation away from any difficult topics. "Guess what?"

"I'm listening."

"I got a letter from that chick who had a thing for me in high school—Tiffany Martinez."

"I'm the one who gave her your address. What'd she say?"

"It was nice. Seems like she turned out to be a decent person. I should've paid more attention to her. I don't think I ever gave her a second look."

"There were a lot of girls who wanted you back then. Read the letter to me, will ya?"

"I don't have it with me, but she sent me a money order for two hundred bucks. And get this—she said Jada Brooks went in half with her on it."

Maddox sat up. "*Jada* sent you money?"

"Yeah. Can you believe it?"

"I can't," he admitted.

"Made me feel… I don't know. Better."

"That was nice of her. Her father died a few months

ago, so she's back in town, trying to help her mother with her cookie shop. Did Tiffany mention that?"

"No. The letter didn't say a whole lot, but she included a cheat sheet so I won't be such a caveman about technology when I get out. I thought that was pretty cool."

"I should have thought of that myself."

"I'm going to hang on to it. She probably thought it was a joke, but I really need it. She said she wants me to heal and be happy."

"That's what I want, too."

"She didn't mention how Jada felt, but she did send that money, right? So I think she's trying to say the same thing."

"So do I."

"Now I have a few bucks, maybe I'll buy *you* that steak tomorrow."

Maddox kicked the covers off so he could get up to go to the bathroom. "No. Dinner is my treat. Use that money to help you get a start. I'm sure that's what it was intended for."

"I will. But can you believe they did that?"

Maddox felt an upwelling of gratitude for Tiffany and, even more so, for Jada. Obviously, her kindness had made a big impact on his brother, made him feel human again, gave him hope. "Jada has always been special."

"Yeah. I'm sorry I screwed up your relationship— along with everything else, of course."

"It's all in the past, bro. We're not going to worry about that anymore, remember?" They'd talked about the necessity of moving on, but now that Tobias was getting out, the crime he'd committed was top of mind again.

"I remember. It's just that sometimes…"

"What?"

"It's hard to forget. That's all."

Maddox felt his throat grow tight. He'd give anything to be able to make Tobias whole and healthy, but he had no idea if his brother would be able to withstand the transition back to regular life or would ultimately go the same way as their mother—and numb the pain. Just thinking about losing the only other member of his family, especially in the same way he'd lost his mother, made him sick at heart. "We'll just take it day by day." He flushed the toilet. "Nothing is that hard if you break it up into small pieces."

"So they say. Anyway, enough of that. Tell me what's going on in your life. You back with Paris?"

"No."

"Why not?"

"I'm not sure, to be honest. She's a nice girl. I just… don't feel what I should for her."

"Have you met someone else?"

Maddox's mind immediately reverted to the woman who'd been texting him. "Not really. Although I did have someone bake me a delicious apple pie last night. Best I've ever had."

"Who?"

"A friend I play chess with now and then."

"My mouth is watering just thinking about homemade pie. Maybe you could bring me a slice."

"You got it."

"Thanks. Well, I'd better get going. Some of the other pricks in here want to use the phone."

"Tomorrow you'll get your own phone."

"Yep. I've got only twenty-four hours left in this hellhole," he said, and then, after a quick goodbye, he was gone.

Maddox washed his hands and brushed his teeth before going to the kitchen to make breakfast. He was halfway through with eating his scrambled eggs and toast when Uriah came to the door.

"Just got back from the farmers' market," he said and handed Maddox a sack of fresh vegetables. "Thought maybe you could use a few things."

"Thanks a lot. I have something for you, too." Maddox held the screen door as he invited Uriah in. Then he put the vegetables on the counter and got out a knife to cut the pie. He'd been planning to drop off a piece when he left the house, so this was perfect.

Uriah was obviously impressed when he saw what Maddox had. "That looks homemade."

"It is."

"Don't tell me *you* baked it."

"No." Maddox chuckled as he covered the plate with plastic wrap. "Someone dropped it off late last night."

"That's what that car was doing here?"

Maddox grew instantly more alert. "Yeah. But…you didn't see it, did you?" He didn't have much hope Uriah would say yes. His landlord went to bed early, but he also didn't sleep well, so Maddox thought there might be a small chance.

"The one that pulled into the orchard around midnight?"

"She didn't come down the drive?"

"Not this gal. She parked on the other side among the trees."

That explained why he hadn't seen her when he ran out. He'd never thought to look around the rest of the property.

"But she wasn't there long," Uriah was saying. "Who are we talking about, anyway? Who's *she*?"

"That's what I'm trying to determine."

"You don't know who made this pie?"

"I don't. Someone dropped it off on my doorstep and was gone before I could answer the door."

"I wish someone would do that for me," he joked.

"*I* wish I would've been able to catch a glimpse of her," Maddox said as he started washing off the knife.

"It was someone in a little sedan. I can tell you that."

He glanced up. "What kind of sedan?"

"I'm trying to remember. The camera on that side of the house recorded a few seconds of it."

Maddox dropped the knife into the sink. "*What* camera?"

"When my son lived here, he hung around with some friends my wife and I didn't trust. We were having such trouble with him, couldn't seem to get along. It got so bad she was afraid we might get robbed, or they'd vandalize the orchard, so she had me put in a surveillance system. I haven't done much with it since he moved out. Some of the motion detectors on the cameras don't work anymore, but the one on that side of the house caught a glimpse of your visitor last night."

The water was still running. Belatedly realizing that, Maddox shut it off. "How clear are the images?"

"I couldn't tell who it was, but you might have better luck. You've got younger eyes, and even if you don't recognize the image, you might recognize the car."

Maddox felt a smile stretch across his face. "Well, isn't that interesting. Let's go have a look."

13

Jada tried to take Sunday off to go to the farmers' market with Atticus and then focus on her own business, but her mother wasn't feeling well enough to get out of bed this morning, and Jada didn't want to close the store when it was supposed to be open. So she canceled her plans and took her computer to Sugar Mama, thinking that after she was finished with the morning baking, if it was slow, she could work on her own stuff.

She managed to get the cases stocked and the store open on time and was glad she'd made the effort when a large party walked in almost immediately. After they left, she had quite a few more customers. The coupon she'd posted online seemed to be driving in extra traffic. She wasn't getting much done on her computer but at least her mother would be able to pay her bills this month.

Atticus brought Maya to the store around three and hung out and talked a bit. He was excited about a job interview he had lined up next week. He brought that up again, even though he'd mentioned it before, probably so that she wouldn't be mad when he left to meet his friend instead of helping at the store.

"Do you think Atticus will be able to get a job?" Maya asked when he was gone.

"I don't see why not."

"He can't walk!"

"He can do other things. You've seen how capable he is."

"So why doesn't Grandma want him to apply?"

"She's afraid they'll tell him no, and it'll hurt his feelings. She doesn't want to see that happen."

"I don't want to see that happen, either."

"Neither do I, but we can't give up for fear of failure. We'll miss every shot we don't take, right? We have to try to build a productive life no matter what we're dealing with."

Maya seemed to consider Jada's answer. "Yeah. You're right."

"Everyone gets rejected, Maya. It's part of life. We have to pick ourselves up and dust ourselves off and keep trying."

"That's easy for us to say, but…he's kind of different."

"Because he has a disability, but that doesn't make him worthless unless he decides to let it."

Again, she took a moment to think. "True…"

"He can find something if he searches hard enough."

A hesitant smile touched her lips. "It'd be really great if he did."

"It sure would. For a lot of reasons."

A mother and child walked in, so Jada headed down the display cases toward them. "Good morning."

"Morning," the woman replied as the child pointed from cookie to cookie, exclaiming that he wanted this one and that one and this one, too.

The woman was laughing when she looked up again.

"I guess he'd like to try them all. Give me a dozen and make it a selection."

"You got it." A young couple entered the store. Seeing her chance to help someone all on her own, Maya hurried closer to them. She'd already served them when someone else came in. Jada heard the bell over the door but didn't pay much attention. She was still waiting on the mother and child, and Maya had proved her competence.

But then Jada heard a voice that sent her stomach plunging to her knees.

The girl had to be Jada's daughter. As far as Maddox was concerned, they looked just alike—both of them beautiful. A smile tugged at his lips as she watched him move closer to the display cases, obviously excited to have another customer. She'd already greeted him with a "Welcome to Sugar Mama" when he walked in and was now trying to be patient so he'd have a chance to decide on his order.

He cast a glance in Jada's direction but she was busy helping a woman with a little boy.

After viewing the video clip from last night on Uriah's computer, it'd taken a couple of hours for Maddox to gather the nerve to come in. The grainy black-and-white image of Jada hurrying toward his house with that pie hadn't been clear enough to say for certain that it was her, but when he considered that image with the type of car that was also in the video, he knew it couldn't be anyone else.

He'd spent the hours since he'd realized pacing across his living room floor, trying to figure out what to do with the information. He was almost afraid to believe that she'd meant any of the things she'd said. He thought she must be playing a cruel joke on him. But then he'd remembered the look on her face when they'd locked gazes at the Blue Suede Shoe and knew it wasn't a joke. He hadn't misread her expression. She still had feelings for him—just as he still had feelings for her. Although he doubted it would or could ever go anywhere, now that he knew, he couldn't just ignore what she'd admitted, not when he was dying to be with her, too. He'd told himself he should wait until she contacted him again. He'd hate it if he scared her away. But now that he knew it was her, he was dying to see her. So here he was.

I'd give almost anything to be able to taste you right now, to run my lips up your warm neck and find those perfect lips.

Those words affected him on a much deeper level now that he knew Jada was the one who'd typed them.

"What can I get for you today?" the girl asked. "If you haven't tried our red velvet cookies, you really should."

"Okay. That sounds good," he told her, and she promptly pulled one from the case and cut it into small pieces, one of which she handed him with a napkin.

"Delicious," he said, but he couldn't really taste it. His stomach was in knots. He could tell Jada knew he was there and that she was nervous about him interacting with her daughter. He could understand why. If Maya went home and told Susan or Atticus he'd come to the store, it could cause problems. He shouldn't have taken the risk, but Jada had been alone the last time he'd seen only her car in the alley. He'd assumed she was alone today, too.

The woman Jada had been helping took her sack and guided the boy out of the store.

"I'll take over now, Maya," Jada said, a strained smile on her face.

"I've got it, Mom," Maya responded, reluctant to hand over her customer.

Jada hesitated as if she wasn't sure whether to push the issue. No doubt she understood that coming off too strong would only create more questions. "Is this your first time in Silver Springs?" Maya asked him.

Maddox got the impression she was mimicking what she'd heard her mother and grandmother do, trying to show Jada that she could do a good job. She had no idea Jada didn't want her near him for other reasons.

Maddox opened his mouth to respond, but Jada answered for him.

"Mr. Richardson is the principal of the girls' school at New Horizons that'll be opening this fall. He lives here."

Maddox waited for recognition of his name to tip Maya off that he might be connected to the person who'd shot her uncle, but no such recognition dawned. "Oh! How do you like it here so far?"

"It's a beautiful area." He indicated the red velvet cookies beneath the glass nearby. "I'll take half a dozen of these."

"Okay! The oatmeal chocolate chip cookies are really good, too," she said. "And if you order a dozen, you save some money."

"That sounds like a deal," he said. "Make it a dozen and put in whatever you think I'd like."

She grinned at her mother, proud of herself, but Jada was too anxious to smile back. She watched him as though he held a loaded gun and might pull the trigger at any second.

"Thank you," he told Maya when she finished boxing up his order and handed him the cookies.

"Would you like to get a loyalty card?" she asked as he pulled out his wallet to pay.

As much as he'd wanted to see Jada, he regretted putting her on the spot. He was about to decline so he could get out of there, but then Maya added, "If you sign up you'll get promotions and other offers via email, and you'll also get free cookies when we've stamped all these little pictures here."

She seemed so hopeful that he'd comply he couldn't resist.

After giving her his information, he paid and was about to leave when he remembered that he'd had a plan when he came in.

"I was thinking about driving over to Santa Barbara sometime this week for dinner. Is there any chance you've been there lately? Maybe you could recommend a good restaurant…"

He'd hoped Jada would show some interest in the topic, that by making it clear he'd meet her out of town she might show a spark of interest. But she just kept her head down, intent on reorganizing some drawer, when she replied, "Sorry. Haven't been there in ages."

Maya must've heard her mother's surly tone and, not understanding the reason for it, tried to smooth over it. "My uncle Atticus goes to Santa Barbara all the time. Would you like me to call and ask him?"

"No, that's okay," Maddox said and, cursing himself for taking a stab at trying to ask Jada out, he left.

Jada's heart continued to pound long after Maddox left. He didn't seem to think anything was up when he saw Maya, didn't seem to notice his own features in her face, and Maya didn't seem to think anything when she saw him, but the whole situation had almost given Jada a heart attack. What had possessed him to come in again? He'd apologized for his part in what happened thirteen years ago, said he'd stay away from her, and then…bam! There he was!

When she didn't have any more customers, she went into the bathroom to see if he'd texted MysteryWoman23 today and found a nice message telling her he was having another piece of pie. Yet he also wanted cookies?

She nibbled on her bottom lip as she deliberated over whether she should say anything in reply and decided she shouldn't.

"Mom? Can I have Uncle Atticus pick me up? There's a show on tonight I want to see."

Jada washed her hands and came out of the bathroom. "Why not have Atticus record it for you?"

"I can't go watch it now? It's slowed down a lot here."

As long as Maya was around, Jada felt confident she could overcome the temptation to interact with Maddox. But if her daughter left, she was afraid her resolve would crumble.

She looked out into the empty lobby. She didn't have a good reason she could state for making Maya stay. "Okay," she said. "As long as Atticus doesn't mind."

"Thanks, Mom!" She texted her uncle and, twenty minutes later, he came by to get her.

Jada cleaned the front of the store, helped a few more customers and started to clean up the back. She had plenty of work to do on her computer, but she was too preoccupied to be creative. She couldn't get Maddox's expression out of her mind when he'd mentioned the restaurant in Santa Barbara. He'd acted as though he'd expected a warmer reception from her and was disappointed when he didn't receive it, but she didn't understand why that would be the case.

She was about to close up when she finally allowed herself to look at her phone again. She'd told Tiffany she might come over tonight and needed to see if she'd heard from her. She had, but Tiffany was only letting her know that she was picking up a shift for someone who was sick, so tonight wouldn't work.

Then Jada's eyes lowered to a new text from Maddox. Are we ever going to finish our game?

No, she wrote.

Why?

I can't.

What harm can a chess game do?

He had a point. Fine, she said, relenting as she advanced one of her pawns. Did you get your nudge? It's your move.

I just tried to make it, came his response.

Jada read that twice. Is something wrong with the app? I don't get it.

Never mind, he wrote and sent her a wink emoji. Let's see if you can beat me tonight.

She played while she gathered her stuff and locked up the shop. She was looking at the game board on her phone trying to decide on her strategy while she walked out to her car, so she'd unlocked the door and tossed her purse on the passenger seat before she noticed the long-stemmed red rose on her windshield.

She looked up and down the alley as she plucked it off. She didn't see anyone, and there was no note attached.

But she knew who it was from.

Maddox made sure he won his chess game with Jada. He was afraid if she beat him she'd quit playing, wanted to be sure he kept that challenge out there. But she was becoming a tougher opponent. He wasn't sure he'd be able to keep up his streak.

You're getting better with each game, he wrote as he lay in bed that night. He hadn't mentioned his visit to the cookie store or the rose he'd left on her windshield because he was still pretending he didn't know who she was. He planned to take it slow, to build up the friendship enough that it wouldn't spook her when he finally let that out of the bag.

When she didn't reply right away, he thought maybe she'd drifted off to sleep. It was one thirty, after all, and she'd put in a full day at Sugar Mama. It seemed she was working day and night, if not for her mother, for her own business. But as anxious as he was about picking up his brother in the morning, he knew he wouldn't get much sleep and wished she could stay up with him.

I'll beat you one day, she responded.

He smiled but felt his smile wilt as he thought about the future. What happens if you do? Will you be satisfied?

Hardly. Lol.

You want more?

I do.

Of what?

Of you. I've told you that already.

He shoved into a sitting position. He could tell she'd been trying to pull back, but when her daughter and her mother and brother weren't top of mind, she was more willing to engage with him, more likely to say the things he wanted so badly to hear. Why don't you take what you want? What's stopping you?

No reply...

If you come over, I'll give you a back rub—and let you dictate what happens from there. He held his breath as he sent that message. He was dying to see her, to touch her as she claimed she wanted to be touched. What they'd had ended much too abruptly and far too soon. Neither one of them had been ready.

Wish I could.

Why can't you? You said you were single and over eighteen. What's stopping you?

No answer.

Don't you trust me? Didn't she know that he wouldn't tell a soul? That he'd protect her with his life, if he had to? He wanted to say so but he doubted she'd believe him, feared it would only give away that he knew who she was.

It's not trust that's the problem.

Can you tell me what is?

Never mind, he wrote before she could text him back. You don't have to answer that. Just come over so we can talk about it. We don't have to do anything. I won't touch you unless you want me to.

I want you to.

Then tell me how it would go if you did come over...

I imagine knocking at your door. It's late—dark and quiet but warm in the orchard. I can smell the tangerines.

He slid back down in his bed. I like it so far.

When you let me in, you're wearing only a pair of jeans. Your hair is mussed from being in bed already, but you don't care about that and neither do I.

What are you wearing?

Cutoffs and a white tank top, no shoes.

Are you shy when you come in, nervous? Or bold, eager?

Definitely nervous. But you slowly pull me up against you, and your hands encircle my waist as I press my cheek to your chest and smell your skin.

Maddox hauled in a deep breath. He was hard as a rock just thinking about her showing up at his door with no one else around, no one to interrupt or say anything about it later. What do I smell like? Cologne? Soap?

You smell like you. And that's exactly how I want you to smell. I press my lips to your bare chest before rising up on tiptoe to slide my mouth up. I find the solid beat of your heart at the base of your neck and feel your pulse beating against my lips, proof your heart is pounding like mine.

It's pounding now. What happens next?

You pull off my shirt.

He swallowed against a dry throat. What are you wearing underneath? Anything?

A lacy bra.

What color?

Black.

Does that come off next or the shorts?

You kiss me first. Your hands move around to grip my ass, pulling me up against your erection, which I can feel through your jeans, as you dip your head.

What does our kiss taste like?

Heaven, she wrote. Nothing I know can describe it. Your mouth is wet and warm and your teeth are slick. I moan as you capture my tongue.

Maddox closed his eyes for a moment to savor what she'd sent him. Then can I take off your bra? he wrote.

Your hands slide up my sides and unhook it from the back but, once it's off, you hold me away from you so you can see what you've uncovered in the light of the moon, which is streaming in from outside.

"Beautiful," he murmured. Tell me what your breasts look like...

My nipples are hard, eager to feel your touch, your mouth.

Then you arch forward and let me taste them.

Yes, one of your hands rests in the spot between my shoulder blades as you dip your head.

I can almost feel the hard buds against my tongue.

Then your other hand slides down inside my shorts.

He groaned at the suggestion. What do I feel?

Bare skin—and then how hot and wet I am. Unable to hold back, you quit worrying about anything other than working the buttons on my shorts so you'll have better access.

Soon you'll be completely naked. Completely available to me.

Yes.

Come over.

She ignored that appeal, but at least she didn't stop building the fantasy. After peeling off my shorts and my thong, you toss them aside. Neither one of us cares where they go. We are so anxious that touching and tasting is all that matters. We can no longer go slow, so you swing me into your arms and carry me to the bed.

Tell me I bury my face between your legs. That I hold your knees apart as I use my mouth to make you squirm and beg for more—right before I make you shudder with the most powerful climax you've ever had.

Yes! I can hardly breathe. The pleasure is so strong.

Then I slide up over your body and bury myself inside you, feel your legs tighten around my hips as you accept me, arch toward me, eager, hungry, still craving more.

And then?

I stare down into your eyes as I begin to thrust.

I like that. I love your eyes, love the intense expression on your face. I want it harder and faster, can't get enough of you.

You're building toward another climax, so I stop to draw it out, make it stronger, better. I don't want it to end too soon. I love the panting of your breath, the half-drunk look on your face. And it nearly makes me come to hear you whisper my name.

So you begin to move again, making me fly higher and

higher each time I feel you push inside me, each time your bare chest rubs against my breasts.

Jada, I want you so badly. We don't have to pretend. Please come over. I won't tell a soul.

He was shaking, both from arousal and from fear that he'd made a mistake sending that last text. He'd been so caught up he hadn't been able to resist, but he knew what it might cost him.

He stared at his phone, awaiting her response. Would she cut him off for good?

When she didn't respond, he cursed. He should've waited longer to let her know. He'd planned to do that, but he didn't want her to think he'd be that hot for a total stranger, for some woman he might never have even met. He already felt like her family believed he was less than she was—white trash with no money, no standards and no promise—and that they'd tried to convince her of the same. He hated to give her reason to believe them, to make her think he'd be glad to have just *anyone* in his bed.

Pretending to make love to her wasn't the same as the real thing, anyway. He knew because he'd been pretending for thirteen years. Dreaming wasn't enough; he wanted to hold her in the flesh.

He spent the next thirty minutes, then an hour, willing her to write him back, to acquiesce, to forgive him for the past enough that she'd give him just one night, if she wouldn't give him more. He even got up and took his phone outside to watch for her car. If she was out there, hiding in the trees like she had been when she delivered the pie, deliberating on whether she should come in, he planned to convince her the answer to that question was yes.

But he got nothing—no sight of her and no answer, either.

14

What had she done?

Nearly paralyzed with fear, Jada stared, wide-awake, at the ceiling above her bed for over an hour and a half. Tiffany had tried to warn her. Heck, she'd warned herself. But she'd contacted Maddox, anyway, and she'd *kept* contacting him, and now he knew it was her.

How? And what was going to happen next? Was that why he'd come to the store out of the blue? Why he'd put that rose on her car?

Had to be. She'd started something she had no business starting. She squeezed her eyes closed as she whispered, *"What do I say to this?"*

A moment later, she pressed the button that would light up the screen on her phone. Maddox had been trying to reach her ever since she stopped responding.

I'm sorry if I scared you.

I won't tell anyone, would never do anything to hurt you.

Please trust me.

Hello? Will you at least answer so I know you're not too upset? We don't have to have sex. We don't even have to touch. Let's just go out to dinner. It can be somewhere in Santa Barbara or LA where no one will see us.

He'd mentioned Santa Barbara at the store, probably with the same idea in mind. He'd known then. She had no doubt of it.

What could be the harm in having a meal together? he'd written last. I miss you.

His offer was tempting. But she knew it wouldn't end there. If she started seeing him, she'd keep seeing him. For Maya's sake, and for the sake of her relationship with her mother and brother, she had to stop what was happening now, *completely*, while there was still a small chance she could.

After deleting their whole string of texts, she also deleted him from her contacts and the chess app she'd downloaded. No more *M.* No more MysteryWoman23. No more trying to be close to him even by text. She'd been a fool to think she could get away with what she'd done.

Praying that he'd let it go, that she hadn't just screwed up her life again, she put her phone on the nightstand and rolled away from it. What she'd been through the past thirteen years—and what her poor brother had been through—had been a high price to pay for going to one party.

This time around, she'd *make* herself do the right thing.

Maddox had a terrible headache when the alarm went off the following morning. In order to arrive at the prison by ten thirty, which was when Tobias guessed he'd be finished with all the searches and paperwork getting released required, he had to leave by six thirty, so the sun was just barely coming up. He'd had only a few hours of sleep.

Bleary-eyed, he lifted his head to stop the racket his alarm was making and dropped back on his pillow. It'd been a rough night. He never did get Jada to respond to him; he figured what small chance he'd had of ever being with her again was gone.

He shouldn't have let her know he knew who she was…

He shoved the covers off as he climbed out of bed. He didn't have time to hang around kicking himself. He had to get on the road. Although he was excited and relieved that his brother would finally be out of prison, worry overshadowed his excitement. The next year, the transition year, would probably be the hardest of Tobias's life. Would he be able to hold out and become productive?

Maddox checked his phone, hoping that he'd heard from Jada after all, but he wasn't surprised to see that he hadn't. He was tempted to text her again, to continue trying to convince her. But pressuring her would only push her farther away. She might even block him. He needed to leave her alone, give her some space. He had enough to worry about without creating more problems for himself. So there'd be no backlash on Aiyana for inviting him back into the community, he needed to mind his own business and just do his job.

With a groan, he put on some coffee and took a long shower, but that didn't help much. He didn't feel a whole lot better after he'd gotten out and eaten a quick breakfast.

He walked out of the house on time at least, but his

day didn't improve. He was only an hour from the prison when he got a call from his mother. She was crying so hard he could barely understand her, and after he finally got her to calm down so that her words would be intelligible, he heard what she was trying to say: she'd been beaten up and robbed.

Jada was determined to act as normal as possible, despite the sleepless night she'd had and the panic that roiled in her gut whenever she thought about Maddox knowing *she* was the one who'd been in touch with him. She'd not only texted him, she'd sexted him! It was *so* reckless, even though leaving it there had required a great deal of restraint. It wasn't as if she'd agreed to visit him or go out to dinner with him. It wasn't even as though she'd told him everything she wanted to say—like how hard it had been for her to let go of him in the first place, how badly she'd missed him and how unhappy she'd been in her marriage, partially because she'd learned the hard lesson that not all loves were created equal.

But there was no use feeling frustrated by her limitations. She could *never* go to his house for the night or tell him those things. She needed to bury the emotions she'd stirred up and forget all about Maddox—put him behind her once again, even though it would be much more difficult this time around, since each day presented a new possibility of seeing him.

She checked her phone. Although she'd deleted him from her contacts, she hadn't blocked him—hadn't been able to bring herself to go that far—and he'd texted her since then. Those messages came in with only his phone number attached, but that didn't create any confusion. She would've known it was him even if he'd only been asking about the weather. Although she couldn't recall memorizing a number in years—smartphones made that unnecessary—she'd memorized his.

She deleted those unanswered messages so she wouldn't have to be quite as paranoid about guarding her phone and got dressed for the day. She needed to focus, had other things to worry about this morning. Although Sugar Mama had had a few strong days over the past month, business hadn't picked up as much as she'd hoped. And if it wasn't doing as well as it needed to during tourist season, they'd never make it through the coming winter, not unless they made a change. Jada believed Maya's idea of adding ice cream to the menu could save the store, and now that she'd investigated the costs, she planned to present the numbers to Susan.

"What are you doing here?" her mother asked after Jada parked in the alley and walked in through the back. "You don't normally come until two."

"I wanted to talk to you and mornings are usually our slowest times."

"That's also when I do all my baking."

"Baking doesn't stop you from talking or listening."

"What is it?" She suddenly lowered her voice. "Don't tell me you've heard from Maddox…"

Jada didn't say one way or the other. "It's about the store."

Her mother didn't seem to relax. She knew things weren't going as well as they needed to be. "What about it?"

"We have to make a few changes."

Susan turned away to pour a bag of chocolate chips into the big bowl of cookie dough she was mixing. "What kind of changes?"

"Something that will draw in more customers."

"I've been thinking of making my frosted pumpkin cookies more than a seasonal offering. They always do well."

"We need something bigger than that."

"Why? It's a bit of a struggle right now, but I'm getting by."

Jada could hear the defensiveness in her voice. "Barely. And what will you do when sales drop in the winter?"

"I'm hoping they won't drop."

Although that wasn't very realistic, Jada didn't say so. "Why not try something new? Something more unexpected than adding a seasonal cookie as a permanent offering?"

"Why would I do that? This is a cookie shop, Jada. That's what we sell."

"It doesn't have to be *all* we sell. Why not go big?"

"If you're talking about adding ice cream, forget it. Maya's already mentioned it. I doubt that's going to help us during the winter, and the summer's halfway over."

"People still eat ice cream in the winter, especially if it's sandwiched between two soft chocolate chip cookies. And it won't take long to get a freezer in here, so we could end the summer with a bang."

"That would require a much bigger investment than I can afford. Maybe when I get this place turned around—"

"You might not get it turned around unless you make the investment," Jada said. "That's the problem."

"It'll be fine."

"It might not be. Look." Jada put down a cloth on the table where her mother typically rolled out the sugar cookies. "Can you stop baking for a few minutes and come over here? I've done an analysis I think you should take a look at."

"An *analysis*? You had to do an analysis to show me that I can't afford to add ice cream?"

"If it boosts sales, you can afford it. It might even save the shop."

"It's a risk," her mother said with a frown.

That was something Susan didn't feel comfortable with. She no longer had Jeremiah with whom to discuss these things and, with her health, she was scared. Jada understood that, but protecting against failure by not trying new things often resulted in failure. "Opening this shop was a risk, but you did it. Now we need to do what it takes to see it through."

Her mother gave her a funny look. "You sound like your father."

"And you miss him. I know that. So do I. But he's not here. So Atticus and I need to step up."

She wiped her hands on a dish towel. "Did Atticus tell you he's looking for a job?"

"He did. But he hasn't mentioned how it's going." And she'd been afraid to ask.

"Nothing so far."

"How many interviews has he had?"

"Just one. He's got another one next week."

"He'll find something," she said, trying to remain positive. "Do you see the projections I've done here?"

Susan's eyes widened as they scanned the graph Jada had created. "You think we can sell this many more cookies if we add ice cream?"

"I believe it's a conservative estimate. It'll give us a chance to put up a new sign, do some fun stuff on social media, get the locals back in to remind them of how good your cookies are. Why not try it?"

"Because we'll be going into debt, spending money we need for necessities."

Jada wondered if she really wanted to take on the liability of convincing her mother. If the ice cream sandwich idea failed, she didn't want to be blamed. Her mother held enough against her. So she backed off a bit. "I would do it if it was my shop, but Sugar Mama belongs to you. You're the one who has to make the decision. I just wanted to get you thinking about it."

"Wow." She pointed to the listing for a freezer Jada had printed out and included with the paperwork. "You've even found someone who's selling an ice cream freezer secondhand."

"There's a place going out of business in Van Nuys. It'd be a drive, but Atticus and I could pick it up in his truck."

"Then I'd better decide soon."

"The freezer could be gone if you don't, and the others I've found are much more expensive."

The expression that settled on her mother's face wasn't exactly *loving*, but it was filled with more respect than Jada had seen there since the shooting. "I'll let you know in the morning."

"Okay."

Jada was just on her way out when her mother called her name. "Yes?"

"Thanks for your help."

Jada nodded. It was difficult to take much praise when she knew how her mother would feel about her contact with Maddox.

* * *

Maddox wasn't going to tell Tobias about their mother. His brother didn't need this kind of news on his first day out. Their mother claimed she had a broken nose and some scrapes and bruises, but her roommate had taken her to the emergency room, so she'd been seen by a doctor and was now resting at home. He hoped she'd be okay until he could spend a good day with Tobias and get over there later. He felt bad making her wait, knew she'd accuse him of not caring as much as he should. But she'd put so many things above him and Tobias over the years. He figured he had the right to do the same—for the sake of his brother. He wasn't even convinced she was as bad off as she said. Knowing her, she was making a bigger deal of it than it was, trying to evoke sympathy so they'd come running. She hated being left out of going to pick up Tobias, so it might even be that she was trying to force herself right into the middle of it.

His brother was already standing outside the gate when Maddox pulled up, but if Maddox hadn't been visiting him regularly, he wouldn't have recognized him. Not only was Tobias taller—he had an inch on Maddox now even though he'd been shorter than him before—he'd spent a great deal of time lifting weights. A tattoo peeked out from beneath the sleeve of the blue polo shirt Maddox had sent with a pair of khaki shorts and flip-flops for when he was released. Maddox had had to send "Dress Out" clothes, as they called it, because what Tobias had been wearing when he went in no longer fit.

"Have you been waiting long?" Maddox asked as he got out of the truck and came around to embrace his brother.

"'Bout an hour. No one else was getting released today, so all the bullshit they put me through went fast."

"What kind of bullshit was it?"

"They searched me. Searched my belongings. Made me sign an endless stack of papers. Gave me fifty dollars of my gate money."

"I thought you were supposed to get a hundred and eighty dollars when you were released."

"My parole officer will dole out the rest over the next sixty days. I might not know what to do with it, after all," he added sarcastically.

Maddox didn't comment. He didn't want to contribute to any negativity. It was important that Tobias get along with his parole officer, so Maddox was hoping the dude would be cool. "So you've got fifty dollars burning a hole in your pocket, huh?"

"No. I have a check for fifty dollars. I also have that two hundred dollars from Tiffany and Jada, so I'd better get a bank account."

"You and Tonya can head to the bank in the morning. It'll be better to open an account close to where you live. Sorry you had to wait so long for me to come, by the way. You should've had me show up sooner."

"Naw. You had to get up early enough as it was." He looked down the road to his right and then his left. "Besides, I liked sitting here, just breathing the air and looking around."

"Oh, so maybe we should hang out a bit longer," Maddox joked.

"Hell, no!" Tobias tossed his small duffel bag—which contained everything he owned in the world except maybe a few keepsakes their mother had stashed away somewhere in her house—in the back of the truck. "Let's blow this dump before they figure out a way to lock me up again."

Maddox would've chuckled except he was concerned by the fact that his brother seemed to believe the justice system was out to get him. No doubt most prisoners talked like that, but the "us" and "them" mentality wasn't going to help him on the outside. "Where should we go first?" he asked as he climbed back behind the wheel.

Tobias didn't answer. He was too busy checking out Maddox's truck. "This is *yours*?"

"Yeah. Bought it a couple of years ago."

He whistled. "It's nice, man."

"Thanks." The disparity between them made Maddox uncomfortable. It all hinged on one night, one night that, if it had gone differently, wouldn't have changed the course of both their lives. "Let's go buy you a phone."

"That'd be great. I want to text Tonya, tell her I'm out."

Maddox did a search with his Around Me app and found a Walmart where they could get a prepaid phone, which was all Tobias could afford until he found work and got on his feet. Maddox was willing to help him out financially, but he didn't want to spend a fortune on a phone when his brother would need other things, as well.

"You still got the cheat sheet Tiffany sent you?"

"Yeah. She's even got the Around Me app on here. That's what you just used, isn't it?"

"It is." As Maddox gave the truck some gas, his brother turned to watch the prison disappear from view. "It's all behind you now."

When he turned back around, he said, "I thought I'd never make it to this day."

Maddox adjusted the air conditioner. "Was it as bad as I imagine?"

His brother rolled down the window and stuck his head out as they sped down the road. "Worse."

Again, Maddox's mind went through all the things he feared had happened to his brother. "You have a new tattoo."

"Yeah."

"I told you to wait until you got out, so you could go to someone with normal supplies, sterilized needles and colored ink."

"I didn't want to wait for this one."

"What is it?" Maddox asked.

Tobias lifted his sleeve to reveal a compass.

Maddox didn't particularly care for Tonya. As soon as they reached her place, after spending the day and having dinner together as they'd planned, she opened the door, flew out and plastered herself all over Tobias. Maddox considered that a good sign. She was obviously happy to see him. But her apartment was so filthy he didn't feel comfortable even sitting on her couch, and his misgivings grew when she proceeded to tell them she'd lost her job working as a receptionist for a construction company a week ago and was going to sue the company for sexual harassment. Although Maddox would've sympathized had he gotten the impression she was truly a victim, the way she talked and laughed about the suit led him to believe she was just trying to get revenge on her boss for letting her go because she wouldn't stay off her cell phone at work.

Maddox was careful not to show his concern. He knew Tobias couldn't think of much beyond her curves and her hot kisses—she'd made certain of it by wearing very little—and Maddox was determined not to ruin his brother's first day out. But when it came time to go, he had a hard time leaving Tobias behind. He was afraid after he was gone Tonya would pull out a crack pipe or something and wondered if Tobias wouldn't be better off staying with their mother.

"Shit," he muttered as he walked to his truck. The last thing Tobias needed was someone who'd get him into trouble again.

Maddox pulled out of his parking space, then almost pulled right back into it but ultimately went ahead and peeled out of the lot. No way would Tobias leave with him even if he did go back. Not right now. They were probably already in bed together.

Traffic was so bad that by the time he reached his mother's, it was almost nine. She'd called him several times and left him angry voice messages, which he'd listened to when Tobias was in the restroom. She was furious that he hadn't brought Tobias directly to her house to make sure she was okay and, truth be told, he felt a little guilty that he hadn't, especially now that he wasn't convinced Tonya was any better for him.

With a sigh, he sat in his parked vehicle and stared at the light shining through the curtains. This wasn't the place where he'd grown up. His mother had moved several times since then. They'd never stayed in one spot longer than a year or two. But it was similar. They were basically all the same.

Before he climbed out, he checked his phone, hoping that Jada had broken down and texted him. He felt like he needed her. At the very least, he wanted her.

When he saw that she hadn't responded to anything he'd sent her last night, he wrote, Just in case you ever doubt it, you're doing the right thing staying away from me. I don't have anything to offer you.

He pressed Send as he prepared himself to deal with the mess that was his mother.

15

It was so hard not to reply to Maddox. Jada knew he'd picked up his brother today, understood it had to have been difficult and worried about what, exactly, had made him send his latest text. She wished she could ask. But cutting him off now might give her a second chance to be smarter and wiser where he was concerned. She was trying so hard to put the needs of her daughter and her family above her own. After all, she and her mother were just starting to get along.

When her phone rang as she was working late in her bedroom that night, she startled and then stared over at it with some trepidation. Could that be him? Was Maddox calling because she hadn't answered his text?

Maya was asleep beside her but, fortunately, the noise didn't even cause her to roll over.

Being careful not to shake the bed too much as she got out of it, Jada crossed to where she'd plugged her phone in to charge and was relieved to find Tiffany's picture on her screen.

"Hey, what's up?" she said, speaking low.

"I'm on break at the hospital, but I wanted to catch you if you were up. I just got a text from Tobias."

"You gave him your number, Tiff?"

"No, Maddox must've given it to him so he could thank me."

She remembered warning Tiffany that it might not be safe to associate with Maddox's brother, but Tiffany didn't seem concerned. "And did he—thank you, I mean?"

"He did. He said…" She put her phone on speaker and read the next part. "'Thank you for the letter you sent. And the money. Both mean a great deal to me.'"

Jada checked to make sure her daughter was still sleeping. "He was released today. You know that, right?"

"I figured he must be out."

"Did he say anything else?"

"Not until I responded. I told him that I hoped it helped and I wished him well, and he asked me if I would thank you for him. He said to tell you he was going to pay us both back when he gets a job."

Would he be able to find work? Jada was afraid it might be as difficult for him to enter the workforce as Atticus. "I hope he won't reach out to me—or, God forbid, send a check to my house."

"I doubt he will. He didn't ask for your number or anything."

"I'm living where I was before he went to prison."

"I'm sure he knows better."

"I wonder how it went when Maddox picked him up this morning."

"Maybe Maddox will tell you when he gets a chance."

Jada felt her face flush hot as she remembered the phone sex she'd had with Maddox last night. She'd been so bold, thinking he didn't know who she was—but the joke had been on her. "We're not talking anymore."

"What happened?"

She hesitated to tell Tiffany he found out who she was, but she figured she'd end up doing it eventually, so she lowered her voice even further and turned away from the bed, just in case Maya was anywhere close to consciousness. "He found out I was MysteryWoman23."

"He *what*?"

"You heard me."

"Holy shit! How?"

"I have no idea."

"He told you he knew it was you?"

"Essentially. And asked me to come over."

"To which you said…"

"No, of course." She'd been so shocked that what she'd done in that moment had been fairly easy. But it wasn't so easy anymore. Since he'd figured out it was her, she couldn't see how one night in his arms would matter. Why couldn't they have that much before going their separate ways?

"*That's* good at least. But will he leave it there?"

She decided not to mention his latest text. She didn't know why he'd sent it, and she hadn't responded to it, so there wasn't much they could gather from it. "Yeah."

"And? How do you feel?"

Like she was missing out. "Unbelievably torn," she admitted.

"I'm sorry, Jada."

"So am I, but there's nothing anyone can do to change the situation. I just need to let go of him and move on, right?"

"I guess. Listen, I have to get back to work. I'll stop by the store tomorrow, though, okay? If you're alone, we can talk."

"Okay." Jada disconnected and tried to return to her work on the computer. She was right in the middle of scheduling Facebook posts for each of her clients. But her mind reverted to Tobias and how grateful he'd seemed for the money. It wasn't much, but when she wasn't thinking about how angry her brother or mother would be over her actions, she was glad she'd sent it. She kept pondering Maddox's latest text, too. She wanted to write him back to see if he was okay.

The only way she was able to stop herself was by sliding down next to Maya and holding her daughter close. *Think of what you stand to lose*, she ordered herself and, finally, nodded off.

Maddox had a stiff neck when he woke up. He'd crashed on his mother's couch. He'd arrived to find her in bed, which was where he'd expected her to be. But she'd been in a stupor. When he roused her enough to get her to mumble a few words to him, she'd told him she'd only taken the pain pills the doctor had prescribed, but he was worried she might've taken those pills in combination with something else, and since her roommate had left to visit family in Virginia after dropping her at the ER, he didn't dare leave her alone. He'd stayed over to make sure she didn't need to go back to the hospital.

It had been a long night of checking on her periodically, but finally he could see the sun slanting through the crack in the drapes that hung, lopsided, from the front window. Sitting up, he kicked off the blanket he'd gotten out of the hall closet and covered a yawn. He felt like shit, but at least his mother looked like she'd be okay as far as her physical injuries went. She had a cut above her eyebrow, with a couple of stitches through it, a fat lip and a bruised cheek, but she'd been exaggerating when she said he'd broken her nose.

Intending to check on her again, he got up and knocked softly on the walls as he moved down the hall so she'd hear him coming. "Mom?" he said through the door to her bedroom. "You awake?"

No answer.

He knocked louder. "Mom? Can I come in?"

Still no answer.

He poked his head into the room, but he couldn't see much. She had shades as well as drapes back here, and both were drawn tight.

His stomach muscles tightened as he approached the bed. Since he was a little boy, he'd worried that he'd find her dead one day, and seeing her lying there unresponsive brought back the old helplessness as well as the current futility of trying to get her to change her life. "Mom?" When he touched her arm, she finally stirred.

"Maddox? Is that you?"

Her words were thick and clumsy, but any drugs she'd taken should've worn off, so he was hoping that was just from sleep. "Yeah, it's me. How do you feel?"

"Okay."

"Good."

She fumbled around to find his hand. "What are you doing here?"

She didn't even remember that he'd spoken to her last night.

"I came by to see how you're doing."

Her free hand went to her head as if it ached, and it probably did. "Did I tell you I was robbed?"

"Yeah. You said a friend forced his way into the house and took all the money from your purse. When you tried to stop him, he knocked you around a bit. Is that what happened?"

"Basically."

"Which friend was it? When I asked for his name, you said you couldn't remember it."

She let go of him to right the covers. "I still can't remember it."

That was a lie. He could tell by the lack of authority in her voice. She just didn't want him to go after the guy, and if that was the case, there had to be a reason. "Because..."

"Because he's more of an acquaintance."

Maddox pinched his neck, trying to ease some of the stiffness. "Was it because you took the money from him first?"

"Meaning what?"

"Did you borrow money from a friend that you didn't pay back?"

"No!"

"Then...did you owe him the money for drugs or something else?"

"What makes you ask that?" She sounded indignant.

"The TV, phone and computer I gave you are all still here."

"Which means what?"

"It wasn't the kind of robbery I at first thought."

"Aren't you the smart one!" she muttered.

He ignored her sarcasm, refused to let her make this conversation about him. "But am I right? If not, give me his name, and I'll find the bastard and get your money back."

She hesitated, seemingly in indecision.

"Mom?"

"I don't want you to get into trouble like your brother."

"Then tell me the truth. Did you owe this man for drugs?"

She didn't answer the question, just asked one of her own. "Where's Tobias?"

"He's where he's supposed to be—at his girlfriend's."

"Did you meet her?"

"I did."

"What's she like?"

Tonya hadn't made the best first impression, but Maddox didn't want to speak poorly of someone he didn't know, especially when it might prejudice his mother's opinion. Tobias needed all the support he could get, especially right now. "She seemed…very excited to see Tobias." That was truthful at least.

"Was he excited to see her?"

"He hasn't been with a woman in thirteen years. I think he was, yeah."

She swatted his leg. "That's not telling me what I want to know. I'm asking if they'll be good together in the long run."

"I wasn't there for more than thirty minutes, Mom. I have no way of judging their chances for a long-term relationship."

"You don't like her."

"Don't put words in my mouth."

"If you thought she was special, you'd be singing her praises right now, because you know I'm just as worried about Tobias as you are."

She had no idea that he was equally worried about her—or she chose to overlook it so she wouldn't have to address her own issues. "We need to give her a chance, okay? Anyway, quit trying to change the subject. Was it your supplier who took your money? Is that how you got hurt, trying to stop him?" It didn't escape Maddox that whoever it was probably could've done a lot more damage than he did, which was why he didn't think it was a concerted "beating" as she'd first described it.

"Life isn't always as easy as you seem to think."

Maddox nearly cursed but managed to refrain. "So it *was* your supplier."

Although he couldn't see her clearly in the dim room, he could tell she was glaring at him.

"Mom?"

"Fine. I owed him the money, but I told him I'd pay him next week and the bastard wouldn't wait."

Maddox could see why the dude wouldn't allow her to put him off. Chances weren't good his mother would have the money then, either. Her response told him what he'd begun to suspect—that what'd happened wasn't entirely the other person's fault. "That's what I thought. And yet you lied to me."

"Only because I didn't want to upset you, especially because I'm going to quit using," she said as she gingerly explored her bruised cheek. "This woke me up. I swear it."

"No, it didn't. You were on something last night."

"Just pain meds!"

He didn't believe that was all, but until she was willing to be honest, there wasn't anything he could do. "I'm missing another day of work. I'm going to make you breakfast and head back to Silver Springs so I can at least make it in to my office by this afternoon."

"When will I see Tobias?" she asked as he stood.

"Hopefully not until after you've healed. I didn't tell

him about this latest *problem*, and I'm hoping you won't, either. Especially now that I know you caused it."

"Okay, I won't. But what am I supposed to do about the money I lost? I needed it for food, rent."

Maddox chuckled without mirth. Here they went again. If he gave it to her, it would mean he'd essentially paid for the drugs she'd taken. If he didn't give it to her, she'd be kicked out of her apartment and would have nowhere else to go, wouldn't even be able to work.

"What you do to me is such bullshit." He got the money he had out of his wallet—two hundred and thirty-four dollars—and tossed it on her nightstand. "That's all I got on me."

"It'll help," she said. "Thank you."

He tried to search her expression for any hint of remorse, regret or even embarrassment, but it wasn't easy to see in the murky shadows of the room. He highly doubted he'd find what he was looking for, anyway. "Don't thank me. And don't count on me bailing you out again. I'm getting sick of it, which means, one day, I'll say no. Understand?"

She didn't respond. She was too busy trying to get the money hidden in a jewelry case in her nightstand. That seemed to be all she cared about, which was why he didn't stay to cook breakfast for her. "On second thought, you seem capable of making your own food. I've got to get back to my life."

Stunned, Maya sank slowly onto the edge of Annie's bed. Her grandmother had given her a ride over to her friend's house first thing in the morning, on her way to open the store. She'd been excited to spend another fun-filled day with Annie, but she'd been greeted almost immediately by terrible news. "So you're not going to Topatopa Junior High?"

Annie frowned. "No. Can you believe it?"

"I can't. I thought we'd be going there together. We've talked about it all summer."

"I know, but my mother *really* wants me to go to the girls' school at New Horizons."

Maya could tell Annie wasn't happy about the change, but that didn't make it any easier. "Why would you go there? You get good grades. You don't need to go to a school like that."

"My mom's friends with Aiyana Turner, who's in charge of the place. She wants to help get the new school off the ground, and she wants me to help other girls who aren't doing as well as I am. She says it's an opportunity to make a difference."

It was certainly going to make a difference to Maya— but not in a good way. "That's nice, but what about all of our plans?" Maya had had fun going to school with Annie the last few months of seventh grade. Leaving the friends she'd had in LA—even her cat, which Eric kept because her grandmother was allergic to pet hair—would've been so much harder had she not met Annie right away. Maya had been looking forward to starting school with her new friend in the fall. How could that have changed even though neither one of them were moving?

Annie plopped down next to her. "I know. I've begged and begged for her to let me decide, but she won't. She says I have to at least *try* it." Annie sent her a concilia-tory glance. "She did promise that we'd still get to see each other a lot, though."

Maya shook her head. "It won't be the same."

A knock sounded at the bedroom door. "Annie?"

It was Annie's mother. Maya turned away so that she wouldn't have to look at her right now. She didn't think she could smile.

"Come in." Annie sounded almost as glum as Maya felt.

The door opened and Mrs. Coates stuck her head through the crack. "Did you tell her?"

Annie stared at her shoes. "Yeah."

Maya forced herself to look over and found Mrs. Coates wearing a sympathetic expression. "I'm sorry. I know you must be disappointed, but I wanted to assure you, as I've assured Annie, that you'll still get to see each other all the time."

Maya wanted to say what she'd said to Annie—that it wouldn't be the same—but as soon as she opened her mouth to reply, tears welled up. "Sorry, I don't mean to be a big baby." She wiped her cheeks. "I've got to go. I'll call you later," she told Annie and scooted around her mom before any more tears could fall.

"I thought you were staying through lunch," Mrs. Coates said. "Do you even have a ride?"

"No, but my mom will come get me. I'm just going to wait for her out front." She started hurrying down the stairs, but Mrs. Coates called after her again.

"What if *you* went to New Horizons, too, Maya? Do you think you'd be interested in doing that?"

Annie appeared at the banister above. "Yes, Maya! Come with me! That'd be so fun!"

Burgeoning hope made it much easier not to cry. Maya couldn't imagine her mother would have any problem with her transferring so long as it was a good school, and Mrs. Coates wouldn't be sending Annie to New Horizons if it wasn't. Mrs. Coates researched everything. "I'd be fine with switching."

"There you go," Mrs. Coates said. "All is not lost quite yet. Let me talk to Aiyana and then we'll approach your mother."

The relief that'd flooded over Maya was suddenly tempered with the realization that changing schools might cost money—money her mother didn't have. "But it's a private school, right? Don't private schools cost a lot?"

"Since this is the first year it'll be open, there might be a slot that won't cost much, if anything. I'll see what I can work out with Aiyana."

If the amount was small enough, Jada *might* go for it. But Maya knew it'd have to be *really* small. They were already worried about how they were going to keep Sugar Mama open. "Okay. I guess it doesn't hurt to see what Mrs. Turner has to say. Maybe when you talk to her, you could tell her I'll work off my tuition by helping the other girls with homework or something."

"It's sweet of you to even think of that," Annie's mother said. "I'll let you know what I find out."

Maya managed a wobbly smile as Annie came down the stairs. "So don't leave. We were going to make cotton candy this morning, remember?"

They were also going to ride bikes down to the barbershop. Annie had said that a lot of older men went there, and maybe one of them would remember someone named Madsen or a motorcycle accident that'd killed someone twelve and a half years ago. They hadn't been able to find out anything at the high school or the library. No one seemed to know who Madsen was or even remember a motorcycle accident where a young man from Silver Springs lost his life. Maya had had to keep bugging

Jada to check old newspapers, but she'd finally said she hadn't been able to find anything.

"I wasn't leaving because I was mad," Maya said, now embarrassed by her reaction.

"I know. You were sad, and so was I. But my mom will fix everything. Won't you, Mom?"

Her mother laughed when they both turned to look up at her. "I'll do my best."

16

Tiffany stopped by the store after she'd slept all morning. Jada liked having the company, especially because as long as she didn't have any customers, they could hang out in the back while she cleaned, and they wouldn't have to watch what they said. There was no danger of Susan, Atticus or Maya showing up today. Atticus was taking Susan to LA to get the freezer her mother had agreed to purchase and Maya had asked to go with them. They'd picked her up from Annie's and left town about twenty minutes ago. Jada had the whole evening to herself.

"We should go out tonight," Tiffany said. "Your family won't be back until late."

"True. But where would we go? By the time I close this place, I won't get off until nine thirty. I'm not sure I'll feel up to a long drive after that, not with as little sleep as I've been getting."

"Why don't we just go to the Blue Suede Shoe? We haven't been out in ages."

Jada's fear of running into Maddox had definitely taken a toll on their social lives, which wasn't fair to Tiffany. "Actually, if you're in the mood, I'll drive to Santa Barbara with you."

To Jada's surprise, Tiffany didn't jump at that concession. *"Actually..."*

When her sentence fell off as though she was searching for the right way to frame what she had to say, Jada asked, "What? You don't want to go to Santa Barbara?"

"It's not that I don't *want* to go. It's that…well, Aaron Andrews texted me this morning."

Aaron was someone they'd both known in high school who lived in San Luis Obispo, a little over two hours away. He used to be on the basketball team—that was where Jada remembered him from—and he'd never been married. He and Tiffany had had a brief fling right after they'd left for college, since they'd both gone to San Diego State. Their relationship hadn't lasted long, but Jada knew they'd been talking again since Tiffany's divorce. "You want to drive to San Luis Obispo? That's even farther than Santa Barbara!"

"There's no need to drive *anywhere*. He's here, visiting his folks."

"Oh!" Jada started laughing. "So what you're *really* saying is that you need me to go to the Blue Suede Shoe with you so that you'll have someone to hang out with until he shows up."

A "you got me" expression claimed her face. "Basically. I'd meet him there on my own, but he set it up so casually I don't think it's a date. And he's bringing someone, too."

"Who?"

"His little brother."

"I don't remember his little brother. Do you?"

"I do, but I was involved with Aaron for a while. Name's Austin. They live in the same house these days—own a construction business together."

Again, Jada considered the possibility of running into

Maddox if she went to the club. But she couldn't leave Tiffany in the lurch. She and Tiffany had talked enough about her and her problems over the past six weeks or so; it was Tiffany's turn for a little support, even if it meant risking an uncomfortable encounter with Maddox.

It was a Tuesday night; hopefully he'd be too busy with work to come out.

"Sure. Okay," she said.

Tiffany smiled in relief. "Thanks. I know you're nervous but, depending on how things go, we won't have to stay long. Once we've been there for a while, if you like his brother well enough and wouldn't mind hanging out longer, I could always suggest we go to my house."

Jada didn't get the chance to respond before someone walked into the store out front. As soon as she heard the bell, she told Tiffany she'd be right back and hurried out to find Annie's mother, Cindy, wearing a tennis outfit and carrying an expensive purse. She always seemed to be toting a new one.

"Hi there!" Cindy was at least fifteen years older than Jada, happily married and financially stable, which meant they didn't have much in common at the moment. But, for the most part, Jada liked her. Cindy could be a little pushy—assertive was the polite way to put it—but she accomplished a lot and was someone Jada respected and appreciated, since she'd been so good to Maya.

"Great to see you," Jada said. "Is Annie with you?" She glanced out front but didn't see Maya's blonde friend in the Ford Explorer Cindy had parked out front.

"No, I asked her to stay home so that you and I could talk in private."

A trickle of concern caused Jada to tense. She thought about mentioning Tiffany, who could, no doubt, hear everything, but didn't bother. She kept nothing from her friend, anyway. "About what? Is something wrong?"

"Not *wrong* exactly. It's just that I wanted to let you know Annie won't be going to Topatopa Junior High this fall, as we'd originally planned."

Jada couldn't say she was happy to hear this news. Maya would be terribly disappointed. "Don't tell me you're moving…"

"No, nothing that drastic. I'm enrolling her at New Horizons, is all."

"New Horizons!" With several elite private schools in the area, Aiyana's brainchild for troubled adolescents was the last school Jada had expected her to name.

Cindy's bracelet slipped up her arm as she adjusted her Michael Kors handbag. "I can understand your surprise, given what we know about New Horizons. This decision is sort of experimental, but I've been thinking it can only help Aiyana to have some well-adjusted girls she can count on to set an example and inspire good behavior in the others. And since this is the start-up year for the girls' side, I'd like to see if Annie's presence there can make a positive impact."

"I see," Jada said.

"The only problem is that Annie doesn't want to go to the new school without Maya and Maya doesn't want Annie to leave Topatopa." She lowered her voice. "Maya started crying this morning when Annie told her, so I promised them both I'd try to find a way to keep them together."

Jada clasped her hands in front of her. "How do you propose to do that?"

"I'm hoping you'd be willing to move Maya, too."

"You mean enroll her at New Horizons."

"Yes. With the low pupil per teacher ratio, they should be able to learn a great deal."

"Do you plan to keep Annie there throughout high school?" Maya had just settled into Silver Springs and was enjoying her friendship with Annie so much.

"No, Aiyana will need those slots for others eventually. I'm thinking of having Annie go there this year and next before transferring over to McGregor."

Jada frowned. "I'm sorry. I'd love to be able to keep the girls together, but New Horizons is a private school, and I'm not in a position to afford the tuition right now. College will come soon enough," she added with a wry chuckle.

Someone in Cindy's income bracket didn't have to worry quite as much about the burden of tuition. "I realize it's an added expense, and no one needs that. I wouldn't be able to afford the normal tuition, either. But I've talked to Aiyana. She agrees with me that it'd be beneficial to have some 'ambassadors,' as we're calling them." She smiled broadly, as though she was about to bestow a fabulous gift. "So she's offering Maya an academic scholarship!"

Jada gripped the counter. "But…surely there are other girls who need that slot more—"

"Since the school isn't at maximum capacity, you don't have to worry about that," she broke in. "Sending Maya to New Horizons would enable our girls to help launch the school and stay together at the same time."

Cindy seemed pleased with the groundwork she'd put in. She'd thought of everything, worked it all out and couldn't imagine any reason Jada would say no. But she didn't fully understand the situation. The Coateses hadn't lived in Silver Springs when Atticus was shot, so they weren't aware of the connection between Maddox and the man who'd crippled Jada's baby brother. And they definitely didn't know Maddox was Maya's biological father. Aiyana knew about Atticus, though, and apparently hadn't shared that information with Cindy. Why not?

"I'm sorry," she said. "I appreciate all you've done—talking to Aiyana and working out the details—but I'm going to keep Maya at Topatopa."

Cindy's self-assured smile wilted. "I don't mean to be rude, but do you mind if I ask *why*?"

"I…I think that's what's best for her. She just started at Topatopa a few months ago. I'd rather not uproot her again so soon."

"But you won't really be uprooting her. She *wants* to go to New Horizons. She told me so this morning."

Jada's mind scrambled to come up with other reasons to bolster her refusal. "I wouldn't feel comfortable taking a scholarship when the school needs money."

"It won't hurt the school to have her enroll. I've donated a great deal of time and effort to New Horizons, so they have been and will be well compensated. And, as I mentioned, the school won't be full this year. It's just getting started. We might as well fill those seats and help the staff, teachers and other pupils get rolling. At this point, it'll be a waste *not* to use those resources."

Jada couldn't help feeling a degree of irritation that Cindy wasn't accepting her answer. "I'm sorry. It's just not an option for us right now."

Cindy's mouth opened and closed twice. Jada could tell she was tempted to try again, but didn't know what to say. "I'm sorry if I've overstepped," she finally mumbled and walked out.

Jada dropped her head to rub her temples only to jerk

it up again when Tiffany came out of the back. "Did I just hear what I thought I heard?"

Jada sighed. "You did."

"Oh jeez. Maya is going to be *so* upset if you don't let her go to New Horizons with Annie. You realize that."

"The Coateses could always change their minds and have Annie go to Topatopa as they originally planned."

"Apparently, you don't know Mrs. Coates very well," Tiffany said, and they both laughed, even though Jada was sure she wouldn't be laughing when her daughter came to her, crying, tomorrow.

Maddox was walking out to his car to head home for the night when Aiyana caught him in the parking lot to tell him that Cindy Coates had just called her. "And? What'd she say?" he asked. "Will Annie be attending in the fall?"

"I think so. At least, Cindy hasn't indicated otherwise. But…there's a wrinkle."

He shifted his briefcase to his other hand. He'd filled it with so many files it was heavy. "What kind of wrinkle?"

"Annie Coates is best friends with Maya Brooks."

Maddox didn't know Maya well enough to have had any idea until Aiyana mentioned it, but he thought he could guess why it might be a problem. "Don't tell me once you told Cindy about my history in this town she changed her mind."

"I didn't tell her about your history. I prefer to keep talk of it to a minimum. You weren't directly involved, anyway."

"So…what, then?"

"Annie doesn't want to change schools without Maya."

Instead of shifting his briefcase again, he set it on

the pavement. "Are you asking me if Maya can come here, too?"

Aiyana's expression revealed a touch of chagrin. "Actually, I'm not. That would've been polite of me. But I took it upon myself to tell Cindy it would be fine. I even told her we'd waive the tuition. I didn't mention it to you because I thought we'd done our part by saying yes and Jada would say no, making it unnecessary for us to even have that conversation."

"And she agreed?" He couldn't imagine she'd let her daughter come to the school *he* was running. Or that Atticus or Susan would ever go along with it, even if she did.

"No, she refused."

As Aiyana had expected. He'd expected the same, so he told himself he shouldn't feel any of the disappointment that hit him so unexpectedly. He picked up his briefcase. "Well, that takes care of it, right?"

"Not really." Aiyana fixed the end of her braid since the tie was coming out. "Cindy's asked me to talk to her. But before I agreed to go that far, I figured it was time to discuss it with you. Would you mind if Maya attended New Horizons? It would mean that you'd have some degree of contact with the Brooks family, of course, including Maya's mother."

He *wanted* contact—at least with Jada. It was the Brookses who wouldn't be interested in what Aiyana proposed. "I'm not sure we should pressure her."

"That's a no?"

He thought about it for a second before nodding to confirm her guess.

She caught him before he could turn away. "But if they let her, they might get to know you, get past what they imagine you to be, and let bygones be bygones. It's time for that to happen. Then you'll be far more comfortable here. I daresay you'll also be more effective."

"I don't want to make Jada uncomfortable just to make myself more comfortable."

"But if they get to know you and forgive and move on, *they'll* feel better about everything, too. Don't you see? It might take some time, but familiarity breeds acceptance. Besides, New Horizons poses a good opportunity for Maya. You're hiring such a talented and devoted staff. I believe she'd love it here."

"I don't think there's any way to convince Jada."

"Not if you refuse to give me a chance. Maddox, Cindy said that Maya started crying when she learned Annie would be going to a different school."

He arched an eyebrow at her. "Now you're just trying to manipulate me."

"That's true," she admitted, and they both laughed.

Sobering, Maddox imagined the sweet girl he'd seen at Sugar Mama. Surely, so that the two friends wouldn't have to be separated, he could give Aiyana the go-ahead to contact Jada. He was fine with having Maya at New Horizons as long as Jada was willing to send her. Maybe Aiyana would say the magic words; his boss was a tough person to resist. Then he'd get to see Jada every now and then.

"It's fine if you call her," he said. "Maybe point out that my position is administrative, that I won't have a lot of daily contact with the students, especially those who don't need the extra attention. Or—" He scratched his head. "Never mind. I'll call her myself."

She tossed her braid over her shoulder. "Do you even have her number?"

He winked.

"Don't tell me you're seeing her again!" she called after him, but he simply waved.

Maddox had hoped to catch Jada at the store. He was figuring out that her mother usually opened, and Jada closed, so evenings were the best time to find her alone. But when he'd arrived home from work, he'd discovered his landlord sitting on the porch, a bit disoriented. Uriah had fallen off a ladder while trying to clean out his rain gutters and was banged up, so Maddox had taken him to the hospital to make sure he was okay.

Fortunately, he didn't have any broken bones. Now he was home in bed with strict orders to take some time off. But the whole emergency room process had taken more than four hours. It was after ten and the store was dark by the time Maddox was free to go into town.

Damn. He'd missed her...

For the second time since he'd known she was back in Silver Springs, he drove past her house. He thought he'd find her car sitting out front, at which point he'd go home with the knowledge that he couldn't have a word with her tonight. He was already considering what he'd send in a text, if that were the case. Maybe he could get her to respond if it was about Maya.

But her car wasn't there, so he drove down the main drag, hoping to spot her. He figured if she wasn't at the grocery store or any of the other businesses, only a few of which were still open, she could be at Tiffany's place. It was possible he could come across her car simply by driving down every street.

He didn't end up having to do that, though. He spotted the Chevy Volt at the Blue Suede Shoe before he could even reach the other end of town.

After pulling into the parking lot, he let his engine idle. Should he try to talk to her here or wait for another opportunity?

He decided to go inside. He doubted she'd respond to a text from him.

Besides, he *wanted* to see her. Their phone sex session had made staying away from her even more difficult. If he went home, he'd just spend half the night fantasizing about her.

The club was busy, especially for midweek, but it was filled mostly with tourists. He didn't recognize anyone until he spotted Tiffany and Jada sitting at a table on the opposite side of the dance floor. Then he wished he hadn't come in: they were both obviously with someone.

He told himself to leave before Jada saw him, but he couldn't seem to make his feet carry him out. A seat opened up at the bar. He took it and ordered a beer. Then he went back to play pool, all the while keeping an eye on Jada and her date. Did she *really* like that dude? How well did they know each other? Where did they meet? Was she going home with him tonight?

The guy looked younger than they were by maybe five or six years. But he was tall, blond and handsome. Dressed as though he had money, too.

Maddox wasn't typically the jealous type, but he couldn't pull his gaze away, which was, no doubt, why she noticed him almost immediately. Her eyes flared as recognition dawned. Still, she kept a determined smile on her face and turned back to whomever she was with.

An onslaught of negative emotions made Maddox slightly ill, a feeling that grew worse with each exchange Jada had with her date. He tried to channel the tension growing inside him into billiards—and decimated every opponent. But that wasn't satisfying enough. When he saw her get up and head toward the bathroom, he put his current game on hold, leaned his cue stick against the wall and made his way over to the hall where the bathrooms were. It was crazy that he'd been staring at her from the corner like some lovesick fool. But he felt somewhat justified. She wanted *him*, not the guy on which she was bestowing so many polite smiles. And watching her with another man so shortly after their intimate exchanges was killing him. Those texts had made him feel a possessiveness he wished he didn't.

What was he going to say to her when he reached her?

He supposed he'd start with the bit about allowing Maya to come to New Horizons. That, at least, gave him an excuse to approach her.

He reached the narrow hallway about the same time she did and opened his mouth to tell her what Aiyana had told him regarding Cindy Coates. But some drunk guy from behind accidentally pushed him into her—and the next thing he knew, he had her up against the wall, his body pressed tightly to hers, his tongue in her mouth.

Jada wasn't sure exactly what happened. She'd been struggling along with Aaron, Austin and Tiffany, trying to act as though she was happy and entertained, for the sake of her best friend. It was clear that Tiffany liked Aaron. But then Jada had excused herself—just for the chance to slip away and catch her breath. When she was in the main part of the club she couldn't pull her gaze away from Maddox. She could tell he didn't like that she was with someone else. Every time she glanced over at him, he was wearing a darker and darker scowl. She wouldn't have liked seeing him with another woman, so she could understand. But what were they supposed to do? They were both single! This was bound to happen again and again if they continued to live in the same town.

And then he'd somehow come up beside her, and in the crush of people trying to jam their way into the back hallway to reach the bathrooms, she'd felt his arm brush hers.

She'd turned; he'd turned. And then he'd kissed her. And she'd kissed him back with every ounce of pent-up longing she felt.

When he'd lifted his head, he'd looked torn, confused, and she must've looked about the same because he'd stepped away and, without a word, pushed through the crowd and out the back door.

"Are you okay?"

At the sound of Tiffany's voice, Jada pulled her gaze away from the door Maddox had used to stalk into the parking lot to find her friend standing beside her, looking concerned. "Yeah. I'm okay," she lied. "Why?"

"You've been gone forever!"

It didn't seem that long. She could still taste Maddox, feel the pressure of his warm, full lips on hers, his big body blocking out everyone and everything else. "There's been a line," she managed to say.

"But you aren't *in* it."

Jada considered telling Tiffany what had just occurred, but she didn't want to put any pressure on her friend to change plans, not when she was having such a great time. "Oh. Right. I'll move over."

As much as she wished Maddox would return, she doubted that would happen and was almost as relieved as she was disappointed when he didn't. It was too hard having him around when she was with someone else.

Heck, just having him back in town was hard, and that had nothing to do with another man.

Forcing herself to move, she slid over, getting in line. "I'll make it as quick as possible," she told Tiffany.

"Thanks—because they're ready to leave."

"The evening's over?"

Tiffany gave her a funny look. "You're acting so strange."

"I've probably had too much to drink."

"You've had one beer! Do you want to go home or something?"

"No!" She pulled her phone from her pocket to check the time. "It's just…it's getting late, so I thought the evening might be winding down."

Disappointment tugged Tiffany's lips into a frown. "Don't you like Austin? He's young but sexy as hell, don't you think?"

That was true. Most women would be eager to be with him, but as far as Jada was concerned, he couldn't compare to Maddox. "Course I like him. He's supernice."

"And you're not too tired?"

Jada mustered a fresh smile. "No. I just assumed they'd be driving back tonight. I wouldn't want them to get too late of a start if they have a couple of hours ahead of them."

"They're staying in Silver Springs until after the weekend, remember? They said that."

"Right," she said as though Tiffany had successfully jogged her memory, but she hadn't heard that at all. She hadn't been listening carefully. She'd been too distracted by the man she *really* wanted, who'd been in the corner playing pool. "I'm down to go to your place, then. Is that the plan?"

"Yeah." Tiffany gave her arm a grateful squeeze and hurried back toward their table.

As Jada faced forward again, she covered her mouth, once again replaying her brief encounter with Maddox. She didn't remember grabbing him or pulling him to her—didn't remember him grabbing her or pulling her to him, either. It was almost as if some outside force, like gravity, had been hard at work. But she couldn't regret what'd happened. His kiss had nearly melted her bones.

17

When Jada left Tiffany's, she wasn't planning on driving straight over to Maddox's house—which was why it was sort of funny that she did. But she didn't turn in at the drive. She crept down between the trees on the far side of the houses, like she had when she delivered the pie.

After she turned off her engine, she sat there, staring at the stars peeking through the leaves here and there as they waved in the warm breeze. Five minutes turned into ten, at which point she decided she needed to do *something*, couldn't sit there all night.

She pulled out her phone to see if Maddox had texted her since leaving the Blue Suede Shoe. Although she'd been checking all night, she hadn't heard a peep from him. And there was nothing waiting for her now.

Was he upset?

Although she'd deleted him as a contact, she easily remembered his number. She typed it in before sending him a message. What happened tonight?

No response. She figured he was asleep.

All the more reason to leave him in peace and go home. She was crazy to make the tug-of-war between them any worse.

She started her car, intending to back up. Instead, she turned it right back off. She was going in. Maddox could send her away if he wanted to…but she didn't think he would.

If you come over, I'll give you a back rub—and let you dictate what happens from there.

Taking a deep breath, she opened her door and shoved her phone and her keys in her pocket as she got out.

She'd wanted to be with him again for *thirteen years*…

She was going to do it. They could always go back to fighting the attraction tomorrow.

Maddox had finally dozed off. He thought he was dreaming when he heard a knock at the door. He imagined it was his brother and his brother's girlfriend, that it was midmorning, sunny and warm outside. They must be going somewhere, he thought, feeling only mildly surprised, as if he should've known they were coming.

Then reality pierced through all of those strange and not entirely consistent images. He was alone in his house, it was late in the night and whoever was knocking on his door probably wasn't his brother. Chances were far greater it was his landlord.

Was Uriah having problems?

Maddox sprang out of bed, just in case. He was anticipating another trip to the ER when he opened his door, so he was shocked to find Jada standing there, wearing the same silky black sleeveless top and tight-fitting jeans she'd had on at the club and rubbing her bare arms as though it was cold, even though it was actually hot and sultry, so hot that he'd been sleeping in his boxers with only a sheet.

They stared at each other for several seconds without

speaking. Then he held the door and stepped aside so she could come in.

She edged past him as though she was afraid to touch him. But he knew why she was there, understood what she wanted. She'd told him via text before she'd quit communicating with him, and he'd felt her response when he was kissing her earlier. She'd been as aroused as he'd been.

"Does this have to go according to the script?" he asked.

She blinked at him. "What script?"

Obviously, her mind was traveling in a different direction than his. "The one you laid out on the phone? Because I'm not sure my brain will be functioning well enough to remember every detail." He was pretty sure he wouldn't be able to think at all, not once he started touching her. Whatever happened from there would be instinctive.

"The details don't matter." She stepped forward, caught his face in her hands and rose up on tiptoe so she could reach his mouth. "I can't wait that long to feel you inside me, anyway."

He heard a guttural sound and realized it had come from his own throat as her body came into full contact with his.

Jada's restraint had snapped completely; she felt oddly reckless. Now that she was no longer holding back, she was going to make sure she got everything she'd ever wanted from Maddox—at least in a physical sense. Maybe she thought it would satisfy her beyond tonight. Put all the temptation he posed behind her. Who could say? She couldn't figure out what was going on inside her head. She just knew that she'd never been quite so aggressive, quite so eager to experience a man's body, to touch and taste him and luxuriate in the way he touched and tasted her.

Fortunately, Maddox didn't seem to mind. His kisses turned frantic and deep almost immediately, and his hands were everywhere—under her blouse, in her pants. When he worked his left hand between her legs and slipped a finger inside her, she felt her knees go weak and had to pull away long enough to gasp for air.

"Are you okay?" he asked.

"I can hardly breathe," she admitted.

"I know the feeling. We have to get rid of these clothes."

He managed to pull her blouse over her head with only a small interruption to the way he was kissing her neck, and she helped him by wiggling out of her jeans while he unfastened her bra.

She felt it come loose as soon as she kicked her jeans aside, so she let it drop at the same time. Then, like him, she was in her underwear—only hers was a black thong.

"That's better," he said.

Jada felt a moment of self-consciousness. It had been a long time since they'd seen each other like this. She'd had a baby since then—*his* baby—which had changed her body in subtle ways. Her hips were a little wider, her breasts larger, fuller. And she had some fine stretch marks along her lower abdomen.

Fortunately, he didn't focus on that, didn't even seem to notice. His nostrils flared slightly as his eyes swept over her. "God, you're even more beautiful than I remembered."

"So are you," she admitted.

He stepped close again, and this time when he touched her, it was with less emergency and more reverence. "I thought I might never have this opportunity again."

She ran her hands over the firm contours and smooth, warm skin of his chest. "I thought the same thing."

His hands came up to hold her head so she had to look at him. "So what does this mean? Anything?"

She wished she could look away. "A time-out from regular life. A break from the resistance. One night of whatever we want."

"Just one night."

He didn't seem to like that she was putting strict limitations on their contact, but as far as she was concerned, something was better than nothing. This was the only way they could be together. "That's all I have to give."

"Then I'd better make it count," he said, and she felt his hands slip around her waist to cup her ass as he brought her back up against him, more possessively now that he understood the rules, and that there weren't any—at least for tonight.

"I can easily get this part of the fantasy right," Maddox said as he swept Jada into his arms and carried her to the bed.

She laughed as he put her down. "That's the only part you remember?"

He remembered a lot more than that. "No. I remember the way it made me feel, knowing you were the one saying those things."

"And how was that?"

He guided her hand back to his chest, where his heart was beating like a drum. "Like this."

One finger from her other hand outlined his erection through the fabric of his boxers. "And this?"

Her touch nearly stole his breath. "And that."

"You don't think we're making a mistake, do you?"

"Hell, no," he said, "but I'm not sure I could admit it, even if I did. Not right now."

She laughed again, until he lowered himself on the bed beside her. Then she sobered as she stared up at him.

As difficult as it was, he refrained from removing her panties. He didn't want this to end too soon. Just being with her, just seeing her so drunk on desire, was intoxicating for him, too, especially after jealousy had nearly eaten him alive at the club.

"It's been thirteen years," she said, her voice wistful.

"Thirteen years too long," he responded and watched her lips part as he cupped her breast and flicked his thumb across the hard nub of her nipple. "You like that?"

The goose bumps that sprang up indicated she did. "Definitely. But please tell me you have protection. I haven't been with anyone since…well, since my divorce. So I'm not on the pill. And I didn't stop and buy anything along the way. I was too busy pretending I wasn't going to do this."

He loved the idea that she hadn't been able to stop herself, couldn't help hoping that if she had a good time, she'd be back for more. "I've got what we need. It's in the nightstand."

"Thank God you're prepared."

"I wasn't when you texted me, but I bought a whole box the morning after."

She grinned as she indicated that she wanted him to remove his boxers. "Then what are you waiting for?"

He felt a fresh deluge of testosterone as he peeled off her panties first. "What if I wasn't prepared?"

"Maybe I would've left."

He ran his lips up her neck. "You're not getting out of here that easily."

She slid her hand inside his boxers. "You have other plans for me?"

"Absolutely." After kicking off his own underwear and rolling on a condom, he used his leg to spread hers and lifted himself on top of her. The prospect of pressing inside her made him a little jittery, a little weak, which was new for him.

"What is it?" she whispered.

"This is going to be good," he replied and heard her groan as he pushed inside her.

It was late and Maddox had drifted off, but Jada didn't plan on sleeping. She wasn't going to waste a moment of her time with Maddox. She smiled as she watched his chest rise and fall. She'd given him quite a workout, but she couldn't seem to get enough of him. Each time they made love was different. After the first time, which became frenzied and intense very fast, they'd made love twice more, once so slow that the climax that finally washed over her was one of the most powerful she'd ever experienced, and the other with her on top. She'd loved the expression on his face when she'd rolled him onto his back. He'd looked a bit surprised that she'd be so assertive. But then he'd given her that sexy smile of his, the one she'd dreamed about as much as anything else where he was concerned, and he'd given up control. As she straddled his hips and took him inside her, he'd whispered, "Oh God," and closed his eyes—and she'd closed hers and abandoned any thought of holding back.

That was the last time. And she wasn't sure there'd be another. The sun would be coming up soon. She couldn't be seen leaving his house.

When she shifted, trying to see the clock on the nightstand, he stirred and muttered, "You're not leaving yet, are you?"

"Not right now, but I have to go soon."

"Tonight was amazing," he said, his words slurred from sleep.

She smiled into the darkness. "Yeah, it was."

He pulled her closer. "Say you'll come back."

"I *can't* come back."

"No one will know, Jada."

"The more I see you, the greater the chances someone will find out."

"We could meet in LA or Santa Barbara."

"I can't leave town." Especially for that. "I have Maya."

He said nothing for a few minutes. When he spoke again, she could tell he was wide-awake. "Are you going to let her come to New Horizons?"

"No."

"Because of me?"

She had her head on his shoulder, so they were still physically very close, but she could feel the emotional distance widening. "Because of my family."

"It's a school, Jada. That's all. Her best friend will be attending. It's not fair to split them up because of something that happened in the past, something that had nothing to do with them. I'm the principal. It's not like your family will have to deal with me one-on-one. I'll just be in the background."

She nibbled at her bottom lip. She wanted to let Maya go, but she was already struggling with her attraction to him. Look how badly she'd failed last night! Could she face bumping into him when she picked Maya up from school? Would increased exposure raise the risk that he might begin to wonder about Maya's paternity?

He slipped his fingers through her hair. "I'll look out for her. Make sure she has a good experience. I promise."

Her stomach twisted into knots. She didn't want to talk about Maya. It was so much easier when she kept Maddox and Maya in separate compartments in her brain, as she'd done last night so she could come over. "I'll talk to my mother. See what she says."

"What about Maya's father? He should have some say."

Jada's heart jumped into her throat. It was all she could do not to pull away, but she didn't want him to think something was wrong, just because he'd mentioned Maya's father. "He does have some say," she muttered.

"So he's involved in her life?"

His fingers were still combing slowly through her hair. Normally, she'd find that kind of touch soothing, but the conversation was putting her on edge. Now that she could think beyond her own needs, she was beginning to realize how selfish it had been to act on her desires. "Not really. He's an alcoholic as well as a workaholic. That didn't leave a lot of room for us."

"Surely he pays child support."

Again, she barely refrained from pulling away. "Of course," she said, although Eric paid nothing. She hadn't asked him to; he wasn't Maya's biological father, so it was never an issue.

"Why don't you talk to him about it? See what he thinks? It shouldn't be up to your mother. It should be up to the two of you."

She finally felt as though she'd waited long enough since the introduction of this subject that she could move away without setting off any alarm bells. "This isn't a usual situation. You know why I have to check with my mother. Anyway, I've got to go," she said as she climbed out of bed.

He leaned on one elbow while watching her dress. "Where'd you park?"

"In the orchard. I wasn't about to pull down the driveway."

"In the future, let me know you're coming. We'll hide your car somewhere, and I'll pick you up."

She kept her back to him. "I'm not coming back."

"If you do."

"Why?" she asked while pulling on her blouse and jeans.

He hesitated long enough that she paused before putting on her sandals. "Maddox?"

Although he answered, she could tell he was reluctant. "There's a security camera on that side of the house. That's how I knew it was you who delivered the pie."

She felt her jaw drop. "You're telling me Uriah will know I was here? He'll see that I pulled in?"

Maddox winced. Obviously, the panic in her voice made him uncomfortable. "He might."

"No! Why didn't you warn me?"

"Because I didn't know you were going to show up."

"You could've told me when I *did* show up," she said. "I could've left right away. At least then he wouldn't think that we…that we…"

"Made love? Whatever he'll think, in my mind it was worth it. I'll never forget tonight."

Neither would she. They'd created so many new memories—probably not a good thing, either. "I can't believe I did this."

"I wasn't going to say anything that might scare you away," he explained. "I wanted you here, in case that isn't obvious by now."

"But I've already hurt my family so much."

"Not by choice."

"*This* was my choice."

"And I, for one, am glad you made it. Please don't worry. It's okay. Uriah's cool. He won't tell anyone."

"He could!"

Maddox got out of bed and put on his boxers. "I shouldn't have brought it up right now. This was exactly what I was trying to avoid."

"That I'm being filmed coming here is, without question, something I need to know."

"Which is why I told you. But please don't regret coming. And don't let it stop you from visiting me in the future. Just communicate with me beforehand, and I'll make sure no one knows." He reached for her, but she stepped away.

"Please…don't tempt me. I don't need that. And pray Uriah doesn't notice it was me or, if he does, that he doesn't tell anyone or… Shit." What were the chances Uriah would keep silent with something that scandalous? Like most small towns, everyone loved a juicy piece of gossip.

She finished dressing and fished her keys from her pocket. She couldn't get out of Maddox's house fast enough.

Maddox shoved a hand through his hair. "I don't like that you're upset, don't want this night to end badly."

"I'm not upset. I just… I can't come back."

"Because…"

"Because I can't screw up my life again!"

He stiffened. "By being with *me. I'm* the big mistake."

"No. Never mind," she said, but she wasn't convincing, and she knew it.

"You realize I didn't pull that trigger, right? I've never done *one thing* to hurt you. Not on purpose, anyway."

She could tell her words had cut him and she felt bad about that. What they'd just shared had been rare and intimate and fulfilling. He deserved some credit for being everything she'd wanted him to be, everything she'd craved. But learning that she'd been caught on tape going into his house and would be seen leaving hours later rattled her so badly she didn't know how to react.

She had to get over him. At last. That was all there was to it.

"I'm sorry," she said and hurried out.

18

When Maddox woke to the scent of Jada's perfume on his sheets, he pulled them off and washed them immediately, while he showered for work. He'd begun to hope he could get her back, and that was dangerous for him. If she didn't want him, she didn't want him.

When he checked his phone, he saw that she'd texted him. I'm sorry. She said nothing more, and that had come in while he was sleeping, so he didn't respond. He didn't want to screw up his life any more than she wanted to screw up hers, and since she seemed to be the only person who possessed the power to hurt him, maybe he needed to wise up and stay away. It wasn't as though she'd ever let herself love him. Too much had happened.

But they were good together. He had to admit that.

Once he arrived at work, he spent half the morning staring off into space, remembering the way she'd kissed him when she first arrived, the small changes in her body, which he found even more attractive, how she'd straddled him the last time they'd made love. He'd enjoyed watching the expressions on her face almost as much as the more direct pleasure she evoked as she—

"Hey, are you going to make it?"

Maddox blinked and turned to see Aiyana poking her head through the doorway. "Where?"

She checked her watch. "We had a staff meeting that was supposed to start fifteen minutes ago."

He shoved away from his desk. "Oh! Right. Sorry."

She gave him a curious look. "Is something wrong?"

"Of course not," he said, but after he reached the conference room on the boys' side of school and greeted Elijah and Gavin, whom he was beginning to eat lunch with if they were around, as well as the other teachers, he had a hard time paying attention. He was so preoccupied that Aiyana pulled him aside when it was over, after everyone had left.

"What's going on with you?" she asked. "Is everything okay with your brother?"

He'd meant to text Tobias to see how his second day of freedom had gone, but he'd been so caught up in Jada since he returned to Silver Springs he hadn't done it yet. "I'll be checking in with him tonight. I'm sure I would've heard if there was a problem, though." He *had* received a message from his mother, thanking him for the money. But he was so angry with her for getting indebted to a pusher and causing her own robbery he hadn't responded.

Instead of being satisfied, Aiyana peered at him a little closer. "So there's nothing going on I should be concerned about?"

He told her Uriah had fallen from a ladder and he'd taken him to the ER, hoping that would satisfy her curiosity enough to stop her from probing further. "So I'm just tired," he said at the end.

He felt slightly guilty when that actually worked to distract her. He was reacting to what'd happened *after* the hospital, not that event at all, so it was sort of misleading.

"Poor guy," she said. "Did you call his son?"

"No. I don't even know his son's name. Should I have asked for it—and his number?"

"Not if Uriah's going to be okay. It's better if Carl doesn't come back."

"You know his son?"

She frowned. "He caused so many problems that most people around here do."

"I take it you don't care for him…" That came as a surprise to Maddox. He'd assumed Aiyana liked everyone.

"He's…extremely difficult."

For Aiyana to say that, it really meant something. "In what way?"

"He couldn't keep a job. Broke into the neighbor's house and stole his guns."

"Was he using?"

"Maybe here and there. I didn't get the impression he was an addict. He came to New Horizons when it first opened, but I couldn't help him."

"That makes him unusual indeed," Maddox joked.

A ghost of a smile curved her lips. "Thanks for saying that, but there are some people who won't ever change, you know? They don't feel the need, don't care about the fact that they are hurting others."

"He was that way?" Maddox couldn't equate that sort of son with such a principled father.

"Dr. Uchtdorf, the psychologist I had on staff in those days, diagnosed Carl with antisocial personality disorder."

"Isn't that close to calling someone a psychopath?"

"Yes. Very. Although some psychologists argue they are two different things, others use the terms interchangeably. Carl was so hard on his mother that Uriah finally kicked him out. Then they had to live in fear, for months, that he'd come back and set their house on fire while they slept."

"So now I know."

"About Carl?"

"I was wondering why Uriah didn't have any contact with his son."

"You're staying in Carl's house. I assumed you knew. Why didn't you ask me before?"

He chuckled. "I guess I should have. I didn't realize you'd have so much information on my landlord's son."

"I almost wish I'd never met him," she said ruefully. "He has that effect on people."

"What forms someone into a psychopath, in your opinion?" Maddox asked. "Nature or nurture?"

"The latest research suggests their brains are wired differently."

"Which means we can't hold them accountable for their actions?" He was desperately hoping his brother wasn't someone who couldn't change. Tobias had always possessed empathy, but he was troubled, seemed to twist certain things in his head. The letters Maddox had received from prison revealed that he still had problems with his thinking.

"I didn't say that. It's probably a combination of both—nature *and* nurture. Those who become serial killers or violent offenders have typically endured some abuse or neglect, but we need more research if we're ever to find a way to treat the untreatable. There's a psychiatrist by the name of Evelyn Talbot doing some groundbreaking work at a new facility called Hanover House. It's in a small town in Alaska. Have you heard of it?"

A dim recollection began to take shape in Maddox's

mind. "Seems like I read something about her in the paper not long ago..."

"They captured the man who attacked her when she was only sixteen. That's probably what you saw. It was big news. They'd been searching for him for over twenty years. It was being tortured for three days and left for dead that made her want to become a psychiatrist in the first place—so that maybe, one day, she could understand why he turned on her."

"She a friend of yours?"

Aiyana's bracelets jangled as she waved a hand. "No. She doesn't know me from Adam. I just make it my business to stay on top of what she and others in the field are doing. I want to know when I run up against someone like Carl, someone who can be dangerous."

"How'd you know I wasn't dangerous?" he asked.

She touched his arm, a tender expression on her face. "It wasn't hard. I could tell you cared too much, not too little."

"What about Tobias?"

"He's going to be fine, too, with time."

He wasn't sure if she was just trying to comfort him or she sincerely meant what she said, but it was exactly what he'd been hoping to hear.

"So how's Uriah today?" she asked. "Any better?"

"I didn't see him up and around this morning, like usual. But the doctors told him to stay down, so I took that as a sign he was listening. I was in a hurry or I would've knocked to be sure." He checked his watch. "It's lunch now. I'll go call him."

Aiyana started toward her office. "Give him my best and be sure to let me know if he needs anything."

"I'll definitely come to you instead of Carl," he said.

She laughed but sobered quickly. "Can you imagine how sad it would be to have a child like that as your only one? They doted on him, but he was *so* abusive."

"Has he ever committed any serious crime? Done time?"

"He might be in prison now, for all I know. When Uriah and Shirley asked him to leave, they cut off all contact with him. Uriah told me it was too hard on Shirley to hear from him, that he'd manipulate her into believing he was repentant, willing to change. He'd say he needed a place to live, so they'd let him move back home, and then he'd start a fire or slash someone's tires or start a fight at the Blue Suede Shoe. The last time they let him come home, Uriah came to me, and we talked about what had to happen for Shirley's sake. Carl was moody at best, but when he got angry he'd start kicking the furniture and throwing things. It took Uriah coming home to find Carl on top of his mother, choking her, to convince him that he had to cut off his son."

"I hope he also pressed charges."

"Yes, but Carl wasn't locked up for long."

And now Shirley was gone and Uriah was alone. Did he miss his son? Want to reconcile? Still hope for change? "Thanks for the insight."

"No problem," she said.

Maddox got Uriah on the phone while he crossed the campus to his own office. "You feeling okay?" he asked when he heard his landlord's gruff voice.

"Bit sore and embarrassed that I let such a dumb thing happen. But I'll be fine."

"Good to hear." Although Maddox was tempted to mention Carl, he didn't. He guessed it was a difficult subject, figured if Uriah wanted to talk about his son, he would've brought him up during one of their many chess games. "Do you have something there at the house to eat? I can bring you something…"

"No, I got plenty of food. No need for you to leave work."

Maddox hesitated. He didn't want to bring up Jada's visit if Uriah hadn't already noticed, but he figured the chances of that were slim. Uriah received a ping when the security cameras were triggered. Even if he were sleeping and didn't hear that, there'd be an alert when he checked his phone or computer. "You probably saw that I had a visitor last night."

"I did."

Maddox scratched his neck. "Is there any way I could convince you not to mention that to anyone?"

"I'm not going to say anything. Long as whoever is coming by doesn't cause any damage to the property, it's none of my business, since you live here, too."

"I'm glad you feel that way. I'm sure Jada will be even happier."

"I did feel a certain amount of surprise that she was back," he admitted. "And I hate to stick my nose where it doesn't belong, but are you sure you know what you're doing where she's concerned?"

"Not entirely."

There were a few moments of silence. "Love makes a man do crazy things, doesn't it?"

Maddox stopped dead in his tracks. "I'm not sure it's *love*. Until I moved back, we hadn't spoken in thirteen years. It's more like…unfinished business. We're just trying to put the fire out, get over each other."

"By spending the night together? Good luck with that," he said, laughing.

"She's not coming back," Maddox explained.

"Is that what she told you?"

"It is, yes."

"Well, I wouldn't take it to heart until she proves it."

"What's that supposed to mean?"

"The way she deliberated last night, opening and shutting her car door, told me she wouldn't have come in the first place if she could help it."

Imagining Jada out in her car, wrestling with herself, made Maddox smile. "Have you ever been unable to get over someone?"

"Sure have."

"What'd you do about it?"

"I married her," he said simply.

It had taken most of the day, which had interrupted business to a degree, but the freezer was installed at one end of the cookie display, and the creamery company they'd chosen was supposed to deliver their first shipment—six flavors of premium ice cream in three-gallon tubs—in the morning. Susan had also ordered a new menu sign that included some pictures Jada had taken herself, one for behind the counter and one for the far wall. Those would take a few more days to get, but Jada was encouraged that they were so close to adding ice cream sandwiches to their menu.

She sure hoped the change would help. She had a lot of ideas on how she wanted to plug the new offerings on social media, but she figured implementing them would have to wait a week or so. She had some catching up to do on work for other clients, and she was exhausted after being up all night with Maddox. She felt guilty, too, for letting her family believe she'd spent the night at Tiffany's.

She hadn't specifically told them that, but they'd assumed it, which was essentially the same thing. It really wasn't any of their business, but telling herself that didn't make her feel a whole lot better.

"It looks great," she said when her mother stood back to examine the new menu signs. Atticus was there, too. He hadn't been able to help lift the freezer off the truck, but he'd served as the driver. Two neighbors had agreed to meet them at the store to unload. Both were gone now, but Maya was there with them. "Can you believe this idea—*your* idea—is actually coming to fruition?" Jada said to her daughter.

Maya shot her a sulky look. Jada had broken the news that she wouldn't be going to New Horizons, so Maya was barely speaking to her or anyone else.

"What's wrong with you?" Susan asked.

Maya folded her arms and stuck out her bottom lip. "My mom won't let me go to New Horizons, even though Annie's going there in the fall and her mom got me a scholarship. I could go to a private school for free! It doesn't make any sense that she won't let me do it. It's not that much farther away. Instead, she's making me stay at dumb old Topatopa, and I don't want to be there without Annie."

Susan lifted her gaze to Jada's. "When did this happen?"

"Cindy came in to talk to me about it yesterday."

"Grandma, will you talk to her?" Maya asked. "I'll be miserable at school without Annie! We have our whole year planned out!"

"Maybe Annie's mother will change her mind," Jada said lamely.

"I know she won't," Maya grumbled.

"I doubt that, too," Susan said. "She's like a…a tornado. She doesn't back off of anything."

"Mom!" Jada cried.

Susan looked a bit sheepish at her negative portrayal. "I'm just saying she's a woman who knows her own mind, that's all. She probably believes world hunger or world peace hinges on letting Annie go to New Horizons, and God forbid we get in the way of that."

"I say you let her go," Atticus said.

Both Jada and Susan pivoted to face him. *"To New Horizons?"* they both said at the same time.

Maya rushed over to his wheelchair. "Yes! Thank you, Uncle Atticus. Mom? *Please?"*

Jada cleared her throat as she tried to think. Didn't they understand that she would have to use her birth certificate to register? Principals didn't typically have anything to do with that process. It wasn't as if they looked through each student's records. But if Maddox ever had reason to wonder, he could easily check her file, and it would be right there. At that point, all he'd have to do is count back nine months.

Although…there would be no way he could know for sure. He didn't know if she'd met someone else in the immediate aftermath of the shooting—or if Maya had been born early.

"Maya, will you go down to the drugstore to get me—" she couldn't come up with anything she needed "—a candy bar?"

Her eyebrows knitted. "You want a candy bar *right now?"*

"No, I want to talk to your grandmother and uncle without you in the room."

"Oh." She straightened, gave Atticus another plead-

ing look, obviously imploring him to continue to be on her side, and got some money from Jada before reluctantly walking out.

"What are you *thinking*?" Jada said to Atticus as soon as she was gone.

"I'm thinking it might seem more strange that you would refuse such an offer than that you would accept it," he replied.

"To *whom*? Anyone who knows us knows about our history with…with Maddox and his brother."

"Cindy isn't aware of it," Atticus said.

"That's because she and her family moved to town a few years after everything went down. Even then she didn't know any of us until Annie and Maya became friends."

"It just seems silly that she would have to miss this opportunity because the brother of the man who shot me is now the principal of the school," he said.

"That's not all," Susan said. "The principal of that school is her *father*!"

"All the more reason for her to have a chance to get to know him. Don't you think?"

"You're saying we should tell her the truth?" Jada asked.

"She's been searching for her father, Jada. Going to the library and trying to look up newspaper articles about a motorcycle wreck. Going through old yearbooks. She even went down to the barbershop because Annie told her that a lot of old men go there and they might remember something. Fortunately, no one did, but…"

Jada felt slightly nauseous. "How do you know?"

"She told me yesterday. Asked me if I could remember any details about him that you couldn't."

"Oh boy," Susan said.

Atticus continued. "This gives you the opportunity to let her be around him, to see how they interact. At some point, maybe you'll want to tell her the truth."

Jada exhaled slowly. "I'm not sure I can do that. Maybe when she's older, but I don't know what he might do or how she might take it—"

"He lost a lot that night, too," Atticus said. "He lost you and doesn't even know about his daughter. Yet he didn't pull the trigger."

"We can't absolve him of *all* responsibility," Susan said. "He was there that night, should never have convinced Jada to sneak out and meet him."

"There were a lot of kids there that night," Atticus said. "They weren't able to stop Tobias, either. And Jada only did what most teenagers would do."

Still Susan seemed hesitant. "I don't know. It's risky."

"Just having him in town is risky," Atticus said. "Had he not moved back, we wouldn't be faced with any of this, but he *is* back, and now Maya's friends with Annie, and…and I don't see any reason she has to suffer because of the past. Kids rarely see the principal of the school, anyway—good kids, that is. I doubt she'll have much interaction with him."

Maya came bursting into the store, out of breath. She must've run the entire way to be back so soon. "Well? What do you think?" she asked as she handed Jada the candy bar and her change in one big fistful. "Can I go?"

"I haven't decided," Jada hedged.

Maya's shoulders slumped. "I don't understand why it's such a big decision."

Susan released an audible sigh. "Neither do I," she said. "If Atticus is okay with it, I say you let her go."

Jada felt her eyebrows shoot up. *Susan* was bending? Apparently, miracles did happen.

"Mom?" Maya put her hands together in a prayer stance. "Did you hear Grandma? She thinks you should let me. *Please?* I'll do *so* good in school. I promise!"

"You already do good, honey. I'm proud of you."

"Then let me go."

Jada glanced at Susan and Atticus before she nodded. She supposed, if Maddox began to suspect, he could easily check the date Maya was born—simply by asking her—regardless of whether she attended his school or not. "Okay. Go ahead and call Annie and see what we need to do to get you enrolled."

"Yay!" After throwing her arms around Jada, she hugged her uncle and grandmother, too. "Thank you *so* much!"

Jada's smile wobbled a bit as memories of making love with Maddox just last night filled her mind. Her family would never have relented on this had they known. It was only because they hadn't seen hide nor hair of him, hadn't heard her speak of him, hadn't known she'd been in touch with him, that they were being so agreeable.

19

Maddox had just finished having dinner with Uriah—he'd stopped and bought some ribs, coleslaw, corn bread and beans on his way home—when Aiyana called. He answered as he cleared the table. "What's up?"

"Jada has agreed to let Maya come to New Horizons."

Maddox turned off the water he'd been using to rinse the dishes. Uriah didn't care for the fact that Maddox was waiting on him—he kept grumbling about it—but he wasn't supposed to be moving around much, so Maddox was trying to do the menial stuff. *"Why?"*

"I don't know. You told me you were going to talk to her, so I assumed you had somehow convinced her."

"I tried. She said no."

"Then something else must've changed her mind. Cindy just called to let me know. Cindy's relieved, Annie and Maya are ecstatic and… I can't even begin to guess what Jada is feeling."

Maddox couldn't, either, but *he* was excited. As far as he was concerned, that Jada would allow her daughter to come to the school where he was the principal—where Maya would run into him, at least on occasion—could only mean good things for their relationship, even if it turned out to be only a friendship. He doubted Susan would ever forgive him, but he hoped the rest of the family would. He wished he could put everything that'd happened that fateful night behind him, even become friends with Atticus, as far-fetched a hope as he knew that was. "I'm shocked."

"Same here. How's Tobias doing, by the way? Did you ever call him?"

"I texted him from the office before I left, but he hasn't responded. I'll call him when I get to my place tonight."

"You're not home?"

"I'm at Uriah's."

"How's he feeling?"

Maddox glanced over his shoulder. Uriah had a scrape on his head from hitting the side of the house when he went down and a couple of stitches on his arm from where he tried to catch himself, but those injuries were already starting to heal. "He's tough. He'll be okay."

"I've never been better," Uriah yelled when he realized Maddox was talking about him. "Tell this young man he doesn't need to coddle me!"

Aiyana heard him without Maddox having to repeat it. "Tell him I said to enjoy it while it lasts."

"I'll get him a meal and clean up afterward, but I won't show him any mercy when we play chess," Maddox joked.

"That knock on the head wasn't hard enough that I can't still beat you," he said.

Maddox signed off with Aiyana and enjoyed the chess game, especially because, to Uriah's chagrin, he *did* win.

"That fall must've rattled my noggin worse than I thought," he complained when Maddox finally put him in check.

"You'd better get some rest, old man."

"*I'd* better get some rest! You were the one who just about fell asleep half a dozen times during the game."

For good reason. He'd had about three hours of sleep last night. "You took forever to move!" he joked, but he could tell Uriah knew the real reason when he said, "You'd better hope she doesn't come back tonight."

The possibility made Maddox smile. "I hope she *does*."

Maddox was still smiling as he walked back to his house. Jada was going to let Maya come to New Horizons. That had to mean something, didn't it? Had to mean he was earning some of her forgiveness, earning some of her trust.

He thought he'd fall into bed and sleep until his alarm went off in the morning. It wasn't even dark, but he didn't care. No *SportsCenter* for him tonight. But just as he was about to let himself into the house, someone stepped out from behind the garage, nearly giving him a heart attack.

"*There* you are! I've been waiting for freaking forever!"

Surprised that he had company—*male* company, anyway—Maddox gaped at his brother. "What are you doing here?"

The soft light of a late summer evening revealed a tentative expression on Tobias's face. "I couldn't take her, dude. You should see what she's like. Such a slob and so fucking needy! She was driving me *crazy*."

"But who brought you here? And how'd you find my house?" He hadn't brought Tobias through Silver Springs. He hadn't wanted him anywhere close to Jada and her family.

"Mom dropped me off down the road, but I could've found it. You sent me letters with this return address, and I have a phone now with maps, remember?"

"Be careful with using those maps. It costs you data. Anyway, she brought you out here but didn't stay to say hello?"

"We were fighting. It made her mad when she offered to let me stay with her and I refused. She's using again. You know that, right? I don't want to get caught up in that crap."

"Why didn't either one of you text me, give me some notice?"

"Like I said, we were fighting. She probably didn't want you to get involved because she knew you'd support my side of the argument. And *I* didn't text you because…" He shoved his hands into his pockets. "I don't know. I guess I was afraid you wouldn't want me to come."

Maddox's chest tightened at the insecurity in his brother's voice and manner. When they were young, they'd had no one but each other. Maddox was still the only person Tobias could rely on to love him. "You've always got a place with me."

"You have room?"

"Only one bedroom, but you can have the pullout couch in the living room. We can make do." As much as his brother's appearance in Silver Springs might screw up everything he had going here, he *had* to make room. If Tobias hadn't been tripping on acid the night he shot Atticus, he would never have harmed a soul—not someone who didn't come at him first. Besides, where else was his poor brother supposed to go? What good would it do to make him feel unwanted?

Maddox *had* to stand by him, but his heart was sinking at the same time.

What was he going to do with Tobias in Silver Springs?

* * *

"The new freezer looks awesome," Tiffany said as she breezed into Sugar Mama with an armful of Chinese take-out not too long before closing. "When will I be able to order an ice cream sandwich?"

It had been a slow day, but Jada was exhausted, so for a change she was grateful for the lack of traffic. She was also happy to see Tiffany. She needed something to distract her from what was going on in her own life, and since Aaron had sent his younger brother home and stayed the night with Tiffany last night, they had plenty to talk about. "As soon as we get the ice cream."

"I bet Maya's excited."

Jada lifted the hinged part of the counter so that Tiffany could slip through and join her on the other side. "Absolutely. Updating the menu was her idea."

"Where is she tonight?"

"Atticus gave her a ride over to Annie's a few hours ago."

They went into the back, where there was a small table they could use. "Those two are even closer than we were at that age."

"They spend every minute they can together. Tonight, I think they're celebrating my reversal on New Horizons and making plans for the school year."

"What reversal?" Obviously preoccupied, Tiffany put down her purse and sat across the table. There were only two chairs and enough space for two plates, which she pulled out of the bag.

"I've decided to let Maya attend New Horizons."

Her friend's hands froze instead of emptying the rest of the sack. "You *what*?"

Trying not to second-guess her decision yet again, Jada frowned. "I know."

"Does that mean you're going to tell Maddox about Maya?"

Jada got them each a bottle of water from the walk-in cooler. "No. I can't. That will tie our two families together forever. And yet I feel guilty for keeping it a secret, especially now that we're in contact again. I'm miserable, no longer know what's fair," she admitted. "I don't want to hurt her *or* him."

Tiffany finished setting out the cartons of food. "It's not just the fact that it will tie your two families together forever that's the problem, Jada. You've lied to Maya about her father for so long you don't know what might happen if you reveal the secret."

"Trust me, I'm fully aware that the consequences could be devastating."

"So why take the risk of letting her associate with him?"

She twisted the top off her water. "Because it feels so selfish *not* to let her know him, as if I'm cheating them both. When I made the decision to keep Maya all to myself, it was because my parents were so sure he wouldn't be good for her. But now that we can see for ourselves how he turned out…"

"Wait—what can we see?"

"We know he's functional. He has a degree, an *advanced* degree, and a good job. He must've stayed out of trouble with the police, or Aiyana couldn't take the risk of hiring him. Except for his relationship with Tobias, he seems as though he'd be a good father."

Tiffany handed her a set of chopsticks. "Boy, and I

thought going through a divorce was bad. You've been through so much. I'm just glad I'm not in your situation."

Steam wafted out of the carton of chow mein Jada opened. "I wish I wasn't in my situation, either."

"What good will it do to send Maya to New Horizons, though? If she doesn't know Maddox is her father, she might just ignore him, anyway. We didn't pay a lot of attention to *our* principals."

"That's what I'm counting on. A casual acquaintance."

"Casual is enough?"

Jada opened a second carton, scooped up some kung pao chicken and dumped it next to her chow mein. "I think so. At least, if she ever learns the truth, she'll have a frame of reference, some general idea of who he was and what he was like. That's better than nothing, isn't it?"

"It might absolve your conscience, but I think the less Maya has to do with Maddox, the better."

"There are other considerations besides my conscience…"

Tiffany's chopsticks snapped as she pulled them apart. "Like…"

"I don't want Annie's mom to make a big deal of the fact that I won't let Maya go to what is likely a vastly superior school. She doesn't understand it, needs a reason, and I don't have a good one, not now that she got Maya a scholarship."

"Tell her about Atticus. Then she'll understand."

"Maybe *she* will, but what about Maddox? He knows Maya has the opportunity to attend for free, so if I don't allow it, he'll know *he's* the reason."

"I can't imagine he'd expect you to let her, not after what happened."

Memories of her time in Maddox's bed flitted across Jada's mind. "It's not that clear-cut."

Tiffany's eyebrows gathered. "Why not?"

"It would seem hard-hearted, given the fact that I slept with him last night."

Tiffany dropped her chopsticks. "Holy shit! We've been talking about me going to bed with Aaron all day, and yet you never mentioned that you went over to Maddox's place after you left mine?"

Jada blew out a sigh. "I didn't want to acknowledge it."

There was a noise outside. Jada hadn't heard the bell, but she hurried out front to see if someone was about to walk in. She *definitely* didn't want anyone overhearing this conversation.

Fortunately, it was only two friends shouting a greeting on the street outside, one from a bike.

When Jada returned to the table, Tiffany lowered her voice even though they were still alone. "So? How was it?"

Jada scowled at her. "Stop."

"Come on! This is the man you've been in love with since forever, and you just had sex with him! Was it amazing? As amazing as my night with Aaron? Or not quite what you'd hoped?"

"It was a *mistake*," she replied. "And, just for the record, I'm *not* in love with him."

Clearly, Tiffany wasn't swayed. "What would you call it, then?"

Jada took a bite of her chicken but could barely taste it. "I just...can't get over him."

"Isn't that the same thing?"

She rested her elbows on the table and leaned her chin on her fists. "I don't know anymore. I don't seem to know anything."

"Does that mean you're *really* not going to tell me how it was?"

Straightening, Jada laughed in spite of herself. "It was everything I dreamed it would be, okay?"

Tiffany swallowed her food. "And yet you don't look happy."

"Because I'm not. I can't be with Maddox the way you can be with Aaron. I don't want the people I love to get hurt, and yet I don't see any other way for this to end."

Tiffany shoveled another bite of kung pao chicken into her mouth. "He didn't ask you anything about Maya, did he?"

Jada started moving her food around her plate. "No. He only said that I should let her come to New Horizons, that he'd look out for her if I did."

"So *that's* why you gave in."

"No, it's not! I told *him* no, too. It wasn't until Atticus and my mother couldn't bear to see how disappointed Maya was that I gave up the fight."

"Whoa, *Atticus* thought you should let her go?"

"He did. Can you believe it? He said it wasn't fair for her to suffer because of something she had nothing to do with."

Tiffany took a sip of the water Jada had given her. "He has a point."

Jada swallowed a piece of chicken. "That's what *I* thought."

"But it wouldn't be an issue if only Cindy would change her mind."

"You know she won't."

"I'm the one who told you that. That woman's a tiger mom."

"I wouldn't call her a 'tiger,' exactly. But she *is* ultra-assertive, and she's so convinced that having some well-adjusted pupils at New Horizons will help those who are less steady that she's determined to see it happen. And I don't have the heart to separate Maya from her best friend. I feel like I've already denied her the opportunity to know her own father. If she finds out, she'll probably hate me."

"She's not going to find out."

"She might. Atticus told me earlier that she's been actively searching for him."

Tiffany's chewing slowed. "For *who*? Her father?"

"Yes."

"Wow. I knew she'd been asking you a lot of questions lately. Moving back here was bound to pique her interest. But this is going a step further."

"It makes me nervous."

She went back to eating. "Still, how effectively can a twelve-year-old search for anyone?"

"She's smart, Tiffany. *Really* smart. She's been going to the library, trying to find newspaper articles on his death, visiting the high schools to ask for old yearbooks, hoping to spot his name—"

"Yikes. That's a lot more than I expected."

Although Jada could usually manage with chopsticks, tonight she was struggling. Tossing them aside, she got a fork from a nearby drawer. "Thank goodness I gave her the wrong name."

"Do you think she'll give up if she doesn't find him?"

"Who can say?"

Tiffany bit her lip. "And now she's going to be right under his nose. You'd better hope Maddox never recognizes how much she looks like him."

"I see that, and you see that, but people tell me all the time that she looks just like me."

"Those people never saw Maddox."

The worry that churned in Jada's stomach along with her food grew almost painful. "He asked me about Eric's involvement in her life, by the way."

Tiffany rocked back. "You don't think he's beginning to suspect…"

Jada shoved her plate away. "No. I didn't get that impression *at all*. He would have no reason to wonder. We didn't always use protection, but he pulled out every time."

"The withdrawal method is hardly reliable."

"I know that now. We were just dumb kids who couldn't keep our hands off each other. But, like I've said before, I finished high school, and I got married right away, which helps. And I never hit him up for child support. Most mothers wouldn't be willing to pay for everything themselves, so the thought that Maya might be his has probably never even crossed his mind."

"True. And you couldn't tell you were pregnant when we were in school, so there's been no talk we have to worry about him getting wind of. I'll never forget how surprised I was when *I* found out."

"You're the only one I told."

Tiffany took a second helping of the kung pao chicken. "You've got all that going for you."

"Let's hope it's enough," she said as she watched Tiffany finish her meal.

It took Maddox the whole day to work up the nerve to talk to Aiyana about his brother. He'd been trying to figure out what to do. Although a small but stubborn part of him was still hoping that Tobias and Tonya would be able to patch things up, so he'd be off the hook and could continue trying to build his own life, deep down he knew that probably wouldn't happen. There was no depth of feeling between Tobias and Tonya, nothing that would bring them back together. Tobias had thought he loved her while he was in prison. But Maddox was beginning to suspect most of that was gratitude and the pleasure of having *some* romantic interest despite being incarcerated. Tonya's letters and visits made him feel as though he was important and mattered to somebody besides the brother he'd relied on for most of his life. It also gave him the illusion he'd have somewhere to go once he was released.

Before walking over to Aiyana's office, Maddox called to check on Tobias and could tell by the cracks in his brother's voice that he'd woken him. The past few days had left Tobias drained. Truth be told, he was likely depressed, which added to his fatigue, although Maddox didn't care to acknowledge that fact. He felt helpless in the face of depression, knew that was partly what had cost them their mother. The drugs Jill took were merely an attempt to self-medicate.

"Hey, you okay?"

Tobias cleared his throat. "Yeah. Why? Somethin' wrong?"

"No, nothing."

"What time is it?"

"Five twenty."

"Isn't that the time you said you'd be home?"

"Yes, and I'll be there soon. What would you like for dinner?"

"There're no groceries here?"

He hadn't even looked through the cupboards, which meant he hadn't eaten all day. "Just the basics. Eggs. Cereal. Bread."

"I'm okay. I can fry an egg, I *think*," he added with a laugh. "I used to fry eggs when I was a kid."

"Don't turn on the stove," Maddox said. "I'll bring dinner."

"Are you sure? I don't want to put you out."

He couldn't help that. But he had no one else. "You're no trouble." Maddox hesitated. He wanted to ask about Tonya, to see if Tobias was feeling any better toward her, but he knew it would come across as though Maddox was anxious for him to make other arrangements, so he bit back the question and signed off before trudging across campus to the administrative building on the boys' side.

Aiyana was working late as always, but fortunately her son Eli was gone for the day, and so was the receptionist who generally sat out front. The place was as quiet as a church.

Since her door stood ajar, Maddox knocked on the doorframe.

She startled as she looked up. "Oh! Maddox! I didn't hear you come in. Are you ready to head home?"

He drew a deep breath as he crossed the threshold and turned to close the door.

She checked the clock on the wall. "We're alone in the building, if you're worried about privacy."

"I'm worried about a lot more than that," he said as he slumped into a chair.

She came around the desk. "Don't tell me this is about having Maya come to New Horizons…"

"No."

"You're okay with that?"

"Of course."

"What is it, then?"

"My brother showed up at my house last night."

Her eyes widened.

"His relationship with that woman—Tonya is her name—has already fallen apart."

"In just two days?"

"They didn't know each other very well to begin with."

"But from what you said, he was really excited about her."

"I believe he was excited to have someone to care about him. It has to be hard, being locked up for so long, wondering if anyone will want you when you get out, or if you've already missed the most important years of your life."

"True. I feel for him in that regard. So what are you going to do?"

He formed his fingers into a steeple as he thought that question over. "I don't know what to do. I feel terrible that you've given me this opportunity when I might not be able to take advantage of it."

Several creases appeared on her forehead. "There has to be *some* way to make it work."

"I don't see how. I don't want Jada and her family to face the prospect of running into Tobias. It was bad enough when *I* moved to town."

"Don't leave yet," she said. "Let's give it some time. See if the problem will resolve itself."

"How will it do that? I'd have him move in with my mother, but…" He hated to admit that Jill was using again, but this was Aiyana. After all she'd done for him, he felt it only fair to level with her. "That wouldn't be a safe environment for him."

"I see…" Thankfully, she seemed to catch on, didn't make him spell it out.

"I'm all he's got," Maddox explained. "I can't let him down."

She came close enough to squeeze his shoulder. "I understand. I would never encourage you to do that, anyway."

Maddox stood. "I'm sorry."

"Don't apologize. This isn't your fault. But, like I said, don't give up just yet. Let him hang out at your place for a couple of weeks. I'll give you whatever time you need to help him get his driver's license and a vehicle and find somewhere for him to stay in LA so that he can get a job."

"Do you think he *will* be able to get a job? Realistically? An ex-con who's never had any experience with... anything?"

"If he can't get something, I'll hire him myself."

"To do *what*? He took some classes in prison, but I'm not sure how applicable auto mechanics will be to whatever you might like him to do around here."

"He can do grounds maintenance. Gavin was just telling me last week that he's going to need help with all the repairs and upkeep now that we've expanded."

"What about the Brookses?"

She lifted her palms up. "Everyone's got to eat, Maddox. I say that takes precedence over all the baggage of the past."

Maddox appreciated her support, was grateful she cared what became of Tobias. But he hated knowing how upset his brother's presence in Silver Springs would make Jada and her family. He was fairly certain that, if she did have any inclination to see him again, learning Tobias was around would destroy it for good. "I'll do everything I can to help him find work in LA."

"I know you will. But if it comes down to it, this is

probably a much better place for him, anyway," she said. "You realize that, don't you? At least here he'd have me, you, Gavin, Eli. It'll be harder for him in LA, without a support system."

Maddox rubbed his temples. "I know," he said with a sigh.

20

Tobias was still in bed watching TV when Maddox got home. "What's going on?" he asked. His brother hadn't even bothered to shower.

"Not a lot."

"Have you heard from Mom?"

"Yeah. She keeps texting me, won't leave me alone," he grumbled.

"Why not?"

"She's still pissed."

"About what?"

"I don't want to talk about it."

Maddox's irritation with their mother shot up like a high striker carnival attraction. Tobias was obviously struggling emotionally, and she was only making it worse. "Do you mind if I take a look at what she's saying?" He indicated Tobias's phone.

"Be my guest. After thirteen years of having someone there every time I so much as took a piss, I'm not used to having any privacy. But why you'd want to read that craziness, I have no idea."

Maddox found the texts from their mother and began to scroll up so he could make sense of the conversation.

Jill: You're a fucking ex-con! How dare you judge me!

Tobias: That's fraud. You want me to go back to prison?

Jill: You won't go back to prison!

Tobias: You don't know that. You don't give a damn if I do or don't, that's the problem. Just leave me alone.

Jill: What have I done? I've never done anything to you!

Tobias: You've never done anything FOR me, either.

Jill: Because you won't let me. I was just trying to help. Why are you turning it into something so negative?

Tobias: Because it's illegal!

"What started this?" Maddox put the phone back on the nightstand. Obviously, the texting had picked up after some kind of conversation or interaction that came before, because it wasn't clear.

"She called me up yesterday, wanted me to hurry and get my driver's license so that Tonya would let me borrow her car."

"Why? Her own car is a bucket of bolts, I admit, but last I heard it was still running."

He didn't answer right away, just kept staring at the TV, but Maddox could tell he was upset, that he wasn't really watching it. Taking the remote, he shut off the distraction. "Tobias?"

He punched the pillow under his head. "You're not

going to like it. She already warned me not to 'turn you against her.'"

"Tell me."

"She wanted me to let her rear-end me. Said I could file a claim on the insurance for whiplash and make something like fifteen thousand dollars. Apparently, her roommate does that sort of thing all the time."

"Insurance fraud. You've got to be kidding me."

"Wish I was. Mom said it was a way for me to come up with the money I need to get a start."

"So the settlement would go to you."

"Not all of it, of course. She'd expect half for setting it all up. Says it'll get her out of debt. She owes someone."

"The guy who robbed her, by any chance?"

"I wouldn't be surprised. She didn't say. But she didn't like it when I told her I wouldn't do it."

"I can't believe she'd ever even suggest it. You're on parole!"

"She claims I couldn't get in trouble, that no one would ever find out it wasn't a legitimate accident. But I don't want to be involved in that shit even if we don't get caught. I want to feel good about myself for a change, you know?"

Maddox felt his muscles bunch. "This started yesterday? That's why you had her bring you here, and why she didn't stay to say hi to me?"

He nodded.

Maddox raked his fingers through his hair. How was he ever going to get his brother on stable ground with a mother like Jill working against them? "Will you get out of bed and get showered?"

"Why? I can't go out. If someone were to see me, word would spread like wildfire that I'm in town, and it would upset the Brooks family." He pinched the bridge of his nose. "Maybe I should try to go back to Tonya..."

"That won't work and you know it—not for more than a night or two."

He dropped his hand. "So what do I do?"

"First of all, I'm telling Mom to quit texting you. I'll change your number if I have to, and make sure she doesn't have it. If she has something to say to you, or something she needs from us, she can come to me."

Tobias sat up. "Wait. I don't want to put you in that position."

"It's fine. Maybe in a few months things can change, become more normal, but not right now. Anyway, get showered. We'll go to Santa Barbara for dinner so you can relax a little and feel better. It's obviously been a rough day."

"I'm not sure dinner out will fix anything. That'll just cost a lot of money."

"The fixing will come, one day at a time. Tomorrow, you'll start the process of getting your driver's license. Once you have that, we'll look for openings at the various auto repair places in LA."

"Meaning what? I'll commute? How will I get a car?"

"I'll move to LA with you and we'll share mine, if we have to."

Obviously frustrated by his situation, Tobias cursed. Maddox guessed he'd expected getting out to be more fun. Instead, he had to face the shambles of life after being locked up for so long. "I'm ruining everything you got set up here, aren't I."

"You're not ruining anything," Maddox said. "We'll get through this together."

"I shouldn't even be here. I'm not doing you any favors."

"Don't worry about it. It's you and me against the world, remember?"

"Just like old times," he muttered with a nostalgic smile and got up but turned back when he reached the doorway to the bathroom. "By the way, your landlord came to the door, but I didn't answer."

"Why not? I'm sure he could hear the TV." Maddox had heard it from the stoop earlier.

"I was hoping he'd think you left it on. I didn't want him to know I was here, didn't want to get you in any trouble."

Maddox remembered what Uriah had said when he'd told him his brother was the one who'd shot Atticus Brooks.

Did you have anything to do with it?

I was there that night, at the same party. But no.

Then I don't regret renting to you.

Uriah might regret it now. Most people wouldn't want an ex-con who'd been convicted for attempted murder living in such close proximity. That would be even more important to someone like Uriah, who'd experienced what he had with his son. "I'll go talk to him while you shower."

Maybe they'd be moving to LA even sooner than Maddox planned…

Maddox found Uriah sitting at his kitchen table, eating a TV dinner. When he knocked on the door he'd started using—the back door that went straight into the kitchen—the old man yelled out for him to come in.

"Would you like a piece of pie?" He motioned toward

the oven. "That slice of apple pie you gave me was so good, I decided to get a blackberry one when I was in town this morning."

"No, I'm fine. Thanks." Uriah's TV dinner didn't look very appetizing. Maddox knew his wife was probably rolling over in her grave, but Maddox had been so preoccupied with his own problems today he hadn't thought to bring Uriah anything better. "Sorry I haven't checked in today."

"Why would you need to check in?"

Maddox hid a smile at the old man's grit. Uriah hated to admit that he was diminished in any way. "No reason. You look like you're doing pretty good."

"I am. How was work? You come over for a game of chess?"

"Not tonight. You probably know this already, but I've got company."

"I wasn't positive but I thought so." He cut off another bite of chicken fried steak. "Heard the TV as I was getting a few items out of the garage, and yet your car was gone. So I stopped by to make sure everything was okay."

"It's my brother."

"The one who was just released from prison?"

"Yes. He would've answered, but he was afraid to. He didn't want to upset you or make things difficult for me."

He made a harrumphing sound. "I was hoping it was Jada."

"Because…"

"I knew you'd like that."

Maddox didn't want to think about Jada. With this new development, he'd probably never see her again—not in the way he'd seen her the other night. "You couldn't tell Tobias from Jada on the security cameras?" he joked.

"There wasn't anything on the cameras."

"That's right. He cut across the property out of range of any of the cameras."

Uriah swallowed his food and took a drink from the glass of milk he had sitting next to his meal. "He could've walked right down the drive. The camera on this side isn't working. It's on my list of things to fix. Maybe I'll get to it in the next week or so."

Uriah didn't sound upset, but Maddox felt bad all the same. "Sounds like you're getting back to work. Does that mean you're feeling better?"

He waved a gnarled hand. "That little spill wasn't anything to worry about."

"It could've been worse. You need to be more careful. But as far as Tobias is concerned, he surprised me, too. I want you to know I had no idea he was coming."

"What are you going to do now that he's here?"

"I'm hoping to find him a room to rent in LA. I'd be grateful if you'd let him stay with me for a couple of weeks until I can do that, though." That was the only way Maddox could salvage his own situation, but even if he came up with a room for Tobias to rent, he wasn't sure he could leave his brother on his own, not so soon. He just didn't want to go into all of that, wasn't quite ready to accept the cold hard truth.

"He can't stay with your mother?"

"No. That would be about the worst place for him."

"I see." He finished his milk. "Okay."

"Okay…what?" Maddox asked.

"He can stay until you figure out a better plan."

"I appreciate it. Despite what happened when my brother was sixteen, he's not a bad person. And now that he's got a second chance, he really wants to get his life on track."

Uriah scraped his tray clean. "Then you're lucky."

"Lucky?" Maddox echoed. "In what way?"

"The only way to change is to want to, right? He can do it if he wants it bad enough. I'd give anything if my son would turn his life around."

Maddox leaned against the doorframe. "What are the chances of that happening?"

"Not very good. There's something missing up here." He knocked lightly on his own head. "But I can always hope. A father never gives up hope."

"Neither does a brother, I guess," Maddox said. "Anyway, I'm sorry to take advantage of your kindness. I didn't expect this, but I probably should have. I wondered if his relationship with his cell mate's sister would last—should've known it wouldn't and planned accordingly."

"This isn't your fault."

"But it does put us both in an awkward position with the Brookses. I hate to do that to you."

"I don't mind giving him a hand. Maybe, if and when my son comes to that point, someone will do the same for him."

Uriah was one of the best men Maddox had ever known. It didn't make sense that he would have such a difficult son, but that was the unpredictability of life. "I can't tell you how much I appreciate it," he said and meant it. If *someone* didn't help Tobias at this particular crossroad, Tobias would never reach his full potential. He might not even reach a small part of it.

When Jada was finally able to close the shop and go home, she walked into her bedroom to find a handful of fresh-picked flowers in a mason jar on her dresser, along with a handmade card that was propped open without an envelope. "What's this?" she asked Maya, who was lying on the bed, reading a book.

Maya lowered her book enough to reveal a sweet smile. "It's for you."

Jada set her purse down so she could read the card, which had a picture of a woman drawn and colored on the front with pencils. Inside, Maya had written, "Thank you for letting me go to New Horizons. I will work *so* hard in school (the *so* was underlined heavily) that you'll be glad you did. Annie thanks you, too." Plenty of hearts and *X*s and *O*s surrounded those words and Annie had also signed her name.

Although Jada was touched, she had to force a smile when she met her daughter's eager gaze. "Thank you. This is beautiful. I'm glad you're happy."

Maya got off the bed to hug her. "I am. I know it's been a hard year with…with the divorce and everything, but you always make sure you're there for me. You're the best mom *ever*."

Jada squeezed her eyes closed as she held her daughter close. "No matter what happens, will you remember one thing?" she asked.

When Maya lifted her head, Jada smoothed her hair back. "I love you and I have always loved you. Okay?"

"I know, Mom. I love you, too."

With a happy hitch in her step, Maya went back to the bed and to reading her book while Jada put on her pajamas and sat at the desk to do her social media work. She was soon so engrossed she didn't notice Maya nodding off until her book dropped onto her chest.

Jada got up to set the book on the nightstand and tuck her daughter in. Then she got back to work, but as it grew later, she kept stopping to check her phone. She'd thought she might hear from Maddox, that he'd react to her allowing Maya to go to the school where he was principal, if nothing else.

But she didn't hear from him. An entire week went by during which he didn't come by the store, leave a note on her car, call or text. They'd had sex for the first time in thirteen years! That had affected her deeply, and yet it didn't seem to have impacted him at all.

Maddox was standing at the stables, giving a handful of the sugar cubes he'd taken from the coffee service in his office to Hannibal, his favorite horse and one of a dozen owned by New Horizons. Although it was getting late and *finally* cooling off, the mosquitoes from the pond nearby, which Aiyana stocked so the students could fish, were out in full force. Hannibal's tail swished every few seconds as the fourteen-hands-high quarter horse did all he could to keep the pests at bay.

When the sugar was gone, he neighed softly and allowed Maddox to pat his strong neck. Maddox remembered how much the animals at New Horizons had soothed him when he was a student here and smiled to think they still had the same effect. Aiyana was brilliant in what she made available to the damaged young men she tried so hard to help.

Before Maddox had realized that Jada was back in town and his brother was released from prison, he'd been considering getting a dog. Now he knew he'd better put that on hold. Having an animal would only make it more difficult if he had to move.

"What are *you* still doing here?"

Surprised to have company, since all the students were in their dorms and the teachers who lived on campus were in their houses on the far side of the property, Maddox turned to see Eli striding toward him wearing a pair of boots, worn jeans, a T-shirt that read Losing My Mind, One Kid at a Time and a friendly smile. Maddox had been lingering at the school because he hadn't been eager to go home. It would be the first of August tomorrow. It was getting closer and closer to the time when the fall semester would start, and yet he was still dithering on whether or not he'd be able to keep his job. The closer it got to the first day of school, the more difficult it would be for Aiyana if he quit, which made him reluctant. He didn't want to let her down. And yet he was beginning to realize that the problems with his brother were going to take a lot longer to fix than he'd first estimated. Maddox had driven Tobias to three different job interviews in Los Angeles, which had cost him one whole day of work, but Tobias hadn't received a call back. Trust for someone so freshly released from prison wasn't easy to come by.

"Not much," he told Eli. "Just thinking."

"You ready for school to start?"

"Getting there. I'm fully staffed at least. We have some great teachers."

"It helps that there are so many top-notch private schools in the area. If any of their teachers get disgruntled or need a change, we're here to scoop them up."

"Your mother's reputation also helps," Maddox said.

Eli rested his arms on top of the fence. From what Maddox had heard, he'd once lived in the house closest to the animals, which was vacant now. After he married Cora and they started having kids, they'd built a larger home, farther out on the periphery. Maddox had once asked Eli if Cora, who was a teacher at New Horizons, wouldn't rather live in town to get a break from the school when she wasn't working, and he'd said no. She liked being able to walk to her classroom, and she liked being close to Aiyana, who was as good a grandmother as she was everything else. He'd said they were far enough from the dorms and other buildings that the students didn't bother them in their off-hours, and yet he could stay late and take care of the animals or help his mother and still spend a lot of time with his own kids. "My mom's a fighter. I never bet against her."

"I wouldn't, either," Maddox said.

"How are things going with your brother?"

He gazed across the pen to where the sun was slowly sinking below the horizon. He liked Eli and his brother Gavin. The rest of their brothers—there were six more Aiyana had adopted, as well—now lived in other towns, cities and even states, except the youngest, who was still in high school and attended New Horizons. "Pretty good."

"Any luck on the job front?"

"Not yet."

Eli showed Hannibal, who kept nudging him, that he didn't have any sugar or other treats, so the horse shook his tail once again and moseyed over to his trough, where he used his lips to carefully pick up the strands of hay left over from his dinner. "I'm sorry to hear that."

"He's not ready to give up yet." Although Maddox feared depression and hopelessness would become a problem if something didn't happen in the next few weeks.

"That's good."

Silence fell. Maddox expected Eli to say good-night and go on about his business, but he didn't.

"Speaking of jobs…"

Maddox felt his eyebrows slide up. "What about them?"

"I received an unexpected application today."

"Unexpected in what way?"

"Atticus Brooks is applying to be our new computer technology teacher."

Maddox, who'd also been leaning on the corral, straightened. "Atticus wants to work *here*? Does he have the education for it?"

"Not exactly. Not for teaching. But he has a BA in computer science, so it wouldn't be too hard for them to get where he needs to be."

"Regardless, I can't believe he'd consider it, especially because he knows *I'm* here."

"That surprised my mother, too. She thinks he's already tried everywhere else and is getting desperate enough to overlook your presence. If we hired him, he'd be employed on the boys' side, anyway, so he wouldn't have a lot of interaction with you. Maybe that's enough separation for him."

"Except we'll all be attending the same faculty meetings, at least when we pull the staff from both schools together. And now that my brother's in town…"

"I'm pretty sure the Brookses aren't aware of that."

Maddox and Tobias had been very careful not to be seen in town. If they went out, they drove to LA or Santa Barbara. Hiding wasn't something they'd be able to pull off indefinitely, but so far, so good—it seemed. "He knows if *anyone* will give him a break, it's Aiyana."

Eli shrugged. "My mom tries to help everybody."

"So she's willing to hire him—even before he works through the student teaching and certification process?"

"She said she could use him as a teacher's aide until he gets that stuff done, so I think she's considering it."

"Why didn't she tell me?"

"She's still trying to figure out how to do that. She

doesn't want it to be the last straw, the thing that makes you leave."

"It won't be the thing that makes me leave."

"But if we hire Atticus, we won't be able to hire Tobias, even if Tobias can't find a job."

"I see. *That* might make me leave."

"Exactly. She wouldn't be happy to know I'm letting the cat out of the bag, but I'd rather she not be put in the position of choosing. I know it'll be hard on her to turn Atticus away."

Maddox bowed his head and kicked at the dirt beneath his feet. Maybe this was one way he and Tobias could try to make up for the past—they could give Tobias's one opportunity to Atticus. Maddox was certainly willing to do that; he had no doubt Tobias would feel the same. "Tell her to give him the job."

"You mean it?" When he looked up, Eli searched his face. "Even though it might make things a bit more difficult for Tobias?"

"Don't worry about Tobias. We'll figure things out."

"And you won't quit?"

He couldn't promise that. If Tobias couldn't find work, and soon, they were going to *have* to leave.

He thought of Jada and the way she'd felt in his arms. That would always be one of the best nights of his life.

At least he'd take away the memory.

"We'll see what happens," he said.

21

When Maddox returned home, Tobias wasn't there. The TV was off; so were the lights.

He grew anxious when he considered all the places his brother could be. Had Tobias called their mother? Had Jill come to pick him up?

He'd told her to leave Tobias alone until Tobias could get on his feet.

He almost called her; then he thought better of it. The last thing he needed was a screaming match with his mother, who was probably still angry with him. First, he was going to be sure Tobias hadn't walked or hitch-hiked to town. Tobias knew to remain scarce here in Silver Springs, but Maddox was usually home by five thirty. He'd been gone an additional three hours tonight, wrestling with all the decisions he had to make. Maybe his brother had been short some ingredient for dinner. Or he'd started to go stir-crazy being cooped up in such a small house for so long. After being in prison, he didn't like tight spaces. No matter how hot it was outside, he preferred that the doors and windows remain open. Said it reminded him that he was a free man and could walk out at any moment. And that was what made it possible for him to breathe right now when he was so wound up about the future.

Maddox quickly changed out of his work clothes and into a pair of jeans and a golf shirt and climbed into his car. He was just backing down the drive when he happened to glance at Uriah's house.

The door and the front windows were open. That struck him as odd; Uriah was usually scrupulous about maximizing the efficiency of his air conditioner.

After coming to an abrupt stop, he jammed his transmission into Park, jumped out and jogged up the walkway.

Before he even reached the stoop, he could hear voices.

"Damn! How'd you do that?"

"Just a little trick I learned in prison."

"I never saw it coming."

"You left yourself vulnerable to it three moves ago. Look. If you hadn't moved your bishop here, I couldn't have moved my queen. And then you went with your rook, so I moved this pawn, and when you responded with that pawn, I used my bishop to slide right over and capture your queen."

Maddox breathed a sigh of relief when he recognized his brother's voice.

"Well, I'll be darned," Uriah said. "That game only lasted five minutes!"

"Sorry about that," Tobias said. "Should I go easier on you?"

"Hell, no! Do your best or beating you won't mean a thing to me."

Maddox chuckled and knocked on the doorframe. "Hey, what's going on in here?" he asked as he let himself inside. "I come home late one night and my brother's already usurped my seat at the chessboard?"

"He's good!" Uriah pointed at Tobias. "*Damn* good! Have you played him?"

"Not yet."

"Well, I suggest you don't, not unless you're ready for a sound beating. He makes winning look easy."

Tobias waved away the praise. "This game saved my sanity in the joint. I've had a lot of experience. That's all."

"Show me your strategy again," Uriah said, but before Tobias could start with that, Uriah motioned at the stove. "There's some spaghetti I made earlier, Maddox. It'll be cold now, but you can warm it up."

There were two dirty plates sitting in the sink. Evidently, Uriah had already fed his brother.

Maddox considered refusing. He didn't want to impose. But he could tell by how animated and engaged Uriah was that he was enjoying having company. So, getting a plate out of the cupboard, Maddox helped himself to that spaghetti and sat down to eat it cold.

"You're not going to heat it up?" Uriah asked.

"It's fine the way it is."

"No, it's not." He grabbed Maddox's plate so he could warm it up himself.

"I've got it," Maddox complained, but Uriah put it in the microwave all the same.

"How long have you been here?" Maddox asked his brother above the steady whir of the fan angled toward them from the opposite corner of the kitchen.

Tobias's forehead glistened with sweat—it was such a hot day—as he glanced at the clock hanging on the wall. "An hour—maybe an hour and a half?"

"It's been two at least," Uriah said. "It was six thirty when I walked back to see if you were hungry."

"Was it that long ago?"

"We've played two other games already." He directed his next comment to Maddox. "I fared better earlier, when he was being careful not to beat me too quickly," he added with a wink.

Maddox noticed the guilty expression on his brother's face. "I had no idea you could play so well. Consider me warned."

"I wish I could get a job playing chess," Tobias grumbled.

Uriah brought Maddox's plate back to the table. "Have you heard back on anything?"

"Not yet."

Maddox thought about his conversation with Eli and how he'd given up the potential opportunity he'd been keeping in his back pocket for Tobias. It'd been nice to know that, worst-case scenario, Tobias might be able to work with Gavin, at least until they could find something else. But it was what it was; he couldn't regret it.

"You could work here for me," Uriah said.

Maddox jerked his gaze to the older man. "*What'd* you say?"

"I said I'll hire him. Can't pay much. Don't have the acreage I used to. But it'd give him a little income until something better comes along."

"Are you serious?" Tobias asked.

Uriah seemed fully committed. "Absolutely."

When Tobias looked to Maddox, Maddox wasn't sure how to respond. "That might help—temporarily, I mean," he said.

"I think so, too," Tobias said. "That'd be really nice."

Uriah shifted the game board to give Maddox more room to eat. "Like I said, I can't pay much…"

Tobias rocked his chair back on two legs. "Whatever you pay has got to be better than the seventy cents an hour I made in prison."

"Maybe you *won't* be disappointed, then. I'll pay you fifteen dollars an hour. I always try to be fair. But you have a young, strong body and an agile mind. You can make a lot more elsewhere, and I know it. So don't feel bad when you find something better. I'm expecting it. This will just give you some work history, experience and, if you do a good job, a recommendation."

"I'll do a good job," Tobias said and seemed so happy that Maddox couldn't bring himself to intervene. *He* was happy, too, especially when he played Uriah and Tobias helped coach on both sides of the board. Having someone who was that good take part made the game last forever, but they were all smiling when they said good-night.

"He's a cool dude, isn't he?" Tobias said as they walked back to the rental house.

"He is."

"What happened to his head—that scrape on his forehead?"

"He fell off a ladder the day before you got here. He tries to do too much, so having you help out while you're here will be smart for both of you." Maddox tilted his head back to look up at the stars. "What made you answer the door when he came to see if you wanted dinner?"

"I thought he was going to demand I move out, but I knew he knew I was there, so I had to let him. It's his property. If he doesn't want me here, he's got the right to tell me to go. But that wasn't what he said. All he wanted was to ask me if I'd like some dinner."

"He's a good guy, all right," Maddox said.

"Can you believe he gave me a job? Just like that?" Tobias snapped his fingers.

As pleased as Maddox was that something good had *finally* happened for his brother, he cringed inside. Tobias couldn't stay in Silver Springs long-term. Building some work history and taking a recommendation with him when he left made sense, though. "I can't," Maddox admitted. "Why do you think he did that?"

"He likes me." Tobias sounded slightly incredulous.

Maddox slugged him in the arm. "I don't know how."

By the time they reached the back door, they were wrestling, trying to throw each other to the ground. Tobias nearly knocked over a dining room chair, and when Maddox tried an arm drag, they hit the wall and rattled everything in the cupboards. It wasn't until Maddox heard his phone ping that he called a truce. He knew it could be his mother, or it could be Jada.

Fortunately, it was Jada. I want to see you.

Maddox had brought a handful of condoms. He wasn't sure he'd have the chance to use any of them tonight, but he wasn't about to see Jada unprepared, just in case. The last time they'd been together had blown his mind. He'd give almost anything for a second encounter. But maybe she only wanted to talk. She could be having second thoughts about allowing her daughter to come to New Horizons. Eli or Aiyana could've called to give Atticus the news that he had a job and Jada could be responding to that. Or Jada could've learned, somehow, that Tobias was in town.

He drew a deep breath as he paced the short length of space at the bottom of the king-size bed in the middle of the room. He'd gone to the expense and trouble of renting a motel so that she wouldn't see Tobias, but he hadn't told her that he had company. He had no doubt she assumed he wanted her to meet him at the Mission Inn so she wouldn't have to worry about the security cameras at the orchard.

He had to tell her what was happening in his life, how things had changed. But he was struggling with the idea of being cut off—*again*—just when she was showing some interest.

The sound of a car engine outside told him she'd arrived. He'd requested a room in the far corner. Although the inn was one of the most popular in town, it was also the biggest and oldest and was built on a large piece of property that backed up to a creek and a thick copse of trees, giving it a somewhat private setting even though it was right in the middle of town.

He parted the drapes to see her get out of her car. When she stood in the floodlights that faced the parking lot, checking the numbers on the doors to make sure she had the right room, he poked his head out. "Right here," he said softly.

She dropped her keys in her purse as she approached. When he stepped back so she could come in, he expected her to berate him for bringing Tobias to town. He knew that was how she and her family would perceive the situation—that he'd duped them by getting them to accept *his* presence before pushing the boundaries and making matters even worse.

But she didn't say a word. As soon as he closed the door and turned to face her, she pulled off her shirt.

Maddox's mouth went dry. So this *was* that kind of meeting. "Jada—" He figured he should speak while he could still think. But he didn't have the chance to get anything else out before she stepped into his arms. Then he *couldn't* speak because they were kissing.

He told himself to stop, to disengage and *tell* her. She needed to hear about Tobias from *him*, before she could find out some other way. And she'd have less reason to be angry if he explained *before* they made love.

In a minute, he told himself. But one minute quickly passed on to the next, and before he knew it, they were both wearing only their jeans. He spoke when he held her away from him long enough to admire the beauty of her body—her breasts, the three freckles on her flat stomach, the curve of her waist—but what came out wasn't what needed to be said. "You're all I've been able to think about. Night and day. The way you look. The way you taste. The way you feel."

A slightly confused expression came over her face as she stared up at him. "Then why didn't you contact me?"

She'd just given him the perfect lead-in to the conversation they needed to have. He opened his mouth to tell her that Tobias was in town. But, ultimately, he couldn't bring himself to ruin something that promised to be so good—every bit as good as the last time they'd spent the night together. "Things are…complicated," he said.

"No kidding. But it doesn't seem to matter. I can't make myself stay away from you."

All thoughts of acting with a more rational head completely disappeared in that moment. *To hell with anything outside this room.*

She locked her legs around his hips as he carried her to the bed. "I don't think what we're doing is so bad," he said. "We're not hurting anyone."

The corners of her lips turned down. "Not unless my family finds out."

* * *

After a week of waiting and wondering, Jada had finally broken down and done the very thing she'd been trying not to do: she'd contacted Maddox again. And that had led immediately to this, just as she'd been afraid it would. But she couldn't feel any regret, not when she was right up against him, when she could feel his heart pounding as fast as hers.

"Where does your mother think you are?" he asked as he dropped her onto the bed and fell along with her.

She let her fingers run over the muscular ridges of his stomach and chest. "I suppose she thinks I'm in my room. It's not like I woke her to tell her I was leaving."

"Where's Maya? Sleeping?"

"Probably not yet. She's staying with Annie. There's an orientation at New Horizons tomorrow afternoon."

He pulled back and gave her a funny look. "I know about the orientation. I work there, remember?"

She was purposely ignoring that, trying to pretend it was just another school year. To do otherwise made her fear she was making the worst mistake of her life. What if he began to suspect he was Maya's father—or *she* did? There was always the possibility. And yet Jada had given in because she *did* want her daughter to know him, hated that, so far, she'd removed the possibility of that from Maya's life. She wished it could be entirely safe, of course, but there was no such thing as a "safe" way to bring them into contact. "They're going to get ready and go together."

"I can't believe you're letting her come to my school."

He seemed pleased, as if he saw that as a concession— a vote of confidence. But Jada preferred not to discuss it, not to even think about it. Especially now.

She'd tackle reality again in the morning. "Neither can I."

He caught her wrists and pinned her hands above her head. "Did you just say 'neither can I'?"

"Huh?" She blinked up at him.

"Should I be offended by that response?"

Twisting her wrists out of his grip, she pulled him down so that she could bite his neck. When she sucked his smooth, warm skin into her mouth, she felt such a rush of satisfaction she couldn't help groaning. "Sorry. I don't know what I'm saying right now," she murmured. Instead of making her content, her last visit to his house had only caused her obsession with him to grow. The second Maya had left for Annie's after they'd had dinner together tonight, she'd nearly raced into her bedroom to text him. At first, she'd fought the urge, thought she'd overcome the temptation. But as soon as the lights went out and the house quieted down, she'd succumbed.

"So what are we doing?" he asked as he shifted onto one elbow so he could slide his hand down her pants.

Closing her eyes, she let her head fall back, welcoming the relief and pleasure he brought her. "Isn't that obvious?"

She nearly jumped when his fingers slipped beneath the thin fabric of her panties.

"If it was, I wouldn't be asking." His other hand fisted in her hair as he leaned forward and kissed her. "Last time, we agreed it would be a one-night stand." He nibbled on her earlobe. "Is this another one?" he whispered, his breath hot, his voice husky. "Or can I hope for something more?"

She gulped for the breath to respond. "Do we—"

When her voice cracked, she cleared her throat. "Do we have to discuss it right now?"

His eyes were heavy-lidded but his focus razor-sharp. She could tell he was aroused. And yet he was holding back. "I think that'd be smart."

"Because…"

His teeth flashed as he smiled. "Because I have a little leverage in this moment, which means I have a better shot at getting what I want."

"You're not interested in *this*?" Covering his hand with hers, she pressed his finger deeper inside her.

His gaze dropped to her mouth. "You know I am. I just don't want to drive home feeling like this was the last time we'll ever be together. There have been enough last times."

Her eyelids felt almost too heavy to lift, and her limbs tingled—not to mention other regions of her body. "This, from the man who didn't call or text me once this week?"

"It wasn't as if I didn't want to."

"Then why didn't you?"

He froze, giving her the impression he was uncomfortable with the question.

"Maddox?"

He undid her pants. "Because what I felt when I lost you in high school was bad enough."

She drew his mouth back to hers, kissing him deeply, hungrily. "Forget high school. Forget everything."

"I'm willing if you are. But that's the problem, isn't it? You *can't* forget. And even if you could, it's asking too much of your family. So where does that leave us?"

Nowhere. But she couldn't say so, didn't want to acknowledge that herself. "How about a torrid affair?"

"*Torrid*'s a great word. I like torrid, especially when

it comes to you, but—" he peeled her jeans all the way off "—give me a few more details. What would I be able to expect?"

She arched her back as his tongue moved over her nipple. "More of this."

He lifted his head. "How often?"

"Two or three times a week. As many times as we can get away."

He didn't accept that as readily as she'd anticipated. "What about dinner every once in a while? Going other places?"

He was letting her know he didn't care to be limited. She could understand why that might be the case. It wasn't particularly gratifying to be anyone's dirty little secret. But he knew the reason they couldn't take their relationship public. It wasn't *her* fault. Slipping away to be with him here and there was dangerous enough. "Maybe. If we go somewhere else."

"Like…"

She could hear the sour note in his voice. "That may not be ideal, but at least we'd be together sometimes. You've offered that before, right?"

Pulling away, he sat up. "I have. But how do you see that ending? When one of us finds someone else?"

She got up on her knees. "Don't make me think that far down the road," she said and pressed him back onto the pillows before undoing his pants and licking her way down his stomach.

She felt his muscles tighten in anticipation.

"Shit. Something tells me I'm a fool to get involved with you again," he said, but she felt his fingers slip through her hair, welcoming what she was offering, as she took him in her mouth.

* * *

They'd wrecked the neatly made bed—kicked the comforter and the top sheet to the floor along with half the pillows.

"That had to be the best sex of my life." Maddox felt utterly boneless as he lay beside Jada, staring up at the ceiling.

She stirred but didn't seem to have any more energy than he did. "No one ever said we weren't good together."

The bitter disappointment he'd endured after Tobias had shot Atticus and he'd lost his brother *and* his girl-friend, and been sent away never to be contacted by Jada again, threatened to ruin his euphoria. He shoved the memory to the back of his mind even though he knew he was probably looking at something similar when their "torrid affair" was over.

"This is a nice motel room." She lifted her head as though she was only now noticing. "How much was it?"

He hadn't been concerned about the price. He'd been so excited to see her, he'd simply found a place that was close and comfortable, somewhere they could meet without being seen. "It wasn't cheap, but I'm not worried about it."

She looked over at him. "How much?"

"Two hundred and fifty dollars."

"Two hundred and fifty dollars?" She sat up. "You paid that, knowing we'd only need it for a couple of hours?"

He couldn't help smiling as he remembered how she'd taken off her top the moment she'd walked through the door. What she proposed wasn't going to be *all* bad—until it ended. "Well, we got started a little sooner than I expected."

She laughed.

"Anyway, it was worth it."

"Do you have Venmo? I'll send you half."

"No, I'll cover the room."

"I want to contribute. Even then, if that's how much seeing each other is going to cost, we can't afford a torrid affair. We need to figure out a way for me to slip past the cameras at your place."

Maddox cringed at the mention of his place. She couldn't come back there, not while Tobias was staying with him. And Maddox sure as hell couldn't show his face at *her* house. "Seeing each other won't be easy."

She rolled onto her side and drew a heart on his chest. "You don't think we can figure it out?"

He wrestled with his conscience for a moment. Then he said, "I need to tell you something."

When she propped her head up, her hair fell in a tangled mass and her lips looked slightly swollen from the feverishness of their kisses, but he thought she was beautiful, liked her this way more than any other. "About what?"

He could hear the wariness in her voice. And for good reason. She wasn't going to like what he had to say.

"My brother's in town."

She blinked several times. "For a visit?"

When he didn't answer right away, she scrambled off the bed and snatched up her panties. "Don't tell me he's going to *live* here. I thought he was going to LA."

Maddox wished he'd waited a bit longer to speak up. Maybe she would've curled against him and gone to sleep for a few hours. They could use the quiet, the calm after the sexual frenzy they'd just experienced. But he also felt as though he was taking advantage of her by making love to her when she didn't know about Tobias. "He was. Things have already fallen apart with the woman he was seeing."

"Because…"

"I guess she's a difficult personality."

"How do you know it wasn't your brother who's to blame?" she asked dryly.

Maddox sat up and combed his fingers through his hair.

"I'm sorry," she muttered before he could respond. "That was uncalled for."

"It's okay." Sometimes it was difficult for *Maddox* not to be angry at what his brother had done. But Tobias couldn't change the past, so at some point, feeding that anger seemed pointless. "I can see why you'd wonder. I honestly don't think so. I met her and… I don't know. I could never be attracted to her. But, either way, he's my brother. I can't turn him out. Where would he go? What would he do?" He held up a hand before she could suggest his mother as a source of support. "My mother's using again. She isn't an option."

Jada pulled the comforter off the floor and covered herself with it as she sank slowly onto the edge of the bed. "Using again…"

"You know my mother's an addict, right?"

She said nothing, just stared down at the carpet.

"This can't be anything you like hearing. I don't come from the kind of family you do, Jada, but it is what it is. I can't walk away from them. They need me too badly."

Instead of getting up to get dressed and leave, she reached for his hand. He hoped, when her fingers curled through his, that it was a good sign. That she wasn't about to tell him their "torrid affair" was already over.

He couldn't blame her if she did. He came with too many problems.

"I'll understand if you don't want to see me again," he said.

She didn't respond, just kept slipping her fingers between his and pulling them out again.

"I honestly didn't come back here to cause trouble for you or your family," he added in case he hadn't made that clear. "I wanted the job Aiyana offered me. That's all. It's a good opportunity, a chance for me to give back. I planned to stay out of your brother's way, hoping your mother and brother wouldn't even notice I was here. But then I found out you were back. And Tobias got out of prison. And the woman he professed to love turned out to be someone he couldn't live with. And my mother relapsed, forcing me to face the fact that *she* couldn't be trusted to help him—story of my life, right? And…there's no easy solution. Eventually, Tobias should be able to work out of the mess he's in, which means *I'll* be able to work out of the mess I'm in, too. But that's not going to happen quickly."

He couldn't see her face. She had her head bowed, and her hair was falling forward. "How long do you think it will take to get his license?"

"Another week or two. But then…we'll see if someone's willing to trust him enough to give him a job. That might not be easy even after he has a license." For all Maddox knew, he might be forced to work for Uriah for several months before the job history Uriah was willing to give him made any difference. For the sake of the Brookses, however, Maddox's goal was still to get Tobias out of town as soon as possible.

She said nothing.

He smoothed her hair back. "Jada?"

"What?"

"Will you tell me what you're thinking?"

"I'm thinking your family is damn lucky to have you. And…"

"Go on…"

"They don't deserve you," she added, more softly.

That was far better than he'd expected. "Do you think we should tell your family about Tobias? How do you suggest we handle the situation?"

She didn't get the chance to answer. His phone rang in the pocket of his jeans, which were lying on the floor where he'd cast them aside. He was about to get up so he could see who it was but that wasn't necessary; Jada handed him his pants.

"It's my brother," he said when he saw caller ID. He wasn't going to answer it. That would sort of bring Tobias into the room with them. Telling Jada Tobias was in town, only two miles away, was bad enough. But when she started grabbing the rest of her things and putting them on, he knew the evening was over, anyway.

She glanced at him over her shoulder when he didn't say hello. "You're not going to pick up?"

"I'll deal with him after you leave."

"Thanks." She was nice, *polite*, but he could feel the sudden distance between them.

"What would you have me do?" he asked.

"There's nothing you can do." She turned to face him. "And, sadly, that goes for me, too."

22

"Where were you?"

Maddox had just let himself into his own house but froze when he heard his brother's voice. He'd left the lights off and had been so quiet when he came through the door, and yet Tobias sounded as though he'd been wide-awake from the start. "Just went out for a bit," he replied and dropped his keys on the counter.

"Was there a specific reason you waited until you thought I was asleep?"

"I couldn't take you with me, if that's what you mean."

"Because…"

"I was meeting someone."

"A woman."

"It certainly wasn't a man," he said, but his brother didn't laugh.

"*Which* woman? That's the question."

Maddox could smell Jada's perfume on his shirt when he pulled it over his head. "I don't want to talk about it."

"You're seeing Jada again, aren't you."

That had been an easy guess. Anyone else and Maddox could've given his brother her name, because it wouldn't have meant anything to him. "I said I don't want to talk about it." He tossed his shirt in the clothes hamper as he peeled off his jeans and walked into the bathroom. He took his time, hoping Tobias would be asleep when he returned, but he wasn't.

"Are you sure you know what you're doing, Maddox?"

"What do you mean?"

"I know you care for her. You always have. I ruined that for you, and I feel terrible because of it. But I can't take back what I did, and given that I can't take it back, has anything really changed? If she won't see you openly, what good is it going to do to meet her late in the night? What will you have in the end?"

"Let me enjoy the memory of what happened tonight before forcing me to face reality, okay?"

"I don't want you to get hurt. I don't want to be to blame for that again."

"Yeah, well, this time it'll be *my* fault," he said.

Butterflies filled Maya's stomach as Annie's mother drove them to their new school Friday afternoon. She was looking forward to orientation and learning what to expect for the coming year, but the prospect of changing to a different junior high wasn't the only reason she was excited today. She was hoping to have a chance to speak with Aiyana Turner. From the way Mrs. Coates talked, Mrs. Turner had lived in Silver Springs for a long time and knew almost everyone. Annie's mother had said Aiyana was a wonderful person, that she'd helped so many troubled young boys—like their principal once was, and look how good he'd turned out—and was now going to do the same for young girls.

Maya thought that was nice and all, but Aiyana's kindness wasn't what got her attention. It was that Aiyana had been in town long enough that she might be able to tell her something about her father. If *anyone* would remember a young man dying in a motorcycle accident, it would be someone who helped young men, wouldn't it?

Annie probably wasn't thinking about Maya's dad like Maya was, but she squeezed Maya's arm in anticipation all the same. "Here we go."

They both peered out the window as Annie's mother slowed down and they rolled beneath a giant wrought-iron arch that said New Horizons.

"It'll be *so* weird going to school without any boys," Maya said and hoped that wouldn't kill any of the fun. If not for Annie, she wouldn't have begged to come here.

"My mom said there will be boys on the other side of the fence," Annie said.

Maya frowned as they passed the outdoor basketball courts, where a few of those boys were playing. One— cute, with curly brown hair blowing across his forehead— looked up as Mrs. Coates turned at the sign that read New Horizons for Girls.

"We won't get to see them very often, though," she said sadly.

Mrs. Coates glanced into the rearview mirror. "There will be dances and joint assemblies now and then."

"But will *we* get to go?" Annie asked. "Won't those be for the older girls?"

"Not necessarily. This year, a section on the boys' side has been designated a junior high, too, so there will be separate activities for the kids your age versus those in high school."

"I hope they have *a lot* of assemblies," Maya said, and she and Annie giggled as a gymnasium came into view. It was smaller than the double-size one by the outdoor courts they'd passed on the boys' side, but it was brand-new and looked nice.

Soon they saw quite a few other buildings. One was a theater, according to the word painted vertically on the side in big orange letters.

Mrs. Coates parked in the lot labeled Administration.

"There's still parking available?" Annie said in surprise. "We had to park all the way down the street at Topatopa Junior High when we went to orientation last year, remember?"

Maya hadn't been there for orientation, so she knew Annie was talking to her mother.

"This school is much smaller than the one you were in," Mrs. Coates said. "And a lot of the girls will be boarders, which means they won't have their parents nearby."

Maya couldn't imagine how weird it would be to be sent away from her mother and immediately felt sorry for the girls who would be in that situation. She would've asked how often they got to go home, or what they did if they had to stay over for Thanksgiving and Christmas, but there wasn't time. Mrs. Coates was speaking to other moms as they converged on the gym, where there were about fifteen rows of seats and a podium at one end with a pulpit.

The principal, Mr. Richardson, stood just inside, saying hello and telling everyone to come in and sit down, that they'd be getting started shortly.

He shook Mrs. Coates's hand and then Annie's. But Maya got the impression he was especially pleased to see *her*. "I'm so glad you'll be joining us this year, Miss Brooks," he said as his large hand closed around hers.

Maya told him she was glad, too, and they found a seat as he greeted the people behind them.

"Do you know Mr. Richardson?" Mrs. Coates asked.

"I met him at the cookie store once," she replied.

After the meeting started, Maya lost a bit of the regret she'd been feeling for insisting on coming to such a small school, especially one without boys. She liked Mr. Richardson and the teachers who introduced themselves. Mrs. Turner was there, too. She spoke at the end and told them how pleased she was to have a school for girls as well as boys, which had always been her dream, and wished them all a good year.

Maya kept an eye on her as the meeting broke up, but she couldn't find an opening to approach her. It seemed as though *everyone* wanted to talk to her; there was always a line.

"Are you feeling okay about coming to New Horizons?"

She turned when she heard a man's voice and realized that Mr. Richardson had walked over to her. She was a little surprised he'd single her out when everyone wanted *his* attention, too—especially the mothers, as Mrs. Coates had predicted. Many of them moved a bit too close to him and smiled a bit too widely, which made it obvious they weren't treating him like a regular old principal. But if he noticed, he didn't act like it.

"I think so," she said. "I'm just going to feel bad for the girls who can't go home—you know, for holidays and stuff."

"This will be a better home for some of them."

"Oh. Then that's even *more* sad."

"It is. But having a good friend can make a big difference, right?"

He meant she could improve their situation; she could tell by his smile. "I hope so," she said and clasped her hands in front of her because she suddenly didn't know where to put them.

"How's your mother?" he asked.

"She's good. Working all the time."

"At the store?"

"And on her computer. I don't know when she sleeps. She's always up so late."

"How long do you think you'll be living with your grandma?"

"I have no idea. My mom feels like she can't leave since my grandma is sick—even though my grandma is sort of mean to her." Maya wasn't sure why she'd added that last part. Her mother and grandmother would call it "family business," and yet she'd just told an outsider—her new principal, no less. But something about Mr. Richardson made her feel as though he cared about her, and that made her trust him. "Sorry, I shouldn't have said that," she told him, feeling even more awkward for having made such a stupid mistake.

He rested a comforting hand on her shoulder. "Don't worry about it. Sometimes it can be hard to get along with family members. It doesn't mean we don't love them."

"Exactly," she said, relieved that he understood. "Don't tell my mom what I said, okay?"

"There's no need for me to repeat it to anyone."

Maya exhaled. "Thanks."

Annie came walking up with her mother. New Horizons offered something most public schools didn't— piano lessons as well as voice lessons—so they'd been speaking to the music teacher.

"Do you have any last questions?" Mr. Richardson asked Mrs. Coates.

"No, I think we're set. I can't believe you're providing such a diverse and rich curriculum. I feel lucky that Annie and Maya will be coming here."

"I'm looking forward to getting to know both girls along with all the other students," he said. Then someone else approached him, and they were ushered by the crowd toward the door.

As they stepped into the bright sunshine of another hot August day, Annie said, "Isn't this going to be a cool place to go to school? Did you hear that they have *horses*?"

"I did." Maya pretended to be happy. She *was* happy about the school, the horses and especially the fact that they had cooking classes, which were of far more interest to her than music lessons. She was just sad that she hadn't been able to find a good opportunity to talk to Mrs. Turner.

But school would start soon. Once everything calmed down, she'd figure out how to get a few minutes of Aiyana's time so that she could ask about her father.

I saw Maya at orientation today.

Jada was sitting up in her bed, working, when that text came in from Maddox. She'd wanted to go to orientation with Maya, but Cindy had that covered, and Jada had been needed at the store, which was doing so much better with the addition of the ice cream sandwiches. Although her mother seemed relieved, Susan hadn't said anything other than that brusque thank-you the day Jada showed her the business plan with the ice cream sandwiches. She probably didn't want Jada to believe what she'd done to help made up for any of the trouble she'd caused in the past.

She came by the store after, she wrote back. Said she was excited.

She's a wonderful girl. I can see why you're so proud of her.

Jada winced as she stared at those words. Maybe she'd helped her mother in various ways financially, but when it came to Maddox and Maya, she was driving them all toward a brick wall and couldn't seem to avoid it.

Everything going okay for you? he asked. Your mother didn't realize you were gone last night or anything, did she?

If she did, she didn't mention it.

You know you can call me if things ever get too tough for you.

What was he referring to? You mean with my mother?

With anything.

She rubbed her temples. What she wanted to do and what she *should* do were moving farther and farther apart. Thanks.

No problem. So when can I see you again?

I don't know, but I don't want to settle for just one night.

Meaning…

Let's go away for an entire weekend.

It's Friday. Not this weekend…

No, next weekend.

Can you get away?

It wouldn't be difficult. She'd been trying to get back to LA. She had some work she needed to do there for her social media clients, which she'd already had to reschedule twice. Maya could stay with Susan while she was gone and help in the store. Susan was paying her a little bit, and she was planning to use the money to buy a few extra school clothes. I'm pretty sure I can. You?

No problem for me.

What about Tobias?

He'll be fine here. Uriah loves him. I swear he likes him more than me.

What's Tobias like these days?

Taller.

She hadn't been asking about the physical changes. But she didn't clarify. She already felt like a traitor for ignoring that he was in town and seeing Maddox, anyway. Where should we go?

Wherever you want.

Her pulse sped up as she imagined spending two whole days with him. They hadn't been together that much since they were teenagers. The beach.

Santa Barbara? Somewhere else?

I've got business in LA. Can we go there?

Of course. Newport?

Perfect.

What will you do with Maya?

She'll stay here with her grandma and uncle.

Then this is for real?

Already, Jada couldn't wait. It's for real.

Maya walked in. "What are you doing?"

Being careful to make sure her daughter couldn't see the screen, Jada set her phone aside. "Just working. You?"

"I was hoping we could do some online shopping so I can start picking out what I'd like for school. Do you have a few minutes?"

Jada slid over to make room for her daughter. "Of course. Where do you want to look first?"

Because she'd spent two hours with Maya instead of working, and then she'd had to make up for it, Jada had

had only three hours of sleep when her door flew open and crashed against the inside wall.

Lifting her head, she blinked to clear her vision and found her brother maneuvering his wheelchair through the opening.

"What's going on?" she asked, confused by his authoritative entrance.

"I couldn't wait to give you the good news."

She pushed the hair out of her face. "*What* good news?"

"I got a job!" A smile stretched across his face as he came close enough to shove an official-looking letter under her nose.

Too excited to even look at it, she let it fall to the floor as she sprang out of bed to hug him. "Are you kidding me? I'm *so* thrilled! Where?"

He gestured at the letter. "I tried to show you."

As soon as she picked it up and saw the New Horizons seal on the letterhead, she felt her joy dim. *"At New Horizons?"*

He shot her a disgruntled look as he snatched the letter away. "Don't say it like that."

"I'm surprised, is all." She couldn't believe he would even apply to New Horizons; she would've thought he'd avoid that at all costs.

"I'll be a teacher's aide on the boys' side. It's not like I'll be working *with* Maddox."

She stared down at the words on the page. *I am pleased to inform you that you have been selected as a teacher's aide in computer technology*... Details about when he would start and what his duties would be followed, and it was signed by Aiyana Turner. "You'll probably bump into him at staff meetings and such," Jada said, looking up again.

"He's not the one who shot me."

That was what *she'd* been trying to tell him and their mother ever since Maddox had come back to town! But she understood it wasn't just Maddox's presence that upset them. They'd been afraid Tobias would come back, too, once he was released. And he had—they just didn't know it yet. She was hoping he'd get his driver's license and a job and move away soon, so they'd never have to know. But if things didn't go that way, Atticus would have a much greater chance of finding out he was in town—and of bumping into him—if he was working at the same school Maddox was. "So you don't mind?" she asked Atticus.

He shrugged. "We won't be working together directly. It should be fine."

She sank back onto the bed so that she'd be eye level with her brother. "Have you seen him yet?"

"Not at the school. He wasn't around when I was there for either of my interviews. Is that what you mean?"

"There or anywhere."

"I ran into him yesterday at the gas station. He was paying for a six-pack when I went in."

"Did he notice you?"

"Of course." He rolled his eyes. "People always notice me. And most of the time they stare."

She knew how uncomfortable that had to be. "Because you're so good-looking," she said with a wink.

"Chicks think it's a damn shame I'm in this chair. Otherwise, a few might be interested in going out with me."

She believed the right woman had to be out there. "If

anything has been holding you up, it's living with your mother and not having a job," she said, refusing to let him feel sorry for himself.

For a change, he didn't get mad. "Now maybe I can fix that."

"Yes, you can." She cleared her throat. "So…did Maddox say anything to you when he saw you?"

"No. He did a double take. Then he lowered his eyes, pivoted and walked out."

"You didn't mention this to me when you came home last night." Maddox hadn't said anything about it when he was texting her, either.

"Why would I? Nothing happened. Anyway, I don't want to talk about Maddox. I want to celebrate my new job."

"And I don't blame you. But—"

"Stop." He put up a hand. "Don't mention Maddox again. I'm just going to ignore him."

"Okay. For what it's worth, I bet you're going to love your job, and that you're going to be fabulous at it."

"I'll be making some money for the first time in my life. Better late than never, eh?"

"Would you ever really get your own place?"

He pursed his lips as he considered the question. "I think so."

Jada knew their mother probably wouldn't like that. She preferred to keep Atticus close. But Jada didn't want what'd happened to lock him into being their mother's security blanket for the rest of his life. "Might be a good time, since I'll be here to take care of Mom."

"Once I save up enough, I'll look around. See what's out there. Anyway, make sure you get everything done you have to do today, because we're going to the Blue Suede Shoe tonight."

"Time to party?"

"Damn right."

Jada needed to work, especially if she was going to be spending next weekend with Maddox. But it wasn't often that Atticus came to her, asking to go out and have fun, and his first job was worth celebrating. "You're on."

As soon as he left, she texted Maddox. Did you know that my brother is going to be working at New Horizons?

It took a few moments to get a response but, finally, she heard the ding that signaled a reply. I did.

Since when?

Thursday. Why?

You didn't mention it to me.

Didn't want you to think I'd arranged it. He got the job on his own.

Jada chuckled at his response. He was trying not to take any of the credit, didn't want her to think Atticus had been given the job out of pity or reparation, which just went to show how aware he was of the needs of others.

He probably *had* helped, but Atticus had applied at New Horizons in spite of Maddox working there, which meant he'd been getting shut out everywhere else. He'd believed Aiyana might give him a chance, since she was known for that sort of thing, and he'd guessed right. She *was* giving him a chance.

Jada felt that a chance was all he needed, that he'd make good.

I'm guessing she at least talked to you about it. I can't imagine she'd hire him without telling you.

Again, he didn't write back right away. But when she got his answer, she smiled again. She did talk to me, but I would never stand in Atticus's way. You know how I feel about what happened. At least I hope you do.

She wished her mother knew how he felt. Instead of letting everything he'd been through break him down, he'd fought back and become stronger because of the adversity. He was also loyal to those he loved, even when that loyalty came at a high price. She admired him far more than some of the other men she'd known who'd always had it good, had no idea what real suffering was like and felt entitled to whatever they wanted. Her ex had had so little empathy and understanding. He'd said he cared about her and Maya, but his actions proved that only *his* goals and desires were important to him. As far as Jada was concerned, he was missing a sensitivity gene, and that was becoming more and more apparent as she got to know Maddox again. He hadn't turned out anything like what her parents had expected.

But Susan had been angry and bitter against Maddox and Tobias for so long, Jada wasn't convinced it would make any difference.

23

Saturday night, Tobias walked around Maddox's house, wishing he were tired enough to shut off his mind and go to bed. He'd spent the evening with Uriah again. Since he'd been helping Uriah in the orchard, he'd had plenty of time to get to know him, not only during the day but in the evenings. For the past two days Uriah had insisted, if Maddox wasn't home, that Tobias join him for dinner. They'd eat together, play some chess and watch the news. Maddox would appear whenever he could and finish out the evening with them. Then Uriah would press them to take something home—the leftover lasagna or even some of his wife's pickled beets from the pantry, which Tobias loved—before he said good-night and turned in.

Tobias *really* liked the old man. He wasn't sure how he would've made it through the week without him. From the beginning, he'd wanted to adjust to regular life and make good, not only for his own sake but for Maddox, so that he wouldn't cause his brother any more problems. Now he wanted to make Uriah proud, too. Uriah seemed to think well of him despite his past, kept telling him he was a good man and he was going to be fine. How a guy who was a total stranger not too long ago could gain

that kind of faith, Tobias couldn't even begin to guess. But the interest and care Uriah offered him made a big difference. Every time Tobias was tempted to call his mother—out of guilt or loneliness or even boredom— he thought of his new job and reminded himself to stay away from Jill. She'd only screw him up, try to get him involved in something he was better off leaving alone. Uriah had given him an anchor to cling to.

Still, keeping his mind where it needed to be was a struggle, especially tonight. Maddox had joined them earlier— until he got a call and rushed off before Uriah went to bed. Although he hadn't told Tobias what was going on and had tried to pretend it was about Jada, Tobias could tell by his brother's reaction that wasn't the case. He was pretty sure it was Jill who'd interrupted Maddox's evening and that something was seriously wrong. His brother had told him to sit tight, that he'd be back in the morning, but now that he was no longer with Uriah, Tobias couldn't decide what to do with himself.

When he turned on the TV, the noise only made his anxiety worse, so he tried to call his brother. He needed to find out exactly what'd gone wrong. But Maddox didn't answer, and although he finally broke down and called Jill, she didn't pick up, either.

"Damn it," he muttered as he paced back and forth in the living room. What was going on? He knew Maddox was trying to act as a firewall between him and their mother, but if she'd been hurt…

Tobias couldn't stay in the house another second. Problem was he didn't have a house key. Since he was home all the time, he hadn't needed one—until now. He left one window cracked open so that he'd be able to get back in when he returned, locked the door behind him

and started the long walk to town. He was supposed to stay out of sight, but it was getting late. What were the chances he'd run into anyone who knew the Brookses? Even if he did, he'd been a skinny teenager the last time anyone from around here had seen him. Chances were he wouldn't be recognized, not if he went to town alone and kept to himself. He just needed an outlet, a distraction, some way to while away the hours and siphon off the excess energy until he heard from Maddox. He hated to even think it, but he was afraid his mother had overdosed and, while he harbored a lot of resentment when it came to her, he also felt a sense of duty, and the desire to love her and be loved by her, despite all of their past differences.

A gentle breeze stirred the trees as he churned up the ground beneath his feet. He was walking so fast he was almost running, but he needed to *move*. He also needed air. Space. To feel he was no longer being restrained.

He wouldn't cause any trouble, wouldn't even interact with anyone.

For a weekend, it was slow at the Blue Suede Shoe. Jada had invited Tiffany to join them, and Atticus had invited Donte, his best friend, but there were only another fifteen or twenty people at the bar.

Jada sort of wished there was one less—that her brother had left Donte at home. But Donte was also celebrating. Although he hadn't been hired by New Horizons, he'd managed to get on at McGregor High School as a PE teacher, and he was proud of that. He kept hitting on her, trying to get her to dance with him—and then trying to pull her too close when she did—but she didn't

find him attractive. It was crazy, but she was too infatu-
ated with Maddox to even look at other guys.

"Have you heard from Maddox?" Tiffany asked.

Jada shot her a look, warning her to be quiet even
though Atticus and Donte were at the bar, talking to
a couple of girls they seemed to know, probably from
school.

"What?" Tiffany spread her hands out as she laughed.
"The music is so loud I can barely hear myself think. I
doubt anyone outside this two-foot circle has any clue
I'm even talking."

Still, Jada was bugged that she would bring it up.
Maybe it was just that she didn't want to tell Tiffany
what she had planned for fear Tiffany would tell her the
truth—that she was just digging herself in deeper. "We've
been keeping in touch a little," she said, downplaying
their interaction as much as possible. "What's going on
with you and Aaron?"

She grimaced. "He hasn't called me, not since he left
town."

"You're kidding! He was so into you."

"Guess not." She rolled her eyes. "I feel like such a
fool. He's burned me before. I shouldn't have trusted
him."

Feeling guilty for being so consumed with her own
problems that she didn't even know her best friend was
suffering disappointment of her own, Jada reached across
the table to squeeze Tiffany's hand. "He doesn't deserve
you."

She opened her mouth to answer, but then she seemed
to spot something across the bar that made her mouth fall
open. "Oh God, is that who I think it is?"

Jada followed Tiffany's line of sight—and her heart

dropped to her stomach. Sure enough, Tobias Richardson was standing right inside the door, only about ten feet from her brother.

Two things hit Tobias at the same time: the fact that Atticus wasn't the only member of the Brooks family at the Blue Suede Shoe—Jada was there, too; the bar was empty enough that he saw her the second he walked in but by then it was too late to change his mind—and the proverb "The road to hell is paved with good intentions."

When he'd first reached town and stumbled upon the Blue Suede Shoe, which was about the only place still open, he'd been careful to check the lot before going in, and had been glad he did. He'd spotted the wheelchair lift on the back of the pickup parked in the accessible spot near the door and had known instantly that it belonged to Atticus. Maddox had mentioned the kind of vehicle Jada's brother drove when he warned Tobias to stay out of sight, so there was no confusion.

Being confronted with it while in his current frame of mind rattled him. He'd turned right around and headed back to the orchard and the house where he was currently staying with Maddox. But the farther he got from the club, the more he'd started to question his motivations in avoiding the victim of his crime. Was he running because he didn't have the courage to face him? Or did he have the guts to stand up and publicly take responsibility for what he'd done? To apologize despite the anger and recriminations he'd likely face?

He hadn't attempted to do anything like that so far. Tobias had sent one letter to the Brooks family, way back when he first went to prison, which they hadn't answered. But he'd done it at the request of his brother—no doubt

Maddox had been praying it would help his own situation with Jada—so it hadn't even been Tobias's idea. And simply writing a note required a lot less effort, energy and risk. To address the man he'd crippled for life in person was far more daunting. It required dropping all of his defenses, opening up and leaving himself completely vulnerable in an emotional sense, and that wasn't his strong suit. He'd spent most of his life keeping his guard up. That was the only way he'd been able to survive his childhood and then prison.

He kept telling himself it wasn't necessary to approach Atticus, that even Atticus would rather he not do it. But he couldn't let himself off that easy. A small but strident voice in his head insisted that he owed Atticus at least that much, especially since his written apology had come before he realized how permanent the destruction he'd caused really was.

So, halfway hoping that Jada's brother would have left and the opportunity to apologize would be gone with him, he'd turned around. And once he'd returned to the bar and could see that Atticus's truck hadn't moved, he'd stood outside, wrestling with his reluctance as well as the fear that announcing his presence in Silver Springs, especially in this way, would only make things worse for his brother.

After fifteen or twenty minutes of stepping back into the shadows every time someone came in or went out of the building, he'd decided that he was tired of hiding out like some kind of coward, and he'd stepped inside.

The moment Atticus saw him, he dropped his drink, which shattered on the floor. But Tobias didn't give him the chance to say or do anything else. If he hesitated for even a split second, he'd lose his nerve.

Careful to keep a respectful distance so that no one would mistake his intentions, he drew a deep breath before forcing the words he'd rehearsed over and over during the previous half hour out of his mouth. "I'm sorry for what I did to you thirteen years ago, Atticus." His pulse was racing so fast he was afraid he might have a heart attack if he didn't get the hell out of there, especially now that the eyes of everyone else in the place had turned to stab him like knives, but he wasn't finished. Clearing his throat so that his voice wouldn't crack—being humiliated by breaking down in addition to causing such a scene was one of his greatest fears—he forged ahead. "I didn't know what I was doing, didn't intend to harm you. But that's no excuse. The ramifications of my actions have been catastrophic, and because of that, I don't expect you to accept my apology. I'm not even asking you to. I just want you to know how badly I wish I could take it back, and that you don't have to worry about me now that I'm out of prison. I will *never* take anything that will impair my judgment again."

He saw Jada bump into a chair and shove it out of the way as she scrambled to reach her brother, but he didn't wait to see if she had something to say to him. After slapping a twenty on the bar to pay for the drink Atticus had dropped, he walked out.

"This is *your* fault, you know," Jill said.

Maddox was trying to distract himself by reading a magazine while waiting for hospital personnel to come get his mother so they could x-ray her shoulder. She'd injured it when she slammed into a Ford Expedition five hours earlier. Fortunately, no one else had been hurt. The other driver had been checked out and released, but there was significant damage to both cars, and his mother would face legal consequences.

He lowered the copy of *People*—his only option for reading material since his phone didn't get good reception inside the hospital. "My fault you were high, ran a red light and could've killed yourself and/or someone else?"

"I was only high because I can't take the stress of what I'm going through. I lost my job yesterday, but you don't care. You don't give a damn about me!"

"I wouldn't be sitting here if that were true," he said. "There are better things I could do on a Saturday night."

"Could've fooled me. You haven't called in forever."

"You mean since I gave you everything I had in my wallet? I wonder why I might not be eager to talk to you again right away."

"You've talked to me once since then—to tell me to leave your brother alone," she grumbled, glaring at him.

"Want to tell me how you lost your job?" Although it required some effort, he was careful to keep his voice mild. Getting angry wouldn't help.

"I was laid off," she mumbled.

"Would your manager use those words if I called him?"

Suddenly, she wouldn't meet his eyes. "He's had it out for me for a long time."

"If I had to guess, that became a problem when you started using again."

"Quit trying to blame me for everything!" She winced because she'd leaned forward and managed to jerk her injured shoulder. "You think you're so clever."

"Not *so* clever. Just clever enough to stay sober. You'd be amazed how much that helps you navigate difficult problems and build a productive life."

"*You* haven't had the challenges I've faced," she grumbled.

He lifted his eyebrows. "No, I've had other challenges." She was one of the biggest and always had been. The hardest part was knowing she always would be.

An orderly parted the drapes that separated his mother's space from everyone else's in the emergency room. "Okay, Ms. Richardson. Time to take you up."

"I need some more meds," she said. "I'm in terrible pain."

Maddox had to grind his teeth to stop from voicing his opinion. He suspected his mother was trying to take advantage of even *this* situation, but he couldn't say for sure that she wasn't in terrible pain, and neither could anyone else.

"I'll talk to your doctor, see if he can give you anything more," the man said, and Maddox held the drape so she could be wheeled out.

"You coming?" She glanced back at him when he didn't fall in step at her side.

"No, I think you can survive an X-ray on your own. But I'll be here when you get back. I'm going to call Tobias." And before he did, he was going to try to think of something he could say that would make this not sound so bad. Since Jill had been driving under the influence and had been cited for it at the scene, she could be facing jail time. At a minimum, she'd have a stiff financial penalty, which she had no way of paying. So, of course, she'd look to him.

He sighed as he watched the orderly roll his mother to the elevator. Then he scrubbed a hand over his face and headed for the exit. For whatever reason, cell reception was better outside.

He stared up at the night sky, so velvety and warm—

in direct contrast to the frustration he felt inside—while he waited for the call to go through.

"Finally!" Tobias said as soon as he picked up.

Maddox walked over to another part of the grass. Someone had come up beside him and lit a cigarette. "You sound pretty wired."

"I am. Haven't you been getting my texts?"

"Probably. Haven't checked. I'm at the hospital and reception isn't the best."

"Is Mom okay? And don't pretend this isn't about her. I know it is."

"She's fine. Fortunately, so is the guy she hit."

"She got hurt doing that insurance scam she tried to get me involved in?"

"No, this was something else entirely. But it could've been a lot worse."

"Is that supposed to make me feel better?"

"It's all I've got," he admitted.

"What happened? Don't tell me the guy who beat her up came back again. Because if he did, he and I are going to have a *serious* conversation."

"That isn't it. We won't be able to help her out of this one." Maddox explained, minimizing where he could, but when he finished, Tobias still cursed.

"It's no wonder I'm so screwed up," he said. "Do you believe this bullshit?"

"Honestly, sometimes I don't."

"You're the only normal one among us."

"Don't say that. You're as normal as I am, if you choose to be. Just don't follow her lead."

"Well, you might not be so encouraging when I tell you that I was also involved in a bit of drama tonight."

Maddox stepped even farther away from the entrance.

"What are you talking about? You and Uriah didn't have a problem…"

"No, but I ran into Atticus at the Blue Suede Shoe."

Maddox sank onto the bench nearby. "What were you doing there?"

"I saw his truck, so…"

"So?"

"I went in to apologize."

Unable to remain sitting, Maddox stood up. "What happened then?"

"He dropped his drink."

"Anything else?" he asked, wincing as he imagined it.

"No. After I said what I was there to say, I paid for his drink and left. I have no idea how he took it."

Maddox stared down at his feet as he tried to figure out if this would turn into a new problem.

"Maddox?" Tobias said.

"I'm still here."

"I felt like I had to do it. I *wanted* to do it. I hope you understand."

He remembered how he'd hovered outside Jada's house, wanting to offer his own apology. Of course he could understand. "You did the right thing," he said. He just wasn't sure that was the best thing for *him*.

24

Susan was on a tear. It had been a long time since Jada had seen her mother's simmering resentment explode into outright anger, but she was going to be late opening the store today, and even that didn't seem to matter. Learning that Tobias had confronted Atticus at the Blue Suede Shoe Saturday night had pushed her over the edge.

"He's *back*? In Silver Springs?" She stopped doing dishes to shift her attention from Atticus, who was sitting at the breakfast table, to Jada, who was standing at the toaster.

"Don't look at me," Jada said. "I didn't invite him to town."

Her eyes narrowed as if Jada *was* somehow responsible. "But you probably don't mind that he's back, just like you don't mind that his handsome brother is back."

"Let's leave Maddox out of this." Jada had just dropped Maya off at a swim party one of the boys she'd met at school last spring was throwing. She was glad her daughter wasn't around to hear this. Had Maddox told their mother yesterday, she would've been. Jada wasn't sure why he'd waited. Maybe he'd been wrestling with himself.

"You want to continue to pretend that his presence in

this town isn't a problem?" Susan cried. "That it doesn't risk the one thing you love more than anything else— your own daughter?"

Problem was…her daughter also happened to be *his* daughter. That should matter. In any other situation, it would matter a great deal, even to her mother. But it almost seemed as though her mother was getting some form of enjoyment from withholding something so precious, something he would want, if only he knew. Jada hated that as much as everything else about her predicament. "He hasn't caused any trouble."

"He could—that's the point. And now his no-good, lousy brother is back, too!"

Jada was tempted to reassure her that Tobias was in town only temporarily, that Maddox was working on trying to help him get a job as well as a place to stay in LA, but that would reveal that she knew far more about the Richardson brothers than she should, and she'd already heard the accusation in her mother's voice. Her mother could tell that, deep down, she still cared about Maddox. "Tobias was trying to *apologize*," she said. "He didn't mean any harm."

"Don't make it sound as though he was being nice." She wagged a wet, soapy finger at Jada. "He was relieving his own conscience, trying to get Atticus to forgive him so that everyone else will do the same. Maybe it's because he plans to stay here, and he thinks it will make things easier for him. Regardless, he can't simply say he's sorry for what he did. Atticus has to live with the consequences of that night. It doesn't just go away."

"I'm sure Tobias understands that. I don't think he expects to be *forgiven*—"

"Don't stand up for him!" she broke in. "Where's your loyalty to your own family, for God's sake?"

That was exactly what she'd said thirteen years ago when Jada had wanted to tell Maddox she was pregnant. Here she was, in the middle again, wanting to try to convince her family not to hate Maddox, regardless of what they thought of his brother. But she knew it was a waste of breath. They saw him as an integral part of what happened, and she couldn't say he wasn't.

"I've been doing everything I can to support the family," she said as her toast popped up. Didn't she get *any* credit for what she'd contributed recently? For how hard she'd tried to relieve her mother's workload since her father died, help with the bills, make sure the store remained afloat?

"What, exactly, did he say to you?" Jada asked, turning to Atticus. After Tobias had walked out of the bar, Atticus had demanded they leave, too. He hadn't been willing to repeat what Tobias had said to him, even though Jada had asked about it, over and over, while they drove home and several times yesterday, as well.

Atticus dropped his head in his hands and kneaded his forehead as if he was feeling more than a little regret for starting this. "You heard what I said to Mom. He told me he was sorry."

"He was there a bit longer than 'I'm sorry.'"

"That was the gist of it."

Obviously, her brother was conflicted. Right when he'd been celebrating a major victory, he'd been confronted by the man who'd shot him. Tobias's sudden appearance had come as a complete surprise. Besides that, Atticus probably felt terrible for the hate and anger that lived inside him still. He didn't want to forgive, just wanted to move on and forget, as much as possible, that there was this person in the world who'd senselessly caused him so much pain and hardship, living and breathing and trying to fulfill his own needs.

"Now that he's had his say, maybe that'll be the end of it." As upset as she was inside, Jada was trying to calm everyone down so that things wouldn't get any worse. "Maybe we can all try to put the past behind us and… and begin to heal."

"This again?" Susan snapped.

Jada widened her eyes. "What else can we do?"

"It's just awfully convenient that *you* keep suggesting we move on, since you aren't the one in the wheelchair."

"You think it's been easy on me?"

"I don't care, since you're the reason we're in this situation to begin with!"

Something snapped inside of Jada. Stunned by the vitriol behind those words, she dropped her toast on the plate where she'd just buttered it.

Susan seemed to realize that perhaps she'd gone too far because she suddenly looked uncertain, on the brink of tears, but Jada knew she'd meant what she said. It was how her mother had felt all along.

Jada looked from Susan to Atticus, who flinched. "She's just upset, Jada," he said.

"So am I," she responded.

"Where are you going?" Susan asked as Jada tossed her uneaten toast in the trash.

"If there is no forgiveness, if I, Maddox and Tobias are terrible people *forever* because of the unfortunate and stupid decisions we made one night—*when we weren't even eighteen*—then what am I doing here?"

"Jada…" Atticus started to wheel closer to her, but she thrust out a hand to stop him.

"I'm sorry, Atticus. I would apologize every day if I thought it would help. But, as you say, nothing can change what happened that night, or the blame Maddox, Tobias and I bear because of it. You shouldn't have to put up with *any* of us. So Maya and I are moving out."

Susan gaped at her. "But where will you go?"

"If I had my way, we'd go back to LA."

"You'd take your daughter away from a loving grandmother? Away from her uncle and…and her best friend, right before school is about to start?"

"You didn't want her in the first place, remember?" Jada said. "Anyway, I'll do what's best for Maya, because no one loves her more than I do. But *I* deserve some consideration, too. Good luck at the store today. If you need help, Atticus will have to step up for a change, because I won't be there. I've fallen so far behind on my own work, trying to help you, that I doubt I'll ever catch up."

"Jada, don't do this." A pained expression contorted Atticus's handsome face, but Jada had no choice. She was beginning to wonder how she'd survived living with her mother for the past six months. She'd been trying so hard to atone for her past mistakes, she hadn't realized that her mother's disapproval and refusal to forgive was sucking all the joy out of life.

"I can't continue to live with Mom, even if you can. You're her favorite, after all. She coddles you like a child, which I think is ridiculous and the last thing you need. So I won't stick around and watch it any longer," she said and went to her room to pack.

When Mrs. Coates picked up Maya and Annie from the swim party, she said she had to stop by New Horizons to check on a delivery for the music department, since the music teacher was stuck at home with a sick baby, which was fine by Maya. Especially because Annie's mom said that, while she was busy, they could walk around campus and find their classes. Although Maya had decided she'd have to wait until school started to talk to Mrs. Turner about her father, it looked like she might have the opportunity sooner than that.

As soon as Mrs. Coates went into the building, Maya and Annie headed straight for the boys' side.

There weren't a lot of students on that campus right now, not as many as during the winter, but it was a year-round school for some, so it wasn't empty, either. Not like the girls' side.

A fence separated the two schools, or halves of one school, which made Maya fear they'd have to walk back the way Mrs. Coates had driven and circle around—until she spotted a gate. Because the girls' side wasn't yet in session, it stood open to make it easier for Mr. Richardson and his faculty to get back and forth whenever they needed to.

Maya glanced at Annie as she slipped through first. "Mrs. Turner's office has to be in that building over there, don't you think?" She pointed at what looked like a small but important building next to a large parking lot.

"I think so, too, since that's where it would be at any other school," Annie replied, but her steps were slowing.

"What's wrong?" Maya asked.

Annie bit her lip. "I'm afraid we'll get caught on the wrong side of the fence when my mom comes out."

"She didn't say we couldn't go over to the boys' side. It's not like we're going to talk to any of the students."

"I know, but…"

Maya gave her a pleading look. "I only need five minutes of Mrs. Turner's time. We'll be back before your mother knows we're gone."

"I hope so. I don't want my mom to ground me from the first dance or something, especially because we don't know that Mrs. Turner will be able to tell us anything. No one else has been able to."

"If *anyone* can help us it's her." Maya spoke with more confidence than she felt, but Mrs. Turner did seem to know a lot of people.

Although Annie fell silent, she allowed Maya to drag her along; Maya was relieved for that.

A gray-haired receptionist—the sign on her desk read Betty May—looked up as soon as they entered the administration building. Maya felt so self-conscious in that moment that she almost grabbed Annie's arm and dragged her right back out. She would have, except she knew she might never have a better opportunity to speak to Mrs. Turner. Once school started, the gate they'd used would be closed and probably locked, which would at the very least make it harder instead of easier.

"How can I help you?" Mrs. May was obviously surprised to see two young women walk in without an adult.

Maya rested her hands on the partition that separated the receptionist area from the waiting area. "I was hoping I could speak to Mrs. Turner."

Mrs. May moved her coffee cup to one side so she wouldn't knock it over when she stood up. "Can I tell her what this is about?"

Maya glanced at Annie with a silent question—*Should I go through with it?*

Annie gave her a "this was your idea" look and shrugged.

Feeling somewhat caught, anyway, Maya drew a deep breath. "Do we have to say?"

The woman's eyebrows, which had been drawn on with a brown pencil, rose almost to her hairline. "Um, I'm not sure, to be honest. I've never had anyone ask me that question. Can I get your names?"

"Maya Brooks." Although Maya had met Aiyana at the cookie store, she doubted her name would mean much to such an important person. She didn't want to say Annie's name—especially her last name. Mrs. Turner would immediately recognize it since Annie's mother did so much volunteering at the school, and Maya didn't want to get her friend in trouble.

"Just a minute."

Betty May plodded to the back of the central area and knocked on a door.

Maya couldn't hear everything that was said, but she thought she made out her name. She held her breath, hoping Mrs. Turner would agree and have time to see her, and sagged in relief as the receptionist returned. "Right this way," she said, beckoning them toward her.

Annie chickened out at the last second. "I'll wait for you here," she said and sat in one of the plastic chairs lining the wall.

Maya didn't have a chance to try to persuade her. She was too interested in seeing if she could find out more about her father to risk missing this opportunity. So she threw back her shoulders and followed Mrs. May into the corner office.

Mrs. Turner was coming around the desk as Maya entered. "Maya. How are you?"

Maya nearly missed a step. She hadn't expected such

a friendly reception, but she was glad for it. It gave her courage. "Good."

"Are you looking forward to coming to New Horizons?"

"I am."

"How's everything at home?"

"Fine."

"I hear your grandmother is now serving ice cream sandwiches made with her famous cookies."

"She is."

"I bet those are good. What a brilliant idea!"

"I'm the one who thought of it." Maya felt herself blush after she said that. It sounded like she was bragging, but she was just excited her idea had worked out.

Fortunately, Mrs. Turner didn't seem to disapprove. If anything, her smile grew wider. "Then your grandmother was smart to listen to you."

Maya shifted from one foot to the other but couldn't decide how to get started on what she'd come to say. "We were hoping we'd be able to sell more cookies that way."

"And? Have you?"

She nodded.

"There you go. Wonderful all the way around." Mrs. Turner waved to a chair. "Would you like to sit down?"

"No, thanks. I just…" She curled her fingernails into her palms. "I wanted to ask you something real quick."

Mrs. Turner leaned against her desk. "What is it?"

"I hope it's okay that I'm here."

"Of course it is. What did you want to ask me?"

"I was wondering if…if you knew my father."

Mrs. Turner blinked several times. "Excuse me?"

"You've lived in this town a long time, so I thought you might have met him."

She straightened. "But your father isn't from here. Your mother married him after she moved to LA."

"That was Eric. He wasn't my father—just my step-dad. I never got to meet my real dad. My mother said he died in a motorcycle accident before I was born."

"In LA?"

"No, right here in Silver Springs."

Looking confused, Mrs. Turner scratched her arm. "I thought... Well, I assumed that Eric was your father."

"So you don't know anything about my real dad..."

"I don't think so. What was his name?"

"Madsen something." Maya felt her face heat when she had to add, "My mother doesn't remember his last name."

Mrs. Turner stared at her for several seconds. Then she smoothed her skirt, and the way she did it, so carefully, gave Maya the impression she was stalling for time, trying to think it over. "And your grandmother? What does she say?"

"What do you mean?"

"Does she also say that your father died in a motor-cycle accident?"

Maya racked her brain, trying to remember what her grandmother had said over the years. It wasn't a lot; she didn't seem to care for the subject. "I guess. She's never said he didn't."

"And your uncle Atticus?"

"He doesn't act like he ever knew him, but he took me to the library so I could look for some information on him not too long ago. I wanted to see if there was a list of people who lived in the area way back then so I could get his last name, but there wasn't such a thing."

"I see." She peered at Maya a little closer. "When were you born, dear?"

"August 26. I'll be turning thirteen right after school starts."

Mrs. Turner used her fingers to count back nine months. "That means your mother got pregnant in…" Suddenly, her voice dropped off and she didn't complete her sentence.

"November," Maya supplied. "I've done the math. My father would've had to be living here in November the year before I was born." She felt a bubble of excitement. This was the first time she hadn't received an immediate no. Maybe coming here wouldn't be a waste; maybe Mrs. Turner had just needed a few details to jog her memory.

"Oh dear," she said.

Eager to understand what the shocked look on her face meant, Maya stepped closer. "You remember a Madsen?"

The warm smile Mrs. Turner had worn when Maya first arrived reappeared. "No. Actually, I don't."

Maya felt her shoulders slump. "Really? But… I thought…"

"I'm sorry," she said. "It took me a moment, but I realize now that I was remembering someone else."

"*Not* a Madsen."

"Definitely not a Madsen."

Something strange was going on, but Maya couldn't figure out what. "You never heard of a young man dying on a motorcycle that year?"

"No," she replied firmly.

"Do you know anyone else who lived here back then I could ask?"

"Not off the top of my head, but…I'll call if I happen to think of anyone."

There was nothing Maya could do except leave, even though she felt Aiyana knew something she wasn't saying. "Thanks for letting me ask."

She was walking out when Mrs. Turner spoke again. "I wish I could've been more help, Maya."

"It's okay," she muttered. "I guess if he's dead I should try to forget about him. It's just that…well, everyone else knows more about their dad than I do mine. I want to know what he looked like at least. Or if he had any family. If so, maybe I could meet them someday."

"I hope you find your answers," she said, her voice so soft and caring that it made Maya wonder if she'd imagined Mrs. Turner's odd reaction a moment before. "Something tells me he is—*was*—a man worth knowing."

"Thank you," she said.

25

Jada was nervous as she pulled in front of Cindy Coates's house to pick up her daughter. There'd already been a lot of changes the past year, and now she was going to have to tell Maya that she'd moved them out of Susan's house. But the decision had been made, and she wasn't going back. She'd put everything she owned—what she didn't sell or give to Eric in the divorce before she even came to Silver Springs—in storage to get it out of her mother's attic and garage, and she'd taken a large suitcase, packed with enough clothes and toiletries to get her and her daughter through a week or so, to Tiffany's.

Although Tiffany had been at work when Jada was moving out, she'd responded to Jada's texts, telling her where she could find a key to the house. So at least they had somewhere to stay. It'd be cramped in that small a house, with Jada sleeping on the couch and Maya sleeping on the floor, but Jada hoped to find a place she could rent in the very near future. Although she was tempted to move away from Silver Springs, as she'd threatened, she knew she couldn't do that to her daughter. Maya was too happy here.

There were things that made Jada happy here, too. She

loved being around Tiffany, for one. She was the closest friend she'd ever had. And then there was Maddox.
Maybe he wasn't the kind of man her mother wanted her
to be with. He came from a humble background and having Tobias as a brother made things complicated, challenging. But he was the only man she'd ever truly loved.
Just being around him made her feel complete.

When Maya didn't come out right away, Jada cursed
under her breath. She'd already texted her daughter twice
to say that she was out front. She didn't want to go to
the door, not after the day she'd had. Her eyes were still
swollen from the tears she'd cried, and she hadn't dressed
with the intention of seeing anyone other than Tiffany.

"Thank goodness," she said on a long exhalation when
Maya finally emerged from the house.

"Hi, Mom," Maya said as she tossed her bag into the
back and climbed into the passenger seat.

"Hi, honey."

She put on her seat belt, but then she caught sight of
Jada's face and grabbed her arm. "Have you been crying? What's wrong?"

Jada forced a smile. "Nothing new. It's going to be
okay."

"Is this about Eric?"

She put the car in Drive and gave it some gas. "No.
Eric doesn't have the power to hurt me anymore."

"So what is it?"

"We're going to be staying with Tiffany for a few days,
until I can find us a new place to live."

"Did you and Grandma have a fight?"

"Not *exactly*. I just don't like the way she treats me."

Maya fell silent as Jada turned out of Annie's sub-
division, but it was only a few seconds later that she said,

"I don't like it, either. I don't think she appreciates you as much as she should."

Surprised that her daughter would take the news so calmly, Jada glanced over at her. "You're okay with moving out?"

"Yeah. I love Grandma, and Uncle Atticus, too, but *you're* the most important person to me."

Fresh tears welled up as Jada reached over to take Maya's hand. "And you're the most important person to me." Which was why she was going to see if Maya could spend next weekend with Annie so she could still go to Newport Beach with Maddox.

If all went well—if she felt it was the right thing to do *and* the right time—maybe she'd tell him he had a daughter.

"So what are we going to do about Mom?" Tobias asked.

Maddox muted the golf tournament he'd been watching and looked up at his brother, who'd just come out of the bathroom wearing nothing but a pair of boxers and carrying a towel he was using to dry his hair. It was Wednesday, but because of his mother's accident, Maddox had taken the day off to move her home from the hospital. After driving home this afternoon, he'd slept a couple of hours and had been eating and watching TV since he woke up.

Tobias hadn't joined him in LA. He'd been out in the orchard with Uriah. Tobias was becoming more and more devoted to their landlord. Uriah was teaching him things that most boys learned in their teens—boys who'd grown up with a father, anyway—and he seemed to be drinking it all up, hanging on every word. Fortunately, Maddox could tell that Uriah liked having an apt pupil as much as Tobias liked being that pupil. When Maddox got home, he'd been able to hear them on one side of the garage and had chuckled at the interaction. Uriah had been teaching Tobias how to care for a lawn, which was something Tobias had never done. They'd always lived in an apartment or in such a crappy house that there wasn't any landscaping to bother with, even if they'd had a lawn mower and other tools, which they never did.

"Her car is pretty much totaled, which is a problem," he said.

"I'm assuming she didn't have insurance."

"Not full coverage."

"So she'll have to pay to replace her car."

"Yes. Except she has no money."

"Of course not."

He went to the sink to scrub his hands again. After coming in from the orchard, he and Uriah had spent several hours tinkering with an old truck Uriah had on the property. That was something Tobias did know about, so he'd been trying to help Uriah get it running again and now he seemed to be having trouble getting all the grease out from under his fingernails. "Maybe she can get a loan."

Maddox grimaced. "With her credit? I doubt it, but we'll deal with that when we have to."

"Do you really think she'll get jail time?"

"I do. And she deserves it. She could've killed someone."

He turned off the water. "How long?"

"Tough to say. Depends on whether the judge decides to throw the book at her. It's her first DUI, so maybe she'll get off with community service and some fines."

"More money. How will she come up with it all?"

"I'll figure it out later. First, I'm going to get her into another good rehab. I think we have to deal with the addiction first, then the car, so she can get another job."

Tobias hung the towel around his neck and sat on the other end of the couch. "The car and the job parts sound familiar," he joked.

"Just be glad you don't have to deal with the addiction part, too."

"I've learned my lesson."

Maddox could only pray that was true. "I'm glad to hear you say it."

He used one end of the towel to rub his hair again. "Do you think I should move to LA so I can take care of her?"

Maddox crushed his empty beer can and threw it at the trash, somehow making it in. "You know what I think."

"That I should stay as far away from her as possible. But I don't want you to feel it's all on you. I'm her son, too."

"You can worry about helping her in a year or two, when you're securely on your feet."

He smiled. "Okay."

Maddox lifted the remote so he could turn the volume back up, but then he hesitated. "How do you feel about how things went with Atticus on Saturday?"

Tobias leaned back and stretched out his legs. "Good. I needed to do it."

"That took guts, man." He admired his brother's courage. Such a public apology could not have been easy. But he was afraid that having Tobias confront Atticus at the bar hadn't done *him* any favors. He'd promised Jada his brother would lie low, wasn't even sure if she'd told her family that Tobias was in town.

After he'd learned about what happened, Maddox had texted her an apology, but she hadn't responded. He didn't know if it was because she'd been too busy the past couple of days—or if she was so angry she wouldn't.

Jada couldn't wait until Maya went to sleep. Moving out had done something to her, made her more determined to pursue her own happiness, and that was intoxicating. She didn't want to be selfish, but she couldn't see how not being with the person she loved helped anyone else. Although she knew this type of thinking was strictly practical and not everything could be boiled down to the practical, especially in a world filled with emotions and trauma the likes of which her brother had suffered, no amount of sacrifice on her part would give Atticus back the use of his legs. And, as a mother, she had other considerations now that she believed Maddox had turned out to be a fully functioning adult—like whether Maya's right to know her father superseded Atticus's right to expect her to cut Maddox out of her life.

"You're going to the orchard?" Tiffany whispered once Maya had gone to bed and Jada started to gather her keys and her purse.

"Yeah."

"Even though Tobias will be there?"

"I'm not sure how I feel about Tobias, to be honest. I'm hoping that getting to know him after what he's been through will make me a better judge of whether or not he should be forgiven and allowed back into my life even in a peripheral way."

"I think you might be pleasantly surprised."

"What makes you say that?"

"I don't know. Just a feeling I have. What he did at the bar was *so* brave."

"My mother thinks he did that for his own benefit—to make people feel sorry for him so they'll be more welcoming."

"We were there. We saw how he was struggling to get the words out without breaking down. *You* think he was sincere, don't you?"

"I do." That was why she found what her mother had said so offensive. As far as she was concerned, Susan's reasoning didn't even make sense. It wasn't as though Tobias wouldn't be allowed to stay in Silver Springs if he *didn't* apologize. He was a free man, could go anywhere, do anything, as long as it was legal. He didn't *have* to care about the person he'd hurt, and he didn't have to apologize. "But we still don't know what he did when he was on the inside that made them lengthen his sentence. Maybe I'll ask him tonight."

Tiffany gave her a brief hug. "I'm glad you're doing this."

"Going to see Maddox?"

"Not allowing your family's disapproval to rob you of something that could be just what you need."

"My mother will be so angry. And Atticus could easily take his cues from her. That's what he's done in the past."

"Don't sell your brother short. He's a man now. He can think for himself."

"If his anger and resentment don't get in the way. Maddox could wind up hating me for costing him thirteen years of Maya's life. Maya could wind up hating me for making her believe she didn't have a father. My mother could wind up hating me for divulging the secret, and Atticus could wind up hating me for bringing the two men he blames for the loss of his legs back into his life." She tossed her keys onto the coffee table and slumped into the closest seat. *"What am I doing, Tiff? Am I destroying my life?"*

Tiffany pulled her back to her feet and handed her the car keys. "No, you're following your heart."

Jada's pulse was racing by the time she reached the orchard and pulled down the long drive. This was the first time she'd come to see Maddox that she wasn't sneaking over. Not making any effort to hide her presence felt daring. So did what she was contemplating telling him. But she didn't plan to mention Maya tonight, not with Tobias around. This was more about getting to know him better, getting to know them both, and trying to decide if telling Maddox about Maya might be the right thing to do. Although she was feeling a great deal of guilt and pressure because of the deception and the number of years he'd already missed of his daughter's life, she didn't want to act too fast.

"Be smart," she muttered to herself and drew a calming breath as she pushed open her door.

A curtain moved in the window looking out on the drive. The sound of her car had apparently alerted Maddox—or maybe Tobias—to her presence. So she wasn't surprised when Maddox met her on the stoop, wearing a T-shirt and a pair of khaki shorts that hung low on his narrow hips with no shoes.

"Are you okay?" he asked, obviously surprised that she'd show up at his house out of the blue when she knew Tobias was staying with him. It was only nine thirty, which meant other people might notice.

"Yeah. I just… I wanted to see you."

"Did I miss a text?"

"No. I didn't text or try to call. I probably should have."

He didn't seem to know what to do. He glanced back at the house but didn't invite her in. Instead, he gestured at her car, since it was behind his. "Should we go for a drive?"

"No. I don't have much to say. I just thought that maybe we could watch a movie or something."

"Here?"

"Yeah. Other than the brief glimpse I caught of Tobias at the Blue Suede Shoe on Saturday, I haven't seen him in thirteen years. I thought I'd say hello."

He coughed, probably to hide his surprise. "Okay. Let me…let me make sure he's dressed."

"If tonight's not a good night, it's no problem," she said. "I mean…if he's not up for company."

"It's not that. He and Uriah were working on an old truck that's behind the barn this evening, and he just showered. Let me see if he's finished."

Jada chewed nervously on her bottom lip while she waited, but it wasn't long before Maddox poked his head out. "He's dressed, and he'd like to see you, too. Come on in."

He held the door as she stepped inside.

Tobias's hair was wet, and he was dressed in a T-shirt and basketball shorts. Although the TV was on, he wasn't sitting down in front of it. He stood in the center of the floor, his shoulders square, his jaw set as though he was determined to take whatever blow she might land. He quite obviously thought she'd come here to let him have it.

"Hello, Tobias," she said and had to admit, at least to herself, that not *everything* in life had gone against him.

He had a magnificent body—looked as though he'd been lifting, which he probably had since there wasn't a lot else to do in prison—and he was incredibly handsome. He had the same thick dark hair and rough-hewn jaw Maddox did, even the same shape to his eyes, but Tobias's were lighter, a pretty green color.

"Hello," he responded.

She swallowed against a dry throat because she could tell he was still waiting for her to unleash on him. "You're looking good."

His eyebrows rose slightly and he glanced over at Maddox. He'd been so prepared for anger and recrimination that he didn't seem to know how to respond to a compliment. "Thank you. So do you," he said, quickly turning the compliment back on her, but he looked down at the floor when he said it.

She gestured at the television. "What are you watching?"

He turned to the TV. "Looks like the news," he said as though he hadn't remembered it was blaring in the background.

"Mind if I join you?"

"Uh, no. Of course not." He moved to quickly gather up some clothes, probably his, that'd been tossed or dropped on the couch. "Sorry. This is such a small place there's nowhere to put anything."

She couldn't imagine he had much, but she didn't say so and neither did he. Perching on one end of the couch, she put her purse on the coffee table.

Maddox had been rubbing his chin while watching them interact, no doubt trying to figure out what had changed since he'd seen her last, but now he spoke up. "Can I get you something to drink?"

"A glass of water would be nice."

"Sure thing."

As he went to the cupboards, Tobias made his way to the front door by edging around the room, as if it might be offensive to her if he got too close. "I'll just…uh… go for a walk and leave you two alone for a bit. Maddox, you can…you know…text me later."

"Actually, I was sort of hoping you'd stay and hang out with us," Jada said.

"Me?" He pressed a hand to his chest.

She jumped to her feet and grabbed her purse. "Or, on second thought, why don't we all go down to the Blue Suede Shoe and have a drink while we play some pool?"

Maddox's jaw dropped and Tobias shook his head. "That's okay. I don't want to get in the way. You two go ahead."

Somehow any negative sentiment—the anger and resentment—she'd harbored against the "monster" who'd shot her brother started to seep away. She would rather be Atticus, the innocent victim, than the person who had to live with the knowledge that he'd cost another human being the ability to walk. That made it possible for her to feel some empathy.

She grinned at him. "What's the matter? 'Fraid I might beat you?"

"Jada, you can't even be seen with *me*, let alone Tobias," Maddox said, his voice low and serious.

Maybe that *was* taking it too far. Showing up in town with the Richardson brothers would send the wrong message to her family. She wasn't out to hurt anyone. She just wanted to put the pain and sadness of the past behind them, as much as possible. "Fine. Maybe we shouldn't go out tonight. But I hope we'll be able to do that one day. For now, I could settle for having a beer and finding something better to watch than the news."

Maddox stretched his neck. "Do you want to tell me what's going on?"

She propped her feet up on the coffee table. "Not right now. Let's just have some fun."

26

Jada had fallen asleep. Maddox was enjoying having her snuggled up against him, could smell the scent of her hair under his chin and feel the slight weight of the hand placed possessively on his chest, when he caught Tobias watching him.

"You're happy, aren't you," he murmured.

Maddox nodded. Making love to Jada in those two frenzied encounters had been wonderful. He could never deny that, couldn't say flat out that he *preferred* this kind of evening. But there was a certain contentment that went with having her come over to spend some time with him, even if it didn't involve sex. He'd never thought this would happen, especially while Tobias was in town. He was almost afraid to trust it. In his mind, hanging out watching TV together in Silver Springs didn't come with the picture she'd painted of a "torrid affair." But he was glad it did.

She'd seemed happy herself. She'd been friendly to Tobias all evening, hadn't even mentioned her family. The three of them had played dominoes and watched *Saturday Night Live* and then put on a movie about a guy who was searching for artifacts in the jungles of Africa, which put her right to sleep.

Keeping his voice barely above a whisper, Tobias asked, "What do you think prompted her to come over? I mean… it was barely nine thirty when she got here. And she parked right behind you. It's not like she's trying to hide anything."

"I can only guess it was your apology." He smiled at his brother. "Thanks for that."

When Tobias smiled back, Maddox felt even better. That Jada would show up and treat him so well made a difference in his life, too.

The movie ended fifteen minutes later, so he nudged Jada. "Can you stay over?"

She blinked up at him.

"Jada?" He could tell she wasn't quite awake, but he loved the dreamy smile she gave him.

"What'd you say?"

"Can you stay over?"

She sobered as full consciousness descended. "No, not tonight. I have to get back to Tiffany's. Maya's there."

"Why are you both staying at Tiffany's?" he asked. "I hope it's just for fun…"

"No, I moved out of my mother's house on Monday."

He felt a moment of uncertainty. "Why?"

"I couldn't take it anymore."

"You weren't getting along?"

"No."

"Do you need a place to stay?"

Her grin slanted sideways. "Are you going to let me move in here—with the two of you?"

"If you don't have any other option."

She touched his face as if she believed him. "I've

got options. Tiff will let us stay there until I can find a place."

"Let me know if you need any help moving."

She got up and twisted her hair into a fresh knot at her nape. "I don't have much to move, but okay."

When she said good-night to Tobias, there was an awkward moment when they acted as though they didn't know whether to hug each other, but Jada must've decided that was going too far for their first night together because she gave him a little wave instead.

Maddox was happy that she'd been able to come over and treat him so kindly. He didn't expect anything more.

He took her hand as he walked her out. "Tonight was really great," he said.

They stopped at her car and she stood on her tiptoes to kiss him. "I think so, too."

"This wasn't really what I was expecting of a 'torrid affair,' but…"

She laughed. "You can have a little more 'torrid' at the beach."

"So we're still on?"

"Of course. But we'll have to put it off by one week, if that's okay. Now that I've moved, I have fewer options for Maya. She can stay with her best friend, but they won't be in town this weekend."

"That's fine. No problem." He kissed her again before reluctantly letting her go. "But it'll be tough to wait."

"For me, too," she said, but then she caught him before he could walk into the house. "Maddox?"

He turned around.

"Can you tell me one thing?"

"What's that?"

She lowered her voice. "What did Tobias do to get his sentence lengthened when he was in prison?"

He walked back to her. "Who told you about that?"

"My dad, before he died."

"He didn't know why?"

"Not yet. And if he found out, he died before he could tell me."

"I see." He shoved his hands into his pockets. "Well… it's like this. There's a hierarchy in prison, right? When you go in, you're tested to see where you're going to fall in that hierarchy. Will you be one of those who call the shots, or will you fall a little lower on the pecking order? When Tobias first went in, he had to face a prison full of much older men, most of them hardened criminals, and that meant he had to fight to avoid being victimized."

"So he got into a fight?"

"He got into a lot of fights. But not because he wanted to. There was this one dude who, for some reason, really had it out for him. He fixated on Tobias from the beginning. To this day, Tobias doesn't know why. But one afternoon, while they were exercising in the yard, he came at Tobias with a homemade knife—what they call a shank—and Tobias wrestled it away and stabbed him."

She couldn't help but grimace at the picture he painted. "So they both got in trouble."

"Not really. Tobias got the blame since the other guy was the one who nearly died, and there was this other inmate, a friend of the guy who got stabbed, who claimed Tobias started it."

She nodded. "Okay."

"I know that might make you afraid of him. But he had to defend himself to establish boundaries, and that cost him a few extra years. I hope you understand."

She thought it over, along with what she'd seen of Tobias when he apologized to Atticus and how he'd behaved tonight. "I do believe you," she said.

"So how was it?"

Maya was in the shower the following morning when Tiffany whispered that question to Jada.

Jada smiled as she stood at the stove, stirring the oatmeal she was making for breakfast. Tiffany insisted she didn't want breakfast, especially oatmeal, but she was making coffee. "Perfect," she whispered.

Tiffany moved closer to her. "It wasn't awkward to see Tobias?"

"A little. As handsome as he is, it would be easy to believe he's a decent guy simply because he looks the part. But I'm trying not to be that easily swayed by something that could mean nothing."

"Do you think he's more handsome than Maddox?" she asked in surprise.

"No one's more handsome than Maddox," Jada replied with a laugh. "But I could see where some women might disagree with me. Tobias is a bit rough around the edges, has that 'bad boy' look and feel, what with those prison tattoos and those mysterious green eyes. When he looks at you, you get the feeling there's so much going on inside his head, but he doesn't share much of what he's thinking."

"Did you get the impression it was hard for him to see you?"

"I could tell he didn't know what to do with himself. But he was very respectful. I had to insist he stay and relax because he kept wanting to leave so that Maddox and I could be alone."

"So you liked him."

Tiffany had a way of netting everything out. "I did," she admitted.

"Do you know what he did to get his sentence lengthened?"

"I do now. I asked Maddox last night. He told me it was because someone tried to jump him with a knife and ended up getting the worst of it."

"Do you believe him?"

"I do. But maybe that's because I *want* to give him another chance. Do you think I'm being too gullible?"

"If so, I'm just as gullible. That apology at the Blue Suede Shoe seemed pretty sincere. I could tell he was fighting tears."

"I got that impression, too. Still, I don't want to alienate my family any further by befriending him if he's not worth the sacrifice."

Tiffany poured her first cup of coffee. "I've been thinking about that."

"You sound worried."

"I am." She poured a second cup for Jada and set it by the stove. "Maybe I've been too encouraging when it comes to the Richardson brothers. I'm a soft touch, quick to forgive. But say you and Maddox get together and then it all blows up after a few months because you realize he's not the man you thought he was. Then you won't have your family *or* Maddox."

Jada listened to be sure the shower was still running and Maya couldn't overhear them. "On the other hand, I haven't been very close to my family for the past thirteen years. So it won't be all that new."

"Trust me, it'll be worse, because you can't just pick up and leave. Maya really likes it here. Maddox could even try to stop you from moving because it'll affect his visitation."

Jada slid the pan of oatmeal off the burner and turned off the stove. "But I've got to tell him, don't I? I was thinking about trying to do it when we go to the beach."

"No way." Tiffany shook her head. "Don't. It's too soon to even *begin* to guess how he might react."

"But the longer I go, the harder it's going to get."

"But if you tell him, your mother may never forgive you. The same goes for Maddox and Maya."

Jada winced as she thought of the possible consequences. The stakes were *so* high. "I'm not sure I care about my mother's reaction."

"You say that now, but come on. Family is family."

"They are the reason I'm in this mess. I'm beginning to wonder if I shouldn't have defied my parents from the start."

"You made the best decision you could at the time. You were only eighteen. Maddox wasn't ready to get married, couldn't have taken care of a family."

They heard the water go off, so Tiffany picked up her cup and headed over to the breakfast table. "Anyway, all I'm trying to say is that you've waited this long. A few more months can't make it any worse."

Jada wasn't sure she believed that. Every time she saw Maddox and didn't tell him, it felt like more of a betrayal. His feelings should matter, too. "We'll see," she said with a sigh.

Maya was sitting on the couch beside Jada, letting Tiffany paint her toenails that evening, when Jada got a text from Atticus.

You still mad?

Fortunately, Tiffany and Maya were engaged in a lively discussion about boys and school and the fact that New Horizons had cooking classes and horses and voice lessons. They didn't seem to be paying attention to Jada or her phone. Still, to be safe, she got up and went into the bathroom. She didn't want Maya to ask who was texting her or what Uncle Atticus was saying. She was trying not to talk about her family at all, because she didn't want to drag her daughter through the upset she was feeling.

Not mad. Fed up, she wrote back once she was alone.

Mom didn't mean what she said, Jada.

Of course she did. Maybe it's time we admit that. Bring it out in the open so she can vent her anger and resentment. Trying to bury it all these years hasn't done anything to improve the way she feels about me.

She's just going through a hard time.

So you're saying she needs a little forgiveness and understanding?

Yes.

You don't see the irony in that?

Stop. She didn't do what Tobias did.

Still, we all make mistakes. Some are just bigger than others.

She doesn't feel well most of the time, she just lost Dad and she's worried about me and whether or not I'll feel comfortable and succeed at my new job.

Maybe their mother needed to have a little more confidence in him, but Jada didn't have it in her to type that. For all the anger she felt, she didn't want to hurt her little brother. I'm not worried about you succeeding, Atticus. I know you'll do great. Anyway, I've tried to be sensitive to what Mom's going through. You saw how hard I was trying.

I know. You've helped her a lot more than I have. I'm sorry. I shouldn't have told her about Tobias. I'm not sure why I did. I knew it would upset her. It's just that I can't figure out how I should feel about him. Sometimes I want to strike back at him, and sometimes I feel like I should just let it go. What does it matter anymore? Things are what they are. People are crippled from accidents all the time, and no one is to blame. If I'd been crippled a different way, I'd still have to live like this.

He'll always feel guilty—even without you making him feel that way. That's the thing. He can't escape what he did regardless of how you feel.

You're saying I should try to make his life a little easier. Be the bigger person.

Do you think Tobias's apology was sincere?

It came across that way, I guess.

If it's easier to forgive him than continue to hold a grudge, you have your answer. No one could blame you if you can't forgive him, but maybe it would be better for YOU if you did.

Even if I could forgive him, Mom will never be able to.

Then she can wrestle with that baggage on her own. You're a full-grown man. You get to make your own decisions.

You make it sound so simple.

I know it's not.

She thinks you're still in love with Maddox.

How did she respond to this? Jada wished she could call him. It was hard texting such lengthy responses. But she was worried Maya might overhear her talking to him.

She might be right.

There. She'd done it. She'd told the truth, even put it in writing.

She held her breath as she stared at the ellipses that meant he was typing a response.

Holy shit. Really? After thirteen years?

Nothing has changed, Atticus.

That explains a lot.

I've done my best to leave him behind—as punishment for taking you to that party. But I'm not the only one I have to consider. What about Maya? What does SHE deserve?

Are you seeing him again? Is that why Tobias apologized to me?

I've seen Maddox a couple of times. But that had nothing to do with what Tobias did. His apology took me as much by surprise as it did you, and I suspect that's true for Maddox, too.

If you get together with Maddox...

She waited but he didn't finish that sentence, so she prodded him. What?

I don't know what I'll do. I can't imagine him as part of my family.

He's not a bad person, Atticus. I don't even think his brother is.

Can you give Mom a few months? Don't do this to her right now.

Will things be any different later? It's been thirteen years. When will Maya get to meet her father?

When are you going to tell him he has a daughter?

I don't know yet, but I hope to do it pretty soon.

She waited for his response to that, but when she didn't receive one, she typed a question mark and sent it.

You're gambling a lot on this guy, he finally wrote. Let's hope you're right and not Mom.

"Amen," she whispered.

Her family was falling apart, and, once again, the Richardson brothers were to blame.

Susan stared out the front windshield, a death grip on the steering wheel, as she raced over to Uriah's tangerine orchard. She had a few things to say to Maddox and Tobias, and she didn't care whether they liked it. Maybe if she'd been stronger and drawn a hard line when Jada first started dating Maddox thirteen years ago, a boy with his background and absolutely nothing to offer, instead of trying to be tolerant and flexible, Atticus would still have the use of his legs. She didn't want to face the same kind of regret for not standing up and fighting harder to protect her family this time around.

Her phone buzzed, drawing her attention to where it lay on the console between the seats of her older-model Lexus, but she made no move to reach for it. Her son's face and number had popped up, were now glowing as brightly as her instrument panel in the dark interior, so she knew who it was. She would've been able to guess even if she couldn't see her phone. Atticus had been calling her nonstop since she'd stormed out of the house after she'd arrived home, already tired from work and still angry from the argument she'd had with Jada three days ago, to hear that he was going to pay Maddox and Tobias a visit sometime in the next few days, as soon as he could gather the nerve, and tell them that he forgave them both. Although he'd broken into tears as he spoke those words, said he was glad they'd come back to Silver Springs because it was forcing him to face his anger and resentment, which he felt he had to overcome if he was ever to move on and be truly happy, she didn't buy it. No doubt Jada had put him up to what he was doing. She must've been crying on his shoulder, trying to elicit sympathy. And he was softhearted enough for it to work. He didn't understand the domino effect forgiving Maddox and Tobias would have on the future for all of them.

"You're not getting her back," she muttered to Maddox, even though she hadn't yet reached his house. She wouldn't allow her daughter to be with someone who'd cost her family so much, not under any circumstances.

The ringing of her phone stopped and started up again. Atticus. He wouldn't give up.

Finally, just as she reached the edge of town, she answered. "What is it?" she snapped.

"What are you doing? Where are you going?"

"That's none of your business." She squinted against the lights of oncoming traffic. She didn't have the energy for this kind of emotional turmoil. It had been so busy at the shop today that, even with Atticus there to help her, she'd worked nearly twelve hours. Now she ached all over. Getting stressed and exhausted caused her lupus to flare up. She hadn't been doing well since Jada moved out. But she couldn't let that stop her tonight. She had to act fast, or this thing would get too far ahead of her.

"Mom, please don't do anything that will hurt Jada."

"*Hurt* Jada! I'm trying to protect her. Maya, too."

"By making it impossible for Jada to be with Maddox? How will that help?"

"Do you know what kind of mother he comes from? She's part of the reason his brother's an ex-con! Do you really want your sister to be associated with people like that? Do you want Maya's *father* to be someone like that? Her grandmother a drug addict, and her uncle a dangerous ex-con—the man who *shot* you? Think of *her*, for crying out loud!"

"I am thinking of her. So is Jada. Maddox isn't his mother or his brother. You have to judge him in his own right."

"Yeah, well, he got your sister pregnant at seventeen years old. It's because of him she married Eric and was so unhappy. It's because of him she doesn't have an education. And it's because of him, taking her to parties where drugs and alcohol were present, that you can't walk!"

"Mom, if you're going to Maddox's house, please stop. I feel bad for him and Jada. If they still love each other, they deserve the chance to be together—regardless of the rest of us."

"Two people who are responsible for what they did don't deserve *anything.*"

"Mom, listen to me! Just…*don't!*" he said, and then she hung up. The way he was speaking to her—so demanding, as if there'd be an "or else" attached if she continued the conversation—wasn't something she would tolerate. She'd been so good to him, nursed him through his injury and waited on him hand and foot ever since. She deserved more loyalty than he was showing her. That was for damn sure.

"See what's happening?" she mumbled, smacking her steering wheel. "Those bastards are already tearing us apart again."

She fishtailed as she pulled into the drive; she was going too fast when the turn came up. But she managed to bring the car under control before slamming on the brakes, cutting the engine and jumping out. Thanks to the rich earth and so many trees, the air just outside of town felt ten degrees cooler. She was glad of that; she was so upset she was damp with sweat.

The rap of her knock seemed to echo against the starry sky overhead. She was breathing heavily as she waited, completely focused on the fight ahead, but she could still hear the croak of a frog nearby and smell the fecund scent of the orchard all around her.

The door opened and an adult Tobias filled the gap. She hadn't seen him since his trial, but she'd spent every day in the courtroom, and she'd read a statement before the judge, asking for the maximum sentence when it was all over. So she knew he knew who she was.

He didn't speak. An expression of resolution, which indicated he thought it might one day come to this, stole over his face. He didn't shut the door, either. He stood there expectantly. Although she could sense that he was wary, there was a respectful, deferential air about him, too. That almost disarmed her. But then she thought about the likelihood of Jada coming forward to tell Maddox Maya was his daughter, of being forever tied to these people who'd cost her so much, if she didn't do something, and felt her resolve return. "Get your brother," she bit out. "I have something to say to the both of you."

"Maddox didn't have anything to do with what happened. If you're here to take some form of retribution, I'm the one you want," he said, stepping outside and closing the door behind him.

"Get Maddox," she said again. "I want to speak to him, too."

"He never did anything wrong."

Everyone seemed so ready to stand up for him. But

she blamed Maddox for what happened even more than Tobias. After all, it was *his* involvement with Jada that'd started the whole thing. He'd also left Jada pregnant at seventeen, which had derailed *her* life, too. "According to you, maybe."

Tobias had seemed so tractable, so penitent, in those first few seconds that it surprised her when he shook his head. "No. If you have something to say, you need to say it to me and leave him out of it. I'm the one who deserves it."

Something inside her snapped. Susan wasn't sure exactly what she said next, but she started screaming and crying and, for the first time in her life, physically attacking someone. She raked her fingernails down his cheeks and hit him wherever she could. She even kicked him.

He never reacted, never even put up his hands to block her. The only thing he did was move to keep her from reaching the door when she'd try to go around him to get to Maddox.

"This is between us," he'd say, his voice soft, calm, but stubborn.

The door opened, anyway, and, finally, there stood Maddox.

"What's going on?" He looked from her to Tobias and back again.

She'd hurt her hand striking his brother, and she was already so exhausted she could barely stand, but she gave Maddox the most baleful glare she could summon. "You leave my daughter alone. I won't allow a piece of trash like you to ruin her life again. Do you understand me? Stay away from her. Don't you come near my granddaughter, either! I know you're probably already trying to get back in Jada's pants, you miserable, worthless—"

"Whoa, whoa!" she heard someone say and turned to see Uriah. She'd been making such a racket that he'd heard the fracas and come out of his house. "You need to get off my property, *now*, or I'm going to call the police."

"On *me*?" She pointed helplessly at Maddox and Tobias. It was *them* who had to go. But then she saw the situation through Uriah's eyes—Maddox and Tobias standing there, Tobias's handsome face bleeding because of how deeply she'd scratched him—and knew it was obvious that neither one of them had so much as lifted their voices or put up a hand to stop her, let alone *harm* her.

"Yes, *you*," Uriah said. "I'm sorry for what you've been through, Mrs. Brooks. I'm sorry for your boy, too. But this isn't the way to handle it. Here, let me help you to your car."

He reached out to take her hand and guide her back over the gravel road, but she refused to let him. She wiped her tears and shook a finger at the Richardson brothers. "You two leave my family alone," she said. "You've done enough. Do you hear me? We don't need you back in our lives, messing it up all over again. What are you *thinking*? Even if you get Jada back, she could never truly be happy without her family. Especially with the family *you* have to offer her!"

"I said, that's enough," Uriah told her, and this time he took firm hold of her arm and escorted her to the car and was unwilling to let go until she was behind the wheel.

"Don't ever come back," he said and shut the door.

27

"Are you okay?" Maddox asked his brother in the silence that ensued after Jada's mom tore down their drive and nearly hit another vehicle trying to get off the property.

Tobias wiped the blood from his face with his T-shirt. "Yeah."

Uriah's feet crunched through the gravel as he walked back toward them. "I never expected that kind of behavior from her," he said, sounding awed.

"She had the right to do a lot worse," Tobias said.

"Let's go up to the house. I'll get some disinfectant to put on that." Uriah tried to catch Tobias's chin so that he could look at the scratches on his face, but Tobias shook him off.

"I'm fine. It's nothing. She's an old lady. Didn't even hurt."

Maybe the pain wasn't substantial enough for him to show it, but he was upset. Maddox knew him well enough to be able to tell.

"I'm sorry you had to get involved," Tobias told Uriah.

"Are you kidding? I'm glad I was here to stop it. Didn't look as though the pair of you were going to do anything."

Tobias shrugged. "Like I said, I deserved it," he said and turned to go inside, leaving Maddox and Uriah to follow him.

"What are you doing?" Maddox asked, watching as his brother shoved what few belongings he owned into an old army-green duffel bag.

"Getting out of here."

Maddox exchanged a look with Uriah before stepping closer to his brother. "What do you mean?"

"I'm leaving, clearing out of this town. I don't want to keep causing you and Uriah trouble."

"You're not," Uriah said. "She's the one who caused the trouble. Besides, you have a job here. I need you."

Tobias laughed bitterly. "You don't need me. Be honest. You gave me a job out of pity. Truth is, I'm a pain in the ass to *everyone*. And I hate that."

"Where will you go?" Maddox asked.

"Mom's, for now. She needs someone to help keep her life in order. She can't seem to manage it herself."

"Mom's fine. She's home recuperating from the accident." She'd have to appear in court to pay for what she'd done, but that had no bearing on this.

"I'd rather you stay," Uriah said. "I admit I was trying to help you when I gave you a job, but the truth is, you've been a hard worker and worth every penny. I don't want to lose you."

"And you're not ready to live with Mom, Tobias," Maddox chimed in. "I don't know if you'll ever be. She's got her life so messed up it can't help but impact everyone around her."

He pulled the drawstrings tight and slung the duffel over his shoulder. "Yeah, well, we have to be there for each other."

"She won't be there for you. That's the point."

Tobias whirled on him. "Maddox, I've seen how much Jada means to you. You'll have a better chance with her if I get out of the picture, and that's what I'm going to do."

Maddox was beginning to think he was a fool to even hope for a relationship with Jada. Did he really want to take her away from her family? As he'd told her before, he didn't have much to offer her, not when he was carrying so much extra baggage from his own family. "I was stupid to get involved with Jada again, Tobias. Stay." He tried to grab the duffel, but Tobias shifted so he couldn't reach it.

"No, man. I'm done. I need to find my own way and quit leaning on you."

"That isn't true," Maddox argued.

"It is." His eyebrows jerked together over stormy eyes as he turned to Uriah. "I appreciate all you've done for me. I really do. But if I don't get out of here, I'll screw up Maddox's job and everything else he's got going. At first I didn't think that was a big deal—his job, I mean. I figured there had to be something he could do in LA that would pay the same or more, and then we could hang out together. But now that I see what's really at risk, I don't want to blow things for him again."

Uriah didn't seem happy to hear what Tobias was saying, but he nodded as though he understood why he was doing it. Maybe he even admired it.

"Tobias, stop," Maddox said. "Who knows if anything serious will ever happen between me and Jada?"

"It's already happening. Last night when she came over here and hung out with us… I've never seen you look at a woman the way you look at her."

"Stop. You heard her mother. I don't have a chance.

The Brookses will never accept me, and I can't pull her away from the people who love her." Any more than he could abandon the ones who loved him. "If you want to leave, give me a couple of weeks. I'll put in my notice and move with you."

Tobias edged past Uriah to reach the door. "That would be a mistake, Maddox. I say you fight for her. *I* would. Don't let anything get in your way," he said and walked out.

"What are you going to do?" Uriah asked Maddox, obviously worried.

Maddox shook his head. "There's nothing I can do."

Throwing up his hands as if that wasn't an answer he liked, Uriah stuck his head out the door and into the night. "At least let one of us give you a ride!" he called after Tobias, but Maddox caught sight of the back of Tobias just as he waved them off.

Maddox didn't sleep at all that night. His brother had made it to their mother's house around four in the morning, after hitchhiking for seven hours, but the echo of Jada's mother's words kept cycling through his head: *I won't allow a piece of trash like you to ruin her life again. Piece of trash... Piece of trash... Piece of trash...*

He had a decision to make, and he couldn't procrastinate it any longer. Did he do what was best for Tobias and his mother and get a job in LA, so he could look after them both? Walk away from Silver Springs and leave the Brookses in peace?

Or did he continue to fight public opinion and the Brookses' negative energy in order to keep the job he loved, with the hope that he might be able to get back with Jada in spite of her mother and brother?

Jada was what he wanted. She was what he'd always wanted. But after last night, it didn't seem very realistic to believe they could be happy together, not with both families pulling them apart. Staying in Silver Springs was the selfish option, the one where he ignored what everyone else needed and reached for what mattered most to *him*.

It was early the next morning when he went into work. He'd reached a decision, but it was probably the hardest decision he'd ever had to make.

"You're here early."

He glanced up at the sound of Aiyana's voice. He'd sent her a text before leaving the house to say he needed to talk to her at her earliest convenience, but he hadn't expected her to walk over as soon as she arrived at work. It was barely eight.

"What's going on? Why are you packing up?" She approached the desk wearing a look that said *This had better not be what I think it is.* "Don't tell me you're quitting. School starts in only two weeks."

"I know. I'm sorry," he said. "I should've realized this wasn't going to work from the beginning. With my brother getting out of prison, and my mother being... well, the person she is, I think I knew, deep down. I just wanted another answer, felt like I could force the issue."

She propped her fists on her hips. "You *can* force it. It's *your* decision, Maddox. You can have whatever you demand out of life."

"You've taught me that, yes. And I believe it. But at what cost? After Jada's mom came to my house last night, I realized—"

"Wait! Susan showed up at your house?"

"She did."

"What did she want?"

"What do you think she wanted?"

"Oh boy. How ugly did it get?"

"*Ugly.* She attacked Tobias. Yelling. Screaming. Hitting. Scratching. Kicking."

A frown tugged at her lips. "Was he hurt?"

"Fortunately, she wasn't strong enough to do much more than gouge his face. But the physical part wasn't the worst of it. It was more what she said. Her fury came across as downright *hate*, and it hit him like a right hook at the worst possible time, just as he was starting to feel a little better about himself after apologizing to Atticus."

"I'm sorry that happened."

Maddox put the plant she'd gifted him his first day of work into one of the boxes he was using to move out. "So am I. Tobias walked off right afterward. Hitchhiked to LA."

"Have you heard from him since? Is he okay?"

He could hear the concern in her voice. "Yeah. He's at our mom's. I don't feel he can stay there for long, though. If I don't do something to help him, I may regret it for the rest of my life. It's one of those things where you have to get in early if you're going to have any impact at all."

"I respect the decision you're making and, somehow, I'll get by without you if I have to. People should come first, before a job, before anything else. But what about Jada? I was under the impression there was still a spark between you two."

He stopped packing and rocked back in his chair. "There's more than a spark," he admitted. "At least on my side. But I can't expect her to turn her back on her family. After last night, I know they'll never accept me— not that I had a lot of hope to begin with but that sort of cemented it. You should've seen her mother. Susan would never forgive Jada if she chose me, and that's a choice I won't ask the woman I care about to make—*ever*. Besides, Jada's got a daughter, so whatever we do will impact her." He got up and started loading his books into the box. "It's just smarter to look down the road a bit and realize that it isn't going to work between us—before our hearts get smashed trying to force the issue."

"I hear what you're saying. And I'm supportive, to a point, since I care about Tobias and your mother. But..."

"But?"

"There are *other* considerations."

"I'll do all I can to help you backfill my position. I worked with someone in Utah who might be interested. He'd be a good choice. And since it could take a while to bring him or someone else up to speed, I'll commute, if necessary, once school starts. I'll make sure you've got the support you need."

"Eli and I can share the load until we find someone else. I'm not talking about the job."

He felt his eyebrows pull together. "What, then?"

She rubbed her forehead. "I'm not at liberty to say."

He couldn't imagine what she was referring to. "There's something you can't tell me?"

"This situation is so difficult," she muttered.

She was talking to herself, but he responded, anyway. "It is. But you're not *directly* involved in it, are you?"

"No. That's part of the problem. Then I'd feel more comfortable voicing my opinion. Just do me one favor..."

"I'll do anything I can. You know I love you like a mother—and that I respect you a great deal more than my real mother."

"You are a wonderful man, Maddox. You deserve to

be happy, and I want that for you so badly. Please promise me you won't leave without speaking to Jada first."

"I would promise that in a heartbeat, if I felt it would do any good. But if I hear her voice, I might change my mind, and where would that leave everyone else, including her?"

"Come on, Maddox. Trust me on this."

"I can't," he said.

Leaving was difficult enough.

Jada hadn't talked to Maddox or even texted with him since she'd been to his house. With Annie and her family out of town visiting grandparents, Maya was home all the time, so Jada had much less privacy than normal. Since she wasn't going to the store anymore, she'd been catching up on her own business and spending all the rest of her time with her daughter, looking for a small rental house, going back-to-school shopping and purchasing books and other supplies.

She wasn't too concerned that she and Maddox weren't communicating like before, though. The evening she'd spent with him and Tobias had gone so well. When she'd left, she'd felt hopeful, even excited, about their relationship, and she was looking forward to spending an entire weekend with him. She figured he was staying out of the way so she could get situated and ready for their trip, which was why the text he sent her on Monday morning took her by complete surprise.

I'm so sorry, Jada. I won't be able to spend the weekend with you. I don't think we've been looking at our situation objectively, and I'm afraid if we don't start, someone is going to get hurt. I want you to know that my feelings for you have always been sincere. And if I could change anything so that we could still see each other, I would. But I won't ask you to choose me over your family. I can't imagine you could be happy like that for long. And I won't saddle you with MY family and their problems. They have no one else to help them get through life, and they don't seem capable of doing it on their own, so I've quit my job and will be moving closer to them. I hope you'll forgive me for being so willing to jump into what we had before, when we can't finish it, yet again. I will never forget you and, to be honest, I doubt I will ever love another woman as much.

A terrible pain radiated through Jada's chest. This was goodbye. And yet he'd barely come back into her life, after she'd missed him and longed for him for *thirteen years*, after she'd learned that no one else would do.

She felt sick, crushed beneath the weight of this sudden reversal. Since she'd moved out of her mother's, she'd been on top of the world—and that was a long way to fall.

After checking to be sure Maya was still asleep on the air mattress on the floor, she kicked off the blankets on the couch where she'd been sleeping and slipped into Tiffany's room, which she had to go through in order to reach the bathroom. Once she was safely inside, she closed and locked the door, then leaned up against it. What had happened? What was going on?

Drawing several deep breaths to stave off the sudden shakiness in her knees, she pushed off the door and sat on the closed lid of the toilet. Why are you doing this?

She waited for what seemed like an eternity, but received no reply, so she tried to call him.

"This is Maddox Richardson. I'm unavailable at the

moment. Leave your name and number and a message, if you'd like, and I'll get back to you as soon as I can."

She cleared her throat in preparation for the beep. "Maddox? It's Jada. Please call me."

She hung up and waited for another fifteen minutes— to no avail. She had a terrible feeling that he'd said what he needed to say and was now cutting her off and moving on.

But it was all so sudden. What had triggered this? Was this about his job, his brother, his mother, *her*?

She had no idea. She figured he'd have to give two weeks' notice at the school, though. He couldn't leave Silver Springs *immediately*.

That brought her a modicum of comfort. She'd have the chance to talk to him. She'd take Maya over to spend some time with Atticus—her mother would be at the store soon, so they wouldn't even have to see each other—and drive to New Horizons. Maddox would *have* to deal with her if she was standing in his office.

She pressed the contact record on her phone that would call her brother.

"Hey," he said, his voice raspy with sleep.

It was almost nine, but they were all enjoying staying up late and sleeping in these last few days before school started. "Sorry to wake you," she said. "But is there any chance you're going to be around this morning? I was hoping to drop Maya off with you for an hour or so. There's something I have to do."

"What is it?"

Since she'd already admitted that she had feelings for Maddox, she decided to be transparent. "I need to talk to Maddox. Something's wrong."

"It doesn't have anything to do with Mom does it?"

Her heart skipped a beat. "What do you mean?"

"We had an...*incident* last Thursday."

"What kind of incident?"

"I told her I was going to pay Tobias and Maddox a visit so I could let them know that I forgive them both for what happened, and she freaked out."

She gripped her phone tighter. "What, exactly, did that entail?"

"I believe she went over to Maddox's house. And I can't say for sure, but I'm guessing it didn't go well. When she came home, her face was puffy from tears and her hand was swelling up."

"Her *hand*? She didn't tell you how she hurt it, did she?"

"If *they'd* injured it, I'm sure I would've heard all about it. She would've called you, too, to tell you how rotten they are. Or she would've just called the police. She had to have been the one at fault. I asked her if she'd hit someone or something, but she wouldn't speak to me at all. Went straight to her room and slammed the door, and when I tried to talk to her, she told me to go away."

Jada came to her feet. "Did she get up and go to the store the next morning?"

"No. Didn't feel up to it. I told her I'd go in for her, but she wouldn't hear of it. She told me to leave the Closed sign in the window."

"And you didn't tell me?"

"I've been trying to let you cut free, Jada. To live your life."

"I appreciate that, but..." She stared at her unhappy face in the bathroom mirror. "What's happened since then? Is her hand okay? Has she mentioned how she hurt it?"

"Her hand is fine. She went back to work yesterday. But she still won't talk about that night."

"So she'll be going to the store today?"

"I assume she's already left. I heard the front door a few minutes ago. I think everything's okay, that it's going to blow over."

She battled the lump in her throat that threatened to choke her. "It's *not* going to blow over, Atticus. Maddox is quitting his job and moving away."

"But I thought he really wanted that job. New Horizons is the whole reason he came to town."

"It is." And then she'd been there, and he'd begun to want something else. That was what had really chased him away.

Atticus whistled. "Mom must've really let loose."

Jada had no doubt about it. For thirteen years, Susan had been dying for the chance to let the Richardson brothers have it. "Can I bring Maya over?"

"Of course. I'll be here."

"I'll see you in an hour."

There was no one in the office. As a matter of fact, the entire administration building on the girls' side was locked and dark. Jada jiggled the door handle before shading her eyes so she could peer out across the deserted campus. Surely, Maddox hadn't left town yet. She'd just received that text from him this morning!

Finally, she spotted a woman hugging some books to her chest and hurrying toward the parking lot.

"Excuse me!" she called.

The woman's head came up and she stopped. "Yes?"

Jada jogged over to her. "Can you tell me where I can find Mr. Richardson, please?"

She pursed her lips in apparent disappointment. "I'm afraid he no longer works here, which is sad. I liked him, thought he was going to do a great job."

"What happened? Do you know?"

"Something came up, something to do with his family. From what I've heard, he'll be living in LA." She shifted her books to her left arm so that she could gesture with her right. "Aiyana should be able to tell you more. You can find her at the building just beyond that gate right there."

Jada felt numb. Maddox was *gone*? *Already?* "Thank you," she mumbled and forced her feet to carry her to the boys' side.

There was a lot more activity here. Jada could see students walking in clumps, laughing and talking and roughhousing as they carried backpacks and responded to teachers who were shepherding them to various places.

Jada could hear the fan of the air conditioner as she stepped inside the administration building, and she could feel its cooling effects, but instead of relief from the heat, she felt chilled.

"Can I help you?"

The heavyset woman sitting at the receptionist station had spotted her.

"Yes. I was hoping to speak with Aiyana."

"I'm pretty sure she's out on campus, but let me check." She walked back, took a peek inside the corner office and immediately returned. "I'm afraid she's not in. If you'd like to sit down, she should be back in a few minutes."

Jada was wrestling with too much anxiety to be able to sit down. "I'll wait outside."

She looked appalled. "In this heat?"

"There's some shade by the building."

"If that's what you prefer."

Once she was back outside, she looked up the number for Honey Hollow Tangerine Orchard on her phone. If she couldn't talk to Aiyana, maybe Uriah could tell her something...

She was afraid he'd have only a land-based phone that would go unanswered because he was out in the orchard. She knew he was getting old, wasn't sure how well he'd adapted to new technology. Her mother was a lot younger than he was and still wasn't particularly conversant. But he picked up on the third ring. "Mr. Lamb?"

"Yes?"

"This is Jada Brooks."

There was a slight pause. Then he said, "Hello, Ms. Brooks," almost as if he'd been expecting her call.

"I've...uh...I've been trying to reach Maddox. You wouldn't happen to know where he is right now, would you?"

"In LA somewhere."

Her stomach muscles tightened. "Will he be coming back?"

"Not according to him."

"He's moved out?"

"After your mother came by Thursday night, Tobias walked off and wouldn't come back. Maddox quit his job and packed his things shortly after."

She dropped her head back and closed her eyes. *No...* "I see. What did my mother say? Do you know?"

"I didn't hear it all. I didn't even know she was on the property until I heard screaming and came out to find her clawing at Tobias's face and neck."

Her eyes snapped open as she covered her mouth.

"Ms. Brooks, are you still there?"

"Yes," she said, dropping her hand. "Just trying to come to terms with it."

"I'm sorry."

"So am I. Can you…can you give me Tobias's number?"

Again, there was a pause.

"Please?"

"I care about that young man and his brother."

"So do I."

"Then just a minute," he said.

She put him on speaker and punched the digits into her phone as he rattled them off, but as soon as she hung up with Uriah, she saw Aiyana coming toward her.

"Jada, it's good to see you." Aiyana seemed as welcoming as ever. "I've been tempted to call you but didn't want to overreach."

"You mean about Maddox."

"Yes."

"I can't believe he's gone. He didn't even tell me he was going to move. I got a text from him this morning and…that was it. He won't respond to me now." She wasn't sure why she was revealing so much, but the words were tumbling out faster than she could stop them.

Aiyana touched her arm. "Would you like to come into my office?"

Jada glanced reluctantly at the door. She would welcome the privacy but hated to walk past the other people who worked there when she was so emotional. "No, I was hoping you could tell me where he went, but I just talked to Uriah, who told me he's in LA. So there's no need for me to waste your time."

Aiyana glanced around as though she was making sure no one could overhear what she was about to say.

"I tried to get him to call you first, to discuss what he was going to do, but he's so stubborn. Once he decided the two of you didn't have a chance, he wouldn't listen to anything. I knew there was only one thing that could stop him, but I didn't feel as though it was my place to speak up. That should come from you."

Jada blinked in surprise. "*What* should come from me?"

"Maya paid me a visit not long ago, Jada, asking if I once knew her father. I thought she was referring to your ex-husband, of course, but she wasn't. She told me her real father was named Madsen, and he died in a motor-cycle accident here in Silver Springs before she was born."

Jada caught her breath.

"But that isn't true, is it?"

Panic shot through her like a lightning bolt, weakening her knees. Aiyana knew her most carefully guarded secret. "You didn't tell her…" she gasped.

"Of course not. I didn't tell *him*, either, although I wanted to. It's dangerous to meddle in other people's lives. I wouldn't want to be responsible for setting something in motion I might live to regret—or, rather, *you* might live to regret. You're facing a very difficult decision. And I can't pretend that the answer I want you to choose is the right one." She lowered her voice but spoke with even more conviction. "But I *can* tell you this—if you love him, if you want him back, you have to give him a reason to fight for you and what the two of you could have together, a reason to believe you might choose him this time around."

"You're saying Maya is that reason."

"Yes."

Jada's heart was pounding so hard it was difficult to

get enough air. "But I'm not ready to tell him. I don't know him all that well, not these days. Maybe we've both changed too much since…since before."

"That's a possibility," she allowed.

"What if I tell him and the challenges we face are still too difficult to overcome?"

"There's no way to predict what would make you the happiest. Life is so uncertain. I can only say that a love like what I believe he feels for you doesn't come around often. And although your mother would disagree with me, it's not easy to find a man as worthy as Maddox. *I* believe he's worth the risk. The question is, do you?"

28

"You're quiet tonight," Tiffany said as Jada sat on the couch, her feet propped up on the coffee table, her computer in her lap.

"Just trying to get a few things done," Jada said, but she hadn't been able to concentrate well enough to work. She'd been watching Maya throughout the day, listening to her excitement over school, hearing her talk to Annie on the phone and thinking about the fact that her daughter had gone to the trouble of visiting Aiyana to see if Aiyana could tell her anything about her father. That took a great deal of desire and effort for a child who would be turning thirteen at the end of the month. Obviously, Maya was sincere in her desire to learn more about the man whose DNA she possessed, was searching for the truth, and Jada wanted to give it to her.

But then what? Would telling Maya about Maddox and everything that'd happened at that party, where so many lives had been changed, make things better—or worse?

She knew her mother wouldn't like it. But Atticus wouldn't mind. How he'd behaved today, taking Maya so she could go look for Maddox, told her as much. He finally seemed to be thinking for himself, establishing some independence. He'd even told their mother he was willing to forgive Tobias and Maddox. *He* was ready to let go of the past, and if he could do that, they should be able to, as well.

Her phone rang. She nearly dropped it as she hurried to snatch it off the coffee table by her feet. She hoped Maddox was finally responding to her attempts to reach him.

It wasn't him; it was Atticus.

"So?" her brother said when she answered.

She tucked her legs underneath her. "So…what?" she asked in confusion.

"What happened with Maddox? I didn't want to say anything in front of Maya when you came to get her this morning, and I haven't texted for fear she'd see it, but you haven't given anything away, and I'm getting tired of waiting. What's the deal?"

"Just a sec." She acted as though the TV was too loud, that she was going into the bedroom so she could hear. Tiffany's gaze followed her; *she'd* probably surmised that the TV had very little to do with it. But Maya didn't catch on. She barely glanced up as Jada slipped into the bedroom and closed the door.

"He wasn't there, Atticus. He quit his job on Friday, has already left Silver Springs."

"Because of Mom…"

"The timing suggests she figured into the decision. But there were probably other things."

"Me?"

"Maybe—as well as some problems he's dealing with when it comes to his own brother and mother."

"So what are you going to do?"

She switched the phone to her other ear. "I don't know."

"What do you mean? You're not going to give him up again, are you?"

"There's a lot to consider…"

"Maybe you should *consider* making it work this time, going all out, giving it everything you've got and holding nothing back, no matter who likes it."

Those words were empowering. She felt a flutter of excitement as she embraced them—and Aiyana's question came back to her: *I believe he's worth the risk. Do you?*

Jada did, but she couldn't bear to hurt her family again. "Mom will cut me off. Did you tell her what I told you about the reason they lengthened Tobias's sentence?"

"I tried."

"But…"

"It didn't do any good."

"Then I doubt we'll ever be able to get beyond it."

"If that's the case, it's her decision. It's not on you."

"Do you think I should try to talk to her?"

"I wouldn't. Like I said, it did me no good."

"So I should just…go after what I want?"

"Yes! Don't let what she might think cost you the happiness you could have."

"Do you mean that?" she asked in surprise.

"It's taken me some time to get to this point, but… yeah, I mean it. I do. I don't want to see you live without the man you love."

"But will it be too difficult for you to know I'm with him? To see us together?"

"It will be *more* difficult knowing you don't have what you want—and Maya doesn't have the father she could have—because of something in the past that has already cost us all too much."

Her heart began to race as she moved to the window and stared out at what she could see via moonlight in

Tiffany's backyard. "But it's too late. He won't return any of my texts or calls."

"There's got to be some way to reach him, to tell him that this time you choose *him*."

"Aiyana can probably get a message to him," she said. "And I have Tobias's number."

"Call Tobias. Ask him where you can find Maddox and go there and talk to him."

"It'll mean telling him about Maya…"

"I think it's time. Don't you?"

"I do," she admitted.

"Then what are you doing still on the phone? Don't you need to be somewhere?"

"Thank you, Atticus. Thank you for loving me enough to forgive me—and him."

"I have to admit it feels good," he said. "If you need me to watch Maya, I'm here."

"I'll accept that offer since the Coateses aren't back yet. I won't take her with me in case he doesn't react well. I don't want her to be hurt if he doesn't seem as excited as she'd want him to be."

"It's smart to give him a chance to come to grips with the surprise first."

"Okay, I'll see if Tobias will help me find him. And if so, I'll bring her by."

"Like I said, I'm here. Mom won't mind if she stays over. She hates that you both moved out."

"She has only herself to blame, but thanks again. You are *so* awesome."

"I know," he said, and they both laughed.

Maddox had always loved the ocean. The sheer dwarfing size of it, the soothing, steady rhythm of the waves, the awesome power it possessed—to sustain life, to take life. Growing up, he and Tobias would drive to the beach all the time; when their mother had men over, sometimes they'd sleep on the sand. He'd always dreamed of owning a home on the coast, so it made sense for him to stay in the small, private cottage he'd rented for the weekend, even though Jada wouldn't be joining him. He'd paid for it, after all, figured he might as well use the time and the privacy to come to grips with all the recent changes in his life. Tobias was spending the weekend with Tonya. She'd been calling him, pleading with him to give her another chance, and he felt obligated to do that, since she'd made his last year in prison so much better than it would've been otherwise. Maddox didn't expect it to work out. Even Tobias wasn't optimistic, but it got Tobias out of their mother's house for a couple of days, doing something that would be, hopefully, fun and engaging, and that allowed Maddox to take a couple of days for himself.

Lord knew he needed the solitude. Walking away from Jada hadn't been easy. She'd texted him a few times, tried to call. But he had to ignore her attempts to reach him. Otherwise, he was afraid he'd give in and see her again, and then it would only get harder from there.

"Better to get it over with in one painful blow," he mumbled as he walked along the shore, picking up seashells and tossing them back into the surf. He saw two lovers holding hands as they waded in the water, and smiled. They were so engrossed in each other they didn't even know he was around, didn't care, either. Being with Jada had been that effortless, that fulfilling, which just went to show he'd made the right decision where Paris was concerned. A mate shouldn't be a chore, an obligation, someone he had to grit his teeth to tolerate. He understood that much better now, hadn't even realized he'd been compromising to such a degree. So maybe he was disappointed that his stint in Silver Springs hadn't worked out the way he'd hoped, but at least now he knew that the love he'd shared with Jada wasn't just something he was remembering through rose-colored glasses.

It was real.

Whether he'd be able to get over her so he could devote himself to someone else was another question. Since he hadn't been able to accomplish that in thirteen years, he figured he might have a long journey ahead.

The sun was sinking below the horizon when he sat down and watched the gulls above him swoop down every now and then to snatch a tidbit off the beach. He'd found a rehab center for his mother, but it was going to cost a fortune, and he'd have to pay her share of the rent on her house while she was in recovery, which meant he had to get another job *fast*.

He hated that he wouldn't be at New Horizons when it opened. He was confident he'd built a great staff, one that could really make a difference to the students they had coming in the fall, which had turned out to be 284, at last count. They had room for 550, but Aiyana wouldn't have any trouble maxing out once word began to spread—

A sound caused him to lift his head. He thought he'd heard his name, but he didn't see anyone nearby. He checked his phone. No activity. He was just sliding it back into his pocket when he saw a figure walking toward him from the direction of the house he'd rented. At first, he thought it was just a random stranger coming out to enjoy the sunset, but something about this woman looked familiar.

Then he heard his name again and realized she *was* familiar. It was Jada. Somehow, she'd figured out where he was and come.

His heart leaped into his throat as she closed the distance between them. Despite everything, all the self-talk about letting her go and doing the right thing for both of them, he was glad to see her. Maybe they could enjoy the weekend together, after all, even if it meant they were only procrastinating the inevitable. Pain was pain. He supposed it could wait.

He got up and started toward her, saw the beautiful smile on her face and smiled in return. "How'd you find me?" he asked when they came together.

She didn't answer. She walked right into his arms and held him so tightly he thought he had to be dreaming. "Here you are," she said as if his embrace was the most comforting thing on earth.

He brought his hand up and pressed her even tighter to him, and when he finally released his hold and leaned back to look into her face, he saw she looked happy but nervous.

"What is it?" he asked.

"I love you," she replied. "I can't live without you."

He caught her hair in one hand to keep it from whipping around them in the breeze. *"Do you mean that?"*

"I never *stopped* loving you."

"But what about your family? Your mother and Atticus? I can't make you choose."

"I already have. And I choose you. I love them. I will always love them. But they will need to accept you, because I won't let you go."

Maddox couldn't believe what was happening. Things that were too good to be true usually were. But she seemed sincere. "I don't know what to say."

"Tell me you'll fight for what we could have."

"Of course I will!" He held the back of her head in

his palm as he kissed her, but she broke away after only a few seconds.

"That's not all."

"What more could there be?" he asked. "As long as I have you, I have everything I've ever wanted."

"There's Maya…"

"She's your daughter, Jada, which means I'll love her, too—just as if I were her real father."

Gripping his arms, she peered worriedly up into his face. "That's just it, Maddox. You *are* her real father."

Maddox felt his knees go weak. If he hadn't been hanging on to her, he would've sunk down into the sand. "What did you say?" He'd heard but, for some reason, he needed her to say it again.

"I was pregnant when Tobias shot Atticus."

He gaped at her. She'd had his child and she hadn't told him? She'd gone thirteen years—all but raised *their* daughter—without saying a word?

The betrayal hit him like a knockout punch, especially after hearing her say she loved him. It was all too much. Suddenly, he couldn't even look at her. Wheeling around, he started to walk away, just left her standing right where she was.

"Maddox, I'm sorry. I didn't know it that night at the party," she called after him. "And when I found out, my parents wouldn't hear of me telling you. They'd already put pressure on Aiyana and your mother to make sure you were transferred to a different school and hoped that would be the end of it." She hurried to close the gap between them, jogging to keep up. "And I let them do it, yes. I hate myself for that now. But I felt so guilty for taking Atticus to that party when I knew we weren't supposed to be there, I felt I was getting what I deserved. That losing you was the price I had to pay for my mistake. I tried to move on, and I tried to create a life, for me and Maya, but there wasn't a day that went by I didn't miss you and want you back."

He didn't stop. He couldn't. He'd never felt so...so *robbed*.

"Please quit walking," she said. "Stop for just a second so we can talk about it, okay? Give me a minute to explain."

He put up a hand to silence her. He needed some time and some space.

As soon as he did that, she stopped following him and, as he pulled away, their separation was almost painful, as if he was leaving half of himself behind.

"I'm sorry!" she said, apologizing again.

But how could "I'm sorry" cover something like this? Those years with Maya were ones he'd never be able to get back.

His breathing grew labored as he marched away. She'd broken his heart into tiny pieces thirteen years ago, and then she'd come back into his life only to demolish it all over again.

"Maddox!"

He heard his name and still kept going.

"Will you please stop and listen to me?"

The tears in her voice caused a lump to rise in his own throat. God, he loved her. He'd always loved her. But that terrible night would always stand between them. Whenever he was with her, the happiness they both felt was like a dream that all too quickly dissipated.

He got all the way to the room before his legs grew so heavy he couldn't take another step. He stood outside, staring at the door, feeling his heart pound against his ribs. He was sweating, too, and it had little to do with his brisk return.

He reached for the handle, but he couldn't bring himself to turn it. If he went inside, the night of that party really would continue to stand between them—and this time it would be partly his fault.

He looked back but couldn't see her. There was a building obstructing his view. They were probably too far apart by now, anyway.

Was she leaving?

Imagining her getting into her car and driving off caused his chest to tighten. She'd just told him she loved him, that she'd *always* loved him.

Maybe, if he expected her to forgive him for his past mistakes, he had to forgive her, too.

That thought shot through him like a lightning bolt, filling him with energy and renewed hope as well as determination. This was painful, but he could bear it. He *would* bear it—for them.

Before he knew it, he was running back down the beach. "Jada!" he called as soon as he caught sight of her slowly trudging away.

When she turned, he could see tears streaking down her cheeks.

"Wait," he yelled and, when he reached her, pulled her back into his arms. "I'm sorry. I just—"

"You don't have to explain," she said. "I was afraid it would make you hate me."

"I don't hate you," he said, feeling the silkiness of her hair against his lips. "What happened was terrible for all of us, but that doesn't mean we should let it cost us what we could have *now*."

She didn't respond, but he could feel her weeping quietly against him. He lifted her chin so he could look down into her face. "We'll get past it."

"Will we, Maddox? *Can* we?"

"I'm sure we'll have difficult moments, especially at first, but we'll work through everything," he replied. "I don't really have a choice."

"Of course you do," she insisted.

"No, I don't—because I couldn't stop loving you if I tried." He wiped the tears from her face. "Does Maya know?"

"Not yet. She thinks her real father died in a motorcycle accident shortly before she was born. I haven't told her for fear… Well, I wanted to make sure you were happy about the news first. If you weren't… I couldn't bear to see her hurt."

He closed his eyes as he pictured the sweet, smart, beautiful girl he'd met. "You don't have to worry about that. I would never do anything to hurt her."

"I know you wouldn't—not on purpose. I just didn't want her to feel you were unhappy about…about learning you were a father."

"I'm unhappy about missing out, not being a father."

"I was afraid she might not be able to tell the difference."

He kissed the top of her head. "I know."

As she clung to him, the anger and hurt that had nearly leveled him at first began to slip away, making room for excitement. "I have a child," he said in wonder. "We have a child together."

"Yes."

"We could be a family."

"*I'd* like that."

"Regardless of Atticus or your mother or my mother or Tobias?"

She nodded.

"And you won't change your mind? Telling me about Maya is…it's a commitment?"

She met his gaze squarely. "It is—if you can forgive me."

"I'm sure I can figure out ways for you to make it up to me," he joked and, cupping her face, he kissed her.

That weekend was probably the best of Jada's life. Since Maddox had rented the beach house through the weekend, and they had a babysitter they could trust for Maya, they decided to stay and enjoy each other and the beautiful scenery. They walked on the beach in the moonlight, made love in the surf and the sand, made love again in the house, woke up and went out for coffee, did a little window-shopping, rented bicycles they rode along the boardwalk and then went back to get ready for a candlelit dinner at a steak place nearby. It felt like a honeymoon and, in a way, it was. They weren't married yet, but they were celebrating their love for each other and the commitment they hoped to make, once Maya knew Maddox better.

Instead of regretting what she'd done, Jada was convinced that she'd made the right choice, and it was a wonderful feeling. She knew there would be difficulties ahead. Maya would probably be angry that she hadn't been told about her father, and it would take time to work through that. Then there was her mother. Susan would be furious. It would still probably get awkward with Atticus at times, too, when he was having a bad day. She doubted his resentment was gone for good; he was only human. But she cared even more for Maddox now that they'd been together every minute of the past two days than she did before.

When Sunday afternoon rolled around, and they were supposed to be out of the rental, she was reluctant to leave, even though she was also excited about what the future might hold. Maddox had called Aiyana yesterday to ask for his job back—and she'd been gracious enough to give it to him. He'd also called Uriah to see if they could move back into his second house until they could find something big enough for all three of them, at which point Tobias would take over. Uriah had been amenable, too, but there were so many other things…

"What are you thinking about?" Maddox asked.

She looked up, hadn't realized he'd stepped back into the room. "I'm scared."

"About…"

"So much."

"Give me an example."

"I'm afraid the peace and contentment we've known here will vanish the second we drive away," she admitted.

He came over and lifted her chin. "Look at me. It's going to be okay."

"But there are still so many unanswered questions. What happens when your mother gets out of rehab?"

"Hopefully, she'll stay clean, be able to get another job and support herself."

"And if she can't?"

"We'll cross that bridge when we come to it."

"What about Tobias?"

"What about him?"

"We told Uriah he'll take over renting the house once we find something else, but how do we know he'll even be willing to return to Silver Springs?"

"I think he'll want to go back. He left when he was upset, but Uriah needs him, and being needed is important to him, especially now."

"Despite my mother?"

"We'll be there to reassure and convince him. And if that doesn't work, I'll do what I can to help him get a car so he can find work in LA."

"What about Maya? I'm nervous about telling her."

"That makes two of us," he said. "How do you think she'll respond?"

"I'm sure she'll be angry, feel just as cheated as you did, right? I can't expect a girl of only twelve to understand how difficult the situation was with Atticus and my mom, and then Eric coming into the picture."

He pressed his lips to her forehead. "Try not to worry too much. She's a smart girl. She'll probably understand better than you think."

"So everything is going to be okay?"

"It might not be, but we'll work through each problem as it arises."

"We won't give up on each other?" She needed to hear him confirm that.

"No. Never," he said, and she rested her cheek against his chest and listened to the solid thump of his heart as he rubbed a hand up and down her back.

Maya wasn't sure why her mother was bringing her to a tangerine orchard. She liked to pick fruit. They'd done that once since moving back to Silver Springs. There were so many small farms and orchards. But her mom had told her that the tangerines she liked so much came on in the *spring*. They were gone by now.

"I don't understand why you won't tell me why we're

coming here." She saw an old man step out of his house and wave at them.

"It's a surprise." Her mother waved back but, to Maya's surprise, didn't stop the car. She kept driving to a second, smaller house and parked behind a truck.

"What kind of surprise?" Maya asked. "A *birthday* surprise?" That made sense. Her birthday was only ten days away. But what kind of present could be out here?

"You'll see." Her mother got out of the car and waited for Maya to come around the front. They hadn't knocked on the door of the second house, but Mr. Richardson came out, anyway. She got the impression he'd been waiting for them.

"My new principal lives here?" she whispered. "Why are we coming to see him?"

Her mother's chest lifted as if she'd just taken a deep breath. But she didn't answer. She took Maya's hand and led her into Mr. Richardson's house without even saying hello to him.

The inside was a little bare but clean and smelled like men's cologne. It was a nice scent. And there was a wooden platter with crackers and slices of cheese, sort of like a school open house.

Her mother indicated that they should sit on the couch, so Maya did.

"Is this about New Horizons?" Maya asked.

Mr. Richardson laughed, but he looked nervous. "No. Actually, this doesn't have anything to do with school."

Maya shifted her gaze to her mother. "So…what's the surprise?"

Her mother exchanged a glance with Mr. Richardson before clearing her throat. "I wanted to tell you about something that happened when I was pregnant with you."

"But…what does this have to do with Mr. Richardson?"

"He was there, too."

"Okay…"

"When I was seventeen, your grandma asked me to watch your uncle Atticus one night. He was eleven. But I didn't want to stay home and babysit. There was a fun party going on, and…"

"…and I asked your mom to come," Mr. Richardson said, picking up when her mother fell silent.

"*You* used to live in Silver Springs, too?"

"Only for a few months."

Maya turned her attention back to her mother. "So did you go?"

"I did. I disobeyed Grandma and took Atticus, and that was a terrible decision. It was that night that—"

"Uncle Atticus was shot?" Maya broke in.

Her mother went pale but nodded. "Yes."

"Your mother came to the party to see me, even though your grandma didn't like me," Mr. Richardson said. "And there were some bad things at that party. Some drugs."

Maya felt her jaw drop. "You took drugs? But you're a principal!"

"No, not me. My brother. I also have a brother, you see. He's just a year younger than me, and he was at the party, too. The drugs messed up what he thought was real, made him feel desperate and under attack. And there was a gun at the party."

Finally, Maya was beginning to understand where this was going—although she didn't see why her mother would present it as a pleasant surprise. "It was your brother who shot Uncle Atticus."

"Yes. I'm afraid it was."

"And he's the guy who went to prison?"

"Yes, for thirteen years. He just got out a few weeks ago."

"Is he *dangerous*?"

"No. He just made a very poor decision, one that has lifelong consequences. There's no excuse for what he did, but there's no taking it back, either. Do you understand?"

She nodded. "You wanted me to know it was your brother who shot my uncle in case I heard about it at school this year."

"Not *exactly*," her mother said. "That's only part of it."

Maya fiddled with the hem on her shirt. "What's the other part?"

"You know how you've been looking for information on your father? Going to the library to see if they have a list of the people who lived here when you were born? Visiting the barbershop to see if they might remember him? You even went to visit Aiyana, didn't you? To ask if she remembered a young man who died on a motor-cycle?"

Maya was slightly embarrassed that her mother knew she'd been hunting that hard. "Yes. But she didn't remember." Suddenly, Maya guessed what she thought was going on. "Oh my gosh! Don't tell me you knew my father!" she cried. "Was he at that party, too?"

Mr. Richardson opened his mouth but didn't seem capable of speech. He looked to her mother again, and her mother said quietly, "Maya, *this* is your father."

Maya stared up at Mr. Richardson, who shifted nervously. "My father's alive?" she said. "*You're* my father?" She turned to her mother. "Why did you lie to me?"

Her mother seemed so scared it made Maya feel sorry for her even though she was mad.

"Because of what happened to Uncle Atticus," she explained. "Because Grandma was sure that Maddox's brother was evil and he and Maddox would come to no good. I found out I was pregnant after that night, and she was so angry. She forbade me to have any contact with Maddox—"

"Maddox! That's your first name? Not Madsen?"

He didn't get a chance to answer before her mother did. "Yes. I didn't want you to be able to find him, Maya. I was afraid if you knew you had a living father, you'd one day go looking for him, and…and I'd lose you."

Maya was surprised that her mom, who'd always been so dependable and good, would lie. And she was sad that she'd had a father her whole life but didn't know it. On top of all that, she was beginning to understand why her mother and grandmother couldn't get along. Grandma blamed her mother for what'd happened to Atticus. That was why she was so mean even though her mother had tried so hard to help at home and the store.

Maya didn't know what to do. Mr. Richardson looked like he didn't know what to do, either.

He came over to her. "I just found out you are my daughter this weekend. But I'm *so* glad to be your father. I hope we can put the sadness and tragedy of the past behind us—the three of us—and move forward. I love your mother, have always loved your mother, and would like to marry her and be part of her life, as well as yours. I couldn't be happier to have a child, especially one as sweet and smart as you."

As she looked into her father's face and saw kindness there, a feeling of excitement and hope cut through the confusion Maya had been feeling and brought tears to her eyes. Stepping forward, she allowed him to draw her into a hug. "Does my mother love you, too?" she asked.

She felt her mother come over to put her arms around both of them. "I do."

"So we'll be living with you instead of Tiffany?"

"If you're willing to try that," Mr. Richardson—*her father*—replied.

She'd lived with Eric, and that had been okay until her mother became so unhappy. Her mother didn't seem the least unhappy now—she seemed the opposite—which made Maya think it might be a good thing. "That would be okay as long as everyone is nice to each other."

He gripped her upper arms as he looked down at her, making what he said more of a promise. "We'll all be nice."

"Will I still get to go to New Horizons with Annie?" she asked.

"You will. And I'll try not to show any partiality to you, even though I think it will be almost impossible," he said with a wink, and they all laughed.

Epilogue

"What do *you* think it is?" Maddox asked, coming up behind her at the window and slipping his hands around to rest on her stomach.

"I have no idea. First I think boy. Then I think girl." So excited she couldn't stay still, Jada slipped out of his arms to fiddle with the settings she'd put out for dinner, straightening a fork here or a glass there. The party to reveal the gender of their child started in only fifteen minutes. Atticus, Tobias, Tiffany, Aiyana, Uriah, Jill—if she'd actually left LA when she claimed; Jill wasn't the most reliable person—Cindy and Annie, and Evangeline, who owned the oil and balsamic vinegar shop near the cookie store and had become a friend as well as a new client for Jada's social media business, would all be arriving shortly. Evangeline would also be bringing her daughter, Erica, who was still troubled but doing better since starting at New Horizons, what with Maddox and Aiyana taking a special interest in her, and Annie's and Maya's friendship helping to support that effort. Susan hadn't responded to the invitation, but Jada hadn't expected her to. Since they'd moved into a three-bedroom, three-bath house—part of the faculty housing at New

Horizons, which had come available shortly after they were married—her mother refused to talk to her. Susan was doing so well at the store with the addition of the ice cream sandwiches that she'd been able to hire a high school student to help out in the afternoons. And Maya occasionally helped on weekends, so grandmother and granddaughter were maintaining a relationship at least. Jada figured that was enough, for now. Maybe, with time, her mother's heart would soften. Even if it didn't, Jada knew she'd made the right choice. She was happier than she'd ever been, and so were Maddox and Maya. She expected the new baby to make their lives even richer.

"Tiffany didn't give anything away. She picked up the ultrasound results, took a quick peek and just smiled," she told Maddox, who remained at the window.

He came over. "Do you think Maya will be disappointed if it's a boy?" he asked, lowering his voice so that Maya, who was still getting ready in the bathroom, wouldn't be able to hear him. "She's really counting on a little sister."

"I'm sure she'll be happy no matter what it is."

He was as excited as Maya was about the new baby. Jada could tell, and found it so endearing. He'd insisted on going to every doctor appointment with her so far and had almost not been able to stop himself from peeking inside the envelope they'd received from the doctor, before she'd passed it along to Tiffany.

Tobias and Uriah were the first to arrive. Tobias had driven, since they were both coming from the orchard, where he was living again. He was helping Aiyana's son Gavin do ground maintenance and repair at New Horizons, but he also did a lot for Uriah at the orchard.

Atticus arrived next. Since he worked at New Horizons with Maddox and Tobias, they had actually become friends. Occasionally, they even hung out together, playing chess, video games, darts at the Blue Suede Shoe or watching sports. That was what gave Jada hope that her mother would eventually soften. Atticus seemed to like Maddox and Tobias and he was thriving.

Tiffany arrived a few minutes after Atticus, at the same time the rest of their guests, except for Jill, converged on the house, so it got loud and crowded very fast. Jada noticed that Tiffany had on new clothes and smiled to herself. She suspected her best friend had a thing for Tobias.

"Do you have the envelope?" Jada asked as she followed Tiffany through the crowd to the kitchen, where Tiffany put down the sacks she'd carried in with her.

"I don't need the envelope," she said. "I have these gender reveal smoke cannon things I found online."

"Smoke cannons?"

She got one out to show Jada. "They're kind of like fireworks. You light them, and instead of exploding, they put out a bunch of pink or blue smoke."

"Wait—don't light that thing yet!" Atticus said, overhearing. "I'm still taking bets." He was going around, getting everyone to commit themselves to a particular gender and giving them the opportunity to put a little money behind it—just a few bucks to make it even more fun.

Maya came out and they all talked and laughed and ate appetizers while waiting for Jill to arrive. Jill was almost an hour late, but she eventually walked through the door. Then, because dinner was going to be ruined if they didn't serve it soon, Tiffany called everyone to attention, Maya got out her cell phone to video the big event, they all got their glasses of sparkling apple cider ready for a toast—and Maddox lit the fuse.

Pink smoke poured out.

"It's a girl!" Maya cried, jumping up and down at having received her wish, and Jada felt her husband pull her into his arms for a kiss.

* * * * *

If you liked Jada and Maddox's story,
don't miss the next book in the series,
featuring Tobias,
Christmas in Silver Springs,
coming soon
from Brenda Novak and MIRA Books.

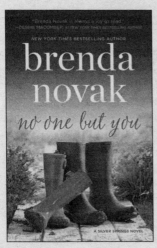

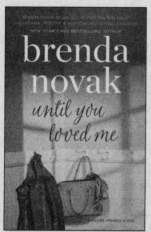

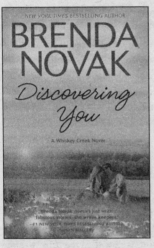

brenda novak

33082	THE SECRETS SHE KEPT	___ $7.99 U.S.	___ $9.99	CAN.
33038	RIGHT WHERE WE BELONG	___ $7.99 U.S.	___ $9.99	CAN.
33025	UNTIL YOU LOVED ME	___ $7.99 U.S.	___ $9.99	CAN.
32877	NO ONE BUT YOU	___ $7.99 U.S.	___ $9.99	CAN.
32831	KILLER HEAT	___ $7.99 U.S.	___ $9.99	CAN.
31962	THE SECRET SISTER	___ $7.99 U.S.	___ $9.99	CAN.
31639	THE HEART OF CHRISTMAS	___ $7.99 U.S.	___ $8.99	CAN.
31546	TAKE ME HOME FOR CHRISTMAS	___ $7.99 U.S.	___ $8.99	CAN.

(limited quantities available)

TOTAL AMOUNT $ _____
POSTAGE & HANDLING $ _____
($1.00 for 1 book, 50¢ for each additional)
APPLICABLE TAXES* $ _____
TOTAL PAYABLE $ _____

(check or money order—please do not send cash)

To order, complete this form and send it, along with a check or money order for the total above, payable to MIRA Books, to: **In the U.S.:** 3010 Walden Avenue, P.O. Box 9077, Buffalo, NY 14269-9077; **In Canada:** P.O. Box 636, Fort Erie, Ontario, L2A 5X3.

Name: _____

Address: _____ City: _____

State/Prov.: _____ Zip/Postal Code: _____

Account Number (if applicable): _____
075 CSAS

mira

Harlequin.com

*New York residents remit applicable sales taxes.
*Canadian residents remit applicable GST and provincial taxes.

MBN0319BL